# Wanted

by

Paula L. Silici

Wanted by Paula L. Silici


ISBN 13: 978-0-88100-169-3
ISBN10: 0-88100-169-4
Library of Congress Number: 2019935803

Cover Design by NZ Graphics

Published by National Writers Press

Library of Congress Cataloging-in-Publication Data

Silici, Paula L.
Wanted by Paula L. Silici

International Standard Book Number 13: 978-0-88100-169-3
International Standard Book Number 10: 0-88100-169-4

1. Fiction/Action Adventure/Romance
2. Fiction/Romance/Western
3. Fiction/Women I. Title 2019935803

*For Frank*

# Chapter One
## The Sierra Nevada Mountains
## July, 1873

"Shooter, you idiot, I said hold her down!"

Jessie Driscoll fought her captors like a wildcat. Her cousin was really going to do this terrible thing. He was. And worse, the whole cursed lot of them were going to stand there, grinning down at her like a pack of tongue-lolling jackals, and do nothing to help her. Through a throat scoured raw from nearly twenty minutes of venting her outrage, Jessie gathered together every shred of courage, every spark of red-hot anger burning inside her and tried one last time to reason with her crazy cousin.

"Curtis, I swear, if you do this to me, I'll never, *ever* forgive you for it. It's sick. And cruel. And meaner than anything you've ever done to me before. Let me go!"

"No."

"Let's be reasonable about this, Driscoll. Order Charlie and Shot off her. Jessie's right. She doesn't deserve this. There has to be another way."

Jessie went still. At the sound of those words, hope bloomed like a springtime crocus. She lifted her head, straining to see around the big oaf sitting on her chest.

"Marty?" she managed to croak. "Thank goodness somebody's come to his senses. Marty, help me! Don't let him do it."

"Stay out of this, Marty." Curtis's sharp rejoinder hit the air like a rifle shot, making her flinch. "Don't interfere unless you're ready to take a bullet over it. If you don't want to watch, then don't. You know I'm doing this for her own good. Now stand clear everybody. This will only take a minute."

As Marty gave in and backed away, Jessie's head lolled back into the dust. She felt helpless. *Helpless and terrified.* Worse, the appalling sting of tears burned behind her eyes. Heaven help her, if she showed any hint of weakness now, Curtis would gloat over it to her dying day.

She'd never before let him see she was afraid of him. Never. Not even when they were children and his cruel pranks had given her nightmares long after the bruises had faded.

She wouldn't cry. She wouldn't. If she cried now it would only give him too much satisfaction. She was nineteen—a grown woman. Not a child. *She would not cry.*

Or then again, maybe she would. Ah, sweet mercy. She simply couldn't help it. A tear slipped past her lashes and slid into her hair. Then another. *Into her hair. Her precious hair.*

Curtis's blonde, bearded face loomed above her now. She could see him clearly because Shooter had shifted off her chest and knelt by her head where he easily shackled her wrists in his big, brawny hands. Charlie had her ankles nailed down tight, and another man, Walt Conner, stood by to press a boot to her waist should she try to buck and squirm. From the corner of her eye she saw a cowed Marty Chase, her last hope, clomping his way toward the sanctuary of the trees. Her heart sank.

"Curtis, please. You don't have to do this."

"Stop your sniveling. Yes I do. It's the only way."

"No." Her voice was a thread of sound.

He bent down on one knee beside her and pulled a knife from the battered leather sheath at his waist. Tracing a tear along her cheek, his eyes briefly glittered with a shock of surprise. And something else. It was almost as if he honestly felt a pang of regret. He hesitated, but only for a moment. Clenching his jaw, he moved his fingers into her hair. "I promised to make this quick and I will," he said gruffly.

Her voice, which had always been a touch on the gravely side, grated now with just plain bitterness. "Is that supposed to make me feel better? Well, it doesn't."

"Shut up and hold still while I get it done. You don't want me to slit your throat or mess up that pretty face of yours by mistake, do you?"

She answered with a hysterical little laugh. As the gleaming hunting knife sliced neatly through the first hank of hair, Jessie tensed and closed her eyes. "Go to the devil, Curtis Driscoll," she whispered, letting the tears fall freely now. "All of you, go straight to the devil and rot."

☙ ☙ ☙

Gazing out over the creek, Jessie sat with her back against the rough tree trunk and pulled her skirt tightly around her drawn-up legs. A warm breeze blew across the gurgling water, tickling her nape where her heavy, mahogany-colored hair used to hang. Now her head felt as light as a soap bubble. Another tear slipped past her lashes, splashing onto her skirt.

"Hey, Jess."

She'd been so lost in her misery she hadn't heard Marty's approach. That he'd dare try to talk to her alone, especially now, not only galled her, it shocked her.

Curtis ruled his gang like an army general. When they'd parted from the wagon train and struck out on their own, he'd made it plain that any sweet talk with his young cousin would be instantly dealt with—by a bullet to the brains. The brains in this case being the ones a man possessed below his belt.

She stiffened, resentment knotting her stomach. "Go away, Marty." Swiping the tears off her cheek, she quickly averted her head.

"I brought you some dinner. Shooter fixed us all some beans and corn bread. Next to you, old Shot's the best cook among us. They're real good."

"I'm not hungry."

You've gotta eat, Jess."

"I said I don't want any."

Marty remained quiet for a moment. "I know you're feeling poorly because of everything what's happened, but if you don't eat you're gonna get sick on us and then it's a sure thing Curtis'll plain up and leave you behind. Come on, Jess. Try, okay?"

Jessie threw her arms over her shorn hair and buried her head in her skirts. She already felt sick. Sick to her soul. And if Curtis walked up to her and told her he'd decided to leave her behind, she wouldn't care one whit.

To get Marty to leave, she said, "Just set the plate down over there. Maybe I'll eat it later." The words were muffled by layers of tear-stained skirt.

An awkward hand gripped her shoulder.

"I brought you something else, Jess. Look at me. Please?"

"I don't want to see anybody just now. Can't you understand that? Go away." Her voice wobbled. Her pride was in shambles. She'd never felt so humiliated and full of shame in all her life.

It wasn't just that her hair was gone. That was horrible enough, but it was the fact that she'd been reduced to begging Curtis for mercy and crying while she'd done it that was making her feel so wretched now. Everyone, including the kind-hearted but spineless Marty, had witnessed her awful humbling. Despite his protests, he'd approved of it even, when all was said and done. How could she ever face them again?

To her dismay, Marty dropped down on his haunches in front of her, took her hands away from her head, and forced her chin up.

"It ain't all that bad, Jess." He tried for a reassuring smile, sweeping his gaze over the damage. "In fact, you look sort of...well, even sweeter than usual."

When she closed her eyes to shut him out, he persisted stubbornly, "Come on. I truly mean it.  Here. Take a look." He stuck his fingers into the breast pocket of his shirt. "I brought you the mirror I use for shaving so you can see for yourself. Aw, Jess. Don't you know all of us think you're still the prettiest little gal this side of heaven? Hair or no hair?"

She parted her lids slightly, surprised she'd just heard such a forbidden declaration. Marty looked over his shoulder toward camp, clearly uneasy that he'd just admitted such a thing aloud. Jessie followed his gaze. Curtis was standing by the fire with his arms crossed over his chest, watching them.

Marty quickly turned back to Jessie and held the mirror up in such a way she had no choice but to look.

Her heart thudded to a halt. Gone were those masses and masses of beautiful hair—her pride, her glory, her one and only vanity. Gone. All gone.

Her fingers trembling, she reached up to touch the short, curly tendrils that hugged her skull like a woolly winter cap. "Shorn sheep" didn't begin to describe it. She watched the mirror image of herself go pale, then paler still. Fresh tears flooded her brown eyes, eyes that looked too huge for her face now that the heavy nut-brown frame no longer lay against her cheeks to offset them.

For the millionth time, she asked herself how she'd gotten into this mess. She should have known better than to trust Curtis. When they'd stopped in the little town of Sulfur Flats for supplies yesterday, why hadn't she trusted her instincts when her cousin had insisted she remain with the horses while he and the men "attended to some business" up the street?

"Stay right here and don't move an inch," Curtis had said in that tone of his that struck terror into even the meanest of men. "Watch the horses."

"Why?" she'd sputtered warily. "Curtis, no. I want to take a walk up to the mercantile. I need—"

"Shut your trap, Jess, and just do as you're told. No sass. Stay put or you'll feel my belt across your backside when I get back."

What else could she do? She stayed put. A half hour later Curtis, a neckerchief tied over the lower half of his face, threw her on her horse, slapping its rump before she even made it all the way into the saddle. In seconds they were all beating it like demons into the hills beyond the sleepy town of Sulfur Flats, a hastily assembled posse of angry citizens hot on their tails not long after. Two hours later found them deep into the Sierra

Nevada foothills, the posse trailing a mile or so behind and losing more and more ground as time went on. Late in the afternoon when Curtis was certain they'd lost the posse, he pushed them for another three hours, then called a halt. They'd come across a stream, a good place to make camp for the night.

She'd been anxiously watching her back trail ever since.

"Aw, now don't cry!" Marty jerked the mirror away. "It ain't like it's permanent. It's gonna grow back."

The words settled into her belly as if she'd just swallowed a pile of stones. Just when would it grow back? In a year? Two years? Maybe even longer than that if Curtis decided to take his knife to it again.

"I would have helped you if I could," Marty stammered. "Honest I would have. But after thinking on it, I figured Curtis was probably right. He did what he had to do to keep you safe."

Her eyes flew wide. She swiped at the tears indignantly. "What do you mean, keep me safe? You know darn well the only reason Curtis took a knife to my hair was to get me back for sassing him about the robbery in front of the men. He wanted to make sure I was good and humbled, that's all."

Marty stood, removed his Stetson, and ran a chubby hand through his unkempt hair. He looked away, gazing off into the distance, his expression grim. After another long pause and a glance over his shoulder, he said, "You gotta know some things about yesterday. Curtis sent me to tell you, and I gotta get it done."

Dread settled over her. "What things?"

He looked down at her, his face hard-set. Clamping his hat back on his head he said, "Back in Sulfur Flats we heard some yahoo yelling his head off that a woman was minding the getaway horses. We figure somebody got a real good look at you—enough to be able to describe you to the law. That's why Curtis cut off your hair. So's you'd look different."

Jessie paled. The world started to tilt. Everything blurred before her eyes into a bluish-green smudge. Steadying herself with one hand on the tree trunk, she stood to her feet, the mirror falling to the grass.

"But I...I didn't even know what you all were up to. I—"

"I know you didn't. Heck, Jess, you're so sweet-hearted you wouldn't even rob a snow bank," he grinned.

In her agitation, she failed to appreciate the joke. "You say somebody saw me?" she stammered. "You all had neckerchiefs tied to your faces and your hats were tipped low, hiding your eyes, but I...I.... Somebody clearly saw me? Marty, if they catch me, I could go to prison!"

Marty's gaze dropped to his boots. He said quickly, "Charlie's sure nobody's following us, and I trust his word. Indians is right canny about them things. For now you're safe enough. Especially if you put these on."

He strode over to a pile of clothes she hadn't noticed before. Scooping them up, he handed them over. "Here. These are some of Charlie's duds. Curtis says you're to dress like a man from now on, and that I'm to wait right here while you change. Told me to tell you to put *everything* on. He's gonna check later to make sure you do."

She snapped her head up, confused.

"Don't know what he meant, but he said *you'd* know as soon as you got to changing."

As Jessie reached for the bundle, a tan Stetson fell out, rolling to a stop just past her left foot. She stared at it for several long moments.

"Why, Marty?" she asked, barely able to speak.

"Because Curtis says you got to. It's for your own good, Jess."

"No, no," she said numbly. "Why did you all have to go and rob a bank? Sweet mercy. Armed robbery! Every one of us might end up in prison."

"It's because we was out of money," Marty said tersely. "And Curtis said it was a sure thing. Said it would be easy as swiping one of your hair ribbons."

Jessie felt the breeze on her nape, felt the short, silky curls, the remnants of her once abundant locks, brushing against her forehead. She wouldn't be wearing hair ribbons for a long time. Anger such as she'd never known bloomed inside her at that moment—the kind of scary anger that caused a body to commit murder.

"That's ridiculous," she cried, crushing the bundle of clothes to her chest. "Curtis has all that money from selling the farm. He—"

"Lost it in a poker game."

Jessie sputtered. "He what? That's impossible!"

"Nope. Lost every dime. I suppose I shouldn't be telling you this, but, well, remember that night Curtis got you that hotel room in Silver Creek? Well, after you turned in we joined a poker game over to the saloon. Lost our shirts. I suspect we was cheated on, but, well shoot, we were all so drunk I suppose the worst was bound to happen."

Her mind reeled. "Spare me. I can imagine the details, Marty." Oh, sweet mercy, Curtis lost the farm money. He'd gone and gambled away their happy future at a poker table.

"Come on now, Jess. Don't cry no more," Marty pleaded. "Things is gonna work out. Now take them clothes and get yourself changed. I gotta get back to camp. Curtis said I was to tell you to get changed, eat your vittles, and be ready to ride in.... Aw, looky there now. The others is breaking camp. We wasted so much time flapping our jaws you ain't got any time left at all."

Hidden behind a broad pine tree while Marty stood by with his back turned, Jessie quickly stripped down to her drawers and camisole. She folded her own clothes as neatly as haste would allow to be packed into her saddlebags later.

Grabbing the jeans, she held them up. Charlie Deerhorn was the smallest of the men in their group. A short, wiry man in his early twenties, he was the by-blow of a Ute Indian and a captive white woman. He'd joined the five of them at Fort Dodge, telling Curtis he knew his way through the mountains just like he knew the way to every whorehouse in the territory. That was all the credentials Curtis needed to take him on.

The jeans and shirt smelled of tobacco, man, and horse sweat. Wrinkling her nose, she decided she would have to wash them at the soonest possible opportunity. The pants were a baggy fit, but not so much that cinching them up with a measure of rope wouldn't take care of the slack. While reaching for the shirt, a wide strip of linen spilled out, causing her to gasp.

Whoa. *A breast binder?* Lifting the garment by her thumb and forefinger, she could hardly believe it. How in heaven's name had Curtis gotten hold of such a thing? A souvenir, perhaps, from one of his numerous late-night romps? Red-faced, she bit her lip, deciding it was probably best she didn't know.

Curtis took pleasure in belittling her figure. Scrawny and shapeless as a flag pole, he'd always told her. She knew she wasn't exactly shapeless, but even so, she didn't have much on top anyway, so why this?

Feeling too scared and defeated to do anything else, she slowly removed her camisole, wrapped the stiff length of fabric around her torso, and fastened the hooks and eyes up the front. *Just let Curtis try to check,* she thought bitterly.

"Uh, Jess? Time's up. The men are ready to ride." She'd no sooner gotten her shirttails tucked in than she heard Marty's summons. With the enormity of her predicament weighing her down, she gathered her things in her arms, shoved the Stetson as far down on her forehead as it would go, and left the shelter of the trees.

# Chapter Two

"Curtis, I don't like this. What are we doing here?"

"Shut up, Jessie, and do as I say. Stay up here behind these rocks and keep your head down. We'll be back before you know it. When you hear us coming, mount up and ride like the devil's on your tail. In a few minutes there'll be plenty of daylight to guide your horse through the trees. Just keep low and follow my lead."

The men were fanned out behind her, nervously standing abreast of their horses in the scant light before dawn. Not one of them would look her in the eyes.

Uneasily, Jessie turned and rose on tiptoes, peering over the shelter of granite boulders, her designated hiding place. Ahead she could just barely make out the silhouette of a crude cabin nestled in a clearing about two-hundred feet away. Beside the cabin stood a makeshift corral, and milling inside the corral she saw a small herd of maybe ten to fifteen horses.

She understood at once. *Curtis is planning to steal those horses*, she thought in a near panic.

She was about to turn and confront him when a tall man wearing nothing but a snug pair of low-riding jeans emerged from the cabin. Startled, Jessie sucked in her breath.

Dark-haired, brawny, and hard-muscled, his broad chest and thick arms gleamed in the half-light like polished stone. Fascinated, her knees suddenly went weak, and a strange, unfamiliar ache curled in the pit of her belly. His undulating, compact muscles shouted strength and danger. Without a doubt, he was the most physically powerful man she'd ever seen.

At the water barrel, he looked about, then set down his rifle. Bending, he splashed his face and chest, making low shivering sounds as he sluiced his upper body with the cold water. Grabbing a nearby towel, he quickly dried himself, retrieved his rifle, glanced toward the corral, and went back inside.

The sight of him shot fear through Jessie. Her woman's eye and woman's soul knew instantly this was not a man to tangle with.

Filled with dread, she turned and whispered fiercely, "Don't do it, Curtis. You'll never get away with it this time. I saw—"

He yanked on her arm, and for a minute it looked as if he was going to slap her. "I said, keep your mouth shut and your head down. That's all you have to do."

Anger flared, hot and quick. She simply couldn't hold her tongue. "Great. This is just great," she spat. "Not only are you a bank robber, but now you're a lowdown horse thief, too!"

He did slap her then. She reeled from the blow, covering her burning cheek with her hand as she stumbled against the rocks. The men shifted uneasily, but when Curtis glowered at them, daring them to interfere, they backed off.

In an angry whisper Curtis said, "Our horses are played out. You know that. We'll never make it to Placerville without fresh mounts." He pitched his bearded jaw toward the cabin. "As you saw, the answer to our problem is right over there, ripe for the plucking."

Afraid he'd hit her again, Jessie tried to keep her voice calm, her nerves steady. Straightening, she dropped her arms to her side and said, "Why don't you just ride up to that cabin and ask the folks inside if they'll sell you some horses? Thanks to the bank robbery, you've got the money to pay for them. Why do you have to steal them?"

"Because it's like this, dummy." He cut her off, his tone sounding as if he were speaking to a simpleton. "Why should we spend money when we don't have to?"

The tall man with the dangerous muscles came to mind. She wanted to tell Curtis exactly why, but this time, she wisely held her tongue. He'd hit her again for sure if she dared offend his manhood.

Curtis turned away from her and headed for his horse. "Do exactly as I told you," he bit out over his shoulder. "Because if you mess this up for us I swear, little cousin, you'll pay for it."

Several minutes later, Jessie's toes were numb from standing on them so long. Cautiously, she peered over the cover of rocks, holding her breath as she watched the group of five men on horseback circle the clearing, inching their way along the trees toward the penned horses. The closer they got to the corral, the more anxious she became. Did Curtis honestly think they could just ride in there and take what they wanted without a fight? Stupid. Stupid!

Curse Curtis and his wild ways! Against her will, he was involving her in his crimes again, and she was powerless to stop him. Even if she wanted to run, where would she go? A woman alone with no money and no prospects...well, she didn't want to think about the dangers of that. Thumping down on her heels, she began to pace, grim images of hangmen and nooses crowding her thoughts.

She was on her fifth pivot when a rifle shot shattered the eerie quiet. Scrambling to the rocks, she inched her head above the ledge, straining to see through the dim half-light.

Somebody'd been shot. She saw that clearly enough. She gave a small scream as the penned horses began thundering through the open corral gate, heading straight toward a figure writhing in the dirt. In vain, Jessie tried to make out the downed man's identity. Was it Curtis? Marty? Who?

Another crack of gunfire rocked the canyon walls. Jessie watched, terrified, as a second man fell from his mount, straight into the path of the stampeding herd.

The others spurred their horses, ducking low in their saddles, struggling to elude the deadly rifle fire. Flanking the frenzied herd as best they could, they raced across the clearing toward Jessie, heading for the cover of the boulders and trees.

Occasionally, the men squeezed off shots over their shoulders, but the bullets flew wild.

As the sun rose higher, enough light shone upon the clearing for Jessie to recognize the survivors. Walt Conner was in the lead to Jessie's left. Marty followed close behind, with Curtis riding drag along the right-hand side of the herd.

Hastily, Jessie mounted her horse. "Please, God, let them be alive," she chanted frantically, realizing Charlie and Shooter were the two downed men lying motionless in the dust-filled clearing. Of course it was those two who'd taken the brunt, she reasoned. The two men most capable of taking care of themselves, Curtis would have placed them in the most dangerous positions—nearest the cabin and behind the herd as the horses broke free of the corral. Not only were both men expert riders, they were excellent marksmen as well.

Jessie clenched her jaw as bitterness washed through her. A lot of good their expertise had done either of them this time. Somewhere down deep, she knew they were dead.

She'd just rounded the boulders when three more shots rang out. Whipping her head up, she watched in horror as Marty's body jerked sideways, then fell in an awkward jackknife to the ground. His terrified horse screamed and bucked, then melted into the stampeding herd.

Clutching his injured thigh with one hand, Marty curled his body into a tight ball until the scores of deadly hooves pounded past him. Then, digging his free elbow and boot into the dirt, he tried desperately to claw his way toward the cover of the trees, ducking bullets as he went.

Why wasn't Curtis trying to help Marty? Her cousin was so close, only a few yards away. It would be dangerous, but all he had to do was cut left, rein in a little, and give Marty a hand up. But no...Curtis was going to stick with the horses and pass right on by.

Without thinking about it another instant, she kicked her horse into a gallop and headed for the downed man, circling to the left and keeping to the edge of the trees to avoid the frenzy of onrushing horses.

The moment Curtis sighted her, he started yelling. "You little fool! Get back to the rocks! Go back!"

She stayed her course. "Marty!" she screamed, yanking hard on the reins as she neared his side. Her horse reared just inches from his legs. A bullet whizzed past her head. "Give me your hand!"

The frantic cowboy scrambled to his knees, reaching wildly for her outstretched arm. The herd was well ahead of them now, their only danger the rapid rifle fire coming from the cabin window.

Gripping the saddle and the horse's flanks with her knees and thighs, Jessie grasped the pommel with one hand and bent low. But when Marty locked onto her forearm and pulled, she hadn't been prepared for the enormity of his strength. As he hoisted himself onto the horse's rump, the agonizing wrench to her shoulder socket nearly sent her flying out of the saddle.

With a startled cry, she felt the hot breath of a second bullet as it tore past her cheek, missing her face by mere inches. Frantically, she tried to gain a steady seat, kicking the horse's flanks as best she could to get them moving.

The next bullet struck Marty in the back, throwing him violently forward. This time the impact of his solid body knocked Jessie to the ground.

A pain such as she'd never known crashed through her skull as her head thudded against a rock imbedded in the dirt. As from a long distance, she heard someone shout her name. She was aware that her horse had wheeled and was galloping away with a bleeding, cursing Marty clinging to its mane.

Now she was the injured one being left behind. Now she was the one the man would discover and shoot on sight once he found her lying helpless in the dirt.

Curtis and Walt had already disappeared with the herd. Marty was twice wounded, probably fatally.

Marty. Because he was the only one of the men who'd ever truly been kind to her, she'd risked her life to help him. But the ungrateful worm had taken off with her horse, abandoning her, too.

*How could they do this to me? How?* She took a deep breath, fighting back hysteria. Especially Curtis. Her own flesh and blood had chased after his precious booty without giving her or the other downed men a backward glance.

She groaned, her whole body turning cold with fear. She tried to get up, but couldn't. Her shoulder was stiff with pain and her head felt like somebody had taken a hammer to it.

In moments the man and whoever else occupied that cabin would come.

"Just like Charlie and Shooter, this is the day I'm going to die," she moaned.

# Chapter Three

Mitch Wyden waited for the dust to settle. Gripping the Winchester near his hip, he creaked open the door and eased into the sunlight.

Nothing stirred. Even the birds kept their silence as he made his way toward the clearing and the man he'd watched fall from his horse only moments before.

He cast a derisive glance at the two battered men lying face down near the corral. While the senselessness of their deaths embittered him, he felt no pity, or any remorse for shooting them. That band of filthy reprobates had stolen his horses.

His eyes swung back to the rustler lying face up near the trees. He could hear the man whimpering like a beaten dog. Briefly, Mitch wondered if he'd shot him after all. He'd hit his target with the larger man, but he'd seen the bullets miss this one. Taking no chances, he steadied his rifle, long strides cutting the distance between them in seconds.

The horse stealer groaned. An unsteady hand reached up to cradle the side of his bleeding head.

Mitch hovered over him, feet braced apart, his muscles tense, ready to shoot with the slightest provocation. "Don't move, you thieving little runt, or I'll blow your head off."

Instantly, the hand stilled.

When he took a good look at the man his heart skipped a beat. The thief had a small, pale face, not the rugged hardened one he'd expected. Large, frightened brown eyes, heavily fringed with dark, smoky lashes stared back at him.

Mitch paused, hauling in a breath, thinking furiously. This one was a mere boy, not much past the front end of his teens. The kid hadn't even sprouted whiskers yet.

A strained voice broke the silence. "Well, what are you waiting for? Go ahead and shoot me. I deserve it for being such a fool. Just...please, mister, do it quick."

Mitch gritted his teeth. The husky voice sounded far too young and scared for his comfort. The flat emptiness of it cooled his anger a little.

He lowered the rifle and squatted down, hooking the Winchester across the crook of one arm. Fighting off the kid's weak protests, he patted down the boy's sides and legs. Satisfied he was weaponless, he scanned the kid's clothing for blood.

"Are you shot? Tell me where it hurts."

Quaking, the boy licked his lips, trying to string a few words together. Those huge eyes pierced Mitch through. "Mister, if you'd just pull that trigger and get it over with, it won't hurt *anywhere* anymore."

Frustrated, Mitch threatened, "Give me another smart answer like that one, kid, and I might still do that." Scowling, he fingered the kid's bloody head wound.

"Ow!"

The boy tried to squirm away. "Keep still," Mitch growled, slamming his palm against the kid's shoulder. The impact sent the boy arching off the ground with an outcry of pain.

"That was your own fault," Mitch said stiffly. "I told you to tell me where it hurts." He let the boy settle, waiting tight-lipped until the pain passed. With an immobilizing knee pressed to the kid's chest, he probed to see if the shoulder was dislocated. It wasn't, but he caused more agony finding out.

After a moment he said in a hard voice, "Where else?"

The kid sputtered pitifully, beads of sweat gathering on his forehead and smooth upper lip. "N-nowhere else. My head and shoulder. That's all. Keep your filthy hands off me!"

Mitch sat back on his heels, his eyes scanning the empty corral. It had taken him over six months to capture and break his small, wild herd. And now, thanks to this mouthy brat and his thieving cohorts, all his toil and sweat had been for nothing.

He glanced back down at the boy. "Get up," he growled, barely able to keep from knocking the kid's teeth down his throat. "Move!"

It took a while, but the boy finally made it to his knees, then staggered to full height.

Disgusted, Mitch scowled. The kid was short and puny. He figured he couldn't weigh more than a hundred pounds. Worse, he carried himself like a sissy.

"M-my hat," the boy sputtered. A tan Stetson lay brim up against a sapling several feet away. Those dark eyes turned on him, pleading, unnerving him.

He jerked the rifle barrel. "Get it. Just don't try anything stupid."

With slow movements, the boy retrieved his hat, wincing as he squashed it onto his injured head. With a sharp tug, he secured the throat latch tightly under his chin.

"Come on," Mitch said, pointing the rifle straight at the kid's midsection. "Into the cabin."

The boy hesitated, his eyes going wide with fear. "What are you going to do with me?"

Hardening his heart, Mitch grated, "Hang you from that tree over there, maybe. Or turn you over to the law. I haven't made up my mind yet. Start walking."

The boy stumbled, then righted himself. Mitch shoved the muzzle of the rifle into the small of his back. The kid didn't stumble again after that.

☙ ☙ ☙

Jessie trembled as the man herded her inside and forced her to sit in a rickety chair set against a rough-hewn pine table. No other people occupied the small, one-room cabin. So. She was alone with him, then.

Her head hurt abominably, but she didn't dare complain. He hovered over her, like a beast guarding its kill. She thought it best to just keep her mouth shut, period.

Feeling faint and nauseated, she struggled to remain upright in the chair. But she forced herself to keep alert, eyeing him warily, fearing his next move. This man with longish dark hair the color of coffee and wide-set blue eyes was far bigger and taller than Curtis. His strong, square jaw, set like stone in anger, terrified her.

He was dressed much the same as she was, in faded jeans and a loose-fitting shirt, though unlike hers, his jeans fit snugly across his muscular thighs and buttocks. Nor did his blue flannel shirt do anything to hide the masculine bulk of his brawny chest and arms. Trying to figure his age, she guessed he was maybe five or six years older than she.

Jessie took a hasty breath, only to curse the binder that made it so difficult to breathe. If he was going to kill her, she wished he'd get it over with. She felt so sick and miserable, death would be a blessing.

His anger was a palpable thing, radiating from him in waves. Yet, beyond her fear of this daunting man, she had to admit she could sympathize with how he felt. Stealing someone's property was a horrible, hateful crime. Every time Curtis had stolen something precious from her she'd—

"I asked you what your name is. Answer me!"

Jessie flinched, snapping her head up. The sudden jerk sent a dizzying shaft of pain through her temple. "What?"

"Your name," he demanded. "What is it?"

She answered the threatening tone automatically, without thinking things through first. "Jessie."

"Jessie what? And if you say James you'll get a mouth full of my fist."

Another wave of dizziness washed over her. She lowered her head and clamped her lips shut. She was scared, but he could beat her to death before she'd tell him her last name. Jessie Driscoll's likeness, thanks to that witness, was probably plastered on wanted posters from Sulfur Flats all the way to San Francisco by now. She had no way of knowing if the authorities knew her name yet or not, but she wasn't about to take any chances. For the time being, this man didn't know she was a woman, and he didn't know her full name. For her own self-preservation, she planned to keep it that way as long as she possibly could.

"Tell me!" he thundered, sounding a lot like Curtis in a rage.

Bracing herself for the blow that was sure to come, she mustered her courage and answered in a tight voice, "James is close enough."

The man stared at her in amazement, as if he couldn't believe her audacity. He turned away and began to pace the cramped area between the table and the cobblestone hearth, cursing under his breath. But within moments he stood before her again, blue fire smoldering in his eyes.

Placing his hands on either side of the chair back, imprisoning her, he leaned into her face. "You'd better start talking, kid, or things are going to go badly for you. If I don't get those horses back, I'll take the price of every single one of them out of your hide. You understand?"

Straightening, he took a step back and studied her again, his blazing eyes scorching her down to her soul. "Tell me, *Jessie*. Before you joined up with that gang and plotted to steal my herd, did you ever think about the consequences? Did you ever think you'd be shot—or hung for your crimes if you got caught?"

She bristled, hating his assumptions, resenting that he was condemning her without knowing the truth. "No! You don't—"

"Or spend the rest of your life in prison? Do you want to go to prison, son? Spend the rest of your days in some rat-infested, airless, stone cage—"

Jessie bolted so fast the chair flew backwards and bounced on the plank floor. She got a foot from the open door before a heavy hand clutched her shirt and hauled her backward. She felt a tremendous sting on her backside, the force of the blow so powerful her hips shot forward, nearly sending her to her knees.

The man jerked her against his chest, holding her there with an arm around her waist. His voice, cold and deadly, froze her in her place. "Try that again, kid, and I'll make it so you'll wish you were never born."

Jessie tried very hard not to cry. Stiffening her spine, she raised her chin and stared straight ahead, out the open doorway toward the verdant trees and great stone walls of the canyon beyond. She tried to ignore the stinging pain in her buttocks, her aching shoulder, and the pounding headache. Most of all, she tried to blink away the hot tears gathering on her lashes. His body was hard and unyielding against her back, his male scent raw and primitive. His hot breath, coming in angry bursts against her cheek, turned her insides to mush.

*I'm innocent,* she wanted to cry out, but the words stuck like wads of cotton in her throat. *I didn't know they were going to steal your horses until just before they did it. Open your eyes, mister. Can't you see I'm a girl, for goodness sakes? What chance did I have of stopping them, a woman alone against five men?*

The man loosened his hold. She turned her head slightly, braving a sideways look at him. "I don't want to go to prison," she whispered tightly, her voice raw with fright and pain. "Nor do I want to get my neck stretched by a hanging rope. But I'm not going to tell you my last name no matter what. So why don't you just kill me now and get it over with? I'd be much obliged if you did."

The band around her waist tightened again. "You stubborn little smart-mouthed brat," he exploded. "Fine. Have it your way. I just ran out of threats."

The man shoved her forward out the door, taking up a coil of rope and his rifle as he followed her out. Nudging her roughly with the rifle butt, he herded her across the yard, past Shooter and Charlie's trampled bodies, to the corral. Keeping her eyes straight ahead, she tried desperately to avoid the horror of those two bodies sprawled face down in the dirt.

Ignoring her discomfort, he pushed her down to a sitting position beside a fence post. Deftly, he deflected her struggles, tied her hands and feet, then tightly wound the rope across her chest, securing her to the post.

Stepping back, he cocked the rifle.

Heart pounding, Jessie tried to prepare herself for death. It was hard, because staring down that rifle barrel, sucking in her last desperate breaths, she knew she didn't want to die. Oh sweet mercy, she just wanted to go to San Francisco and start a new life. She wanted to dip her bare toes into the grand Pacific Ocean, wanted to feel the cold, damp San Francisco fog she'd heard so much about caress her face. She wanted to leave her miserable life with Curtis far behind—to marry someday and have children. She wanted to find a man like kind Thomas Fowler who'd attempted to court her back in Missouri until Uncle Thaddeus put an end to things. Oh dear heaven. She wanted to marry a man like Thomas, or the fantasy one she'd always dreamed of finding someday in California.

She tore her eyes from the rifle and looked up. The man's jaw was set at a grim angle, his big hands gripping the stock, steadying it, taking aim. Their gazes locked. The man sucked in his breath.

She cried out as the shot boomed then echoed through the canyon, her whole body jerking as the powerful firearm exploded. *How strange*, she thought, as the last echo faded away and a peaceful calm settled over her. She felt no wrenching pain, and when she looked down she saw no blood streaming from a gaping wound in her chest.

Dumbfounded, Jessie raised her eyes. He'd shot over her head! Staring blankly at the man, her mind froze. He stared back, but only for a moment. Tight-lipped, he spun on his heel and left her there as he stalked off into the trees with determined, angry strides.

☙ ☙ ☙

Nearing noon, the sun blazed at its zenith, fat and orange and hotter than a bushel of chili peppers. Drenched in perspiration, Jessie sat slumped against the fence post, her whole body one aching, steaming mass of discomfort.

Trying to loosen the knots binding her wrists had proved futile. Scraped raw from her efforts, her delicate skin burned beneath the rough hemp, the abrasions oozing blood. The headache had gotten worse, her bottom still stung, and her shoulder throbbed whenever she shifted positions.

Yet, she was alive.

Her head lolled forward, the brim of her Stetson brushing her knees, knocking it slightly askew. The hat was the only thing protecting her face from the sun's blistering rays, and now she'd nearly lost it. Desperately, she straightened up again, struggling to stay alert.

Why had the man spared her? For hours she'd pondered that riddle, coming up empty every time she thought about it. For the hundredth time, the man's searing blue eyes floated before her. Those unrelenting eyes that had suddenly softened for one, heart-stopping moment just before his finger squeezed the trigger.

Moaning softly, she forced her mind to concentrate on other things. *Okay, so he hadn't killed her. But how long did he plan to keep her tied up like this?* The relentless sun beating down on her was nigh to unbearable. Her whole body ached worse than that time she'd tried to run away from home and Uncle Thaddeus had taken his belt to her.

And.... And.... More than anything, she needed to use the privy.

Charlie Deerhorn's body lie not twenty feet away, his crushed and bloody skull abuzz with hungry flies. A few yards farther on, Shooter's corpse lie bloating in the heat. Had the man done this on purpose? Positioned her so that she was forced to look at the horrific consequence of her "crime" before she died?

He had. She was sure of it.

She closed her eyes tightly, forcing her thoughts to drift elsewhere. They landed on her cousin Curtis. For a while she'd thought maybe he would come back for her. She'd been tied out here in the open, unguarded, for hours. Sadly, she realized that if Curtis had ever been going to rescue her, he'd have done it by now. But when had her cousin ever cared about what happened to her? For as long as she could remember, from the first day she'd come to live with her aunt and uncle, she and her jealous cousin Curtis had been adversaries.

She sighed, thinking about Missouri. Thinking about the farm, the only home she'd ever known. Uncle Thaddeus had died eight months ago, a mere six months after Aunt Cora passed on. Her uncle's body hadn't lain in the ground even two days before Curtis began making grand plans.

Since Uncle Thaddeus hadn't provided for her in his will, his death had left her destitute, totally dependent upon Curtis's almost non-existent sense of charity. When Curtis sold the farm to finance his trip west, he hadn't given Jessie one penny of the proceeds. Her only option had been to beg him to take her with him to San Francisco.

He objected, of course. Never thinking beyond his own selfish ambition, he didn't give a hoot about what would happen to her should he leave her behind.

"It's a grueling trip and you'll slow me down," he'd argued. "You're too puny and inept, Jess. You'd never make it. So the answer is no."

If Curtis hadn't drunk too much that night so long ago, if she hadn't caught him at a very weak moment, convincing him she'd be useful doing all the camp chores during the trip, she never would have gotten him to agree to take her along.

Now she wished she hadn't begged so hard.

After the bank robbery, following Charlie Deerhorn's advice and relying on the Indian's wilderness experience, Curtis had led his gang deep into the Sierra Nevada Mountains. They'd successfully outrun the Sulfur Flats posse, but Jessie couldn't help but worry that somehow, someday, the law would catch up with them—with her.

"Stop your fretting, Jess," Curtis had told her one evening not long ago when she was feeling particularly anxious. She hadn't eaten or slept much in days, worrying about that posse. All her waking hours and all her midnight dreams kept filling up with hangmen, nooses, and prison cells.

Her cousin had finally gotten fed up and threatened to shoot her if she didn't stop worrying. "I did a good job turning you into a boy," he'd said. "Your appearance is so different from what you used to look like, I bet if that yahoo witness was standing square in front of you he'd swear you weren't the one he saw that day."

But Jessie wasn't so sure. She was still the same height, weight, and coloring....

Her eyes flew open. Somebody was coming. She could hear footfalls thrashing through the undergrowth just beyond the trees. Hope surged through her. Maybe she'd underestimated Curtis, been too quick to disparage him. Maybe he'd come back for her after all!

She moistened her parched lips with her tongue and tried to shout for help, but her mouth and throat were too dry. Sucking in a breath, concentrating, she attempted a second time to force a strangled plea past her lips.

But the words died in her throat. She slumped forward against the ropes that bound her, more heartsick and miserable than she'd ever been in her life. It wasn't Curtis coming to rescue her at all. The man was back, and he looked meaner and more determined to do her harm than ever.

# Chapter Four

The kid looked half dead. Mitch clenched his jaw, holding back a curse. Why the devil hadn't he shot the brat hours ago like he'd meant to? Because...because the kid was just that. A snot-nosed, misguided *kid* who'd ridden down the wrong trail and got caught. A schoolboy outlaw whose desperate, pleading eyes would have haunted his dreams for the rest of his life had he pulled that trigger.

He'd been watching the clearing and the corral for the last few minutes to make sure the area was clear of trouble before he walked out of the trees. Frowning, he shook his head, then laughed a bitter little laugh. Yep. This nightmare was real, all right. Nothing had changed. His horses were still gone, and nobody'd come to snatch the brat back.

He gazed at the suffering boy again. He hadn't meant to be gone this long, but he'd needed to track his animals and determine the direction they were headed before the signs disappeared. Without a horse, it had been slow going. He glanced at the sky, worried. Every afternoon this week, thunder clouds had rolled in, dumping rain. The violent squalls lasted only an hour or so, but if another storm gathered today, all hope of tracking the herd would vanish. As it was, unless he could force Jessie to tell him the thieves' destination, he had about as much of a chance of finding them on foot as finding a virgin in a whore house.

"I see nobody came to your rescue while I was away," he taunted when he reached the corral. The boy recoiled at the barb.

Mitch was feeling mean and angry enough to bite the head off a rattler. Angry at himself, mostly, for not guarding his horses better, for letting a band of criminals steal his precious stock. For allowing sentiment to get between him and this scrawny, horse-thief kid before he'd stalked off to track the rest of the bunch this morning.

"Sure looks like your friends deserted you, doesn't it? Dry gulched you good, didn't they?" Taunting the kid and watching him flinch felt good. Real good.

He set the Winchester against a fence post out of his prisoner's reach. Pulling his hunting knife from his belt, he squatted down. Sunlight flashed off the wide blade, catching the kid in the eyes.

"Hold still," Mitch ordered as he reached behind the boy's back and sliced through the hemp. Noticing the bloody abrasions, he inwardly winced, feeling some of his temper ease. He sucked in a breath. The little runt did it to him every time.

"Hey, you awake?" he prompted roughly.

The kid didn't answer. Gripping the boy's jaw, he tipped it up to study the hot, sweaty face beneath the hat brim. Leaving the ankles tied, Mitch snagged the rifle and headed for the water barrel.

"Here," he said moments later, holding out a dipper of cool water. The boy clutched it awkwardly, drinking hastily, spilling some down the front of his shirt. "Take it easy. Drink it slow or you'll puke it all back up."

When the cup was empty, Mitch cut the ankle bonds and sheathed the knife. "Can you stand?"

"I-I don't know," came the shaky answer.

Mitch didn't wait to find out. Hauling him up by the shirt front, he said gruffly, "Get into the cabin before you keel over from sunstroke." He didn't let go of the shirt.

"Wait," Jessie cried, unsteady and stumbling so much Mitch had to watch his own steps or go sprawling in the dirt himself. "Please."

"What now?"

"I...I have to use the privy."

Mitch yanked the kid to a halt. He'd never seen a body so sissified in all his life. He'd said, "use the privy" shyly, just like a girl would. And was that smooth, little-boy face flushing crimson now after saying it? One thing for sure, if this kid didn't toughen up and soon, he'd never make it to adulthood before some bully bashed his brains in.

Reining in his temper, he roughly changed directions, prodding him with the rifle butt. "Over there. Leave the door open. I'm in no mood for shenanigans."

The boy stammered, turning even redder. "I...I won't try anything, mister. Please. Let me shut the door."

"Not a chance."

"Then forget it. If you're going to watch, I...I won't…."

Exasperated, Mitch clenched his jaw. "Get in there, Jessie. Shut the door if you must, but I swear, if you so much as grunt wrong…." He didn't need to finish the threat. The kid got the point.

☙ ☙ ☙

Mortified, Jessie hurried into the privy, shutting the door with an unintentional bang. Praying the man wouldn't change his mind and barge in on her, she quickly took care of business.

The smelly, airless chamber nearly suffocated her. Her head hurt so bad it was hard to hang onto consciousness. She wanted to faint. She wanted to throw up. The breast binder was squeezing her to death. If she didn't get a full breath of air quickly, she was going to pass out and fall head first into the cesspit.

At that moment she hated Curtis for the way he'd always controlled her life, loathed and despised him for abandoning her to that terrifying beast lurking just beyond the privy door. Not able to stand it one more second, Jessie allowed the rage to obliterate her self-pity.

Unbuttoning her shirt and removing it, she tore at the cursed hooks and eyes until at last she was free of the suffocating binder. With shaking fingers, she tossed the symbol of her bondage down the privy.

Despite the stench, she took a deep breath. Bending slightly, she peered down the hole at the white linen floating in the filth below. She groaned inwardly, having second thoughts. What if the man discovered her secret because of what she'd just done? What if Charlie's bulky shirt failed to hide her curves? Would the man try to rape her?

Curtis always told her she wasn't much to look at, but that if a man wanted a woman badly enough, any female would do. Her considerable deficiencies wouldn't matter, he'd insisted. That's the reason her cousin always enforced such strict rules between her and the men.

"You fall in, kid? Hurry up."

A loud thump on the door spurred her into action.

"I'm coming," she cried in a strangled voice, shrugging on the shirt and fumbling to button it. After stuffing the tails into her pants, she hastily opened the door.

"Come on," the man said, pointing the rifle at her.

Breathing deeply for the first time in days, she gratefully filled her lungs with pure, sweet, mountain air. Not even fear of this towering, rifle-brandishing brute diminished this blessed moment of freedom.

Inside the cabin he pressed her down into the same chair she'd occupied that morning. His blue eyes were on fire again, and when he glared down at her, the flames scorched her near to cinders. He kept her there for a good ten minutes, pacing back and forth, not saying a word.

She was grateful for the respite. The cabin was blessedly cool, and she began to feel a little better. He'd allowed her to see to her creature comforts, the water had slaked her thirst, and at last she could breathe properly. Thank heaven for small blessings.

Jessie passed the time staring at her folded hands in her lap. But when the man turned to glare at her again, a bolt of terror shook her. What was he thinking?

Finally, she couldn't stand his dark scrutiny any longer. With an upward tilt to her chin, she said with all the courage she could muster, "You didn't kill me. Why?"

"Shut up."

She hesitated, but only for a moment.

She'd had hours to think things through. Since he hadn't pulled the trigger this morning, she doubted he ever would. Which meant there might be a slight chance she could redeem herself, possibly go free. She decided to offer the proposition she'd fashioned earlier, now before her courage failed her.

She said, "I'm sorry about your horses, mister. Truly. I know they were valuable to you. I've been thinking. What if I work off the value of the horses? What if you just set a price and...and I agree to do any job you say until we're square? Then afterward I'll go on my way and you—"

"Ha!" he snorted, his gaze traveling the length and breadth of her. His eyebrows drew together and his scowl became a monstrous thing.

Jessie felt herself shriveling, her voice growing faint. Quickly, she insisted, "I'm stronger than I look. I'm a hard worker and know how to do most everything. I'm a great cook—"

The man slammed the flat of his hand on the table, rounding on her as if next he was going to slam it into her face.

"All I want from you, kid, is information. Tell me where your friends have taken my horses. What were their plans?"

Eyes wide, Jessie met his scorching glare. "I don't know," she cried in a rush, pressing her hands to her throbbing temples. "I swear I don't know!"

"Sure you don't," he laughed derisively. Pacing the length of the table and back he said, "I didn't shoot you, Jessie, but that doesn't mean I won't make your life miserable from now on as punishment for what you've done. Okay. You say you want to work for me? I had fifteen of the finest mustangs west of the Rockies out there in that corral. Plus my own, near priceless saddle horse. The mustangs were broke and ready for sale. The army was willing to pay big for them. A hundred dollars apiece. You got well over fifteen hundred dollars' worth of work in you, kid?"

Jessie nearly swooned. White faced, she stared up at the man, open-mouthed. It would take her years to work off such a huge sum.

"Stand up!" The sudden, vicious command came like a whiplash. "So you're strong are you? Willing to do any job I say? Well, come with me then. We're going to find out just what a stinking liar you are. Move!"

Outside, he snagged a shovel leaning against the wall and stalked over to Shooter's prone body.

Jessie scurried to follow his angry strides—until she saw where he was headed. She hesitated, primal instinct urging her to bolt.

The man snarled over his shoulder, "Try running, kid, and I'll shoot you down like a rabid animal. I won't kill you, but the wound will cripple you for life. Get over here. Now."

After turning the body over, the man hunkered down and motioned for Jessie to kneel down on the other side. The sight of Shooter's bullet-riddled body made her stomach roil and her pulse race. She struggled to keep from heaving.

"Go through his pockets. Whatever we find we'll save for the authorities."

Jessie stared at the man's implacable face. He was going to force her to do this, and she didn't think she could. Biting her lip, it took her a moment to gather the courage to obey him.

*Oh Shooter, I'm so sorry. So sorry,* she moaned silently.

The man finished on his side before she'd pushed her fingers into even the first pocket on hers. Somehow in the next few moments she made it through the grisly search, but just barely.

"Shooter Gant," the man mumbled, thumbing through a thin leather envelope full of Shooter's personal papers. He looked up at Jessie for confirmation. "That's who this letter's addressed to. Is this man Gant?"

Jessie nodded, too heartsick to speak.

After sorting through the rest of the papers, the man pulled a long lock of hair out of the envelope, holding it up to the sun. The strands were the color of mahogany and tied in the middle with a yellow ribbon. He studied it only for a moment before tucking it back into the envelope.

Jessie held her breath, her thoughts careening back to those moments when Shooter had held her down while Curtis cut her hair. The big, brooding cowboy had kept a lock of her hair! Hot tears stung the backs of her lids, and she rapidly blinked them away.

"Help me drag him over to the trees. Take his feet."

The blunt command left no room for argument. With tears still threatening to spill, she sucked in a breath and did as she was told.

Shooter was heavy. She felt the painful pull to her injured shoulder with every difficult step. It was a miracle that she managed not to drop her end even once.

"Now the other one," the man said grimly.

Because of the position he'd held during the raid, Charlie's body was badly battered, one side of his skull nearly crushed flat. He'd been shot twice in the back; the bullets exiting the chest. His shirt was drenched with blood, the gaping holes black and ugly. Shaking with revulsion, Jessie bent to the task, again desperately swallowing bile.

One by one, they extracted Charlie's meager possessions: a deerskin beaded medicine pouch, a hunting knife, a turquoise amulet carved in the shape of a turtle. All these things Jessie had seen many times during the weeks Charlie had been a part of their group.

"Well, look here," the man said, holding up a goodly length of braided brown hair. The strands were decorated with bits of feathers and beads, tied at the ends with thin strips of rawhide. "Another lock of hair."

The man studied her briefly. Jessie remained silent, praying the man wasn't making any connections.

A sweet, awkward rush of awe flooded her. Had each of the men taken a trophy that day? Men sometimes kept a lock of their sweetheart's hair....

He motioned for her to stand, and they dragged the gruesome body to the trees.

Easing down onto a fallen pine limb and cradling the Winchester across his arms, the man said, "I figure burying those two is worth a dollar apiece." He thrust his chin toward the shovel lying in the dirt. "Get started."

Jessie stared at the shovel, worn to the bone with disgust and resentment.

"You heard me," he barked. "I said, get started."

Picking up the heavy spade, she shoved it hard into the loamy earth. Recent rains had softened the ground, making the task easier than she thought it would be. Still, lifting the heavy dirt began to take its toll. After the tenth shovelful, her shoulder felt as if an invisible hand were trying to wrench it from her body. Blisters were beginning to form on the palms of her hands.

It was cooler under the trees, though, and she was thankful for that. She was terribly thirsty, but was afraid to ask for a drink, determined not to show any kind of weakness. Bullies like this man only got meaner if their victims showed weakness. Concentrating, she began to chant silently, *Place, push, lift and swing. Place, push, lift and swing.* The chant helped to keep a steady rhythm, helped her to keep her sanity, but to her dismay, progress proved terribly slow.

She'd been concentrating so hard, she hadn't noticed the man had left her. Emptying the shovel, Jessie looked up to see him sauntering across the yard toward her, a canteen dangling from one hand. Reaching her side, he took the spade and handed her the canteen.

Gratefully, Jessie drank, sinking to her knees before she could stop herself.

Within moments, a sure, steady rhythm filled her ears. Dragging the back of her hand across her lips, she looked up. The man was continuing where she'd left off.

"No!" Jessie cried out, staggering to her feet. "You can't. I won't let you cheat me out of those two dollars."

"You're worth nothing to me dead, kid. And that's what you're gonna be if you keep digging. You're done in. So drink that water and shut up."

"No," Jessie cried again, staggering forward and nearly toppling into the grave.

"Stop it, Jessie. You're so blasted puny and weak you can barely lift the shovel. Now sit your sissy rump down by that tree and keep your trap shut."

Puny. Weak. Those had always been Curtis's words for her. This man had added another one: sissy. The worst insult one man could hurl at another man.

*If she were a man.*

It was too much. She'd had enough. Wildly, she searched the ground, the world turning blood-red. Heart galloping out of control, she stooped to grab the first stout limb she saw. Like a screeching she-cat, she sprang in reckless fury.

"You lousy, stinking, rotten, sorry excuse for a man," she screamed, going for the man's belly. But he was quicker, knocking the limb aside with the shovel as she lunged. The limb almost flew from her hands, but she held on. Gripping the rough wood in her bloody palms, she tried again. With all her might she spun and thrust again, this time barely catching him in the upper arm, tearing his shirt.

He made no move to strike back at her with the shovel. He just stood there, as if dumbfounded that she would even try such a stunt. Anger such as she'd never known overcame her. "You stinking, mangy cur! You lousy skunk," she snarled, thrusting again. "I'm not weak! I'm not puny! What I've endured the last months would have *broken* a lesser person." Scalding tears streamed down her cheeks but she didn't care. She was going to kill him.

With one, swift, flawless twist of his powerful body, the man knocked the limb from her hands, threw down the shovel, and grappled her to the ground. Fighting like a madwoman, Jessie kicked and clawed, writhing beneath his enormous weight.

She saw the slap coming and tried to turn her head, but she wasn't fast enough. His open palm connected with her cheek, the stinging crack making her ears ring. Pulsing with adrenaline, Jessie raised her own hand, raking her ragged fingernails across his neck. Catching him unprepared, there came a moment when the grip on her shoulders slackened and his weight shifted. In a flash she kneed his groin, then rolled to the side. She heard him grunt, swearing at the pain. Freedom was almost hers....

Viciously, he yanked her back. "Stop it," he shouted, holding his crotch with one hand, the scruff of her shirt collar with the other. Jessie heard a tremendous rip, saw buttons flying every which way as she flew backwards. She felt the cool breeze on her belly and breasts. Then she was beneath him again, panting and sobbing, her wrists imprisoned above her head, held there in one of his huge hands. He straddled her, his thighs pinning hers as he panted swear words above her face.

He looked down.

The world froze.

Their eyes locked.

He sucked in a deep, ragged breath.

*Oh, God. He knows.*

# Chapter Five

"I'll kill you," Jessie choked out the words. "I swear, mister, I'll k—"

"Easy. Take it easy." Holding her down, the man let her struggle until she ran out of fight.

After a while, he relaxed his thighs and loosened his grip on her wrists. Weary beyond any weariness she'd ever known, Jessie lay there, feeling exposed, helpless, and lost. *What would happen to her now? What would he do now that he knew? He was a man, and men....* She couldn't think about it.

He seemed to read her thoughts.

With his free hand, he pulled her tattered shirt together, covering her naked breasts. "I didn't know," he rasped, shaking his head. "I swear I didn't know."

Jessie's Stetson had long ago tumbled off her head, leaving her cropped hair vulnerable to his scrutiny. Studying her hard, his gaze wandered over her face, her hair, her upper body, delving into the depths of her desperate glare. She knew his anger still simmered dangerously beneath the surface. He was scowling so darkly she wondered if he would strike her again.

"Why didn't you tell me right off?" he ground out at last, his face so close to hers their breath mingled. "Don't you have any sense at all, girl? I hit you. Twice." Unsteady fingers traced the curve of her stinging cheek, sending uncontrollable tremors through her limbs. "I nearly shot you. I left you out there alone for hours this morning. Ah, Jessie girl, you should have told me."

Rolling off her, he lifted her in his arms and stood. She squirmed, but soon gave it up when he pressed her hard to his chest, shutting off her protests like nothing else could. She was too exhausted to fight that awesome strength anymore.

"I'm taking you into the cabin," he said. "You can rest there." His voice was pitched low, its cadence almost gentle as he met her gaze. "Later, when you're feeling better, we'll talk."

She tried to speak, tried to protest, but the words wouldn't come. Kindness from him was unexpected, throwing her off center. Her poor, battered wits didn't know how to deal with this new kind of animal.

His powerful arms were holding her now, not as a prisoner, but as if she were fragile, precious. The sensation went totally beyond her experience. It was almost as if suddenly his raw masculinity were there to protect her instead of do her harm. And that didn't make sense.

She closed her eyes. Too worn out to understand anything happening to her now, she reluctantly yielded to his overwhelming dominance, her exhausted body at last going slack in the strange, gentle security of his embrace.

☙ ☙ ☙

Mitch slouched in one of the uncomfortable wooden chairs, his booted feet propped on the hearth ledge, crossed at the ankles. Between savage drags on the cheroot clenched between his teeth, he sent frequent glances toward the fragile, dark-haired *girl* asleep like a curled-up kitten on his bed. Too spent to fight him further, she'd fallen asleep almost at once as soon as he'd placed her there.

Why him? How had things turned so crazy upside down in so short a time? Curse the little scamp for her duplicity. And curse her all over again for making a fool of him, first by stealing his horses, then by hiding her gender.

Didn't she know what a dangerous game she'd played? Twice he could have killed her, first with a bullet, then with his bare hands. If he hadn't reined in his temper out there by the grave site, he might have struck her with his closed fist instead of his open palm. He might have hit her with all his strength, breaking her jaw. Hit her like he would hit a man deserving a killing.

The girl groaned, shifting onto her back. The thin sheet he'd covered her with didn't do much to disguise the shape of her trim woman's body beneath it. It took some effort to rein in the sudden, hot surge of desire that coursed through him. Cursing didn't help.

It had been a year or more since he'd had a woman, way too long since he'd enjoyed the pleasure of female company in his bed.... *Whoa! Stop it right there, Mitch*, he warned himself. He shifted uncomfortably, making the rickety chair creak. Taking another long drag on the thin cigar he'd lit moments before, he exhaled the smoke in twin streams through his nostrils, forcing his thoughts to head in another direction. What was her story, anyway? Where had she come from? And how'd she get mixed up with an outlaw gang of horse thieves?

While she slept, he'd taken a lot of time studying her face. She was older than he'd first thought—maybe twenty or so, now that he knew it was a female face he was looking at. Was she the sister of one of those men? A wife? Or, more like it, he thought grimly with a shudder of disgust, the camp whore? And why the devil had she cut her hair off like that? And those hideous britches....

There were a million questions he wanted to ask her. *Would* ask her as soon as she recovered enough to talk.

Meanwhile, he flipped the cheroot butt into the hearth, then lit another, just to give his itching hands something to do. To keep them from reaching out and touching her silky cheek, maybe more. Jessie whatever-her-last-name-was, was making his blood sing.

His gaze lingered on the outline of her slim, graceful figure beneath the sheet. Another surge of heat flooded his body, but this time from anger more than desire. He felt like a fool. How had he missed all the signs? She was a pretty little thing, small and delicate like a prairie flower, not mannish at all. Shoot, he figured she'd be downright *beautiful* once he got her cleaned up.

She groaned again, then murmured a few more disjointed words he couldn't decipher. Her dusky voice had an appealing, grainy edge to it. It sort of reminded him of sawdust and warm whiskey and long nights in smoky saloons.

She fidgeted, no doubt in the throes of a dream, arching a slender arm above her head. When a muffled cry escaped her lips, he wanted more than ever to reach out and touch her. Instead, he sucked in a full lungful of smoke, holding it there to near bursting.

"Currrrtis?"

He blew out the smoke. Well, he understood that word perfectly. *Who the devil is Curtis?*

"Neeeed...you...Curtis. Don't...want to die. The...man. Dangerous. No! Can't go to prison. I don't know...swear I don't know...."

He flipped the cheroot into the cold hearth. In one swift move he was by her side, shaking her awake. "Jessie, wake up. You're having a bad dream."

Her eyes flew wide and she cried out, struggling to escape his grip. Mitch's mind raced. "Easy," he said, keeping his tone even. "You were having a nightmare." He let go of her and held his hands up in the age-old gesture of surrender. "It's okay, Jessie. Easy now."

The sheet fell away as she scrambled to the edge of the bed until she couldn't retreat any farther. Pressing her back against the wall, she clutched the edges of her shirt together and cried, "Don't touch me. Leave me alone!"

Not moving a muscle, Mitch said, "It wasn't my intent to hurt you just now. You were having a nightmare. I woke you up to spare you from it. If I hurt your shoulder again, I swear I didn't mean to."

Warily, she eyed him, her body rigid, her face a pale cameo against the backdrop of the wooden wall.

Mitch felt like the animal she thought he was. Holding her gaze, he stood, then after a few moments turned his back on her. Casually, as if his heart weren't pounding nearly out of his chest, he said, "There's a pot of beans in the warmer. When's the last time you had something to eat?"

He glanced over his shoulder. Nothing moved but those dark eyes, following him as he made his way over to the cook stove. Taking two bowls and two spoons off the shelf above the dry sink, he set them down on the table, then headed for the pot of beans. Removing a cast-iron skillet from the warmer with a dish-towel-covered hand, he ladled some of the spicy, aromatic beans into his bowl. After plunking the pot in the middle of the table, he fetched two cups of coffee, then sat down and began to eat.

He could tell the tempting aroma of baked beans was driving her crazy; he could hear her stomach rumble all the way across the room.

"You gonna cower over there like a scared kitten, or are you gonna come over here and have something to eat? Come on, Jessie. Let's call a truce." He attempted a smile, hoping to put her at ease. All of a sudden it wasn't gratifying anymore, having her scared of him. "At least until after dinner," he added dryly.

Slowly, warily, she edged off the bed. Keeping the table between them, she clutched her shirt together with one hand, dragging out a chair with the other. Keeping one eye on him at all times, with her free hand she dipped repeatedly into the pot, filling her bowl nearly to the brim.

He laughed. "Hungry, are you, brat? Been a while?"

Her gaze dropped to the bowl as she lifted the spoon. Shrugging, she said, "Nearly two days."

Mitch dragged his chair back and she flinched.

"It's all right," he assured her quickly. "Take it easy. I'm only getting the leftover biscuits from this morning's breakfast. Here," he said, setting a tin plate piled with biscuits in front of her. "Eat your fill."

He didn't say anything again until her bowl was empty and the biscuits nearly gone. Obviously, it was awkward for her, eating one-handed while trying to hold the ruined shirt in place with the other. He thought of teasing her about it, but held his tongue. Instead, he left the table to rummage around in his clothes trunk.

Keeping a good couple of feet between them, which would force her to meet him halfway, he held out one of his old shirts, the tight expression on his face daring her to refuse it. "This won't fit you properly either, but at least it'll cover you up. Since I did the damage to *your* shirt, I'm making you a present of one of mine."

She hesitated, and he could read her thoughts. Clearly, she didn't trust him. Well, he supposed he couldn't very well blame her for that.

"I won't bite you," he promised. "Neither will the shirt. Come on over here and take it."

"No," she said. "I'll take the shirt, but I want you to put it on the table then step away."

He thought about refusing, but changed his mind. If he was to gain her trust, if he were going to get any information out of her about his stolen horses, he'd allow her to call the shots for now. He approached the table and laid the shirt where she could easily reach it, then stepped away.

Rising, Jessie snatched up the garment and clutched it to her chest. "Turn around," she demanded, and waited until he complied.

He could hear the soft rustle of fabric as she pulled on the new shirt. When she gave the all clear, he turned around to find that in a matter of seconds she had not only donned the shirt, but had it buttoned clear up to her throat. The old tattered shirt lay at her feet on the floor.

Mitch laughed, though his gut tightened at the sight of her smallness, her obvious vulnerability, her pinched, wary face with those big eyes peering out at him above the collar. His blue chambray shirt nearly swallowed her up.

Sobering, he sighed. *So now what? What the devil was he going to do with the little horse thief now?*

# Chapter Six

When Jessie finally managed to get the fresh shirt fastened and told him it was okay to turn back around, she never in her life felt so grateful to be completely covered again. She sat back down at the table, considering whether to have one more ladleful of beans. After a moment, the man sat again, as well. When next she looked up, he was staring at her across the table as if she were a bug in a glass jar. She stared back, trying her darnedest not to show how terrified of him she was. He sat there, elbows on the table, looking full and satisfied after his dinner of beans and biscuits, and...so very frighteningly male.

"Are you feeling better?" he asked, the chair groaning that familiar groan as he shifted forward toward her. Inanely, she wondered how the frail wood managed to support his solid bulk.

She wasn't feeling better at all. Even after the much-needed nap, her bottom and cheek still stung, her shoulder hurt, and her head was pounding like hammer blows to an anvil. But she refused to let him know it. She wouldn't complain. Just then, she thought of Curtis. He always said men hated for a woman to complain and got angry whenever he assumed she was. No, it would be far more prudent to just keep silent.

He tried again. "How's the shoulder?"

Mercy, the man was persistent. She wet her lips, weighing the odds. His eyes lazily followed the path of her tongue, sending heat to her cheeks.

"Come on, brat," he teased. "Talk to me."

"My head hurts," she finally admitted. "But not much," she added quickly.

"Sure. And my name's Rumpelstiltskin." The man rose and started around the table toward her. Alarmed, Jessie stood too, ready to bolt.

The man stopped cold. "Look," he said, sighing. "I told you I won't bite, and I meant it. I can't help you if you won't let me see the wound."

Jessie hesitated, and when she did, he stepped closer and snagged her wrist. Their eyes locked. He wouldn't let her pull away. Then, just like that, something changed between them. Jessie saw a shadow of sympathy mixed with frustration cross his features, and when she did, some deep inner voice told her he was telling the truth, that she could allow his touch, accept his offer of help. All she could do now was pray she was right, that he wasn't going to hurt her again.

She let out a long breath. "Okay," she said. "But promise you'll stop if I tell you to."

"Deal." With gentle fingers, he began to probe the scalp high above her right temple. "That's quite a gash and knot. It's bled some. No wonder you've got a blinding headache."

She raised her eyelashes in surprise. "Who said anything about a headache?"

His lips twitched. "Nice try."

"Okay, you're right. It hurts something awful. I...hit a rock when I fell from my horse."

He nodded, dropping his hand to his side. His other hand still held her wrist.

"And your shoulder?"

"It hurts, too." She hesitated. "I...hurt it trying to...trying to help a friend." To her mortification, tears threatened as she thought of Marty. Thought of how he'd abandoned her after she'd risked her life to help him. Mentally, she gave herself a good shake. Mercy sakes, she'd done more crying and feeling sorry for herself in the past week than she had in her entire lifetime, but right at this moment, no matter how much she wanted to, she simply couldn't keep the tears from welling up. She felt so broken and betrayed. The whole lot of them had abandoned her!

The man noticed the tears and frowned, but clearly, he misunderstood her reasons for shedding them. "The shoulder isn't dislocated, you know. You'd be hollering like a mad woman if it was. It's just badly bruised. It'll feel much better in a couple of days." He glanced at the shelves above the dry sink. "I've got some laudanum around here somewhere. Later I'll find it for you. It'll ease the pain."

She swiped her eyes with the back of her shirt sleeve. *In a couple of days.* Would she still be alive in a couple of days? Or would she be on her way to jail? Facing a hangman's noose, perhaps? A sore shoulder and a bad headache were the least of her troubles. Losing her confidence again, she asked, desperately, "What are you going to do with me?"

She felt a leathery thumb brush a lazy circle across the underside of her wrist. He remained silent for a moment, studying her dewy lashes. To her frustration, he didn't answer her directly.

"I think you'll feel a lot better once we get you cleaned up." He bent toward her and sniffed. "Whew," he added, wrinkling his nose. "Girl, you sure do need a thorough wash."

Jessie raised her chin and set her jaw. She knew she smelled less than rosy, but that wasn't her fault. It had been days since she'd had a proper bath because Curtis had pushed them so hard, barely allowing them enough time for a meal and a short rest. To cover her injured feelings, she squared her shoulders and tried hard to feign indifference.

He merely laughed at her. "Come on," he said, dropping her wrist and snatching up his rifle. "Maybe you don't mind smelling like a hog waller, but I sure do. Follow me, and no protests," he ordered.

He led her outside to the rain barrel where he grabbed a sliver of soap and a towel hanging on a nail. Snagging her wrist again, he began moving toward the trees.

*A hog waller? How dare he say such a thing?* "Wait," she cried, digging in her heels. "Where are you taking me?"

"Down to the river. You're going to take a bath and wash those britches and whatever else you've got on that smells like you haven't washed in weeks. And if you put up a fight, I'll haul you over my shoulder and dump you into the river myself."

Jessie followed, sure he'd carry out his threat if she showed any further resistance. Once this morning, she thought she'd heard the roar of rushing water in the distance, but she'd dismissed it, thinking it was just the roaring of her injured temple. Now she knew better. Within five minutes, he'd brought her to the edge of a sizable stream, its clear, glimmering water tumbling over an impressive bed of smooth rocks and boulders. Jessie caught her breath. In spite of her distress, the sun-drenched beauty of the spot drew her, beckoned her like a siren's call.

The man dropped her wrist, but then quickly gripped her upper arm, turning her to face him. "There's nowhere to run," he warned, the flinty set of his jaw daring her to try. Gone was any hint of the gentleness she'd felt from him just moments ago. "If you run, I'll find you. Count on it."

She hung there, silent, weighing the warning, then wishing the ground would swallow her as another horror struck her. Would he watch while she removed her clothes? Would he watch her bathe?

He squeezed her arm, studying her. As if reading her thoughts he said, "I'm going to leave you here to bathe in private and wash your clothes, but I won't be far away. No need to wash my shirt. It's clean. Put it on after your bath, then spread your clean clothes out to dry on that boulder over there."

He handed her the soap and towel. She wanted to resist, and he saw.

"No arguments. When you wash your hair, pay close attention to that scalp wound. Don't scrub too hard or it'll start bleeding again. All you need do is cleanse the matted blood away. Got that?"

She nodded.

"Good. Now start singing."

Her head snapped up. "Singing?"

"Yeah. Loud enough so I can hear you from over there behind those trees." He jerked his jaw toward a stand of pines several yards away. "I'll have my back to you, so I want to be able to hear you. Understand?"

"You...promise you won't watch?" The words rushed out before she could stop them.

He looked down at her, his expression grim. "Maybe I will, maybe I won't." He paused, as if thinking things over. "Tell you what. If you promise not to run, I'll promise not to watch."

She didn't trust him an inch. She felt vulnerable and trapped with no way out. "I haven't got any real choice, do I?" she mumbled bitterly.

"Nope," he drawled. "So quit dawdling. Pick a song and start singing. I'm giving you twenty minutes. No more. If you aren't finished up by then, all promises are off."

The man abruptly turned to head for the trees. Biting her lip, she began unbuttoning the shirt. She also began to sing the first song that popped into her head, a tune Uncle Thaddeus always requested Aunt Cora play on the piano back home: "Aura Lee." She felt foolish. Ridiculous. Humiliated. Still, she managed to roughly croak out the melody.

Well, the man was in for a real treat now. She couldn't sing worth spit, had always been told to keep silent whenever the family gathered at the piano.

"Louder," she heard him call, and she could tell by the diminished sound that he had his back to her. He'd kept his promise, then, and hadn't turned around. Encouraged only slightly, she forced her fingers to move, her numb mind to concentrate on how good it would feel to be washed clean again. Lifting her voice, she nearly shouted the lyrics, faltering only slightly when he answered her warbling with a guffaw so loud she heard it over the din of the roaring water.

Shrugging off embarrassment, she gazed at the dancing river, the water lively and inviting. She'd felt grimy for days, ever since Curtis had forced her to wear Charlie's clothes. It would be heaven to feel truly clean again. To put fresh-smelling clothes next to her skin again.

She gazed longingly at the river. He'd said he wouldn't look if she didn't try to run. Maybe she could believe him….

By the time she reached the plaintive chorus of the song, she was naked and thigh-deep in the frigid water, glorying in sudsy lather, reveling in the warm kiss of the sun on her back while the swirling river washed every speck of grime away. Best of all, the cool water soothed the awful ache in her temple.

He'd given her twenty precious minutes. She decided she was going to enjoy every single second of them.

☙ ☙ ☙

Mitch took off for the trees at a slow, easy pace, hesitating only briefly when the girl's smoky voice began singing the old Civil War song, "Aura Lee." Woefully off key, her clumsy crooning actually hurt his ears.

"Louder!" he shouted, unable to keep from chuckling when she instantly obeyed. At last they were making progress.

Satisfied, he quickened his steps, and when he'd gone several yards into the trees, he settled in atop a flat granite boulder, his back to the river, keeping his rifle close. The temptation to watch Jessie bathe tortured him. What red-blooded male wouldn't want to feast on a banquet such as the one set before him now? After several minutes of fierce internal battle, he'd almost convinced himself that he'd be a fool not to look. But as he listened to her sing, as he listened to her *try* to sing, a pang of sympathy overtook him. That and a stab of conscience. What was he thinking? He'd just made her a promise. He was an honorable man. His word had always been his bond.

But, he told himself reasonably, since when did a promise to a horse thief carry any weight? Why was he torturing himself? He owed her nothing, and she owed him everything.

About to give in and look his fill, in the next instant the decision to look was stolen from him. All of a sudden the gawdawful singing came to a halt. He tensed. Grabbing his rifle, he turned and scanned the churning river through a break in the trees but saw no sign of the girl anywhere. Where had she gone?

Had she tricked him and run? Or had she lost her balance somehow and the current had pulled her under?

Just as he was about to go after her one way or the other, she came up sputtering and coughing, madly swiping the stinging soap from her eyes. Clambering toward the shallows, he heard her angry mumbling and relaxed. She'd fought the current and won.

She sure had grit. Not a soul could say otherwise. All the women he'd ever known, including his own sister whom he loved and respected dearly, couldn't hold a candle to Jessie when it came to courage and sheer determination. Jessie. This morning she'd come after him, a man three times her size and weight, with nothing but a broken tree branch for a weapon. With that injured shoulder and throbbing head, she'd wielded the shovel and dug that grave with a determination he could only call downright amazing. And then he'd made her suffer in the sun for hours after he'd tied her to the fence post....

Recovered from her mishap, she dunked her head once more to rinse the soap from her hair and eyes, straightened, and started that awful warbling again.

Watching her, Mitch held his breath, stunned. She was lovelier than any woman he'd ever known. Lovelier than he could ever have imagined. Shorn hair aside, he wondered how in the world he'd ever mistakened her for a boy.

But the next moment, to his great disappointment, the show ended. As if assessing the time, she splashed the rest of the way to shore, slipped on the shirt, and gathered up her dirty clothes. Choosing a flat rock to use as a washboard, she began to soap and scrub her things with a vengeance.

Sighing, he settled back down and let her finish up her laundry, this time, watching her like a hawk. When he decided the twenty minutes he'd given her were just about spent, he eased off the boulder and headed for the river.

She sure looked good in his shirt. The hem hit the bottoms of her calves, which left a fine view of her dainty ankles and bare feet. She was bending over, laying her drawers out to dry, when he came up quietly behind her.

"You can stop singing now," he said, his tone a bit more unsteady than he liked.

She spun around, startled. A discordant note stuck in her throat. Obviously, she hadn't heard him coming.

Angry at himself that she could rattle him so, he said the first thing that popped into his mind. "Anybody ever tell you you've got one doozy of a tin ear, Jessie? Remind me never to order you to sing again. I nearly died from the torture."

She colored and turned away, but not before he saw a flash of hurt in her eyes. Immediately, he regretted his taunt. He'd only meant to tease her, but instead he'd bruised her feelings. Again, he caught himself. Why should hurting a horse thief's feelings matter to him?

"Let me see your head," he said, shoving aside the guilt. He took her by the arm, turned her around, and pulled her close, fully expecting her to put up a fuss, surprised when she didn't. Instead, she stood stiffly before him, shivering slightly from the breeze on her damp skin, waiting for him to do whatever it was she thought he was going to do. She refused to meet his eyes. He could feel her tense muscles, the evidence of her simmering anger—or was it fear?—beneath his fingers, but he ignored it.

Drawing her near was a mistake. She smelled sweet and clean, just like the herbs in the soap he'd made her use. That, combined with her own womanly perfume nearly sent him to his knees. He set his rifle down, then carefully lifted her chin and turned her head toward the sun so he could better study the wound.

"It looks pretty good. I was afraid the gash might reopen when you washed it, but it didn't. Lucky you."

She turned her head away. "Yeah," she replied dully. "Lucky me."

She sounded so bleak and dispirited it startled him. "Jessie," he began, but wasn't sure how to finish, or even what he wanted to say. Why should he apologize? She was a thief. A criminal. He didn't have to lend her any quarter at all.

Looking at her scrubbed, sun-kissed cheeks, her glistening hair, her dark, sad eyes, Mitch all of a sudden went weak in the knees. He'd seen her naked; he knew she was naked now beneath the shirt. Her scent, her deep, sultry voice, the unique cap of short chestnut hair, her waiflike vulnerability—all of it caused such desire to course through him he could barely stand.

He cupped her cheek, tenderly rubbing his thumb over the slight bruise along the cheekbone. The bruise he had given her earlier when he'd lost his temper.

His voice sounded far too gruff when he asked, "Why do you wear men's clothes? And why do you keep your hair short like that? If I'd known you were a woman, I wouldn't have been so rough on you. I...caused a bruise here." The words left his mouth even before he'd consciously completed the thoughts. Hearing the apology in his tone irritated him. She didn't deserve an apology for any of his actions, yet he couldn't seem to mask the guilt he felt because he'd hurt her that way.

She just shrugged and once again attempted to turn away. He wouldn't let her. He narrowed his eyes as a sudden, uncomfortable thought struck him. "Is it that you wish you were born a man, Jessie? Are you...do you...prefer women? Is that it?"

"Certainly not!" she sputtered, taken aback. And somehow, given that immediate, emphatic response, he knew in his gut she was telling the truth.

He heaved a sigh of relief, laughing a little, throwing his arms around her when she tried to squirm away. "Well, at least that put the fire back in your eyes." When she settled down, he pressed her head against his chest and tilted her chin up, rubbing his thumb across her full, lower lip. "So. You prefer men. That's a relief."

She was warm beneath his hands. Soft and warm and infinitely feminine. He wanted her, the need to possess her so strong he reeled with it. It had been a long time for him, he told himself again. Far too long. Devilishly, he began to think of one-thousand-five-hundred blissful ways she could repay the money she owed him.

She was very young and looked the innocent, but for all he knew, what appeared to be so might just be an act. A ruse. A woman traveling with a band of outlaws? He couldn't be certain of anything. So, looking deep into those huge brown eyes, he couldn't help himself. Slowly, slowly, he bent his head and brushed his mouth against her full, moist lips.

Startled, she moved to stop him, wedging her hands between them against his chest, trying to push him away.

He held her tighter. "I want you, Jessie," he murmured against her cheek. "Sweet Jessie girl, horse thief or no, I want you."

He pressed her closer, thwarting her struggles. She felt so small and fragile against him, so easy to dominate. He heard her muffled protests against his chest, but he ignored them.

She tasted like warm peaches doused in brandy. So unbearably sweet and intoxicating his whole body trembled with need for her. But, of course she wasn't with him, wasn't where he wanted her to be. He could feel her resistance, her fear of him. She didn't want this, and knowing she didn't extinguished his ardor like nothing else could. He was a lot of things, but he was no rapist. No matter how much he ached to make love to her, he could never take her against her will, camp whore or no.

Frustrated, he tried to reason with her. "I'm a man like any other," he told her. "And you're a woman who just assured me she prefers men. I want you, Jessie. Can't you pretend I'm just one of the boys in the gang?"

He tried to kiss her again, but her lips were stiff and unyielding, her mouth closed firmly against him. Pulling away, he studied her upturned face, annoyed to see that her eyes were full of fury.

"What is it?" he asked, hauling in a lungful of air. She actually looked stunned, as if he'd hit her.

In a flash she answered him. "I said no! You've got some crazy idea I'm something I'm not. Stay away from me!"

He released her arms and reached for her hand, intending to talk some sense into her. But quicker than a blink, the next thing he saw was little bubble-like stars floating crazily before his eyes. For the second time that day, Jessie whatever-her-last-name-was, had kneed him hard, dead center in the groin.

# Chapter Seven

Jessie spun and ran. She prayed she'd injured him badly enough to get a decent head start. Sharp pine needles and jagged stones stabbed her bare feet, slowing her. Heart pounding, she stumbled blindly through the woods, not knowing where to go, but certain she needed to put as much distance between them as she possibly could.

Because he'd kill her for sure—or worse—if he found her.

A sharp rock pierced her left foot. Immediately, she felt a warm trickle of blood flow from the wound. Ignoring the pain, she pushed on, panting and stumbling, crashing through the woods as if the Sulfur Flats posse were hot on her tail.

As she reached down to press her hand to the stitch in her side, she heard it: heavy, swift footfalls pounding the ground behind her. She panicked, darting behind a tree, desperate to quiet her heaving breaths.

*Please, God, don't let him find me!* Pressing her back against the tree trunk, she tried to make herself small, prayed that she would somehow blend in with the shadows dappling the forest floor.

*Curtis was right. When a man's need was strong enough, any female body would do.*

And then he was there. Right in front of her, chest heaving, his features so fierce her bones seemed to turn to dust beneath his angry glare. Desperate, she heaved against him, taking him by surprise, briefly knocking him off balance. Like a slippery sprite, she ducked and ran, but he was right behind her, his heavy hand snatching her shirt, catching her easily. Pinning her against a tree, he locked her arms above her head in a vicious grip, pressing the lower half of his body against her so she couldn't move.

His blue eyes turned the color of midnight as she struggled against his iron hold. Through clenched teeth, he cursed.

"Hold still, you little wildcat. Stop it!"

Surely he would kill her now. Not even Curtis had ever looked at her with such fury in his eyes. She stilled, paralyzed with terror, preparing for the death blow. Oh how she cursed her feminine impotence against the overwhelming power of this dangerous mountain of a man. If only she had his strength. If only....

Abruptly, he dragged her from the tree and wrenched her around, pinning her hard against his chest. She understood the tactic immediately. With her arms locked behind her and her knees facing outward, there was no way she could attempt to hurt him a second time. She tried kicking his shins with her bare feet, but quickly gave that up. She only hurt herself.

She felt his hot, rapid breath at her temple, felt the rasp of his rough chin against her cheek as he moved his lips near her ear. Another foul curse escaped him, sending fresh ripples of terror through her.

"*Who are you*?" he demanded.

She couldn't speak. Her voice wouldn't work. She closed her eyes, desperately, trying to think of a way to save herself.

His breathing slowed. Then he moved, and a stab of pain shot through her shoulder. Instantly, he released her, spun her around, and imprisoned her wrists.

"Move," he said, nudging her forward. "I want answers, and I swear by all that's holy, you're going to give them to me."

He hauled her back to the cabin, heedless of her bare feet and discomfort. She had to run to keep up with his long, angry strides.

Once there, he ordered her to sit in a chair while he towered over her with his booted feet braced apart and his heavy arms crossed over his chest. Sweet mercy, he was huge. His broad shoulders filled her vision so completely, she saw nothing else.

"We're going to have a talk, Jessie. I'm going to ask the questions, and I swear, you're going to give me the answers or pay the consequences."

Slumping into the chair, she tried to catch her heaving breath. If she wasn't so exhausted, so utterly spent, maybe she could continue the fight, maybe even win somehow. But she was so tired and hurting she didn't know how she was managing to keep from sinking to the floor.

"First, I want to know who you are," he thundered. "And I mean your full name."

She stared at the man's heaving chest, thinking of Curtis. She wondered if her cousin had made it to Placerville by now. Wondered if he'd even once thought of her again after she'd fallen to misfortune. Ha! No doubt he'd been relieved to have gotten rid of her so easily.

Well, whatever happened now simply didn't matter anymore. Nothing did. She had no money, no clothes, no horse, no hope. What did it matter if this man abused her or killed her or kept her prisoner? She had no future. Even if she did manage to escape somehow, she'd be looking over her shoulder for the rest of her life, waiting for the day when the law—or this madman—would finally catch up with her.

"Answer me!"

She flinched. Her eyes locked with his. And in that instant, weary down to the center of her bones, she gave up. "Jessie Driscoll," she answered dully.

He stared at her, seeming to roll the name around in his brain. In the silence, she looked away and stole a glance at her injured foot. The cut throbbed, but it had stopped bleeding, she noticed, relieved.

"Jessie Driscoll," he repeated in a gruff whisper. More loudly he asked, "Where were they taking my horses?"

She lifted her good shoulder. "I don't know."

"Jessie—"

"Look, mister. Rape me. Kill me if you must. But I still don't know what Curtis's plans were! I have no idea where your horses are, and that's the truth. The only thing I can tell you is that when last I heard, we were headed for Placerville."

He shifted a little, glaring down at her. "Mitch," he said, finally, evenly.

"What?"

"My name is Mitch. Mitch Wyden. Not Mister."

Well, that tore it. She almost giggled. Why in the world was he telling her that now? At this point, what did it matter if she knew his name or not? She didn't care if it was Andrew Jackson or Abraham Lincoln or Humpty Dumpty.

She pulled at the hem of the shirt to better cover her bare legs. She felt exposed and vulnerable. Exactly the way he wanted it, she supposed.

"Who's Curtis?" he demanded.

Startled, she asked, "How did you—?"

"Just answer the question."

She hesitated, but only for a moment. Why should she try to protect her cousin? He'd abandoned her. Left her for dead. He cared nothing about her now, if ever he did.

"My cousin," she answered, biting her lip.

"Your cousin?"

Clearly, that threw him off balance, and she briefly wondered why.

"Yes. We were traveling together. To...to San Francisco. We were going to start a new life there."

He paused, mulling that over. "And where did you live before heading west?" he finally asked.

"Missouri. On a farm With Curtis and my Aunt Cora and Uncle Thaddeus. Right after my aunt and uncle died, Curtis made plans to come west."

"Don't you have parents? Brothers and sisters?"

She stared at her lap, remembering the dismal rainy day her father had dumped her off at her aunt and uncle's doorstep. After her mama died from a fever, her pa had had no use for a little girl of four. He'd asked his brother and sister-in-law to keep his child while he went off to deal with his grief and find a new life for himself.

Jessie never saw him again. She became a charity case, never quite belonging, never loved, never fitting in to the Driscoll household. She was always made to feel beholden to her relatives because they'd "been so kind" as to clothe her and feed her while her worthless, irresponsible father was off adventuring.

And then there was Cousin Curtis. He was a big boy, as blond as she was a dark brunette, as large as she was petite. Total opposites in looks, temperament, and in personality, they had grown up at odds with each other, sharing nothing whatsoever in common but their last names.

Her cousin had always been bigger than she. That had been Jessie's first impression of six-year-old Curtis the moment she'd seen him standing stiffly beside his mother's skirts, glaring at her as if he wanted to pound her four-year-old little body into the dust: that he was big and dangerous and full of a strength her female body could never hope to possess.

She looked up at Mitch Wyden, jerking her thoughts back to the present. Studying him, comparing him to Curtis, she thought that Mitch Wyden was a fitting handle for him, a solid, masculine name befitting a strong, virile man....

"Jessie—"

"No," she answered truthfully. "I haven't any parents or brothers and sisters. Just Curtis." Briefly, she told him the facts of her childhood, but only just enough to satisfy his immediate curiosity. He clearly was in no mood for long, sad stories, but even if he was, she didn't have the energy to tell him everything anyway.

A worried frown crossed his face. "Describe Curtis."

"What? Why?"

"Because I want to know what he looks like."

"Well, he's a big man. Not quite as big as you, but almost. He's blond and bearded and has blue eyes."

Mitch sighed. "I shot him, Jessie. I only winged him, but if he's the one who was riding drag behind the herd, I know I put a bullet in him before he got away."

Jessie sucked in a breath. Curtis had taken a bullet? Maybe that was why he hadn't come back for her. Maybe he'd been too weak from the wound to attempt a rescue. Maybe...maybe there was still a chance he'd come back for her.

He must have seen the stricken look on her face because he said quickly, "I said I winged him, Jessie. I didn't kill him. I'm sure of that."

She didn't say anything. She couldn't.

"So, you think they're headed for Placerville," he repeated, stroking the dark stubble on his chin.

"That's what Curtis said the last time we talked."

Fishing into his shirt pocket, he pulled out a cheroot. Striking a sulfur match on the seam of his jeans, he cupped the flame in his palm and lit up, deeply inhaling the smoke. With a flick of his fingers, he extinguished the flame and dropped the match.

"Tell me why a pretty woman like you would choose to wear men's clothes. Tell me why those chestnut locks aren't hanging long and thick down your back, or piled up in curls on the top of your head. That's how a decent, God-fearing woman would wear her hair."

The accusations and his pious tone hurt. As if she would ever choose this humiliation for herself! Filled with indignation, she almost didn't answer him. But when she looked up and saw the no-nonsense determination in his eyes, the fight went out of her again. Besides, she reasoned, what did she have to lose? If Curtis had been shot, that was all the more reason he would only watch out for his own hide and ditch his troublesome cousin. With a sinking heart, she realized that Curtis surely wouldn't be coming back for her.

"Curtis and the men robbed a bank in Sulfur Flats. He swore nobody got hurt, and the worst thing that happened was that the townsfolk lost a little money."

The story came tumbling out. All of it. How her cousin had made her hold the horses while they pulled the robbery, how she'd been spotted, how they'd fled from the posse, barely escaping into the mountains. How she'd worried day and night that the posse was going to catch them and hang her or put her in prison for the rest of her life.

"That's why Curtis put a knife to my hair and made me wear Charlie's clothes. The men held me down, and I begged him not to do it, but Curtis kept cutting and cutting." Her voice faltered as a shiver overtook her. "I don't think he realized how bad I'd feel afterwards. A woman without her hair is like...like.... Well, anyway, he gave me Charlie's clothes and a Stetson to wear, swearing that nobody would recognize me after that."

She ran out of words. With shaky fingers, she brushed the tears from her cheeks. She hadn't even realized she'd started to cry. Again, curse it!

Mitch took a long drag on the cheroot. "Are you telling me you had no idea what they were up to in Sulfur Flats?" he asked her softly, suddenly going very still.

She nodded, dropping her gaze.

"And when they stole my horses. You didn't know what they were about to do?"

"No. I swear it. I only figured things out moments before they rode. I...I even tried to stop my cousin." She took a deep breath, not fully understanding why she felt obliged to reveal this next bit of information. "A lot of good that did me. You didn't hit me hard enough to leave this bruise on my cheek. Curtis did. Just before dawn this morning."

The man, Mitch Wyden, softly swore, dropping the cheroot to the rough-planked floor, grinding it beneath his boot heel. He paced, as was his habit, Jessie realized, when he was upset. Suddenly, he turned to her again, piercing her through with his cobalt glare.

"What was your relationship to the rest of the men?"

"What?"

"You heard me. Answer the question."

She hesitated. "Well, I...I cooked for them and I mended their clothes when they needed it, and I had other camp chores, of course."

"And?"

"And what? That was about the extent of it."

"Describe the 'camp chores'," he insisted.

She suddenly understood his meaning. It wasn't very hard, since she clearly remembered how he'd treated her at the river, the words he'd used when he'd told her he wanted to lie with her. She stiffened, her injured pride and sense of dignity making her bolder than wisdom should have dictated.

She lifted her chin and shot him a frosty glare. "I'm *not* a harlot, sir. Unlike present company, the men Curtis chose to ride with were perfect gentlemen at all times. My cousin demanded it."

A faint tide of crimson spilled into his cheeks, evidence her barb had hit its mark.

"I see," he said, abruptly turning his back on her.

She followed his every move as he stalked over to the dry sink and rummaged through the shelves above it. The cabin was small, a shack really, with a tiny kitchen area, a table and chairs at one end, and a bed and hearth at the other. A crude night stand and an oil lamp stood beside the oversized rope bed. She saw another small room curtained off near the kitchen, which she supposed was the pantry and storage area. The place was confining, with no decoration on the walls of any kind to make it cheerful or more like a home. She wondered how such an imposing man as he would choose to live alone in a cramped, Spartan place like this.

Presently, he returned with a small vial in his hand. "Here," he said. "I found the laudanum. Take a swig now and another one later on. It'll ease your pain."

She doubted that very much; some kinds of pain simply couldn't be eased. Thanks to Curtis, her battered, disillusioned heart might never mend, she reasoned. But her pounding headache was another matter. She was willing to try almost anything if it would take away the throbbing ache.

Leaving her, he went to the stove and poured himself a cup of coffee, not bothering to offer her any. Dragging a chair out from beneath the table, he sat down heavily next to her. Not looking at her, he said, "The tracks point northwest. I'm going to choose to believe what you said about your cousin heading for Placerville. The trouble is, without horses, we're stuck here for a while."

He looked at her then, tossing her a disgruntled frown when she didn't comment back.

"I'd walk out of here on my own, but the *gentleman* in me won't let me leave you, *a lady*, here all alone to fend for yourself. There's no telling what kind of trouble you'd get yourself into next."

Tipping the vial to her lips, Jessie took a stout sip of the laudanum, choking delicately as the bitter fluid coursed down her throat. She made a face. Her grimace, she noticed, made him almost smile. "Ugh! Mercy, that stuff's revolting."

A long moment passed while she tried to swallow away the nasty taste from her mouth. The narcotic sang in her veins almost instantaneously, she noticed, making her feel light as a balloon. The room began to spin a little as she considered his last comment. Replacing the stopper, she retorted glibly, the drug giving her Dutch courage, "Well now, Mr. Mitch Wyden. Don't give little old me another thought. Feel free to leave any time you want."

Apparently he didn't appreciate her retort. "You'd like that, wouldn't you? And as soon as I'm gone what will you do?"

"Walk out of here myself, of course."

"And you wouldn't get farther than a mile or so before you realized the extent of your foolishness and gave it up." He took a sip of coffee.

"You think so? We should make a bet on that."

"I've been watching you," he said, banging the coffee cup down on the table. "I know your head hurts like the devil. And your shoulder aches only a little less. Add to all that a cut foot, and I'd say Miss Jessie Driscoll is in no shape to travel on her own to the outhouse and back, let alone make it all the way to San Francisco."

Jessie laughed, in spite of the insult. She was feeling very brave and reckless all of a sudden. In no uncertain terms, she told him, "Now that's where you're wrong, mister."

"Mitch," he corrected.

"Mitch. I've come miles and miles already. Endured hardships you couldn't dream about in your worst nightmares. A little bump on the head and a cut foot wouldn't stop me from trying."

"Oh? Then maybe to keep you here I'll just have to take you out and tie you up to that fence post again." He pushed to his feet.

Her eyes flew wide. "No," she whispered, stricken. The confidence and bravery she'd felt just moments before vanished.

Oh, why had she provoked him? Why hadn't she kept her runaway mouth shut instead of taunting him like that?

Her stomach began to churn and she started to feel sick. She couldn't endure it if he trussed her up to that post again. She just couldn't.

He was at her side in an instant. "Jessie?"

"No!" she cried, pushing him away, but the powerful opiate was working on her in earnest now. She felt drowsy and lethargic, her limbs so leaden she could barely raise them to fight him off.

In the next instant her body grew light as a hummingbird's wings, floating up, up, as he lifted her high off the chair and into his arms.

"Please, no. I promise I won't try—"

"Hush," he said, holding her close. She expected him to take her outside and head for the corral, but instead he made his way toward the bed, bent, and holding her tight with one arm, threw back the bedclothes.

The hay-stuffed mattress engulfed her like a mama's tender embrace when he placed her between the sheets. Her body drifted like a pile of feathers into its soft comfort. Through half-closed eyes, she searched his face, bewildered. *What now?*

"Go to sleep," he whispered as he pulled the covers up and tucked her in. "No more fence posts. The outlaw Jessie Driscoll's been through quite enough for one day, I think."

# Chapter Eight

Jessie dreamed. The man was there, holding her close, gazing into her eyes, his rough fingers stroking the delicate curve of her jaw. His lips—his firm man's lips—slowly descended to brush her mouth with a feather-soft kiss that caused her heart to pound and desire like she'd never known to course through her body. It felt so good to be enfolded in his warm embrace, to succumb to the tenderness of his kiss. For just this little while, her terrors didn't exist. Nothing could harm her. This man and his powerful, dangerous muscles would protect her and keep her safe.

A loud clatter crashed through her dream, and she groaned, burrowing further beneath the covers. No, no, no. She didn't want to wake up. She wanted these exquisite feelings and his kiss to go on and on.

A curse, then more clatter. Her eyes flew wide as she jerked alert. Dear heaven, where was she? And then...and then she knew.

She saw the man hunkered down by the table, reaching toward a spoon, tin plates and utensils scattered like shrapnel all over the floor.

"Sorry," he called, his worried gaze finding hers. "Now I woke you up."

Rubbing the laudanum-induced sleep from her eyes, she struggled to sit up.

He forgot about the mess on the floor, rose, and came to her aid.

"Take it easy," he warned, slipping an arm around her shoulders. His movements were slow, careful, nonthreatening. After plumping a pillow behind her back, he studied her face. "How do you feel?"

She took a moment to think about that. Her entire body tingled in the most delicious way, but she couldn't seem to recall just exactly why that should be. Was he talking about this pleasant lassitude drifting through her?

"What?" she croaked, finding her voice with a bit of difficulty.

He drew himself upright and studied her some more. "Your head. And shoulder. How do they feel?"

"Oh." She carefully rolled her shoulder and put tentative fingers to her temple. To her amazement, both felt pretty good. Her head still throbbed dully, but nothing like it had before she'd taken the laudanum. She managed a small smile. "Much better, thanks. How...how long have I been asleep?"

"Almost eighteen hours."

She sucked in her breath. "Mercy."

He laughed. "I know. For a while there I thought you'd died on me. How big a swig of that laudanum did you swallow, anyway?"

She looked away, embarrassed. "Too big a one, I guess. I've never taken it before. Aunt Cora was of a mind that one's aches and pains should be silently suffered. The endurance of pain strengthened a person's character, she always said."

His expression softened. "Ah. Well, next time you'll know to take a smaller swallow."

Things turned suddenly uncomfortable and she tensed beneath his lingering scrutiny. She remembered his name was Mitch Wyden, and that before he'd tucked her into his bed she'd thought he was going to tie her to the fence post again. She remembered her terror, her lethargy as she tried to resist him, and she remembered how he'd lifted her into his arms and pressed her to his solid chest.... Dear heaven, and she remembered the dream.

Tearing her eyes away, she drew the blanket to her neck, hoping he wouldn't notice her sudden discomfort.

She cleared her throat. "I suppose I needed waking," she answered feebly. Goodness, was that an understatement.

"Are you hungry? I've got a slab of ham frying in the skillet."

The sizzling meat smelled heavenly. She nodded.

"That's a good sign. You being hungry, I mean. As soon as I clean up that mess I dropped on the floor, we'll eat."

As he turned and bent to the task, Jessie studied him. He'd changed into clean clothes and shaved, she noticed, and realizing it, a shaft of pleasure darted through her. The sight of this new Mitch Wyden pleased her very much, she decided.

She knew she was staring, but she couldn't help it. Gone was the shadowy stubble on his strong, angular jaw that had given him a frightening, savage appearance. With smooth cheeks and his longish dark hair neatly brushed back away from his face, he looked almost approachable.

She brought her thoughts up short, confused. There was something very wrong here.

"Mister? Uh, Mitch," she corrected, fingering the bedclothes. "How come you're being so nice to me all of a sudden?"

Her question gave him pause. After a moment he stood, tin plates and silverware clutched in his hands. "Never kick a sleeping dog, Jessie. It'll come up snarling every time."

Her question had put a scowl back on his face. Chastened, she didn't say anymore.

"Give me a minute to set the table," he finally said in a more pleasant tone. "Then I'll leave you while you get dressed. Your clothes and hat are over there, along with a few other things I scraped together." He nodded toward the items on the night stand and the pile of clothes laid out on the hearth.

Swallowing hard, she nodded back, then waited until he'd gone outside.

*Her foot was bandaged. And her chafed wrists and palms no longer stung.* Slowly, she swung her legs over the side of the bed and set her feet on the floor. He must have doctored her foot and tended her hands while she slept. In her drugged sleep she hadn't felt a thing.

She carefully placed her full weight on the cut, testing for pain. Not too bad. She had to limp a little to the hearth, but all things considered, the injury could have been worse.

A wave of uneasiness rippled through her as she gazed down at her clean underclothes spread out beside Charlie's britches. The torn shirt, she noticed, had been washed, too, one more thing he must have done while she slept. Then another alarming thought struck her: he'd had to touch her drawers and stockings, her intimate things, when he'd brought them from the river and laid them out for her.

Well, she didn't want to think about that. Nor did she wish to recall the dream, or those confusing moments down by the river when he'd kissed her. No, she certainly didn't want that forbidden, sweet warmth to curl through the pit of her belly again.

Shaking such disturbing thoughts aside, her gaze swung to the nightstand. Atop its scarred surface, right beside the oil lamp, lay six wooden shirt buttons, two shiny needles jabbed into a swatch of cloth, and a spool of dark thread. Next to the thread, he'd laid out what was obviously a woman's silver-backed brush and comb. Puzzled, her thoughts spun. *Where had he gotten those?*

She fingered the pretty brush and comb. Had he laid those out to mock her? But then she raked her fingers through her thatch of tousled hair and encountered a sizeable snarl. Mercy, she must look a fright. Maybe he hadn't meant to be cruel after all. Her hair had grown some—long enough to tangle.

Reaching out, she lightly ran her fingers over each of the other items on the table, as if it all might disappear if she made the wrong move.

"He found all the buttons for me," she whispered aloud, picturing his bulky frame stooping to search the ground near the grave site. "And because he did, he's given me back the use of the smaller shirt." She smiled. "That is," she corrected, "I'll have it back the moment I repair it." Then another thought struck her. The needle and thread gave her a way to make the other clothes fit properly as well.

Her heart took a little tumble. Kindness and thoughtfulness from others weren't something she was used to. Though this sudden reversal perplexed her, she decided not to "kick the sleeping dog." She wouldn't try to figure out why he'd done it; she'd just be grateful he had.

Mercy. Now she almost felt guilty for kneeing him earlier.

Almost.

In minutes she was fully dressed and pulling on the second boot over her bandaged foot. If she hurried, she just might have time to hobble to the privy and back before he walked through the door.

☙ ☙ ☙

Swallowing a mouthful of salty ham and a morsel of biscuit, she reached for the tin cup by her plate, her unsteady fingers nearly upsetting the cup. Sitting across the table from him, trying to remain calm in his intimidating presence was difficult. Since he'd returned to the cabin, he hadn't said one word, and his taciturn manner was starting to needle her.

She took a swallow of water, deciding it was time to break the silence between them. Mustering her courage, she offered tentatively, "I owe you a thank you."

He looked up, a forkful of ham poised halfway to his mouth. That apparently had done the trick. His mood seemed to shift, and he actually grinned. "Several," he agreed. Taking a bite, he chewed the meat slowly while Jessie stared.

She had a hard time keeping her eyes off him. She'd never known a man could look so appealing while doing something as mundane as chewing and swallowing food. It was the pleasant way his Adam's apple bobbed when he swallowed, she decided.

"Okay, several," she allowed.

A long pause ensued while she gathered her thoughts.

"Well, so thank me," he said, tired of the wait. But amusement lurked in his voice, taking away the sting.

He was teasing her, she realized, and unbelievably, that pleased her. When he wasn't wearing that scowl, he wasn't quite so terrifying.

She risked a small smile. "Thank you for bandaging my foot and doctoring my hands."

"And?"

"And for finding the buttons and bringing in my clothes. Oh, and for washing Charlie's shirt for me."

"And?"

She hesitated, lightly drumming her fingers on the table. What more did he want, a pound of flesh? "And for giving me the needles and thread."

He forked another slice of ham from the skillet sitting in the middle of the table, then reached for the plate of biscuits. "And what else, brat?" he insisted, spooning pan grease on the biscuit.

She looked at him, puzzled, her smile slipping.

He spoke for her. "And thanks, Mitch, for not tying me to the fence post, even though I deserved it for threatening to walk out of here. Not to mention for near crippling you with my knee. Twice."

Piqued that he would mention *that*, she rallied hotly in defense. "I couldn't have hurt you that badly. I don't see you bent over and hobbling, after all. And anyway, you deserved it. You...you did worse things to me first."

As he swallowed the chunk of biscuit, a thoughtful expression crossed his face. Jessie's gaze again slid to his Adam's apple. "Maybe," he allowed.

Uncomfortable, she changed the subject. "Where did the comb and brush come from? Um, they obviously belong to a woman."

"Out of that trunk over there."

"No, I mean...." Her voice faltered. But then she realized he was teasing her again.

His blue eyes glittered as his dark head moved into a shaft of sunlight slanting through the kitchen window. "A miner and his woman lived here before me. Must have been in a hurry when they moved on because the woman left some of her things behind."

Jessie looked up at him hopefully, but he shook his head. "Sorry, no clothes. Just several cakes of fancy soap, some sewing supplies, and that comb and brush."

"You haven't got a wife tucked away somewhere, then?" The moment the words were out, she wanted to bite her tongue off. Why had she asked such a thing? What did she care if he was married or not? Quickly, she dropped her gaze to her plate and took a bite of food.

He chuckled. "Nope. Look around, brat. You see a wife hiding in the corner?"

"No." She kept her head down, determined to stifle the tiny twinge of elation his answer gave her. With a sudden spurt of spunk she said, "But it did cross my mind that maybe you've got her tied up to a fence post somewhere."

He laughed at that. Actually laughed. Around another mouthful of ham, he countered, "How about you? You married?"

He was teasing her yet again, turning the tables on her. It was the question, though, not the teasing that caused a certain wistfulness to enter her voice when she replied. "I almost was once. His name was Thomas Fowler. But things didn't work out." Oh dear, thinking about how Uncle Thaddeus had quashed her starry-eyed dreams of marrying Thomas Fowler was far too painful a memory.

He looked at her oddly then, like he sensed he'd touched a raw spot. Before he could comment further, she said, "Does your family live anywhere close by? In Virginia City or Sacramento, maybe?"

The warm atmosphere between them abruptly chilled. Slowly, he laid down his fork, then wiped his lips with the bit of cloth he used for a napkin.

"No."

The depth of rancor in that stiff, one-word reply startled her. Uneasy again, she braced herself. What had she said? "I didn't mean to pry," she told him quickly. "I...I was just making conversation."

He hauled in a breath and placed the napkin on the table. "I've got family in Denver," he said after a long, uncomfortable pause. "A ma, a pa, two brothers, and a sister. We aren't exactly what you'd call one big happy family. Satisficd?"

His biting tone stung worse than she was prepared for. "Yes," was all she could think of to say.

But mentally, she shook her head, unkindly judging him, she supposed. Some people just didn't know the value of what they had. What she wouldn't give to belong to a large family. Even one like his, a family apparently at odds with each other.

She shoved back her chair and began clearing the dirty plates. Trailing the heels of their light banter, his unexpected shift toward animosity hurt. Throat tight, she rushed to carry everything to the dry sink before he saw.

When she passed his chair, he grabbed a fistful of her shirt and tugged her back. "I hurt your feelings just now. I shouldn't have growled at you like that, Jessie. My family is a sore subject, is all."

She held her breath. He hadn't exactly said the words, "I'm sorry," but there he went again. Being nice to her. And charming. Confusing her.

Abruptly he stood, releasing the wad of shirt. Towering above her like a great, shadowy mountain, she had to strain her neck to meet his eyes. When he lifted his fingers, she thought he meant to touch her cheek. But he must have changed his mind because he lowered them again and said instead, his lips twitching with wry amusement, "You wash, I'll dry. Washing the dishes is worth a dime. Afterwards, if you still want to hear, I'll tell you about my family."

She let out a long breath, forcing her stiff limbs to relax. "So what's drying worth? Shouldn't I do both?"

Was that a spark of approval she saw in his eyes?

"A nickel. You'll earn it next time."

# Chapter Nine

Sunlight, warm and comforting, splashed through a canopy of green, spattering the forest floor, illuminating the wild lupines growing beneath the pines. Two squirrels scampered across the clearing, heading for cover, then chattered loudly as they scrambled up a tree. Mitch watched Jessie. She'd abandoned her sewing for a moment to watch the squirrels.

"Aren't they cute?" she murmured once the animals vanished and the sound of their squabbling faded against the huffing summer breeze.

When she smiled like that she looked exactly like one of those curly-topped, Renaissance seraphs he'd once seen reproduced in *Harper's Weekly*. "Yeah, cute."

She caught him staring at her and quickly returned to her sewing. He loved it when she went all shy on him like that.

Once they'd finished up the dishes, he'd brought two chairs outside to the porch, if one could call the narrow covered area in front of the cabin a porch. He'd encouraged Jessie to do her mending outdoors where the light was better. She didn't object to his suggestion, anxious as she was to exchange his over-sized shirt for the smaller one.

Mitch lit a smoke. The sun wasn't as intense as it had been the day before, and a slight breeze blowing from the north kept things comfortable. Tipping his chair back against the wall, he stretched out his legs, crossed his ankles, and settled in. Sitting out here with her felt good. Mighty good.

Jessie said, "Sometimes in the morning, just before breaking camp, I used to feed the squirrels bits of cornbread and bacon. Curtis didn't like that much because he said I was wasting food, but when he wasn't looking I did it anyway. The little critters were so cute, I just couldn't resist. One time I even coaxed one to eat out of my palm."

"That so?"

She nodded. Then a frown wrinkled her brow. He saw it just before she ducked her head, trying to hide it beneath the brim of her Stetson.

"And the squirrel didn't bite you?" he prompted when she remained silent. Why had her mood gone south all of a sudden?

"No...." When she looked up at him there were shadows in her eyes. "Curtis shot it. Said that with all the cornbread I'd just fed it, it would make choice eating that night for supper."

Mitch swore silently. Cousin Curtis was a real charmer, it seemed.

"So, tell me about your family," she said, much too quickly.

He was glad she'd changed the subject. He had an urge to take her in his arms and kiss away her bad memories. Instead, he took a long, calming drag off the cheroot.

Where should he begin? How much should he tell her? "What do you want to know?" he asked, blowing a stream of smoke through his nose.

"I don't know," she shrugged. "Are you the youngest, oldest, or middle child? Tell me about your parents. What do they do in Denver?"

Mitch sucked in another drag, allowing the smoke swirl through his lungs longer than he should have. The subject annoyed him, made him uncomfortable. But he'd told her he'd talk, so he did.

"Pa owns a dry goods store. Ma and the rest of the family help out. I'm the youngest of four. And the black sheep. Couldn't abide the thought of tallying sacks of beans and parched corn for the rest of my life, so one day I turned tail and joined the army. Broke everybody's heart."

There was more to it than that, of course. Things he had no intention of telling her. Like his father's fury that their youngest son would abandon the business, and thus the secure future he'd so painstakingly built for his children. Like his mother's anguish the day he left to join the troops fighting the Indian wars. So many bitter words spoken among them....

"You were in the army?"

"Four years."

Tying a knot, Jessie bit off the thread with her teeth. "Does your sister help out at the store, too?" she asked.

"Yep. A real nice family effort is Pa's general store. Laurie's smarter than all of us put together. She loves working figures. Keeps the books, does the ordering and inventory, that sort of thing. At least she did. Maybe she's married by now and has a couple of kids. Had herself a beau just before I left home."

"You don't keep in touch, then?"

"No."

She peeked at him thoughtfully, then resumed sewing. "When I get to San Francisco, I'll try to find work. Maybe at a mercantile, like your sister. I can read and write and do figures some."

"You can?" As he replied, he tried to keep his voice neutral. He doubted Jessie would ever make it to San Francisco. Most likely the law would catch up with her before then. But not if he could help it.

"Mm hm. Uncle Thaddeus didn't think a girl needed schooling, but I'd watch Curtis practice his letters and numbers and I just sort of picked things up on my own. I like books," she commented wistfully. "Dime novels, especially. Shooter bought one for me one time." Her gaze darted to the grave beneath the trees and back again. "*Nora and the Outlaws,* it was called. Can you read and write?"

Mitch faked a smile, pretending he hadn't seen the direction of that look. "Some."

She chewed on her lower lip, anchoring a fresh button with her thumb until she maneuvered the needle through one of the holes in it. "Nobody minds that your sister helps out at the store?"

"No," Mitch replied, wondering where she was heading with all this. "Ma and Pa are grateful she's so handy. You sound surprised."

"Well, Uncle Thaddeus was of a mind that women don't have the brains for such things. That their place is tending to home and babies."

"Don't ever tell Laurie that." Mitch laughed. "Most likely she'd come at you with a carving knife. Not that she objects to home and babies; she just feels that women should be allowed to explore other interests, too."

Jessie looked up, her brown eyes shining. "I think I like your sister very much," she said.

They fell into a companionable silence. Mitch's mind drifted toward his stolen horses. Where they were, if they were lost to him forever. His stomach clenched thinking about the cash he'd lost. Not to mention the futility of all that time, work, and sweat.

He looked up to find Jessie studying him.

"You're thinking about the horses, aren't you?" she asked gently.

"How'd you guess?"

"By that grim, faraway look on your face."

"If you really want to know, I was thinking about how I'm gonna have to spend another year up here, living in this godforsaken run-down shack."

She tied off another knot, again severing the thread with her teeth. Shaking out the shirt to examine her work, she asked, sounding surprised, "You don't like your home?"

He gave a little laugh. "Darlin', this shack isn't home. I only come up here to work the horses. No. I've got my eye on a sweet little spread for sale in Crystal Springs, just across the Nevada/California border near Lake Tahoe. Until you and your cousin showed up, I was two weeks and fifteen hundred dollars away from making the down payment."

He'd tried to keep the bitterness out of his voice, but he could tell by the way her cheeks drained of color that she'd picked up on it anyway. She folded the shirt in her lap, then met his gaze, remorse in her eyes.

"I'm sorry."

He sighed. "Nothing to do about it now, except get you better so we can walk out of here."

Her brow wrinkled. "I told you, you can leave me here. You want to track your horses, so do it."

Mitch shook his head. "No."

"I'll be okay, honest." She glanced around the clearing, cocking her head slightly when a couple of blue jays began a ruckus in the trees. "I like it here. I'd do just fine all by myself."

What she didn't say, what he could read behind the words, was that she considered this shack and canyon to be a perfect hiding place, tucked away in the mountains and secluded from outsiders as it was. But she deluded herself to think the law would have a hard time tracking her here. He knew better. Any good lawman worth his badge wouldn't give up until he finished the job.

Scowling, Mitch gestured toward the kitchen. "In three days, five if we stretch it, the food's gonna run out. You handy with a firearm, brat?"

She hesitated. "Well, no, but—"

"Then without me you wouldn't make it past next week."

"I would if you went hunting first. Before you left, I mean."

"I'll do that anyway. Jessie, let me make this clear. We leave together, or we don't leave at all."

She seemed to have trouble handling that. Rocking forward, he ground the cheroot beneath his heel. "That's the way it's gonna be, brat. Get used to the idea."

"I...there's a tear in your shirt."

"What?"

"Right there." She pointed at his chest. "The pocket's torn. And there's another little tear in the sleeve. Want me to mend it?"

He looked at her, frustrated, thinking he'd never understand the workings of a woman's brain. "I thought we were talking about walking out of here."

"We were. But now I'm saying I'll fix your shirt." She smiled one of those innocent smiles of hers and his chest tightened.

He unbuttoned his high-collared shirt while she set aside her mended one. He'd no sooner shrugged it off his shoulders than he heard her gasp.

"Those marks on your neck," she cried. "What in heaven's name happened?"

He grinned, handing over the shirt. "A spitting little hellcat scratched me, that's what. Tore my shirt in a couple of places, too."

"Wait a minute. I did that?"

"During our squabble under the trees."

Crimson flooded her cheeks. "I don't remember that part."

"No, I don't suppose you do."

She reached for the shirt and said so quietly he barely heard her, "I'll have it mended in no time."

During the next half hour, they didn't talk. Mitch noticed that Jessie scrupulously avoided looking at his naked chest, preferring to keep her eyes on her work. He grinned with satisfaction, knowing she was having a hard time of it.

As he was.

Desire burned in him, making him shift uncomfortably in his chair. He wished she'd take off that Stetson so he could see her face better. He wanted to look his fill at her, memorize her expressions, catch her smiles.

"You don't have to wear that blasted hat all the time, you know," he said irritably, watching as she tied a final knot. "I've seen your haircut. Remember?"

Her head snapped up. She didn't reply. She just looked at him with those huge brown eyes of hers, as if he'd just thrown a dead rodent in her lap.

He knew how sensitive she was about her hair, so why had he tried to provoke her like that? Because he wanted her, that's why. And she'd made it crystal clear he couldn't have her—not the way he dreamed about having her, anyway.

Frustrated, he said more forcefully than he'd intended, "You finished?"

He stood, and in one stride, he reached her side and tore the Stetson from her head. Tossing it aside, he lifted her chin. "You're hiding under there, Jessie, and I don't like it. I want to look at your pretty face while we talk, not at a hat band." The silk of her skin beneath his fingers was almost his undoing. Inwardly cursing, he tightened his hold.

Immediately, he regretted his anger when he saw the fear in her eyes. He eased the grip on her chin and moved his hand upward to the lump above her temple. Sorry he'd frightened her, he let out a long breath, fingering the swelling, trying to be gentle. "Are you okay?" he asked gruffly, hoping she could hear the apology in his voice. "Does it still hurt?"

She didn't answer right away, but then she said, "Not so much anymore. Only when you poke at it."

He looked down. She'd dropped the needle. Both hands tightly fisted the shirt. Her lips trembled and her throat worked, but she couldn't say anything more. He felt like a monster.

Dropping to one knee, throwing caution aside, he took her face in his hands and kissed her. "Ah, Jessie girl, don't be scared of me," he breathed. "I don't want to hurt you. I shouldn't have said anything about your hat. I know that now. Kiss me back, sweetheart. Kiss me back."

He waited for a response, taking his time. Holding her still, his fingers buried in her thick, silky curls, he teased her lips with his, silently begging her to open up. The shirt rustled as it slid off her lap onto the porch.

Then something magical happened, just as he was about to despair it ever would. Jessie groaned deep in her throat. And when he felt the tension in her ease, he knew she'd begun to surrender.

Her hands were warm, feather-light as she tentatively explored his hair-roughened chest, and her innocent curiosity moved him like nothing else could. Heart hammering, he drew her closer and deepened the kiss. She'd opened her mouth and let him in at last.

Outlaw or not, Jessie Driscoll was his, and he wanted her.

This time he would take things slowly, play by her rules, bide his time. No more scaring her or threatening her. No more misunderstandings.

"Mitch," she murmured as he drew his head back slightly to look at her. Her body edged forward, chasing his retreat, and he smiled.

Kissing her cheek, he asked, "What? What do you want, Jessie?"

She hesitated, her eyes glazed, her pretty lips kiss-swollen. "What's happening to me? First you make me so afraid. And then you...you make me feel hot and boneless, like I'm melting away."

He teased her lips with his again. "Didn't Thomas Fowler ever kiss you like this?"

"Who?"

He chuckled softly. "Thomas Fowler. The man you almost married. Remember him?"

"Oh." She shook her head, bemused. "No. Not like this. We were never allowed any privacy, you see. And anyway, Uncle Thaddeus put an end to things even before they really got started. He told Thomas that he'd never give him permission to marry me. He told him I was needed too much on the farm."

"And Fowler didn't challenge your uncle? Fight for you?"

She turned her head away, but he reached out and forced her to look at him. Slowly, she answered. "No. I think the last time Thomas came courting, Uncle Thaddeus threatened him in some way. He never came around again."

"And no other beaux did either?"

She gave him a delicate shrug. "No."

He rubbed his thumb along her lower lip. Unable to resist, he kissed her again. "I'm thinking that's a good thing, Jessie girl. A real good thing."

Reluctantly, he stood. Barely. His knees were so weak he felt as if he'd just busted ten wild broncs in a row. Snatching up his shirt, he shrugged it on.

"Where are you going?" she asked, her husky voice swirling over him like a cloud of smoke and honey.

"Finish up your mending," he said, indicating Charlie Deerhorn's britches. She'd have to take them off to fix them. Reaching behind his back, he pulled his hunting knife from its sheath. "Here," he said. "Use this to cut the threads instead of your teeth." He placed the knife, hilt first, in her palm. Wide-eyed, she stared at it as if she couldn't believe he'd trust her with such a wicked-looking weapon. He touched the tip of her nose. "I trust you not to throw it at me the moment I turn around. Holler if you need me. I won't be far away."

ꕤ ꕤ ꕤ

At the river, Mitch set down his rifle against a boulder, shucked his clothes, and dove into the chilly water. He needed to think. He needed to cool off. He needed to rid his body of all this pent-up tension.

For the thousandth time he asked himself how the devil, within two brief days, his life had been turned so completely inside out.

He moved through the water steadily, his strokes determined, powerful against the tugging current. He made it to the opposite shore, then turned and swam back, making the crossings five more times before trudging, out of breath and nearly out of strength, onto the bank. Chest heaving, he used his shirt for a towel, dressed, then made his way back to the clearing. Stopping just short of the tree line, he eased down on a fallen tree trunk, situating himself comfortably where he could easily keep an eye on Jessie.

Where was Jessie's fool cousin and the rest of that gang of his? Mitch had expected Curtis to ride in, guns blazing, to rescue Jessie long before now. Didn't that sadistic excuse for a man care about her at all? All three remaining rustlers had seen her fall. Plain and simple, Curtis and his cohorts had left her for dead. And if Curtis had somehow known that Jessie hadn't taken any bullets, then that meant he'd abandoned his female cousin to an even worse fate. Mitch made a vow to someday even the score with Curtis Driscoll.

He scanned the clearing, settling his gaze on the sun-drenched porch where Jessie sat. As if she sensed his scrutiny, she looked up from her mending, squinting into the distance. But he knew she couldn't see him; he was well-hidden in the shadows. She studied the empty forest a few moments, nudged the hunting knife at her feet with the toe of her boot, then continued sewing.

An hour or two passed. With his horses gone, there wasn't much else for him to do, so he contented himself by sitting in the shadows and simply watching her.

It seemed it had been forever since he'd shared company with a female. He smiled wryly. No, mares and fillies just didn't come close to the heady company of the human kind of female. Somehow, watching Jessie's gentle ways eased the ever-present bite of loneliness residing deep in his soul.

He realized something profound and disturbing, sitting there, observing her, wanting her as he did. Suddenly, he knew that Jessie Driscoll was the woman he'd been searching for all his life. Jessie was a woman as sweet and lovely as Adam's Eve, yet full of strength, grit, and determination to face anything life threw at her. Not once had he heard her complain. Not even when she was badly hurting and so worn out she could barely hold her head up.

Jessie had the kind of determination his sister Laurie had, he realized. Even more so, since Jessie'd had the will and stamina to trek miles and miles across the frontier, all the while coping with her devious cousin Curtis. Thinking about that, he made a vow.

*I swear I'll protect you, brat. Nobody's gonna hurt you or push you around ever again. You've got me on your side now. Together we'll get this robbery mess cleared up. Count on it!*

Before long Jessie shook out the britches, put them on, and stood. Limping heavily, she walked the length of the porch and back, stretched, then gathered her things and entered the cabin. Mitch cursed softly. The cut on her foot hurt her more than she'd let on, he realized with a jolt. If that were the case, her head and shoulder were probably giving her more trouble than she'd admitted, too. And if *that* were also the case, which he didn't doubt, there was no way he was going to get her out of here any time soon.

Killing time, he formed a plan of sorts. The little town of Sweet Glenn was only fifteen miles south. The moment Jessie was well enough to walk it, he'd take her there. Sweet Glenn didn't boast a lawman, but the town did have a telegraph station. The moment they arrived, he'd wire the sheriff in Sulfur Flats, report the theft of his horses, and at the same time inform the authorities that he was holding Jessie Driscoll.

He had no doubt about Jessie's innocence. Not anymore. He was convinced she'd merely been a victim of circumstances. He hoped that if Jessie voluntarily turned herself in and told her story to the authorities, they also would believe she had nothing to do with that bank robbery and let her go free.

The problem was, the more time he took reporting everything to the law, the greater the danger and risk for Jessie. A posse might have already caught up with Curtis and his gang, so it was imperative he reach the sheriff in Sulfur Flats before they weaseled out of Curtis where Jessie was and caught up with her, too. If Jessie could turn herself in first, her story would carry far more credibility than if she tried to explain things after an arrest.

Forty-five minutes later, Jessie appeared at the cabin door wearing a new set of altered clothes. A slow, wolfish grin curled the corners of Mitch's mouth as she stepped out into the sunlight. Britches on a woman weren't such a bad thing after all, he decided. Those men's pants he'd hated so much before now hugged her shapely limbs like bark on a tree. And the shirt fit her better, too. Now he could clearly see the jut of her small breasts through the fabric.

Just as he was experiencing a satisfying jolt of pure lust, Jessie happened to turn her head his way. The wary caution in her expression beneath the Stetson startled him back to earth. After taking a careful, worried look around, she left the cabin, heavily favoring her left foot as she limped across the clearing, heading for the forest.

Mitch rose, uneasy. In her right hand the thick knife blade flashed, reflecting the sun like a polished mirror.

Surely she wouldn't try anything foolish. Like running. Would she?

Anger hot and fierce rose in him. He'd trusted her! And the moment she thought his back was turned she'd betrayed that trust.

Snatching his Winchester, he followed several yards behind her, keeping to the shadows. Once she turned and cocked her head, as if she sensed his presence, but failing to see anything, she continued on. Hurriedly. As if she had no time to lose.

When Jessie reached a patch of sunlight, she stopped to rest. She turned, and it was obvious that she was measuring the distance between herself and the cabin. Clearly, she thought she was safe from pursuit, because as if she didn't have a worry in the world, she bent down with her back toward him to pick up something near her boot.

His heart sank.

Not bothering to hide any longer, he stepped from the trees. The sudden move startled her.

"Mitch!" she cried, then gave a nervous little laugh, her hand rising to her chest. "You scared me!"

He said, menacingly low, "Did I? I told you if you tried to run, I'd find you."

"What?"

"And I also told you what the consequences would be. I meant it when I said you'd be sorry."

She was looking at him oddly, as if she thought he'd taken leave of his senses.

"What in the world are you saying?"

"You know full well what I'm saying. Get back to the cabin, Jessie. Now."

"But I was just—"

"Now!"

The knife slipped from her fingers. Dumbly, she watched it thump to the ground to land flat against the carpet of pine needles and wildflowers beneath her feet. A couple of blue lupines clutched in her fist fell next. Giving a little cry, she threw a fierce look at Mitch, then dropped to her knees, scrambling to retrieve the fallen weapon.

Mitch was faster. Before she could grab the hilt, he covered the flat of the blade with a quick stomp of his boot.

She looked up at him in stunned disbelief. "You're mad," she said, giving her head a quick shake.

"Furious," he thundered back.

"That's not what I meant."

"Get up."

She rose to her feet slowly, her eyes never leaving his. Her fierce glare threw him a little. It wasn't fear he saw in her eyes, as he'd expected. By the looks of things, she was furious, too.

Tight-lipped, she slipped in front of him and marched—if one could call that painful, lopsided gait marching—back to the cabin. Once inside, she went directly to the hearth, crossed her arms over her stomach, and turned her back on him.

Mitch entered the cabin, fully intending to set her straight about the dangers of a lone woman, a lone *injured* woman, traipsing through the mountains alone. But at the portal he froze. And took a double-take. And a deep breath. Was that stew he smelled simmering on the stove? He sniffed again. It *was* stew.

Heart pounding, his gaze settled on the kitchen table. It was set for two, complete with table cloth and napkins. What the...where had the table cloth come from?

And then he remembered. At the bottom of the pantry closet, that's where. More leftovers, compliments of the miner's woman.

An empty wide-mouthed mason jar filled with water sat directly in the middle of the table.

*And then he knew.* He shifted uncomfortably. She hadn't been running at all. She'd gone out to pick wildflowers to fancy up the table.

He raised his eyes, his gaze colliding with her stiff back. She stood at the hearth, arms hugging her middle, not saying a word.

"Jessie," he said, his voice rough, contrite. "I guess I owe you.... I owe you an apology, brat."

She spun around, her dark eyes smoldering. "Don't bother," she rounded on him. "I don't want one."

"Too bad. You're getting one anyway. I jumped to the wrong conclusions out there. Did I scare you again?"

She bit her lip, clearly trying to keep it from trembling. "No," she said sharply. "I'm never going to be scared of a man again. Especially not you."

Mitch set his rifle against the wall. "You aren't, huh?"

"No, I'm not."

"Well, that's a good thing, because I don't want you to be scared of me." He took another deep breath. "It sure smells good in here. I guess you found that mason jar of stew I was saving for my celebration dinner."

She studied him blankly, clearly confused.

"I was going to open it," he explained, "along with my last jug of whiskey, the day I sold the horses to the army."

Jessie let out a long, soft groan and sank to the ledge of the hearth, covering her face with her hands. "Oh, Mitch. I made a mess of things again, didn't I? I only meant...I wanted to thank you for giving me the needles and thread, and for doctoring me. And for—"

"I know, brat. I know." Squatting before her, he took her hands away from her face and made her look at him. "I *know*, Jessie. And I appreciate it." He gave her a small kiss on the forehead, knocking the Stetson askew. "Wait right here. Don't move."

When he returned several minutes later, his arms were filled to overflowing with wild lupines. So many, Jessie couldn't fit them all in the Mason jar.

# Chapter Ten

By evening, just before sundown, a storm gathered, chilling the air and blanketing the forest and canyon walls in deep shadows. Jessie stood hatless at the open kitchen window watching the black clouds gather, listening to the wind roar in the towering pines. When lightning flashed, followed by a boom of thunder, she flinched. Its report echoed like a mighty cannon blast through the canyon.

"Thunder and lightning bother you?" Mitch came up behind her to share the view. This time, the warmth of his hands on her shoulders soothed instead of disconcerted her.

"Not really," she said. When she turned to face him, her nose almost bumped his chest. He laughed.

"That's good, because things get pretty noisy around here when a storm hits."

"I was just listening to the wind in the trees. Can you hear it? It sounds like a thousand voices murmuring all at once."

"I always thought it sounded more like the roar of the ocean. Like miles and miles of surf crashing against the shore."

Jessie smiled, thinking that over. "Is that what the ocean sounds like? Truly?"

"Yes, truly. You've never been to the ocean?"

"No, but it's always been one of my fondest dreams to—" She fell silent, biting her lower lip.

"To what?"

She hesitated. “I don’t want to tell you. You’ll laugh. Just like Curtis always does.”

“I’m not Curtis, Jessie. I won’t ever laugh at anything you say is important to you. Tell me.”

“Well,” she said, taking a chance. “One of the reasons I can’t wait to get to San Francisco is so I can run barefoot in the Pacific Ocean. There was a woman at Fort Hays who told me all about San Francisco. She said it’s foggy there a lot, but when the sun comes out the city is as pretty as a bouquet of buttercups in springtime. She said the beach is the best place of all. That you can find seashells in the sand as big as sun hats, that when the cold sea water floods your bare toes there isn’t another sensation like it in the whole world.” She stopped rambling to sneak a peek at Mitch. “Have you ever been to San Francisco?”

“Once or twice,” he said, grinning. But she noticed a tightness around his eyes, a slight stiffness to his jaw, and she wondered what she’d said to cause it.

Another flash of lightning lit the sky, and a few seconds later a mighty clap of thunder shook the cabin.

“We’d better move away and shut the window now. It isn’t safe to stand here anymore. The storm’s right overhead.”

She shivered.

“Cold?” he asked, running a rough finger down her nose, sending a different kind of tremor racing toward her toes. “Come on, I’ll build a fire. That’ll take the chill out of the air in here.”

When he’d set the pine logs ablaze in the hearth and the cabin had warmed up some, Mitch strode over to the bed and patted the blankets.

“Come here, Jessie.”

“What?” she asked, startled. She was just about to pull up a chair and get cozy near the hearth. She caught his eyes, and apprehension made her hesitate.

“I just want to take a look at that foot. No doubt the cut needs cleaning again and a fresh bandage.”

“I can do it,” she said, much too quickly.

Mitch frowned. “What’s the matter, brat? You aren’t still afraid of me, are you?”

His challenge was unmistakable.

"No," she said, lifting her chin. "I told you before, I'm done with being afraid."

She limped over to him, easing down on the edge of the mattress.

"So why the hesitation?"

She could think of several reasons, but she gave him the most important one. "It's just that...it isn't proper for a lady," she cleared her throat, "to show her ankles to a man."

His booming laugh caught her off guard.

"I've seen a whole lot more than your ankles, sweetheart." She bristled at that, and he instantly sobered, as if he regretted his words. "I mean, I've already seen your ankles. If the sight of them didn't send me into seizures of lust the first time, I doubt it will this time, either. Come on. Trust me. All I want to do is make sure that cut is healing properly. Why don't you lie back? You'll be more comfortable, and it'll make things easier for me."

He was smiling at her. That smile he used when he was in one of his "charming" moods. Jessie felt that familiar sweet stab of desire shoot through her middle. Confused by it, she tried to push it away, but wasn't very successful. She found she really loved it when Mitch Wyden was in a charming mood.

She eyed him through her lashes. "I'll lie back, Mitch, only if you'll tell me about San Francisco while you're working on my foot."

"Ultimatums don't sit well with me. You ought to know that by now."

Jessie grinned, scooting back and settling on her elbows. Choosing to ignore that last statement, she told him again, nodding toward her boot, "I'm perfectly capable of doing that myself, you know."

"I'm sure you could, but I'm doing it for you." He tugged off her boot and let it drop. "Take off your stocking while I fetch some water."

He turned his back and went to the cook stove to pour hot water from the kettle into a crockery bowl. While he was gone, she peeled off her sock.

After setting the bowl and a clean cloth on the nightstand, he sat on the edge of the bed near her feet and reached for her left ankle. His big hands swallowed the heel, and only when his thumbs briefly massaged her arch, did she begin to relax.

Slowly, he unraveled the makeshift bandage, tugging slightly at the last turn to release the cloth from the dried blood surrounding the wound. Examining the cut, he frowned, swearing softly beneath his breath.

"What is it," she asked, a curl of alarm bolting her upright. "Let me see."

"Take it easy, Jessie. Just lie back and relax."

"It's *my* foot; I want to see it."

Expelling a long breath, he let her foot fall back onto the bed. "Suit yourself."

The sight made her gasp. She hadn't expected the cut, which made a long, ragged zigzag along the ball of her foot, to look so angry. The skin surrounding it appeared puffy and yellowish-blue.

"If we're not careful," Mitch stated grimly, "infection's going to settle in."

She heard anger in his voice, and frustration. Jessie sank back onto her elbows again. "I'm sorry," she whispered. "Sweet mercy, Mitch, I'm sorry to be such trouble to you."

Mitch's expression softened. "Don't, Jessie. I scared you and you ran. This was all my fault, not yours."

He reached for the cloth, dipped it in the hot water, and gently applied it to her tender foot. When the heated cloth touched the wound, she clenched her jaw, refusing to recoil, just barely managing to hold in a groan.

"What are you thinking?" she asked when she'd recovered a little and saw the worried look on his face.

He didn't reply.

"Tell me, Mitch. What aren't you saying?"

He shook his head. "I don't have anything but whiskey and a jar of horse salve to doctor it with, Jessie. I don't want to hurt you further, but there just isn't any getting around it. I'll have to douse the cut in alcohol, and that's gonna sting like the devil."

She'd been favoring the foot, trying hard not to let on to Mitch how painful it really was, and so far she thought she'd pretty much succeeded. She took a breath for courage. "Oh. Well, is that all? I can take the pain," she said, praying he didn't detect the tremor in her tone. "Just do what you have to do and don't worry about me."

The gash already hurt more than she wanted to admit. Most likely, by the looks of things, infection had already set in. Dousing the wound in spirits, she knew, was going to be like taking a trip to hell.

Mitch didn't say anything more. When he was through cleansing the wound, he rose to empty the water bowl and find the whiskey jug. It took only a moment before he was back at her side.

"Hold your foot out over the bowl, sweetheart. I'll be as quick about it as I can. And don't give even a moment's thought to all that 'pain builds character' nonsense your Aunt Cora spouted. Go right ahead and yell the roof down if you want. Won't be any shame in it. Ready?"

Jessie screwed her eyes shut and gripped the bedclothes in both fists. She hadn't meant to cry out and writhe like that when the fiery alcohol hit the wound. Or for those blasted tears to rush into her eyes and nearly fall. She'd wanted to prove to him that she wasn't a sissy who couldn't take a little pain. A man like Mitch respected strength, not weakness, and she wanted to prove once and for all that she was stronger than he thought, that she could take anything he dished out. How else could she make him believe that he could leave her here to track his horses without giving her a second thought? But now she'd gone and ruined everything.

"Easy, Jessie. It's over now. All over."

And then he was beside her, gathering her up, kissing her cheeks, her forehead, her lips, pressing her close until the pain faded and her breathing turned normal again.

"It near killed me to hurt you like that." He covered her mouth with his own and kissed her deeply then, as if taking away her pain was the most important thing in the world to him. And right then, Jessie almost believed it was.

She'd never in her life experienced anything as sweet and wonderful as Mitch's lips pressed to hers, his body pressed close, and those capable arms cradling her as if she were truly something precious.

"You really meant that, didn't you?" she whispered when he ended the kiss. "That it hurt you to hurt me?"

"I meant it, all right. And I'll kill anyone who ever tries to hurt you again."

A rush of emotion filled her, sweet and powerful. In all her days, nobody had ever told her such nice things. Gently, she touched his face, smoothing out the frown creasing his brow. "Mitch Wyden," she told him seriously, "if you killed anybody over me, I'd be sorely upset with you."

His blue eyes swept her face. And then he said, in that implacable tone he used whenever he truly meant business, "Well, you'd just have to be upset with me, Jessie."

And that settled that.

He kissed her again, his mouth easing down on hers, the gentle invasion drowning her in sensation. The pleasure she felt as his hands idly roamed her waist and back was simply like no other pleasure she'd ever known before. Through this wondrous haze of pleasure she suddenly realized that there was nothing she wanted more than for these new, exciting sensations to never end.

She ran her hands over his broad, chambray-covered torso, delighting in the contours of his massive chest. The smell of his dusky maleness as she drew a deep breath, the firm press of his hands upon her heated flesh, all brought her such exquisite joy she could barely keep from crying out.

When he pressed her backward to the mattress and his hands moved slowly from the short curls of her hair, down, down, past the slope of her shoulders to the curve of her breasts, Jessie sucked in her breath. In a small moment of sanity, she realized that not only had she entered turbulent waters, she'd begun to wade out deeper and deeper, getting in over her head. That if things continued going along as they were, there might not be any turning back. What was she doing? *What was she allowing him to do?*

"Mitch," she breathed.

"What?" he asked. His voice sounded lazy-rough. Firelight leaped across his dark features, turning his face into sharp angles and shadows. His fierce blue eyes studied her, waiting for her to answer him. Taking his time, he nuzzled her neck and pressed his lips to the sensitive spot just under her ear. Lightning flashed. Thunder boomed.

Jessie closed her eyes as another sharp thrill of pleasure rolled through her. "Mitch, maybe we shouldn't be doing this."

"Why not?" he asked, his warm breath teasing her skin.

"Because...because a lady doesn't do things like this." To her horror, her voice broke.

He laughed softly and nuzzled her neck again. "Hmm. Now that's where you're wrong, brat. *Ladies* do this all the time." He smoothed a glossy curl from her forehead, then kissed the tip of her nose. "There isn't anything wrong with two people loving each other, Jessie. This," he gave her a quick, hard kiss on the mouth as his hand moved to caress her breast, "is one of God's greatest gifts to mankind. It's called making love. You *do* like it, don't you?"

"Yes, very much. But Mitch?" She could barely speak.

"What?"

"I feel a little dizzy and...like my bones are melting. And I'm not so sure that's a proper way for a lady to feel. It's all so confusing."

"It's supposed to feel that way, Jessie. You've got feelings for me, just as I have for you, and this is how two people who care for each other best express those feelings. Surely you aren't so naïve that you don't know by now what's what between a man and a woman? I want you, Jessie. And by the way you're responding, sweetheart, I've got a sneaking hunch you want me too."

*He's done this plenty of times before.* The disturbing thought rocked her, and though she wanted to dash it away, she found she couldn't. Oh, how she wanted to let him love her and allow herself to love him right back, but when she thought of Mitch lying with other women....

She stiffened and tried to pull away. When he'd first started kissing her, touching her, making her melt, yes, she'd had a prick of conscience about the liberties she was allowing him to take. But mercy, everything he did to her made her feel wanted and cherished. His touch thrilled her, his kisses made her dizzy, taking her into exciting, uncharted waters. She wanted to explore those waters, find out for herself if what she'd overheard those young women on the wagon train whispering among themselves was really true. She wanted to know what Curtis and the other men had whispered about when they'd come back to camp so giddy after a night on the town. Of course, she wasn't entirely ignorant of what went on between men and women, the birds and animals. She'd grown up on a farm, after all. But these startling new feelings she had toward Mitch, the way he made her feel inside when he kissed her, compelled her to abandon caution, listen to her heart and not her head.

By caressing and kissing her, by simply holding her close, Mitch was making her feel special and wanted. Something she'd never felt in her life before. When he touched her with those big, work-roughened hands, caressed her, whispered praises against her skin, he did so as if he truly cared for her, truly considered her precious and worthy of his affection.

A woman could love a man like that. Love him to the ends of the earth and back. And oh how that woman's heart would break if it turned out that she was just one more of his passing fancies.

With that terrible thought, reality slammed into her. Men simply couldn't be counted on. Hadn't experience taught her that? Eventually, they all broke their promises and left you shattered. Could she allow herself to believe that Mitch was any different from any of the other men she'd ever known?

A hard rain had begun to fall. She could hear it now, like a thousand pairs of boots thumping the roof. And then, in another moment of crystal clarity, she realized there was no use debating the issue. In the short while they'd been together, Mitch Wyden had stolen her heart. Heaven help her, she'd already fallen in love with him.

The revelation stunned her, stealing her breath. What should she do? If she surrendered her body now, let her passions and her heart rule, would Mitch, too, desert her once his own passion cooled? Could she honestly take that risk? Right now, this moment, did Mitch only see her as just another golden opportunity?

"What's the matter, Jessie? What did I say?"

She shook her head, a tight knot forming in her throat making it difficult to speak.

"Nothing," she finally managed.

"Yes there is. Tell me what I did to cause that sigh."

"Nothing, I said."

Propping himself up on one elbow, he gazed down at her, his brows deeply furrowed. "Come on, Jessie. Tell me."

She hesitated, searching his eyes. When she couldn't bear the awkward stillness any longer, she blurted, "How many other women have you done this with, Mitch?"

"Ah, so that's it," he said, studying her.

"Just tell me."

"All right," he shrugged, "You asked, so I won't lie to you. I'm twenty-six years old, Jessie. I haven't been exactly celibate all that time. So the answer is yes, there have been a few women here and there."

"And after. Afterward you just left them? Walked away as if nothing important had happened?"

"Whoa, brat. What the devil are you thinking? With you the rules are different. Those others were...well, most of them were working girls. You understand what I mean by that?"

"Oh, yes. I understand. You once thought *I* was a working girl, remember?"

Swearing under his breath, he gripped a wad of pillow at the side of her head. "Well, that was before. And this is now."

☙ ☙ ☙

Jessie was his, and that was all there was to it. She just hadn't realized it yet. How could he make her understand that if he made love to her now there would be no turning back for him? That he would be committed to protecting and providing for her from now on?

He never had been very good with words, and now was no exception. He just couldn't seem to draw the right ones out at important times like this.

Though he couldn't be absolutely sure, he suspected Jessie was babe-innocent. In so many words, she'd admitted as much when she'd told him about that yellow-bellied beau of hers, Thomas Fowler. He could understand her maiden's fears, even her difficulty in trusting him. Hadn't every man she'd ever put her trust in let her down? Even her own pa had pawned her off, leaving her in the hands of an uncaring aunt and uncle who'd used her for cheap farm and household help.

"I won't hurt you, Jessie," was all he could manage to say. It wasn't enough, but he meant the words. She simply looked at him with dark, searching eyes. "I swear it," he finished on a note of frustration.

That look. Like a wary child who's been offered candy by a stranger. If it was the last thing he did tonight, he swore he was going to remove that uncertainty from those pretty brown eyes.

"You can trust me, Jessie," he whispered. He could tell she wasn't certain of that at all, but right now that didn't matter. Just like working with wild horses, he understood that her learning to trust him would take time. But he also knew that in matters such as this, he was a very patient man.

"So, are you with me on this, Jessie girl? Because if you aren't, then we'll stop right here."

She didn't say anything for several long moments, and waiting for her reply nearly killed him. She had no idea what it had cost him to tell her that. But at last she expelled a long breath and said, "I'm with you, Mitch. Yes, I'm with you."

Her smoke-and-honey voice drifted through his senses, curling like heady incense around the bed. Gathering her up, he rolled onto his back, taking her with him. When she lay sprawled along his length, he drew her close, and for the next several hours, while the storm outside raged, he proceeded to prove his words.

# Chapter Eleven

"Mitch?" she rasped under the weight of his chest when their heartbeats had slowed and they'd both come back down to earth. She squirmed slightly, then settled down again.

He shifted a little to hear her better. "Hmm?"

"Sweet mercy, Mitch. I think I just died. I went to heaven. But that can't be because now I'm back here. Unless...did the angels kick me out?"

She loved it when she made him laugh. Except right now the increased pressure on her lungs as his chest heaved was making the situation downright intolerable. Thankfully, he must have realized this, because he pushed himself upright, eased out of her, and the next thing she knew he'd lit the oil lamp.

"What are you doing?"

"I want to see your face when I ask you this."

"What?"

Pausing, he ran his fingers through her hair, then down to trace the curve of her cheek. "I'm a big man. I tried hard not to hurt you, Jessie."

"I know."

"Did I?"

"A little," she said honestly. "But only at first."

She wondered what he was thinking. "What is it?" she asked. "Why the worried frown?" She took his hand away from her cheek and tenderly kissed his palm.

"I promised never to hurt you again, and you just said I did. Even if it was just 'a little,' I feel bad about that. Now I know for sure that you've never been with a man before. I should have been more careful."

Jessie bristled. "So, you didn't believe me, then?"

"I wanted to. You'll never know how much. And stop looking at me like that, brat. I've never been so pleased in my life that I've been wrong about so many things about you."

She thought about that, and decided she wasn't going to allow anything to spoil the wonder of what she and Mitch had just shared together. "I'm fine, Mitch. And if truth be told, I'm way more than fine." She smiled, meaning that with all her heart.

"How's the shoulder?" he asked.

"It's all right."

He shifted her slightly so that he could study the injury better. Jessie looked down at the ugly yellowish bruise spread across her upper chest and arm. It looked horrible in the lamplight, much worse than it actually felt.

"You sure it doesn't pain you anymore?" Mitch asked, looking worried.

"Not much."

"And how about your head?" Next his fingers were in her hair, probing the lump.

"I don't have the headache anymore. It only hurts when somebody touches the bump." She slanted him a smile, hoping to ease his worry by teasing him.

He dropped his hand. "Sorry."

Shivering, he got up and piled more logs onto the fire, blew out the lamp, then got back into bed beside her.

"Storm's easing up," he commented, covering them with the blankets.

"Seems that way," she answered, listening for the patter of rain on the roof and barely able to hear it.

He scooped her up, arranging her in the circle of his arms so that she lay on his chest with her head tucked beneath his chin.

"Sleepy?" he asked.

"Not really. Mitch?"

"Hmm?"

"Can I ask you something?"

She felt him smile against the top of her head. "What now?"

"This is hard," she said. "Embarrassing because I don't want you to think me vain."

"Just say it."

"Well, I was wondering. Once, when you were kissing me here," she touched the curve of her jaw at the hollow just beneath her ear, "you called me your 'beautiful Jessie'. Did you mean it? Or is that what's usually done when a man sports with a woman—he nuzzles her neck and cheek and whispers that she's beautiful."

He didn't respond right away.

Firelight danced off the hard angles of his face. She feared she'd made him angry, but she had to know. After the haircut, Marty had called her pretty just to make her feel better. So that didn't count. Nobody, ever, had called her beautiful. Nobody'd ever held her or had even given her so much as a kiss on the cheek. It wouldn't do to carry around a swelled head if Mitch had told her such a thing but hadn't really meant it.

"Please don't be angry, Mitch. I was just wondering because I know I don't have any...well what Nora in *Nora and the Outlaws* called 'endearing charms.' Especially on top. Curtis is always telling me I've got a shape like a flagpole." She sighed. "Oh, I know that when a man's need is powerful enough, things like what the woman looks like don't matter to him, but...Mitch? Ow! Mitch, you're crushing me!"

Pushing against his chest, she struggled to break free of his iron grip. Shoving Mitch was like trying to shove a mountain.

"I should have killed that miserable blond devil when I had the chance," Mitch murmured tightly. "He got lucky, or I would have."

She suffered a long silence, but finally Mitch eased his hold. Jessie was afraid to move for fear he'd start squeezing her again.

"Curtis told you lies," he said flatly, his tone resolute. "Jessie, listen to me. You've got a fine body. More than fine. You've got enough *endearing charms* to drive every man from here to China and back plumb out of his senses. No man could ask for better."

Jessie swallowed, her chest constricting. "You really mean it?"

"I don't say things I don't mean."

He tilted her chin up.

"And another thing. I was *not* sporting with you. We were making love. There's a big difference."

"But you've had other women, and most likely you're comparing me to them."

"Nothing could be farther from the truth. Forget about those other women, Jessie. If I could go back and change the past I would. For your sake. But I can't, so I never want to hear you mention them again." He waggled her chin a little. "Promise me."

She sighed. "All right. I promise."

"One more thing, brat. Listen close. I don't ever recall my telling any woman before that she was beautiful. Only you. Understand?"

She nodded, but barely, because he was holding onto her chin so tight.

"All right then." He let her loose and expelled a long breath.

Jessie lay there breathing in his scent, absorbing his comforting warmth, listening to his heartbeat while his words tumbled over and over in her mind.

She said after a while, "I wish I could change the past, too. I wish Curtis and I never left the wagon train. Then he and the men wouldn't have robbed the bank, stolen your horses, and I wouldn't—"

"Wouldn't be lying here with me right now." He cut off her words, as if the thought that they might never have met pained him. Pressing her near, he lazily massaged her nape and shoulders, attempting to soothe her. "I don't want you worrying about that robbery business anymore, either. As soon as I get you to Sweet Glenn, I'll take care of everything."

"How?" she asked, raising her chin and wrinkling her brow, a million other questions hovering in her mind. But he remained silent, his jaw clenched tight. "Mitch? Please answer me."

“I’ll let you know when we get to Sweet Glenn,” he replied stiffly.

Jessie looked beyond Mitch into the fire. One of the crumbling embers resembled a roan horse leaping across a landscape of blistering mountains and blazing canyons.

How she wished she had a horse. She’d give it to Mitch so that he could track his horses on his own.

She didn’t want to go anywhere. She wanted to take her chances here in the mountains where she felt safe and protected among the comforting forest of pines and wild lupines. Thoughts of entering a town scared her.

Her stomach knotted, a fist of uncertainty gripping her hard. She didn’t want to think that Mitch would abandon her, but he might, and she had to prepare herself for the worst.

Mentally pulling herself up short, she forced her thoughts onto a different track. She was through feeling sorry for herself. No matter what, she had to remember that she had only herself to depend on, that no man, not even Mitch, could be fully trusted.

The desperate state of her poverty gnawed at her. But she couldn’t let the fact that she was destitute get her down, either. True, she possessed nothing of value to get by on once she was on her own, but she did have brains and gumption. If by some miracle the posse from Sulfur Flats had given up, she could make her way to some little no-name town and stay there for a while. Get a job. Save her money and eventually make her way to San Francisco.

Thinking about the down side of things frightened her. If the posse *was* still after her, would she and Mitch arrive in Sweet Glenn only to find wanted posters with her picture on the front tacked up all over town? If so, she’d be recognized and arrested on the spot.

The wound on her foot began to throb. She squeezed her eyes shut, forcing the terror away, forcing the ache away. Concentrating on the warmth of Mitch’s body, on the reassuring beat of his heart beneath her cheek, her limbs eventually relaxed. A lovely feeling of safety enveloped her as she lay in the circle of his strength, the delicious pressure of his fingers continuing to work their magic on her nape. For now she was safe, and that's all that mattered.

She must have dozed, because the next thing she knew, Mitch's hands were stroking her breasts, his lips pressed firmly to hers in a deep, erotic kiss. Luscious liquid warmth pooled in her belly, spread, then flooded like a tide of warmed molasses through her limbs.

"I just want you to know, sweet Jessie girl," he said, his voice rough and unsteady, "that you're perfect. Everything you've got on top and otherwise is all that this man could ever want or ask for."

☙ ☙ ☙

Jessie awoke the next morning to find herself curled up against Mitch's length, her back and bottom nestled against his broad chest and lap, his sheltering arms hugging her close.

A wide wedge of sunlight spilled through the kitchen window, splashing onto the floor, turning dust motes into golden spangles. Red embers smoldered in the hearth. Blue jays chattered in the verdant pines outside, so loud she could hear their ruckus through the cabin's walls.

Had she ever felt more alive? More content?

"Morning." Mitch's breath tickled the fine hairs on the back of her neck making delicious little shivers race across her nape and down her spine. "Sleep well?"

"Mmm," she murmured, shifting lazily to face him. "Did you?"

"Like a rancher after putting in a sixteen-hour day." He smiled crookedly, sliding a long finger down her nose. "You wore me out."

She blushed. She couldn't help it. Didn't he know he shouldn't say such things? Ah, well. Reaching up, she brushed a lock of teak-colored hair away from his brow. "Me too," she admitted quietly.

He kissed her.

"I love you, Mitch," she whispered against the crook of his neck.

His fingers feathered a trail down the length of her arm and back, and then his arms tightened to press her close. He kissed the top of her head.

Silence.

No echoing love words from him. No declarations. Her heart sank.

When she could finally trust herself to keep the hurt out of her voice, she spoke. "Are you hungry?" she asked. "I'll fix us some breakfast if you want. There's a bit of ham left and a few cups of oats in the sack to make porridge." The words tumbled off her tongue like a rock slide, piling up on top of each other. She hated it that she cared so much.

If Mitch noticed anything amiss, he didn't indicate it. Right away he said, "Let me check your foot first. I've been thinking it'll heal faster if you stay off it."

Not giving her a chance to object, which she sorely wanted to do, he bade her scoot over, threw the covers back, and swung to his feet. The light from the window didn't stretch to this part of the room well enough to see properly, so he lit the lamp.

His hands were gentle as he pressed his thumb against the edge of the wound. Jessie winced.

"The oozing's stopped," he commented encouragingly, "but it's still pretty swollen. Keeping the bandage off and letting it air out last night helped, I think. The color's better."

He reached across to the hearth ledge for the whiskey jug.

"Oh please, Mitch. Not again," Jessie groaned, collapsing onto her back and covering her eyes with her arm.

"Sorry, honey. Grit your teeth. I'll do it fast."

The sting wasn't as ferocious this time. She managed to keep the howl behind her teeth, and by blinking rapidly several times, her eyes remained dry.

"Good girl," Mitch praised her, massaging the arch with the pads of his thumbs. Softly, he blew on the cut, helping to take the sting away. It felt heavenly when he did that. Almost making the near torture worth it.

"I'll put some salve on the cut, but we'll leave the bandage off," he continued. "That goes for stockings and boots, too."

"Wait a minute. Mitch?"

He rose, retrieved his pants, and tossed her her clothes. When her drawers smacked her in the face dead center, he laughed. "No sass, Jessie." Amusement glittered in his eyes. "Get dressed while I fix breakfast."

"I'll get you for this," she said, tearing the garment away, trying her darnedest to sound annoyed.

"You can try."

In the middle of stepping into his jeans, he paused to watch her as she slipped an arm into her shirt. His curious, narrow gaze unnerved her because it was different from the purely male, appreciative looks he usually sent her way. What was he thinking now? Nervously, she hurried to pull the shirt closed and get it buttoned.

"How come you don't wear one of those ladies' under tops, Jessie? The kind all fancied up with lace and ribbons? Most women do."

So that was it. Jessie looked away, too mortified to hold his gaze. She couldn't tell him about the breast binder. She just couldn't.

Stifling the anger that reared its head every time she thought about that torture contraption Curtis had forced her to wear, she answered in a tight voice. "They're called camisoles. As a matter of fact, I own two of them," she informed him. "They're in the same place my skirts and blouses are. In my saddlebags. Which are with my horse. Which Marty rode off on."

Mitch reached for his shirt and shrugged it on. "How come?"

"How come what? How come Marty rode off with my horse?"

"Jessie, stop it. Why were your undertops packed in your saddlebags?"

"Camisoles."

"All right, *camisoles*. Your cousin forced you to dress like a man, but a *camisole* wouldn't show under your shirt any more than those pretty drawers show under your trousers."

Mitch was giving her one of those cross, uncompromising looks that told her he wasn't going to let up until she explained.

"He...he made me wear something else," she grumbled, tugging on her pants.

"Like what?"

"I don't want to say."

"Tell me."

"You aren't going to let me be until I do, are you?" she huffed.

"No."

Swinging her legs over the edge of the bed, she pressed her palms to her knees, struggling to find the words. When they came, she said them in a rush. "Curtis made me wear a breast binder—to flatten my chest. I tore it off and threw it in your privy the first chance I got—which was right after you cut me loose from the fence post."

When she heard him curse under his breath, she tried to change the subject. "I'm hungry, Mitch. Really hungry."

"In a minute, brat."

And then he was there, cradling her snugly between his parted legs, pressing her cheek into his hard belly, his fingers burrowed in her hair.

Quietly, he said, "I'll buy you new clothes when we get to Sweet Glenn. Dresses, skirts, whatever you want. Camisoles and everything. Hundreds of them."

She looked up, intending to ask him if he'd suddenly gone insane, but before she could say a word, his lips were covering hers, drawing the protests right out of her mind.

# Chapter Twelve

Jessie lifted the tin cup to her lips with those graceful fingers of hers and took a small sip of coffee. She looked so utterly sweet to him, all love-tousled and slightly worn out from their long night of lovemaking. *Just the way a woman should look after she'd been thoroughly loved by her man*, he thought.

The first order of business once he got her to Sweet Glenn, Mitch decided, was to hunt down a preacher. There was no doubt in his mind that he'd found the woman he wanted to spend the rest of his life with. He'd settled that even before they'd made love. He still wasn't sure how he'd fallen so hard in such a short time, but he'd lived long enough, and had looked long enough, to know that no other woman would ever satisfy the empty places inside him like Jessie did. She loved him. Those three, dusky, soft-spoken words had gone straight to his heart, lodging there like fire glow, thawing all the frozen places he'd ignored for so long.

Maybe it was her delicacy, or the fact that she was all alone in the world and had no one to look after her that stirred such strong protective instincts in him. All he wanted to do was shield her and keep her safe from harm. He wanted to rescue her from men like Curtis and people like her aunt and uncle, and from lawmen who wanted to track her down and lock her away for the rest of her life.

He knew that when he took her out of here they'd be facing trouble, but no matter what the future held, he was determined they'd face their trials together as Mr. and Mrs. Mitchell Wyden. The pleasant sound of that made him feel giddier than a drunken fool.

The more he thought about it, the surer he was he'd be able to clear her name with the authorities. All anybody needed to do was get one glimpse of Jessie's delicate frame and guileless face to be convinced of her innocence. And once she told her story in that smoke-and-honey voice of hers, well, the sheriff would be reduced to potter's clay in her hands.

All he had to do was get her *there* before trouble showed up *here.* For the thousandth time, he cursed himself for all the mistakes he'd made about her, which had ultimately caused the cut on her foot.

She truly did look angelic this morning. He chuckled to himself. If he looked hard enough, he could almost see the halo glowing around her silky chestnut curls. Briefly, he thought about his horses, and for the first time he realized that losing them hadn't been such a tragedy after all. Not when the theft had led him to Jessie. Jessie was more important to him than a thousand horses, and he'd lose them all again if it meant having her in his life and keeping her close.

He grinned, watching her as she lifted another spoonful of porridge to her lips.

*His beautiful Jessie.* They'd make a fine pair, the two of them. He thought of the spread he'd someday own, with Jessie and their children beside him working the land, cattle, and horses. She appeared fragile, but now he knew better. When provoked, inside Jessie Driscoll lie a lioness poised to pounce. Hadn't she challenged him again and again since the moment he'd laid eyes on her? He admired that part of her most of all. She had more daring and fierce courage than he ever would have figured.

"I wish you wouldn't stare at me like that," she scolded him peevishly, shifting in her chair.

"Why?" He grinned. "I like watching you."

"It makes me nervous."

"It does, huh?"

"Yes. So would you please eat your breakfast and stop it?"

"No. I was just thinking how good it was between us last night. I like watching you and thinking about what we did. How your body fits so well against mine. How fine you feel beneath my hands when I touch you. How when I move inside you your soft moans set my blood on fire." She nearly dropped her spoon and he laughed at her prudish discomfiture. "Ever the blushing Jessie. It's okay to talk about it, honey. That's how it's done."

She gave him a disgruntled look and took another bite of porridge. After swallowing, she cleared her throat and said, "It's going to be impossible for me to stay off my foot for the next couple of days, you know. I can't just sit here twiddling my thumbs waiting for the time to pass. There will be times when I'll *have* to get up."

He decided to be a gentleman and let her change the subject. Still, he couldn't resist teasing her. She looked way too pretty when she blushed. "I don't mind carrying you wherever you want to go."

"Don't be ridiculous," she retorted hotly. "That's out of the question."

"I'm not being ridiculous. Holding you is like holding my sweetest dreams in my arms. No trouble at all."

She was looking at him with those huge brown eyes of hers, her lips parted slightly, her spoon poised half way between the bowl and her chin. The sudden rush of love he saw shining in her eyes stole his breath. Presently, she put down the spoon and pushed the bowl away.

His voice had gone so thick he had to clear his throat before he could speak again.

"Finished?"

She gave him a slight nod.

"Guess I'll go outside and see about making you a crutch, then." He smiled crookedly, getting ready to tease her again. "Meanwhile," he added, piling up the empty plates in front of him, "you're just going to have to sit here and twiddle your thumbs."

ଔ ଔ ଔ

"I won't be far away, Jessie. Stay out here on the porch where I can keep an eye on you. Just in case there's trouble," he added. He looked over his shoulder, scanning the clearing and the trees beyond. "It's been a couple of days now, and I'm thinking this peace and quiet can't last forever. I'd be stupid to let my guard down at this point."

She wished he wouldn't say things like that. Things that reminded her the posse might show up any time. Or Curtis. Mitch was gripping his rifle and the hatchet a little too fiercely. And for a fleeting moment, he looked worried, which made her stomach knot with worry, too.

She gazed past him at the dark shadows beyond the clearing.

"Keep the knife handy. If you need me for anything—look at me Jessie. If you need me for anything, call out and I'll come. Understand?"

She met his eyes. "I'll be all right, Mitch. I can take care of myself."

"Sure you can. I know from experience you've got a demon lethal knee." He chuckled, but his attempt to lighten the moment didn't set Jessie any more at ease. She didn't smile back. More seriously he said, "Stay off the foot. Don't get up for any reason. I won't be gone long."

He wasn't. In no time at all, he came walking back carrying a sturdy, T-shaped pine limb.

"Stand up," he instructed, "and lean on me. That's it."

The crutch was too long; it wouldn't fit under her arm comfortably.

"No problem," he said. Sitting her back down, he hefted the hatchet and chopped the end off the limb, measured again, and whittled some more.

"How does it feel now?" he asked, fitting it for the last time under her arm. "Later I'll wrap the top with some rags to make it even more comfortable for you."

"Perfect," she said, smiling.

"Try it out. Down the porch and back."

The crutch made a loud thump on the crude boards, the succeeding thud-scrape-thuds and her own clumsiness making Jessie laugh. "Well, at least I'm not chair-bound anymore. With a little practice, I'm sure I'll get the hang of this."

Mitch stayed one step beside her while she made a few more lurching passes up and down the porch, preparing to catch her if she lost her balance.

"Was the thought of me carrying you wherever you wanted to go so bad, Jessie?" he asked when she paused to catch her breath.

Balancing on her good foot, she grinned up at him, swinging the crutch so it caught him lightly on the shin.

"My worst nightmare," she said quietly, stretching to give him a kiss on the cheek.

His hands circled her waist, holding her steady. Every time he touched her she felt a little safer, a little more cherished. He jerked her close. The crutch clattered to the floor.

"Your worst nightmare, huh?" he growled, scooping her up and lifting her high. "Now you've gone and hurt my feelings. Think I'll just have to punish you for that."

"Oh no," she squealed, laughing. "Not the fence post, please, Mitch!"

He spun her around in crazy circles, pretending a couple of times like he was going to drop her. Jessie wrapped her arms around his neck, pressed her body close, and held on tight. She didn't yelp another word about nightmares or fence posts. He was kissing her so thoroughly and crushing her so close she could barely manage to breathe.

☙ ☙ ☙

Another night and day passed. A night and day of pleasant discovery for Jessie, where she learned to use the crutch, and Mitch continued to watch over her like a guardian angel.

He took her to the river again to bathe, but this time he arranged her in the shallows and washed her himself, carrying her in and out of the water, drying her off and dressing her afterward in one of his roomy shirts. It didn't do any good to protest, to tell him she was perfectly capable of bathing and dressing herself.

Afterward, to get him back for his high-handedness, she tortured him by singing a few rousing bars of "Aura Lee" in his ear.

Now she lay on a blanket, the sweet scent of pines, sunshine, and earthy loam filling her senses. Mitch, dressed only in a worn pair of jeans he hadn't bothered to button, was busy at the river's edge finishing up their laundry. She could have lain there and watched the play of his powerful arm, chest, and back muscles all day long.

Desire tightened her insides. Every glance, every smile, every word he spoke, made the wanting start all over again.

Rolling onto her stomach, she propped her chin in her hands and allowed her gaze to wander past him to the other side of the river where the shadows lurked. Mitch's concern for her welfare thrilled her, yet she couldn't help but be puzzled by it. That someone should care about her feelings and the state of her health to the extent that Mitch did was a whole new experience for her. No one had ever pampered her like that before.

Curtis and the others, with the exception of Marty sometimes, had never once considered her needs. Or her feelings. At least no farther beyond what would benefit them in some way. If she'd cut her foot, say, while traveling with Curtis, he'd have cursed her for her clumsiness, then let her tend the wound herself. And if she'd been hurt badly enough, he'd certainly have left her behind on the trail somewhere rather than deal with an injured woman who couldn't pull her own weight any longer.

Through years of bitter experience, she'd come to believe all men possessed that same mean-spiritedness and indifference toward women.

*Was Mitch Wyden the exception?*

Her eyes returned to the big, dangerous-looking man who, sensing her scrutiny, lifted his head and tossed her a playful, white-toothed grin. Jessie pushed aside her dark thoughts and, grinning like a besotted fool right back, blew him a kiss. Mercy, how she loved him.

☙ ☙ ☙

On the morning of the fifth day, Mitch announced it was time they start preparing to walk out. Jessie had just finished cleaning her teeth and brushing her hair when he casually broke the news, taking the brush from her hand and carefully replacing it on the table.

"Your foot's healed up enough, I think."

Jessie stiffened. Another nightmare about hangmen and prison cells had haunted her sleep last night. She'd woken on the cusp of a scream, hot, sweaty, and shaking. It had taken her ages to convince Mitch it was nothing but a bad dream, that she was fine and would have no trouble going back to sleep. He'd tried to make sure of that by making love to her and holding her close to his heart afterward. But she'd lain wide awake the rest of the night anyway.

"Do we have to leave?" Jessie asked, struggling to keep her nerves steady, her voice calm.

"Yeah. We do. We're almost out of grub, Jessie. As it is, I'll have to do some hunting today if we're to eat a decent supper tonight. Maybe I'll get lucky and bag a deer. If I do, I won't have to waste time hunting during the next two days."

"Is that how long it's going to take us to get to Sweet Glenn?"

"Depends on that foot of yours. But yeah," he said, fingering the stubble on his chin thoughtfully, "two days ought to do it. Three at the most unless something goes wrong."

Her distress spilled over. Added to all her other worries, getting to town depended on her ability to walk the fifteen miles it took to get there. She felt pressured and uncertain. What if her foot gave out before they got there? What if the law apprehended her the moment they set foot in the town?

"What's the all-fire rush, anyway?" Jessie blurted, turning away and thumping nearer the hearth so he wouldn't see on her face the depth of her anxiety.

Mitch remained quiet a long time. Finally, she heard the snap of a sulfur match as he lit a cheroot. The extinguished match sailed past her shoulder, landing soundlessly in the grate beside her.

"The rush is, brat," he said, exhaling forcefully, "that we've been mighty lucky up until now. I've got a feeling deep in my gut. It's telling me to skedaddle out of here. The sooner the better."

"Do you think they're still after me, then?" She darted a glance over her shoulder, unable to hide the tremor in her voice anymore. Her grip tightened on the crutch and Mitch noticed.

"Take it easy, Jessie. I can't be sure about anything."

"But you have a feeling."

"My instincts have never let me down before. I just want to get you somewhere safe. Here, in this place," he waved the cheroot, "isn't it."

"Why not? It's hidden well and miles from the nearest town."

"And any good tracker worth his sand could find it eventually. I'm not willing to take that chance." Then, under his breath he added, "I sure won't be sorry to leave this gawdawful mess behind me, either."

Though he thought she hadn't, Jessie heard that last remark and wondered just what he'd meant by it. She suffered a deeper stab of uncertainty.

Despondent, she turned to face him fully, no longer caring whether he saw the magnitude of her distress or not. The thud of the crutch on the plank floor boomed like she'd dropped a cast-iron pot. Hugging her middle as if wrapping her arms around herself could keep her from falling apart, she said, "I know you well enough by now to understand that when you've made up your mind about something, there's no talking you out of it. My trying to change your mind won't do any good, will it?"

He gave his head a small shake, stubbornly setting the angle of his jaw. "Trust me, Jessie. I'm right about this. It's the only way."

Grinding out the cheroot beneath his boot, he strode to the old clothes trunk and began rummaging through its contents.

"What are you looking for?" Jessie asked, her heart heavy. She felt as if he'd just sentenced her to death, and here he was blithely going on about his business as if nothing had changed.

"This." He held up a revolver. "It's an old Civil War relic, but it still fires well enough. I told you I'm going hunting. You'll need some protection while I'm gone."

Startled, she swayed on the crutch a little.

"Come with me, Jessie." Brooking no argument, he helped her outside to the clearing and extended the gun to her.

"What are you doing? I don't even want to touch that thing."

"I remember you telling me you aren't very good with firearms. You're going to learn how to shoot it."

"Oh no I'm not."

"Yes you are. Just point it and squeeze the trigger. Lean on the crutch to steady yourself," he ordered, pressing the revolver into her hand. He covered her fingers when she attempted to let the weapon drop to the ground.

She faltered, expelling a long breath. "Mitch, I *hate* guns."

He didn't seem to care that she hated guns in the least. He gripped her hand a little tighter.

"Point it," he demanded again.

Her shoulders sagged. "Point it where?" she asked thinly, knowing she was fighting a losing battle.

"Toward the trees."

"But don't I have to aim at something?"

"I just told you where to aim. Aim for the trees," he repeated.

"Which one?" she snapped, exasperated.

Clearly, his patience was wearing thin, too. "The whole blasted forest, Jessie. See it out there?"

She gave him a freezing look.

"I don't want you to hit anything in particular right now. I just want you to get used to the feel of the gun."

"Well, you could have said that to begin with."

She stood quiet for a moment as perspiration trickled down her back and a slight wave of dizziness passed over her. Thoughts of shooting and possibly killing someone terrified her.

"Mitch?"

"What?"

"You ought to know something."

"What now?"

"I'd never have the stomach to shoot somebody."

His glare unnerved her, but she held her ground. After a moment his features softened as he considered her choppy breathing and blanched complexion. His shoulders, so tense just a moment before, suddenly relaxed. Smoothing a hand across her hip, he patted her bottom reassuringly.

"The idea is to frighten the enemy off with a warning blast," he explained gently. "Let him know you're armed and dangerous. Come on, brat. Don't worry so much. This piece isn't very accurate. The target would have to be standing nose to nose with you before it'd do much damage."

Jessie digested that. After a moment she cleared her throat, then commented lamely, "It's heavy."

"I know. Hold it with both hands, like this." He stood behind her, wrapped her hands around the pistol, positioned her finger over the trigger, and helped her level it toward the trees. "Now gently squeeze the trigger."

The recoil slammed her backward into Mitch's chest. The crutch flew from beneath her arm, landing almost a yard away. Laughing, he steadied her, retrieved the crutch, then made her shoot a couple more times until she got the hang of it without keeling over anymore. Patiently, he taught her how to load it between tries.

"Good girl," he praised after she shot the final round. Taking the gun from her hands, he reloaded it himself for the last time. "You're a quick study."

Once back inside the cabin, Mitch tacked on that grim, serious expression again. "I want you to keep the gun within reach at all times while I'm gone. Understand?"

"Mitch, please. Why can't you leave the knife with me like before?"

"Because I'll need it myself this time."

Her face crumpled with worry. "But guns scare me."

"Don't argue with me anymore, Jessie. If someone should show up and threaten you while I'm gone, I won't be within hollering distance this time. I won't be able to reach you quickly if you should need my help."

A small, terrifying silence followed, Mitch's words hanging in the air like black smoke. Jessie crumpled into a chair.

The pulse in Mitch's temple throbbed. "I'll be able to hear gunfire, Jessie. If you get scared or need me for any reason, you're to pull that trigger."

He stared at her, resolute, until she at last gave him a nod.

He turned to go. "Just one more thing. Stay inside the cabin as much as possible. No wandering off to pick posies." His hard, steady gaze told her he wasn't joking.

Jessie knew it was useless to argue. With a sinking heart, she sat mute while he shouldered his rifle and grabbed a canteen.

"All right then," he said. "Just sit tight. I'll be back before sundown."

Before he left he drew her to her feet, kissed her and held her close, but his embrace and murmured reassurances did little to ease the awful foreboding lodged in her heart. What if something happened to him and he never came back?

Oh, mercy. What if...what if he'd lied to her? What if *everything* he'd said and done had been a lie and now it was over and he was leaving for good?

She remembered his words and flinched. *"I sure won't be sorry to leave this gawdawful mess behind me,"* he'd said when he thought she hadn't heard.

She watched after him until his long strides took him deep into the trees and, finally, out of sight.

# Chapter Thirteen

The day crawled by on caterpillar feet. Jessie tried to stay occupied, but found that difficult. The cabin was quiet without him, empty and cheerless; the silence gnawed at her until she thought she'd go crazy missing him so much. Even the two *Harper's Weekly* magazines she'd found in Mitch's trunk hadn't kept her interest for very long.

Nights turned cold in the mountains, but the days yawned warm and endless beneath the bright summer sun, making a fire during the day unnecessary. Nevertheless, out of desperation to liven the place up, Jessie built a fire in the hearth. Something about a fire always made her feel a little less lonesome, a little more at peace inside.

Because it was habit, she stayed off her foot during the morning, but by early afternoon, with nothing to do but stare into the fire and count the passing minutes, Jessie decided enough was enough. Sitting on the hearth ledge, she cradled her injured foot, turning it toward the flames for a closer inspection. The cut had fused together with no further infection, she observed with relief. The surrounding skin now had a pink, healthy look to it. In a week a scar would be all she'd be able to see.

Tentatively, she lowered her foot to the floor and tried putting a little pressure on the cut.

"Not bad," she commented aloud.

When Mitch came back—and he *was* coming back, she reassured herself sternly—she was going to show him how well she could walk on it now. Without the crutch. She'd convince him he didn't have to worry about her foot giving out on their way to town. He'd be proud of her, and, she hoped, relieved by her progress. She found a clean rag for a bandage and wrapped the injury tightly, convinced that today would be a turning point. She'd use her foot normally, without the help of the crutch.

Slipping on her stockings and both boots for the first time in days, Jessie decided to survey the pantry for anything that she could add to a pot of broth. She frowned a little when full pressure on the cut caused her to limp a bit, but she was determined to try getting around without the crutch for a while, something she knew Mitch wouldn't allow if he were here.

Their foodstuffs were painfully low, she admitted, pulling aside the curtain and perusing the shelves. Yesterday, Mitch had revealed that the morning the horses were stolen he'd planned to ride into town after daybreak for supplies. His horse had been saddled and ready. She couldn't help but realize the irony of it. If Curtis had just waited another few minutes, Mitch would have been gone and nobody would have gotten killed....

She sighed and studied the shelves, taking inventory. A couple of tins of beans, a small slab of bacon, an almost empty sack of flour, a little sugar, coffee and corn meal, a handful of dried apples, and four pieces of jerked deer meat. Mitch had been right. It was walk out of here now or waste away from starvation. You couldn't survive on meat and grains alone. A body needed fresh vegetables and other foodstuffs, as well.

As she turned away, her hand knocked a small canister to the floor. Coins and greenbacks spilled out, the lid and the coins rolling every which way. Surprised, Jessie dropped to her hands and knees, mentally counting the money as she hastily stuffed it back into the canister. She'd had no idea Mitch had kept a stash of money on the shelf.

A shaft of apprehension straightened her spine. Had Mitch known she'd find that canister eventually? Had he left without it, knowing that when he didn't return, she'd need a little something to get by on? She counted only thirty dollars or so, but that would be enough money to see her through for a week or two if she needed it.

She slid the canister back onto the shelf as if it burned her fingers to touch it. She mustn't think like that. Mitch *hadn't* left her. He's gone hunting, just as he'd said, and he would be coming back with supper on his back in just a few more hours. She wouldn't allow herself to think anything otherwise.

Slowly, Jessie rose to her feet, added a log to the fire, and nudged the ashes with the poker. This time she saw a cameo in the red embers, its Romanesque features sharply defined, etched in gray and black. A woman's image; a woman with curly, flaming hair piled on the top of her head. Her mother had worn her hair like that, Jessie recalled as a wave of sadness washed through her. Abruptly, she turned away.

She spent the rest of the day cleaning an already clean cabin. She swept, then hauled water into the house from the barrel outside to scrub the floor. She dusted. She gathered the blankets and sheets off the bed and aired them over the porch railing, all the while aware that Mitch never would have approved of her doing these things if he were here. *But Mitch isn't here*, Jessie sighed heavily.

By sundown, she began to worry. Mitch had promised to be back by now. She kept pacing to the window, searching past the clearing into the deepening shadows for any sign of him, but every time she looked, emptiness met her gaze.

Well past midnight, fraught with worry, Jessie curled up, still fully dressed, into a fetal ball on the bed. She couldn't bear to think that something might have happened to him. Brown bears and cougars were plentiful in these mountains. Mitch might have been attacked by any sort of wild animal. He could be lying out there, cold and injured and bleeding.

She covered her ears, trying to shut out the torment, struggling to keep her imagination tamed. Because, deep inside she knew Mitch could take care of himself, wild animals or no. That cruel, nagging voice she'd been hearing all day ever since she'd found the canister full of money, kept telling her that Mitch had left her for good. That he wasn't coming back. That he'd never planned to come back for her at all.

Why had she begun to trust him? Why had she set herself up for such a devastating fall? *Because he made you fall in love with him, that's why. You lost your heart because he was kind to you and pampered you and made you feel wanted and cared for.*

But he'd never once said he loved her, and that fact gnawed at her now. What a fool she'd been to give her heart away like that. Mitch had even told her once that he was a man, just like any other. Why hadn't she remembered that before now? Now it was too late. He was gone, and with him he'd taken all the vital parts of herself. Not just her heart, but her pride, her dignity, her maiden's innocence.

She thought about firing the pistol. But if he'd truly left her, the gunshot wouldn't bring him back. *Stop it, Jesse!* she scolded herself in desperation. Maybe the hunt had taken him farther away than he'd figured. No doubt he was on his way back right this minute. And if he wasn't able, for some good reason, to make it back tonight, surely Mitch would come back for her tomorrow.

She fell into a fitful sleep a few hours before dawn to the sounds of crackling embers and the endless chirp of crickets mating in the empty clearing beyond the cabin walls.

☙ ☙ ☙

*What in blazes had happened?*

Mitch awoke to the sound of his own groaning, a bleached full moon staring down at him from the star-studded blackness above. His head was pounding, as if a horse with a burr beneath its saddle bucked inside it. He shivered with cold.

As he rolled over, nausea roiled in his stomach. Pushing to his knees, he gingerly pressed his throbbing head, cursing when his fingers came away bloody.

*What had happened?* he asked himself again. When his vision cleared, he scanned the moonlit ground for his rifle, spotting it three feet away, half buried in a pile of rubble. The buck deer he'd shot lay in an inky pool of blood beside it.

And then everything came rushing back. Around the third hour out, he'd spotted the buck and its doe on the lip of a rocky ravine, ambling toward a stand of pines. Moving fast but cautiously, Mitch moved into position to get a clear shot, hoping the buck wouldn't dart suddenly for the woods.

He'd gotten a clean shot. The bullet ripped through the buck's chest, the report sending flocks of birds to flight and the startled doe scrambling for the trees.

With dismay, Mitch watched as his prey staggered several steps the wrong way toward the lip of the shallow gorge. At the edge, its front legs buckled, pitching it head first into the ravine. As the bulky body bounced against the jagged granite outcroppings, several of its antlers broke on the way down.

He'd stood there frozen and contemplated the arduous task of reaching the fallen buck and hauling it, or parts of it anyway, back up those forbidding walls. The drop wasn't impossibly steep, just treacherous, and for a moment he considered leaving the buck and going after the doe. But reciting the old proverb about the bird in the hand, he'd decided to take the risk.

He'd been on his way down, slowly, cautiously placing his footing on the natural depressions of stone and exposed roots, when one of the stones gave way, sending him tumbling, willy-nilly, to the bottom. He must have taken the blow to his head on the way down because he neither remembered striking the ground nor the moment he'd passed out.

He raised his eyes to the sky, the quick movement causing another wave of nausea. Perspiration poured from his body, the cold, dangerous kind. Doggedly, he pushed the dizziness away, gulping in the frigid air until his vision cleared and his hammering heart settled back down. The set of the Dipper told him it was well past midnight.

*Jessie.* She'd be bone-deep worried about him by now. Alone and scared, he could only imagine the state of mind she'd be in. And if she'd needed him.... The terrible thought momentarily paralyzed him: had she fired the pistol while he'd been unconscious?

He had to finish this business quickly and get back to her. Setting his jaw, he rose to his feet, his gaze traveling first to the bleeding buck and then to the surrounding granite walls. With slow deliberation, by the light of the full moon, he planned a safer route out.

Determined, he drew his knife and set to work on the buck's right hind quarter. The meat would have a strong gamy taste since it had been far too long since the kill, but to waste so much meat seemed criminal.

He glanced at the Dipper again. With luck and no more mishaps, and if he could keep from passing out from the bucking bronco gone wild in his brain, he could make it back to the cabin—and Jessie—by mid-morning.

☙ ☙ ☙

Jessie awoke with a start. *What was that?*

"Mitch?" She sat up, hugging her knees, a cold knot of fear settling in her stomach. She quickly glanced around, only to find the cabin desolate, empty. *As empty as the place beside her in the bed.* No. It wasn't Mitch who had made that sound. Mitch hadn't come back.

The sound came again, not from inside the cabin but from outside, a faraway snuffle, like that of a— *Sweet mercy, a horse!*

She scrambled from the bed, grabbed the heavy gun off the night stand, and headed for the window. Carefully, she peeked from the edge of the sill, straining to get a glimpse of whatever or whoever was outside.

Dawn had broken over the canyon rim, washing the clearing in morning light. A riderless horse broke from the trees at a trot, heading straight for the corral. The silver conchos studding the empty saddle glinted in the sunlight like tiny mirrors; the loose reins streamed behind it like two black ribbons.

Jessie held her breath, searching the trees. Would the fallen rider come staggering into the clearing next? After ten minutes of motionless silence, she decided it was safe to venture outside and inspect the horse milling about at the corral fence. It had been pacing and stomping the ground in frustration all this time, eyeing the hay bales and the water trough beyond the gate.

"Hello, fella," she said softly, approaching the skittish chestnut-colored horse with caution, suppressing her limp as best she could. She couldn't think of anything worse than scaring the stallion and causing it to bolt. The animal was her ticket out of here. *Or Mitch's if he hadn't left her.*

Laying the gun on the ground, she gently extended her hand and began stroking the chestnut's neck, crooning nonsense to gentle him. The stallion snorted, rearing a little, but soon Jessie had hold of the reins and was leading him like a gentled lamb into the corral. Once inside, she let him go, and laughed a little as he headed straight for the water trough. Quickly, she secured the gate latch.

That was an awfully expensive saddle on him, Jessie noticed, as her eyes scanned the animal's fine lines. An expensive saddle for an expensive horse. Where had he come from?

And then she noticed the bulging saddlebags hanging heavily across the horse's flanks. Curious, she stepped closer, anxious for the horse to finish drinking so that she could remove the saddle and saddlebags without him putting up a fuss.

Behind her a horse neighed. The chestnut raised his head, water dripping from his muzzle, and snorted an amiable reply.

Jessie froze, just for a heartbeat, before spinning around, nearly losing her balance when her vulnerable foot took her full weight. A man on horseback, his hat pitched low over his eyes, entered the clearing, walking his horse at a leisurely pace. Backlit by the sun as he was, she couldn't make out his face. But there was something familiar about the loose-jointed way the man sat his horse, the lazy attitude of his shoulders as he approached.

"Hello, cousin."

*Dear God. Curtis!*

# Chapter Fourteen

"Curtis!" Jessie slipped through the corral gate and approached him, apprehension keeping her steps slow.

Halting his horse in front of the cabin, he made no attempt to dismount, but instead, shifted forward in the saddle, lazily propping one forearm on the pommel. Pushing the brim of his hat back with his thumb, he grinned down at her, his teeth very white against the frame of his tawny beard.

"Well, you're still alive, I see," he said, sounding bored and a little disappointed.

Jessie took a step backward. It was her mare he was riding, she realized. She was overjoyed to see her old friend, Belle, yet inside she fumed at the callous way Curtis had greeted her.

The small smile she was prepared to give him died at its inception. "No thanks to you," she snapped instead, her voice cold.

Curtis slid from Belle, tied the reins to the porch railing, and climbed the stairs. Jessie moved to block him, slipping between him and the door. The motion stopped him, but only for a moment.

"Aw come on, Jess. Aren't you happy to see me?"

"No," she told him frankly, stumbling backward as he shouldered her aside.

"And after all the trouble I went through to get back here. I've come to rescue you."

"I don't want to be rescued," Jessie said, pushing down her panic.

Curtis gave her a dry laugh. "Well isn't that just too bad. Get inside."

He grabbed her arm and spun her around, giving her a smart slap on the rump to get her moving. The grin on his face vanished the moment he got her inside.

"Cozy," he commented, looking around, squinting to see the layout of the place in the dim light. He was favoring his right side, Jessie noticed, and he absently pressed a hand to his back, just above the kidney.

"If you know what's good for you, you'll get out of here fast, Curtis. Mitch will be back any time now, and if he catches you here, he'll kill you."

He studied her hard, a muscle twitching in his cheek. "So, that murderer's name is Mitch, is it? Mitch what?"

"Wyden. I'm warning you, Curtis. He's not a man to trifle with."

"How long's he been gone, Jess?"

She remained silent. *Let him sweat*, she thought.

"I watched the clearing for a good ten minutes after the chestnut ran for the corral. When nobody came out after that horse but you, I figured you were alone. Where'd he go? Tell me before my patience runs out."

"I told you, he'll be back soon. Any moment."

"Yeah, I heard you the first time." Apparently he was willing to drop it for the time being. Spying the lamp, he said, "Light that lamp. I can't see a blasted thing in here."

She stood where she was, not moving a muscle.

"Do it! We don't have much time."

"*I* have all the time in the world," she retorted hotly, folding her arms and taking a combative stance. "It's you whose time is running out."

He gave her a chilling look. "Don't give me any trouble, Jess. Believe me, I'm not in the mood."

Striding past her, he headed for the bed, snatched a pillow and tore off its case. Grabbing the oil lamp on his way back, he shoved it into her hands. "I told you to light the lamp." He towered above her, the threat in his voice unmistakable.

Grudgingly, she did as she was told. While she searched for the matches and lit the lamp, out of the corner of her eye she watched as Curtis surveyed the cabin's tiny interior. She saw him rip back the pantry curtain just as the lamp wick caught.

Setting the lamp on the edge of the dry sink, Jessie braced herself for a confrontation.

"Don't just stand there gawking at me like a dummy," he said, "Get me that other pillow case." He began sorting through the pantry shelves, piling everything onto the table.

"What do you think you're doing?" A mixture of alarm and anger made her voice crack.

Curtis turned on her, his face dark with contempt. "You were never the one with the brains in the family, were you? What's it look like I'm doing? We need food if we're ever gonna reach—"

He didn't finish, which didn't bode well.

"Reach where?" Jessie demanded. "Curtis, tell me!"

He turned back to what he was doing, taking his time before answering, as if he were weighing how much to tell her and how much not to, or even to tell her at all. "Mexico," he said finally, apparently deciding she ought to know.

Jessie laughed, incredulous. "Mexico? Curtis, you're crazy if you think I'm going with you to Mexico."

"Just gather up whatever you want to bring with you and shut up. Make sure you pack that comb and brush over there. Looks like they might be made of silver." He glanced at her mop of painfully short curls, a derisive smirk on his lips. "We can sell them somewhere."

His meaning was clear. Until her hair grew out, she wouldn't be needing them.

Enraged, instead of obeying orders, she limped over to the bed and sat down, her legs suddenly too wobbly to support her. She wasn't going anywhere with Curtis. She doubted she'd be able to stop him from taking the comb and brush when he left, but she'd sure as heaven try. They were precious to her. She'd received few gifts in her life, and certainly none as fine as those given to her by the man she loved.

Curtis had found the money canister and was greedily stuffing its contents into his pockets. But it wasn't long before he turned and spotted her sitting on the bed.

Angrily, he said, "I guess I'm gonna have to spell things out for you. We didn't make out so good with the horses. With three of our men down, over half of 'em ran off. A rancher bought a few, but Walt had trouble getting a good price because the rancher suspected something wasn't square."

"Where *were* you all this time?" Jessie demanded. "It's been days since you rode off and left me here." She didn't want to hear about how they'd tried to sell Mitch's horses. It made her too sick inside to hear it.

Curtis gave her a cold look. "Marty and I were laid up with gunshot wounds; Marty's were so bad, for a while there he was in no shape to help at all." He paused. "Anyway, since Walt ended up not getting much for the horses, we pulled another robbery."

"Oh Curtis, no. You didn't!"

"Some idiot got brave and I had to shoot a man. Aw, now don't start with me, Jessie. I didn't kill him, just busted up the man's leg a little. So anyway, California's out for the time being. I figure Mexico's the safest place for us right now."

"Where is Walt?" Jessie asked, her voice wobbling like a kite tail in a high wind.

"We split up."

"And Marty?"

"Dead."

She gasped, another piece of her dying inside. In spite of his cowardice and the rotten thing he'd done to her, Marty, in his own way, had always been kind to her.

"Enough now. Get up and hand me that pillow case."

Out of habit, or maybe because she was too rattled not to, Jessie obeyed him, snatching the other pillow and tossing it across the room. It caught him on the side of the head.

He turned on her with fury in his eyes. "Don't get smart. And if you're gonna leave here with anything of your own, you'd better get a move on."

"I'm not going with you," Jessie said stiffly. "Mitch will be back soon and I prefer to stay here with him."

Curtis stared at her. "Mitch." He spat the name like a curse. "Gather up your things, Jessie. Now."

Wildly, she remembered the revolver she'd left at the corral. How could she have been so stupid? Mitch had warned her to keep it handy at all times, but she'd been careless.

She eyed her cousin like a cornered animal. Curtis was going to force her to leave here. For the thousandth time, he was forcing her to do something she didn't want to do. *No!* her mind screamed. Somehow she had to convince him to leave without her.

Her eyes darted to the hearth. She'd bash Curtis with the poker if she had to.

Silently, she got up and reached out, her hand curling around the cold iron rod, her resolve firm, determined. Curtis saw, but there was a startled look on his face, as if he couldn't believe she had the audacity to do such a thing. Then he took a step forward, his lips twisted in a snarl.

Whirling, she wielded the poker, gripping it in both hands like a battle sword. "Stay away from me, Curtis! I told you, I'm not going with you."

"Oh yes you are." He moved to grab her.

She swung the poker at him, narrowly missing the side of his head.

Curtis cursed, dodging the thrust. "What's gotten into you?" he shouted.

"I've come to my senses, that's what," she said, swinging again. "I'm tired of being bullied into doing things I don't want to do. Tired of you bossing me around as if I'm some brainless simpleton set here on earth for the sole purpose of doing your bidding."

Curtis feinted left, dodging her swing, and paused, keeping a wary eye on the poker. "Ha! That's not it at all, is it?" he ground out in disgust. "I've already figured things out, Jessie." His smirk unnerved her. "You let that murderer bed you, didn't you? And by your ridiculous little show of defiance, I can only assume you enjoyed it. Jessie, how *could* you? He killed three of your friends!"

He lunged for her again. This time the poker struck him squarely in the forearm, making him yelp. Furiously, he came at her with all his strength, tackling her to the floor, wrenching the poker from her hands before she had the chance to strike out at him again.

"Curse your hide," he spat, hurling the poker to the other side of the room. It crashed against a shelf, smashing crockery.

As his weight slammed into her, the breath momentarily whooshed from her lungs, sending her into panic. Strong hands pinned her wrists above her head as she fought with all her strength to free herself.

Curtis easily held her down, letting her struggle until she exhausted herself. Straight into her face, his hot, stale breath assaulting her nose and cheeks, he growled, "You're coming with me, Jess."

"I won't."

A slow, menacing smile curled his narrow lips. "You don't have a choice."

He raised his doubled fist.

"No!" Jessie cried as pain exploded in her cheek and jaw. Curtis's satisfied smile faded into the blackness.

They were several miles away when Jessie finally came to. The side of her face, especially her jaw, hurt like the devil. To make matters worse, it felt like a hot band of barbed wire circled her wrists. She looked down to discover that Curtis had tied her to her horse.

"Curtis," she groaned, feeling sick.

He halted his horse—the chestnut—and swung around in the saddle. Belle's reins were in his hands.

"You finally came to," he said, giving her a cursory once over.

"Why am I tied up like this?" Jessie barely managed to push the words past her swollen lips and aching jaw.

"Didn't want you falling off." He pushed the brim of his hat higher on his forehead to take a better look at her. The gesture made her aware that her own hat sat atop her head. "You okay?"

"No."

For some reason, her reply made him chuckle. Which made her furious.

His smile vanished. "Next time, maybe you'll do as you're told. Don't ever pull a stunt like that on me again, little cousin. Next time I won't be so lenient."

"Lenient?" she cried with difficulty. "The side of my face feels like a balloon. And my wrists hurt. Untie me, Curtis."

"You should be thanking me I didn't just throw you over the saddle and let your bat-brained head dangle over the side. Then you'd really have a load of pain to complain about." There was a short pause while he studied her some more. "Want some water?"

She shook her head and silence fell between them.

"Come on, then. We're wasting time."

"Curtis, untie me!"

"Later." He nudged his horse. Jessie winced as Belle jerked to follow.

They'd been riding, the horses picking through the rough landscape at a steady walk, for hours. Jessie kept her eyes in front of her, too miserable over her defeat to do much else. Somehow, she'd escape her cousin, she vowed. She'd just have to be patient and wait for the perfect opportunity. She had Belle now, and her own saddlebags filled with her belongings. The going might be difficult, but somehow she would slip from under Curtis's watchful eyes and make her way to San Francisco.

She'd been staring at the chestnut's rump and saddle for over an hour, wincing every time one of the silver conchos flashed sun in her eyes.

It was a beautiful saddle, she mused absently. Lots of scroll work and fancy rigging. Where in the world had it come from? She nudged Belle closer with her knees when she noticed the lettering. Hand-tooled into the underside of the cantle she saw the initials M. W.

ଔ ଔ ଔ

"Jessie?"

*Where is she?*

Reeling with pain and fatigue, Mitch dropped the heavy haunch of venison just inside the door, gripping the jamb to keep from keeling over. Slowly, his eyes adjusted to the dim light. No Jessie.

*She was gone.*

His mind raced. What had happened to her? When he hadn't returned at the appointed time, had she wandered off to search for him?

Worried, he gave his head a gentle shake to clear his vision and surveyed the room. The pantry was empty; by the looks of things it had been ransacked. Shards of a crockery bowl lay scattered on the floor where she must have knocked it from the shelf in her haste. Two caseless pillows lay tossed in the corner of the kitchen. She'd left her extra shirt—his shirt—folded neatly at the foot of the bed, and the crutch was propped against the wall, but just about everything else of value was missing. Including the lamp and the silver comb and brush.

His blood froze, then rushed to pound in his temples. Doggedly, he fought for control. Had she planned to leave all along and had simply been waiting for a good opportunity to make a getaway?

He knew she'd been scared to leave here for fear she'd be arrested the moment she stepped foot in a town. And he'd insisted that's just where he was going to take her, willing or not. He'd dismissed her apprehensions, ignored her worries and pleas, even her nightmares, certain he knew what was best. And now she'd run off because of his bullheaded stubbornness.

"Little fool," he whispered into the empty room, picturing her alone, on an injured foot, making her way through the dangerous woods....

But as he glanced around again, his gaze sliding to a halt on the broken pottery and the poker lying among the shards, another explanation occurred to him. These were signs of a struggle. What if she'd been taken?

Had she fired a warning shot while he'd been unconscious? What if the posse had shown up? He held his throbbing temples, trying to reason things out, fighting the roaring in his head.

No, a posse wouldn't have cleaned out the cabin like this.

*Curtis!*

The pain in his temples intensified, causing his knees to buckle, his grip on the door jamb to slip. Threatening shadows crossed his vision as the roaring in his ears swelled louder and louder, climbing toward a deafening crescendo.

He covered his ears, sinking to the floor. Moments later he sank into the shadows.

☙ ☙ ☙

Jessie stared into the cold face of the full moon, her thoughts in a jumble. Where was Mitch tonight? For the millionth time she mulled the possibilities. Was he alone and hurt somewhere, and that's why he hadn't returned on time? Or had he truly abandoned her and had made his way to a town by now? She still couldn't fully give in to that notion. To do so hurt too much. That would mean that everything precious they'd shared between them had been a lie on his part. No! Mitch had given her the gun. He'd spent time teaching her how to use it. He knew she needed food. He'd sworn he'd be back—

"I'll take another piece of that jerky," Curtis said, nudging her thigh with the toe of his boot. They were cold camping; Curtis hadn't wanted to risk a fire.

Her back stiffened. She was saddle sore, tired, and irritable. She couldn't talk, or chew very well, or move her jaw without discomfort, all because of the beast of a man sitting across from her. He hadn't broken any of her bones, but he might as well have, given the way the side of her face felt.

"The sack's right in front of you. Get it yourself," she snapped through her teeth.

Curtis shifted and narrowed his eyes on her. "Watch your step, Jess. I'm in no mood for sass."

She stiffened, preparing for retaliation, but he surprised her. In a huff, he snagged the sack, tore off a piece of the tough meat with his teeth, and rolled it around in his cheek. With each pass of his tongue, moonlight glinted off his pale beard.

Jessie went back to studying the moon.

After a long silence Curtis said, "You've got the cleaning up to do. Best get to it. Afterwards you can lay out our bedrolls while I check the horses a final time."

Jessie tore her gaze from the moon and her dismal thoughts. "Not quite yet, Curtis,' she told him. "We need to talk." She'd been too upset, in too much pain to talk much all day, but now there were things she wanted to know.

She said through her stiff jaw, "Why'd you come back for me? You could have been halfway to Mexico by now. As you say, all I've ever been is a bother to you. Won't I slow you down?"

Curtis tore off another bite of meat, rolled it around in his mouth a while, chewed it slowly. "Let's see if you can figure it out," he said, his tone surly.

It took a while, but finally, she did. In a flash of insight, everything became crystal clear. The tin cup she'd been holding slipped from her fingers, spilling cold water onto her lap. In a low voice rife with a fury she couldn't hide she said, "You didn't come back for me at all, did you? You came for the chestnut!"

Curtis grinned at her, maddeningly unmoved by her outrage. Lazily, he leaned back on his elbows, crossed his ankles, and watched her. "Seems you got a few brains after all."

She clenched her fists, grinding them into her thighs. Fixing him with her own stare, she inquired through her teeth, "So what happened? *How* did it happen?"

"That chestnut devil threw me, that's what. One minute I was teaching him a little discipline, and the next...." He let the words trail off, but Jessie pictured a furious Curtis planted butt first into the dirt. It took effort to stifle a laugh.

"I don't understand," she said instead, cupping a hand to her painful jaw. "Where were you when that happened?"

"Outside the cave we were holed up in. Something spooked the chestnut and he bucked me off."

"And you decided to chase after him?"

"Yeah. The good part was that only minutes before the chestnut threw me, Marty'd finally cashed in from those gunshot wounds. Truth be known, I don't know how he made it as far as he did. Had to hand it to him, though. He held up his end of the robbery well enough. I'd have shot him myself if he hadn't."

Jessie flinched at Curtis's callousness. "Where is Walt?"

"After the Murryville robbery, we divided the loot and Walt cut out. I opted to take my chances and stay with Marty. In the shape he was in, I couldn't just leave him."

She almost laughed out loud again. *You're such a liar, Curtis! You were hoping he'd die so you could get your hands on his share of the loot. I wouldn't put it past you to have even helped him along some.*

Curtis's next words confirmed her thoughts.

"When Marty expired, I helped myself to his saddlebags, mounted up on Belle, and tracked the chestnut back to the shack."

"Why track the chestnut at all?" Jessie asked, the familiar sadness over Marty's death seeping into her again. "Weren't you taking a big risk?"

"You can be so stupid sometimes, Jessie. You could win a stupid contest, you know that? My cut of the booty was strapped to that fancy saddle on his back, that's why. Besides, that horse was the best of the lot. I couldn't lose him."

Curtis glanced at the two horses hobbled by a patch of grass beneath a stand of lodge pole pines. "He's been well trained," he commented with a touch of awe. "It wasn't hard to figure out where he'd run off to. I figured, along with everything else, in a pinch he'd been trained to head for home. I was right. Smartest horse I've ever owned," he mused.

"You don't own him," Jessie corrected him hotly. "He's Mitch Wyden's personal mount."

Curtis shot her a look, his expression closed and cold. "And how could you possibly know that?"

"Mitch's initials are engraved in the saddle. I put two and two together." She remembered Mitch saying that he'd planned to take a trip into town the morning the horses were stolen. In preparation, he'd saddled his horse.

Curtis shot her a cocky grin. "Lucky for me Wyden was bent on taking an early morning ride. I not only got the chestnut, but a fine saddle too, didn't I?" The grin faded like the light of a dying candle. Clearly, Curtis had long ago "put two and two together" himself to realize that if he'd waited mere minutes that fateful morning, Mitch would have been gone and three of his friends wouldn't have been shot to death. "Anyway, who cares? I'm sick of talking about all this."

"*I* care, Curtis. And so does Mitch."

Gliding to his feet, Curtis threw down the last bit of jerky he'd been working on and came to stand over her, his feet planted apart. An unholy glint shone in his glacier-blue eyes as he glared down at her. "Ah yes, your Mitch," he ground out coldly. "The man you played the harlot for."

Jessie threw her head back, startled at the sudden change of subject. It took a moment before she found her voice. "It wasn't like that. I love him," she stammered, her whole body tightening in defense.

He laughed at that. "And I suppose he told you he loved you too."

She remained quiet. Not for the world would she admit Mitch hadn't told her anything of the sort.

But Curtis must have read the disquiet on her face because he sneered, "You've been played for a fool, Jessie. Don't you know it wouldn't have meant anything if he had? A man will say whatever he has to to get a woman to give him what he wants."

"You're wrong, Curtis. I told you it wasn't like that. I got hurt during the raid and he took care of me," Jessie protested. Curtis's words had cut her in two; they mirrored what she'd been fearing all along. "We were going to walk to Sweet Glenn but I cut my foot so we couldn't go right away. He was good to me. He treated my foot and—"

"So that's why you've got that limp." His gaze slid briefly to her foot, then back to her pale face. "I wondered." Sighing impatiently, he said, "Of course he treated your foot. He wanted you well enough to get you to a town on your own steam so he could turn you in and collect the reward money. You said before you'd told him about the bank robbery. My guess is, he was counting on the citizens of Sulfur Flats putting up a ransom for our capture. Anyway, he had nothing to lose by hauling you to a town to find out one way or the other."

Jessie's breath caught, an acute stab of pain piercing her heart. "R-reward money?"

Is that why Mitch had been so insistent they walk out *together*? Why he'd ignored her pleading every time she'd begged him to leave her behind?

Curtis shook his head, giving her a pitying look. "You really should enter a contest, you know that? We're *wanted*, Cousin. Wanted with a capital W."

"Mitch wouldn't have done that!" Jessie insisted, her heart breaking.

"Think, Jesse. He'd already killed Charlie and Shooter, and he had a third thief, *you*, in his clutches. After you gave him all that information about the robbery, all he had to do was turn you in, lead the law back to that shack to exhume Charlie and Shooter's bodies for identification, collect the reward money, and ride off a rich man.

"In the meantime, he made the best of a bad situation by taking his pleasure with his captured lady horse thief. His *willing*, captured lady horse thief. Tell me, did he know right off you were a woman? Or did it take him a while to figure things out?"

Jessie remained mute, dying inside. Tears stung the backs of her eyelids but she blinked them back, refusing to let him see her anguish.

Curtis lifted her chin with the dirty toe of his boot, forcing her to look up at him. For a moment, she was afraid he was going to kick her in the throat.

Softly, chillingly, he said, "In Bible times they stoned harlots to death. Did you know that, Jessie?"

She tried to scoot away from him, but he easily caught her. Grabbing her upper arms in a cruel grip, he hauled her to her feet. His whole body shook with anger, his chilling tone freezing her where she stood. Lifting her so that her toes dangled and her face hung directly in front of his he said, "Get to your chores, girl. Not another word from you tonight. I like you a whole lot better with your mouth shut."

☙ ☙ ☙

The next morning Jessie remained sullen and quiet, going about her chores in a numb daze. She'd slept badly, having rehashed a million times everything Curtis had told her the night before.

She'd finally figured out that Mitch had truly gone hunting that day, and that he hadn't abandoned her at all. If what Curtis had said was true, Mitch had wanted her for the reward money. He wouldn't have left her, in that case, for anything. Burning with humiliation, she realized how wrong her conclusions had been that night when he hadn't returned. How ridiculous her reasoning sounded now that she'd had the time to think things through.

It had been her own insecurities that had led her to believe he'd abandoned her. Experience had taught her well that the moment she trusted, gave herself over to deep feelings for somebody, she ended up being kicked aside and forgotten.

But if Mitch *had* gone hunting, then that meant maybe something bad had happened to him out there. And even now that she'd figured out the truth, for the life of her she couldn't stop herself from worrying about him. Sweet mercy, she was a sorry case. The man had used her, trampled her feelings and heart, and yet she couldn't stop loving him. Couldn't stop the sweet ache of desire from overtaking her every time she thought about him.

"Come here, Jessie, and help me with this."

Curtis sat bare-chested on the edge of a boulder, a canteen in one hand, his shirt dangling from the other. The blonde whorls of hair covering his broad chest glistened like a golden fleece in the morning light. Jessie watched him as he laid the shirt next to Mitch's pistol—he'd spotted it near the corral and had taken it—

and his own .45 on the boulder, then carefully fingered the white sash of bandage wrapped around his middle.

Jessie's mind wandered to focus on another broad chest, much finer and far more masculine than Curtis's could ever be.

"Move it," he barked. "I need tending and we don't have all day." Another reason he'd brought her with him, Jessie reasoned, fresh fury replacing some of her despondency. He figured he could use her to do the camp chores, just like he always had, and while she was at it, she could take over the doctoring of his wound. He'd always told her that, nuisance or not, at times she did have her uses.

"Got any whiskey in your saddlebags?" she asked with forced sweetness through her tight jaw. Her face felt a little better today after she'd kept a cold cloth pressed to it during the night, but it still hurt to talk.

Curtis eyed her warily. "What for?"

"To douse the wound with. I've heard tell whiskey helps keep infection away."

"Thanks, but I'll take my chances," he retorted sourly. "Wipe that smirk off your face. If you don't want to be tied to your horse again today, you'll get over here and do as I say."

Curtis was buttoning his shirt, the flesh wound on the edge of his back cleaned and freshly bandaged, when he ordered her to finish picking up the camp and go get her saddlebags. Her hackles rose at his dictatorial tone, but since her wrists still stung from yesterday's rope burns, and she didn't want a repeat of yesterday's tortures, she pretended a meekness she didn't feel. It was important she remain untied today, in case a chance to escape presented itself.

She stopped what she was doing and stared at him. "What do you want my saddlebags for?"

"I want you out of those britches," he said. "It's time you start dressing like a woman again."

"Why?" The word was past her teeth before she gave it thought.

"Because we're being chased," he answered irritably, strapping on his gun belt. "Whoever's after us will think twice before shooting if they see it's a woman they've got in their sights. Curse it, Jess, don't look at me like that. Just do as I say and hurry up about it. I'm giving you five minutes."

So that was the real reason he'd insisted on bringing her with him, had gone to the lengths of knocking her unconscious to do it. She turned away so he wouldn't be able to see the loathing in her eyes.

ଓ ଓ ଓ

Mitch awoke to the sound of voices. And somebody shaking his shoulders.

"He's coming to. Give him room, boys. He ain't dead after all."

"Coming to" felt like somebody hauling him up from the ocean floor and slamming him head first into the boat. He heard somebody groan, then a meaty pair of hands lifted him by the armpits, dragged him to the nearest corner, and sat him on the floor with his back against the wall.

"Who are you, mister?" came a deep voice floating in the air around four feet above his head.

"Leave him be a minute, Tally. He ain't all here yet."

Mitch cracked an eye open, and immediately wished he hadn't. A wave of dizziness nearly swept him back into unconsciousness. Where was he? And who were these men? Survival instincts kicked in, and he braced himself for trouble, forcing his eyes open again.

He saw four of them when his vision cleared. They stood in a semicircle near his feet, all eyes riveted on him, their expressions grim. Mitch groped for his rifle, but his arms and fingers wouldn't work properly. He soon realized he could have saved himself the effort. His rifle was now in the possession of one of those men.

"Easy there," the tallest man who looked to be in his late forties and sporting a walrus mustache said, squatting down on his haunches near Mitch's side. A silver badge gleamed at his chest. "You've got quite a bump on the head there. Can you tell us what happened?"

"Who are you?" Mitch's throat felt tight and dry as ashes.

"Get him some water," the tall man ordered.

In seconds, somebody placed a tin cup against his lips. Cool, blessed water spilled into his mouth, moistening his tongue and parched throat. When he finished gulping it down, the tall man took the empty cup and handed it to one of the others.

"Name's Frank Baylor," the man said. "Sheriff Frank Baylor out of Sulfur Flats. These men are my deputies. We're here on official business. Do you feel good enough to talk, or do we give you a few more minutes?"

"Depends on what you want to talk about," Mitch rasped.

"Seems fine enough to me, Frank," one of the others observed.

Baylor dismissed the comment with a curt wave of his hand, then turned his full attention back to Mitch. "This your place?"

Mitch nodded. The instant explosion in his head sent his hands rushing to cradle his temples. The move apparently made everybody nervous. When next he looked, all four men had their guns cocked and pointed straight at his heart.

"Hey," Mitch croaked. "Take it easy. Give me time to...gather...my wits, will you?"

Baylor motioned, and the men holstered their weapons.

Mitch strove to clear his thoughts. *Jessie*, his mind raced, *they've come to take Jessie away.* But then his brain began to work properly again and he remembered. All of it. Jessie wasn't here. She....

Carefully, he shifted, intending to rise. Still somewhat dizzy, Baylor attempted to steady him. Dismissing the help with a curt shrug, Mitch rolled to his knees and struggled to his feet, determined to face these men squarely, by his own power.

"I'll need your name," Baylor said.

"Mitch Wyden."

"How'd you injure your head?"

"Bet Driscoll or Conner done it," a surly voice boomed.

"Mind keeping your voice down?" Mitch groaned. His voice still sounded eerily raw and hollow in his ears. "I took a fall." He pointed to the hind quarter by the door. "Going after a buck I shot."

"Let's sit down over there and talk about it," Baylor suggested in a voice that told Mitch he didn't have a choice. "Tally, get me that cup." Mitch made it to a chair, then collapsed into it heavily. Baylor refilled the tin cup from a canteen and pushed it in front of Mitch, taking the seat opposite him. The other three took up wall space in various spots around the room.

"So, state your business," Mitch said, taking a sip of water. His tone finally sounded crisp and clear, he was pleased to note. Feeling better now, and getting better by the minute, he faced Baylor squarely.

Baylor fingered his mustache, then settled back. "These men and I are trailing a band of bank robbers. The Driscoll gang. Ever hear of them?"

Mitch kept his face blank.

"Driscoll and his men robbed our bank in Sulfur Flats," Baylor continued, reaching into his pocket. He pulled out a tobacco pouch and papers, laying them casually on the table. "Mind if I smoke?"

Gingerly, Mitch shook his head.

As Baylor rolled his cigarette and lit up, he continued, "They gave us the slip for a while there. But then we got lucky. Found a rancher not too far from here by the name of Trueblood who said he'd recently bought six horses off a stranger. Described the stranger in detail.

"Driscoll and another man named Walt Conner, and possibly a third, eventually pulled a second robbery in Murryville. There were witnesses. Conner fit the description Trueblood gave us to a tee."

The sheriff took a long drag off his cigarette, then settled his rump more comfortably in the rickety chair.

"During the Murryville holdup Driscoll shot a man. Hit an artery in the man's thigh, bustin' it pretty bad. Doc did his best to patch him up, but things is iffy. If that man dies, we elevate the charges against Driscoll to murder."

Mitch's heart was beating so hard, he thought it would pound right out of his chest.

"Why aren't you and your men tracking Driscoll closer to Murryville? You're a little out of your way down here, aren't you?"

Baylor squinted through a stream of blue smoke. "Frankly, no," he answered bluntly. "We've been tracking the signs."

Mitch didn't comment.

Ashes fell from the tip of Baylor's cigarette, splashing on the table in an explosion of tiny red sparks, leaving burn marks on the scarred surface. Not that Mitch was all that particular, but in deference to Jessie, he shoved the tin cup in front of Baylor to use as an ashtray. Jessie was always getting after him about the careless way he dropped ashes, matches, and butts all over the place. *Jessie!*

"We found a cave several miles outside of Murryville," Baylor continued. "We think it was the cave Driscoll and his men used as a hideout. I've got a dead man outside, belly down on one of the pack horses. Had a letter on him addressed to Martin Albert Chase, so we're assuming that's who he is for now. Found him in the cave, dead from gunshot wounds. Ever hear of him?"

Mitch spilled a long breath, considering his options. He might just as well tell them what he knew. No point misleading the sheriff and his men. He'd need their help to track Jessie. For certain, these lawmen wouldn't quit until they found her, and Mitch planned to be right there with them when they did. Jessie's future was at stake, if not her very life.

"Yeah. I've heard of him," Mitch admitted, reaching for Baylor's tobacco pouch and papers. He didn't bother to ask permission. His fingers shook as he held a paper in one hand and tapped the pouch with the other. After rolling and licking the paper, Baylor passed him a match. "It was my bullets that killed him. If it is Chase you've got outside, I'll know it."

Restless now, the three deputies shifted. Baylor sent them a stern, keep-your-mouths-shut look and they settled down.

"That rancher, Trueblood?" Mitch continued. "Those were most likely my stolen horses he bought. Driscoll and his men rode in here a little over a week ago and made off with my stock. Sixteen horses in all. Two of Driscoll's men, Charlie Deerhorn and Shooter Gant, are buried outside. I shot them defending my property. Marty Chase took a couple of bullets, but he got away, along with Curtis Driscoll and Walt Conner."

Mitch heaved himself up and went to the shelf above the dry sink, hoping what he was looking for hadn't been disturbed when the place had been ransacked. He found what he wanted. "Here's their personal effects. I would have brought them to the authorities before now, but I'm fresh out of transportation."

Baylor dropped the cigarette butt into the cup. The hiss as it hit the water filled the brittle silence. He reached for the items Mitch handed him, then took a minute to sort through them.

Thoughtfully, the sheriff studied the items in his palm. "Martin Chase had a lock of hair just like these on him, too. Found it in his breast pocket. Right over his heart." He didn't comment further, just eyed Mitch with another thoughtful look. When Mitch didn't offer any explanation, Baylor said, "Fellow in Sulfur Flats says he saw a woman minding the getaway horses. You know anything about her? Was she with the gang when they stole your horses, Wyden?"

Mitch took a long, calming drag off the cigarette. His time was up. He had to plead Jessie's cause, and plead it well or neither of them would have a future.

Baylor seemed like a fair man. As first impressions went, Mitch figured Baylor was as decent a law enforcement officer as any. He seemed tough, thorough, and from the way he looked a person straight in the eyes, most likely honest.

"That'd be Jessie Driscoll," Mitch admitted slowly. "Curtis Driscoll's cousin. And she wasn't exactly 'with' them."

It took a while, but Mitch told Baylor the story, disclosing everything important, except for his intimate involvement with Jessie. Mitch knew Baylor was smart enough to fill in all the blanks without him having to spell things out. What bothered him, though, was that his men—who were holding up the cabin walls and listening to every word he said—probably were smart enough, too. Inwardly he cringed. These men already assumed Jessie had participated in the bank robbery. It angered him to think, just as he himself had at first, that they also had tagged Jessie as a woman of easy virtue.

Baylor listened, his face inscrutable while Mitch plead Jessie's case. Finally Baylor said, carefully smoothing out his mustache with a thumb and forefinger, "And you don't know where Miss Driscoll is now?"

Mitch shook his head. "No. I wish I did." A small silence followed.

Then Baylor said, "Tally over there is an expert tracker. He found a place near the cave where it looked as if somebody had been thrown from his horse. Dirt all churned up and the bushes crushed, that sort of thing. After studying the ground, Tally figured somebody took off after the empty horse. The tracks led us here. Which was a puzzle, because we found ourselves backtracking toward Sulfur Flats instead of south toward Mexico, or west out of the mountains, which would be the logical directions they'd run."

Baylor paused, thinking.

"You a good horse trainer, Wyden? Do you train your horses to return to the barn?"

Mitch gave a curt nod. "The best," he replied without conceit. "And yeah. The horses I keep might as well be homing pigeons."

The sheriff arranged the dead men's personal effects in a pile in front of him. "My guess is, that horse threw its rider, then headed straight for the barn, so to speak. One of those men, Driscoll or Conner, showed up here while you were away hunting and took Jessie Driscoll back, right along with that horse."

Mitch glanced around the trashed cabin. He could see the plausibility of that. If he'd thought things through properly at first, he'd have concluded that Jessie would never have left here on her own, or left the place in such a mess. He realized that now. She'd considered this cabin a hiding place, a sanctuary.

She'd left her extra shirt behind, and her crutch was propped up in the corner by the hearth. Which didn't make sense. And without a horse, she never would have managed to carry everything out of here. Especially with that injured foot and no crutch.

Every time she'd looked at him lately, he'd seen the love she had for him shining in her eyes. And he was certain she'd begun to trust him. After all they'd shared together, she had to know he'd surrender his own life before he'd see her come to any harm.

No. Any way he looked at it, it just didn't make sense that she would have left here on her own. The only question that tormented him now was: had Curtis—or Conner—taken her against her will, or after a little coercion had she left with them voluntarily? He glanced at the broken crockery and the conspicuous poker lying on the floor at the wrong end of the cabin and answered his own question. These things weren't just evidence of a hasty departure, they were signs of a fierce struggle.

If Curtis or Conner had hurt Jessie they were dead men.

"Jessie had nothing to do with any of this," he insisted. "You've got to believe me, Sheriff. She's Curtis Driscoll's victim. I swear, that's the long and short of it."

"She's a wanted fugitive," Sheriff Baylor refuted calmly, unmoved by Mitch's vehemence. Slowly, he removed a folded piece of paper from his breast pocket, pressed out the creases, and handed it to Mitch. "This is a drawing of the woman we believe to be Jessie Driscoll. Can you confirm that?"

Mitch stared numbly at the wanted poster, fighting the urge to rip it to shreds. It was Jessie, all right, but then again, it wasn't Jessie. Her image stared back at him, her enormous dark eyes too big for her face, her full lips parted slightly, her long, lustrous hair gathered up in a ribbon at the top of her head. A few stray curls had busted loose, framing her face. In his mind he imagined what those rich, silken skeins would look like unmoored and loose about her shoulders, smelling like flowers, spilling across his naked chest.... He expelled his breath, barely suppressing a groan.

"Witnesses saw her aiding a gang of bank robbers. If we find her, we'll have to arrest her and bring her in."

"She's innocent," Mitch said, his stomach twisting into knots. "Didn't you hear me when I told you Driscoll forced her? She didn't even know they were going to rob that bank."

"Just like she didn't know they were going to steal your horses?"

"That's right!"

"That's for the judge to decide, Wyden. My job is to find the alleged thieves and bring them in. Jessie Driscoll's one of them."

"I'm going with you," Mitch stated flatly, shoving his chair back. The sudden motion sent his head spinning again, but he recovered quickly and held his ground.

"It doesn't appear you're in good enough shape to travel, Wyden. Best you stay put right here and heal up." Baylor glanced around, noting the empty pantry shelves. "We can swap staples for some of your venison to last you a couple of days. When we get to the next town I'll send a man and a horse back for you."

Mitch slowly rose to his feet. "No." He crumpled the wanted poster in his fist. "Swear me in. Those were my horses Driscoll stole. I have a huge stake in this, Sheriff. I'm feeling fine now. All I need's a little something to eat and we can all be on our way. I'll ride the pack horse you've got Martin Chase mounted on—I've even got an extra saddle for it."

"I don't think so," Baylor said, shaking his head and rising to his feet.

Mitch had never been one to plead, but he'd get down flat on his belly and grovel if he had to in order to get the sheriff to see reason. "If Jessie's with Driscoll like you think she is, then I'm telling you, she's in danger. When you find them, she's gonna be even more scared than I suppose she is right now.

"Let me go along. I already told you I'd planned to bring her in myself. If and when you find Driscoll, I'll be able to help you capture him. Jessie'll come to me willingly, without any trouble, I'm certain of it. When she does, we'll take her and her cousin back to Sulfur Flats together. All I want is to be there to make sure Jessie doesn't get hurt."

"You've really got it bad for her, don't you, son?" Baylor gave Mitch a rueful half-grin.

Mitch plowed his hands through his hair, wincing when his fingers touched the bloody gash at the back of his head. "Wait 'till you meet her, Sheriff," he said. "You'll never be the same again, either."

Baylor gave a little laugh. "I'll meet her, all right. Sooner or later."

"Sheriff?"

"What now?"

"When the time comes, I'm asking you to help me watch out for her. Tell your men there's to be no rough treatment of her. She's young, no bigger than a mite, and bound to be scared. Most important, as much as possible, if there's any gunplay, I want her protected, not shot at."

"None of us wants bloodshed," Baylor said, shifting as if uncomfortable with the idea of a woman getting caught in the middle of a gun battle. "We're hoping to take the Driscolls and Conner back alive to stand trial."

"I couldn't agree more. Let me help you do that."

Baylor glanced at the three deputies. The one called Tally, who was minding Mitch's rifle, caught his eye and gave him a curt nod.

"So you'll swear me in?" Mitch asked, seconds after he observed the exchange.

"Yeah, I'll do it, but I'm warning you. You give me one stitch of trouble, and it'll be you we haul to the gallows. Do I make myself clear?"

"Fair enough."

"All right then. Raise your right hand."

As if on cue, the three deputies heaved themselves off the various walls they were leaning against and ambled over to stand behind Mitch.

"By the way," Baylor said, rubbing his palm across his badge. "Once we get verification and finish up the paperwork in Sulfur Flats, you'll be free to collect the reward money."

"Reward money? What reward money?"

"Didn't you read that poster before you crumpled it up? Two hundred dollars apiece for the Driscoll gang, dead or alive. You got two dead bodies buried outside, and if you can prove you were the one who shot Martin Chase, that makes three. So as things stand right now, you've got six hundred coming your way."

Mitch winced, but it didn't take him more than a few seconds to think things through. On the one hand, the prospect of taking blood money repulsed him, but on the other, he had to be practical. His horses were lost to him for good, and the ranch he had his eye on in Crystal Springs wasn't going to stay up for sale forever. The reward money would partially compensate for his loss and all the hard work he'd put in these past months. Besides, soon he'd have a wife to support. Buying that ranch was more important than ever now.

"That's okay by me," he allowed.

Baylor exchanged another look with his men. "All right then," he said. "Let's do this."

Mitch threw the wanted poster across the room and raised his right hand.

# Chapter Fifteen

Out of practice, pain screamed through Jessie's muscles from hours of riding. Curtis had driven them hard for the last two days and nights. They'd covered more miles over rugged mountain terrain than she cared to count. When she paused to think about it, she wondered how she'd made it. Anger, resentment, and loathing for her cousin drove her, she supposed.

They were pushing due south. Toward Mexico. With every jolt and jog of her horse, the bones in her rear end and spine protested. Hunger and thirst gnawed at her. If they didn't stop soon, Jessie feared she was going to end up falling out of the saddle from fatigue.

Several yards ahead, Curtis looked back at her and scowled. "Give that horse of yours a kick, Jess. You're lagging behind."

"We need to rest for a while, Curtis. Belle's almost done in. The chestnut doesn't look too chipper, either."

Jessie observed her cousin as he looked past her into the distance. It was midafternoon, and they were crossing a long stretch of open ground, which left them little cover.

The sun blazed overhead, hot and merciless. Jessie squinted beneath the brim of her Stetson, then swiped the moisture off her forehead with the back of her sleeve. She saw the nervousness Curtis kept trying to mask and knew the reason for it. Their present position left them vulnerable to rifle fire.

"I said get a move on. We'll rest soon enough."

"Why don't you just leave me behind? You'll be able to cover a lot more ground a whole lot quicker by yourself. I've told you a million times I don't want to go to Mexico. I'd rather take my chances right here."

She hadn't quite been able to keep the irritation out of her voice. Her testy attitude nudged Curtis's temper.

"You'll do as I say, and I say you're coming with me. Once again, do I have to spell it out? The law's looking for two men now, Jess. Walt and me. I need you in order to throw them off."

Jessie gripped the reins so tightly the leather creased her palm. Before now, she hadn't formed the word "hostage" in her thoughts, but the ugly word took shape in her brain now.

She'd been watching for escape opportunities all this time, but Curtis had pushed them so hard, both she and Belle had been in no shape to try. During the brief hours Curtis did stop to rest, Jessie felt too worn out to attempt anything more than drop from her horse and collapse onto her back in a bit of welcome shade.

Another half hour passed. Trees dotted the land now, as well as clusters of granite, but truly adequate cover remained scarce. Jessie could see denser forest a mile or so ahead, and she knew it was this cover Curtis was pushing for.

Perspiration dampened her blouse along her spine and trickled between her breasts. She was feeling somewhat faint, but she didn't dare complain anymore for fear Curtis's temper would explode. If she said the wrong thing and he decided to come at her swinging, she doubted she had the energy to defend herself.

So she kept her eyes on Mitch's saddle, her thoughts on the man himself. She focused on his strength, on the wonders of his virile body, on the sweet way he made her feel inside whenever she lay cradled in his arms.

Mitch. Where was he now? If only she knew what had happened to him. Was he alive and thinking of her? Somehow, even though she couldn't be entirely certain of anything, in the deepest part of her she wanted to believe he hadn't been using her, hadn't been biding his time in order to collect the reward money. Their intimacy together had been too precious, too soul deep between them. He may have never told her he loved her, but certainly he must have cared, even if just a little. When she thought about it, there were too many times that Mitch had, in his gruff but gentle way, pampered her and watched over her. She surely would have known it if he'd been deceiving her for his own selfish reasons. *Wouldn't she?*

Curtis gave a shout.

Startled, Jessie's head jerked up. Her cousin had reined in, his worried gaze riveted on a spot somewhere over her shoulder. She turned, her eyes sweeping their back trail.

There. A faint, smudgy line in the not-so-far-off distance. Horses? Riders?

*Sweet mercy!*

Curtis yelled at her again, shocking her out of her momentary paralysis. "Come on, Jessie! Ride!"

The safest cover lie only a mile or so ahead, but the horses, like Jessie, were already well past exhaustion. When Jessie refused to prod Belle, Curtis wheeled about and yanked the reins from her numb fingers, forcing Belle to follow as he spurred the chestnut into a run.

The rocky, uneven ground strewn with boulders here and there was far too dangerous for this savage pace, yet Curtis drove the horses onward like a madman.

Jessie, holding tight to the saddle horn, risked a quick glance back. The riders had begun to gain ground.

And then Curtis reined in, bringing both horses to an abrupt halt. Throwing Jessie's reins back to her, he said, "Stick close. We'll take cover over there."

The safety of the trees still lie quite a distance away. With the horses lathered and near collapse, Jessie realized that unless Curtis wanted to risk killing their mounts, he had no choice but to make a desperate stand. By "over there," Curtis meant a stout heap of boulders off to the left, just adequate enough to hide them and the horses behind.

A tight, sick knot formed in Jessie's stomach as she followed Curtis until they reached the limited safety of their cover. When they were adequately concealed, he slid from the saddle, pulled Jessie to the ground, then slipped the reins of both horses under a heavy rock. The animals blew and snorted; sweat and lather flew from their withers as they tossed and stomped in agitation.

"What are you going to do?" Jessie demanded.

Curtis reached behind his back and pulled out Mitch's Civil War pistol. "Take it!" he ordered, shoving the gun into her hands. "I'll tell you when to shoot."

Jessie gasped, reeling. "You can't just shoot them, Curtis! You don't even know who they are. Maybe they're just regular folks."

"Shut up and do as I say," he snapped. "They're the law, all right."

Jessie paled. "And I suppose you know that from past experience?"

"That's right, smart mouth."

He didn't say anything more until he'd dragged her behind a good-sized rock and pushed her to her knees, facing the riders. "You know how to use that thing?" he asked, squeezing her arm.

"Ow! Yes, but—"

"*Mitch* teach you?"

"You're hurting me!"

She heaved her body in defense and he dropped his hand. "When I tell you, point it at the knot of horses, then pull the trigger. Maybe you'll get lucky and hit somebody. But if you learned anything or gained any competency at all in target practice, you know to pick your target and aim for the center of the chest. You got that?"

"Oh, I got it just fine, Curtis." She lifted the revolver and pointed it at his chest.

Fuming, he shoved her gun hand down to her side. "Don't you have any brains at all? You shoot me and you lose your ticket out of here. I'm the only one keeping you out of the hands of those lawmen, and if they catch us it means prison or a hanging, Jess. Think about it."

She did think about it. All her nightmares had suddenly come upon her, and it took every ounce of her remaining strength to keep from falling apart. She gripped the gun tighter, but kept it lowered at her side.

She wanted to shoot someone, all right. She really did. Namely, Curtis. Shoot him point blank, between the eyes. But somehow, the decent, God-fearing side of her wouldn't allow it. Curtis was vermin, but vermin or not, he was her only living relative. She couldn't murder *anyone*, let alone her own blood.

Apparently satisfied she wasn't going to shoot him, Curtis eased over to his own chosen cover, a flat-topped boulder positioned slightly to the right and behind Jessie. From this vantage point, her cousin had a clear view of the terrain and the approaching riders. They were close now.

"With luck, they'll think we made it to the trees. They won't be expecting an ambush. But Lord help us if they get past us, Jess. We won't have any place else to hide."

Curtis's words trailed off as a wave of dizziness swept through Jessie. This wasn't happening. It couldn't be. Desperate, she retraced the events of the past months since leaving the wagon train, thinking that nothing, ever, had prepared her for this kind of terror.

"Keep low, Jess, until I tell you to start shooting. And don't go all worm-bellied on me at the last minute, either. For once in your life buck up and do as you're told. I expect you to take out as many of those men as you can. Our lives depend on it."

The pistol lay heavy as an andiron in her hand. Head and heart pounding, she swiped the sweat from her eyes and squinted into the distance. She could see the shapes of the men now. She counted five of them in all, coming at them fast.

"Steady, Jess. Don't you dare panic or I'll shoot you myself."

Jessie heard a quaver in his voice, stark desperation that he couldn't hide, which affirmed that Curtis was not as calm as he wanted her to believe he was. Not at all.

"Steady...steady...."

The men were only about thirty yards away now. Peeping over the edge of the boulder, she could see the grim determination on each face as they spurred their horses onward. Her gaze settled on one rider in particular, on the confident way the man sat his horse and those broad shoulders leaning over the pommel.

*Mitch?*

"Fire, Jess, *fire*!"

Curtis's Colt exploded, startling her so much she nearly sprang to her feet. All else forgotten, Jessie raised her weapon high and squeezed off a couple of shots, intentionally missing the men.

When first the posse's leader, then his men, realized they were heading straight into an ambush, they split up, scattering like rabbits, drawing their guns and shooting as they fled beyond range toward the safety of the trees. One of Curtis's bullets had hit a man, staggering him. But the lawman stuck to his saddle and, like the others, within minutes had hastened out of harm's way.

Wildly, Curtis fired, again and again, but his handgun had little distance power. He needed a rifle for this kind of shooting if he ever hoped to eliminate anyone now.

Jessie drew in a long breath. For the moment the gunfire had stopped, and blessed stillness prevailed.

Curtis broke the silence. "I told you to shoot, Jessie," he hissed. Scrabbling to her side, he gave her a killing look. "You let them get past us! Thanks to you, now they've got the advantage, and we don't have any chance whatsoever of getting out of here alive."

Her mouth went dry. She could barely push her next words past her thick tongue. Not that she was even *trying* to hit anybody, but in her opinion, Curtis hadn't done much to hinder the posse, either. "I did fire the gun," she protested, reaction setting in, making her teeth chatter.

The smell of gun powder hung in the heated air. Desperate for control, Jessie looked away to stare at the peeling bark of a twisted manzanita bush growing, impossibly, between two massive rocks nearby. *A beautiful survivor*, she thought. Like her own limbs, its glossy gray-green leaves trembled in the breathy stillness.

Curtis snatched her gun and smelled the barrel, then checked the chamber. A shot rang out in the distance. Jessie heard a faint curse from one of the lawmen, making her think of Mitch.

Was Mitch out there? Had she truly seen him for that one brief moment before all hell had broken loose? Or was it just her overwrought brain playing tricks on her?

She sent her cousin a wary glance. She *had* fired her pistol. But she'd aimed the gun high, deliberately. Did he suspect as much?

"Next time," Curtis warned, shoving the pistol back into her hands, "try to hit something. You're a lousy shot, you know that?"

"The gun isn't very accurate. Mitch said so. It's an old Civil War Colt .44 dragoon, not much good anymore."

The stifling air pressed in on her, thick and heavy. Curtis gave her another one of his dark looks, then crouched and made his way toward the horses. Using Belle for cover, he reached up for the canteens hanging from the horn of his own mount. Slipping back to Jessie, he threw one of the canteens at her. It landed near her foot.

"Either I got lucky just now, or they've decided not to waste any more ammunition on us for the time being. I guess this is gonna turn out to be a wait-and-see situation." He squinted past the shoulder she was rubbing, his ice-blue eyes scanning the distant tree line. In a blink, he took aim and shot.

"Sneaky devil," he swore under his breath. "Stupid move!" he yelled into the distance. "Try that again and you're a dead man!"

Jessie picked up the canteen and took a sip of water, then another. Somewhere out there she heard a horse whinny.

Curtis said, "They're trying to sneak back and surround us, Jess. So either you take better aim with that pistol and pray it isn't as worthless as you say, or in the next few hours it's gonna be all over for us."

Curtis looked more worried than ever now. Jessie was just plain terrified. "Curtis, this just isn't worth it. Why don't we just give ourselves up?"

"Not a chance. I won't hang, and I don't intend to spend the rest of my life in prison, either. They're gonna have to kill me first."

*What about me?* Jessie wanted to scream. *I haven't committed any crimes. I want to live.*

Curtis fired off another shot. Jessie flinched as a terrible premonition of doom settled over her.

"Get over here and peel your eyeballs. When one of those jackals gets close enough, shoot to kill."

If only it truly was Mitch with those men out there, she thought. If he was with the posse, maybe he could find a way to help her before she came to any real harm. But why would he be with the posse in the first place unless...unless....

Pain filled her as the words "reward money" twisted through her mind like a tangle of serpents.

☙ ☙ ☙

Mitch crouched behind his meager cover and struggled to rein in his anger. That no-good cousin of hers was trying to get her killed. And it *was* Curtis with her out there. Baylor carried a pair of field glasses. A half hour ago, they'd gotten close enough to clearly see Curtis's blonde head and beard.

Not long after they'd started out, Ned Tally informed them that they were tracking only two of the three fugitives, and that "the woman" was most likely the second rider. Said he could tell from the shallow hoof imprints that someone weighing no more than a hundred pounds rode the second horse. Even with the added weight of the saddlebags and gear, the sum total left out hefty Walt Conner. It was anybody's guess where Conner was at the moment.

Mitch squinted, wishing he could see through stone. *Jessie.*

When the initial gunfire started, at Baylor's command they'd scattered and raced for the safety of the trees, all of them making it unscathed except one.

"We're going to get those two," Baylor had boasted while tying his horse to a pine limb. "This time, we'll get 'em for sure."

Mitch took offence. "Those two" meant that the sheriff had no intention of sheltering Jessie when the time came. He halted the sheriff with a firm hand on the man's shoulder. "Jessie's innocent in all this," he insisted, his palms beginning to sweat. "I told you she isn't one of them. You and your men promised to watch out for her, and I'm holding you to it."

"We're gonna do what's necessary," Baylor replied, shrugging off Mitch's grip. "All of us are well aware there's a woman out there." Dismissing Mitch, he turned to address his men, Ned Tally, Shorty Blake, and Edgar Simms. Smoothing two fingers down his bushy mustache, Baylor said, "Ned, you circle east. Get as close as you can. Shorty, you do the same, only veer west of 'em. That's their most vulnerable side. You both know what to do once you get into position."

Both men nodded. Shorty began rechecking his rifle parts.

Baylor narrowed his eyes on Simms. "Simms, that arm of yours doesn't look too good." He cocked his head to listen a moment. "Sounds like there's a stream nearby. Take care of the wound, then rest by the horses until we get back."

"My arm's fine," Simms protested, taking his bloody fingers away from the streaming wound. Baylor ended the argument with a dark look. Simms huffed but held his tongue, then trounced off toward the gurgle of the stream.

"Wyden, you and I are going to ease in toward those boulders, front and center, taking cover where we can. That okay with you?"

Mitch gave Baylor a curt nod.

Baylor drew his Colt and began shoving bullets into the chamber. Without looking up he said to the whole group, "Aim to wound, not to kill unless it's absolutely necessary. That crystal clear to everybody?"

He threw a hard glance at Mitch while everyone mumbled his respective "yeah."

"All right then. Let's go."

That had been over an hour ago. The closer they got to the Driscolls' cover, the more dangerous the situation became. Uneasiness roiled inside Mitch each time he thought about Jessie. She had to be scared out of her mind by now. Somehow he had to keep her safe. Had to get her out of this alive.

Baylor crawled on his belly toward Mitch, rolling the final yard when a burst of bullets just missed his legs. They'd hopscotched from rock to rock, inching closer to the Driscolls' position, taking cover where they could.

"That was close," Baylor huffed, hauling in his legs.

"Had to have been Curtis," Mitch commented, making room for Baylor. "Jessie's scared of guns. No good at all with a firearm. Can't hit the ground, even when she's aiming at it."

Baylor chuckled dryly. "That so?" Then he said, "Shorty and Ned are in place. It's time to talk the Driscolls out of there. I figure I'll take a stab at it first, then you can give it a go if Driscoll doesn't cooperate. That all right with you?"

*It had to be all right*, Mitch thought grimly.

He'd never been much of a praying man, but suddenly he found himself pleading with the Almighty to keep Jessie safe. What if she'd already been hurt? The prospect nearly paralyzed him.

Baylor's husky voice boomed like a sudden burst of thunder. "Driscoll? This is Sheriff Frank Baylor. There isn't anywhere for you and your cousin to run. We've got men covering you at three compass points. And I guarantee you're done for if you try to escape toward the fourth."

"Save your breath!" Curtis yelled.

"Come on now, Curtis. Think of Jessie. You want to see her end up dead? Why don't you just give yourselves up? We can end this right now without anybody else getting hurt."

Curtis's dry laugh cut the air. "Nobody over this way's been hurt," he mocked. "*You* got somebody hurt out there?"

Mitch closed his eyes. If he could believe Curtis, so far Jessie was all right. Thank God.

"We've been deliberately shooting around you both, Driscoll. None of us wants any bloodshed. But you ought to know something. My man Blake's a sharpshooter. Could have taken you and your cousin out an hour ago, had I given the word." Baylor flashed a small mirror toward Blake's cover. Immediately, a rifle shot split the stillness, followed by a woman's short scream.

"What are you doing?" Mitch snapped in hushed tones, angry enough to shoot Baylor's head off. "Have you lost your mind?"

"Relax, Wyden. Shorty can blast the wing off a gnat at one hundred yards. He won't hurt anybody until I give the order for it. Keep your head about you now, or I'm gonna send you back to the trees to baby-sit Simms."

"Your man missed!" Curtis sneered before Mitch could reply. "That sharpshooter you got's a mighty poor shot," he taunted.

Baylor flashed the mirror and Blake shot again. This time they heard Curtis grunt. A small cry burst from Jessie.

"Missed again," Curtis said, but they heard terror in his voice.

"Jessie? Jessie, it's Mitch," Mitch boomed, his heart nearly beating out of his chest. "Don't be scared, honey. We're gonna get you out of there!"

Baylor swore, turning on Mitch with fury in his eyes. "Now, what did you go and do that for?"

"Because you're scaring Jessie, that's why. I keep telling you, she's innocent."

A horse screamed. Both men froze as Curtis charged from the rocks on the chestnut's back, heading north. And then everything exploded at once. Rifle and pistol shots split the air in a deafening cacophony. As Mitch watched, a bullet slammed into Curtis's shoulder nearly pitching him from the saddle, but somehow he managed to hold on. Spurring the horse again and again, he'd soon slipped out of rifle range.

Mitch held his breath, praying Jessie wouldn't follow her brainless cousin. She didn't. He turned to Baylor, but the sheriff had already set out for the trees to retrieve his horse. *Fine. Let Baylor go after him,* he thought.

With his heart in his throat, Mitch yelled, "Jessie? Honey, if you've got a weapon, I want you to throw it out where we can see it."

Silence.

"Jessie? Can you hear me? Are you all right?"

"Mitch?"

"Yeah, it's me, Jessie. I know you're scared, but just do as I say and everything's going to be all right. Trust me, okay?"

Out of the corner of his eye he saw Ned Tally crawling toward the boulders, and Shorty Blake doing the same on the west end. For a moment Mitch experienced a sharp pang of uncertainty. If Curtis had left Jessie a gun, was she scared enough to shoot him if he stood, mistaking him for one of the others? She hadn't yet taken any potshots, but there was always the chance she might.

He decided not to take the chance. Sweating, he waited several minutes, praying Tally and Blake would hold their fire.

*You told me once you'd never have the stomach to shoot somebody, Jessie. Please, please, if you do have a gun, don't change your mind now.*

Tally had reached the edge of the boulders, coming up on Jessie's blind side. Mitch still couldn't see her, hidden as she was behind the rocks. He glanced at Blake. Blake had drawn near also. Mitch could sense the tension in both men, as enormous as his own.

He yelled again. "Jessie, honey, listen to me. I want you to raise your hands up over your head and come on out of there. Don't be afraid. Just do as I say and everything'll be all right."

No response.

*Come on, sweetheart. Answer me!*

Mitch eased forward. In the next instant he heard Tally shout, "Drop the gun, Miss Driscoll. Don't force me to shoot you."

Mitch leaped up and tore toward the boulders at a dead run, rifle cocked, his heart in his mouth. When he reached the scene, the two lawmen had Jessie backed against the boulder, their rifles steadied squarely at her heart.

Pale and hatless, Jessie stood, her legs braced apart just like he'd taught her, the old relic pistol clutched in both hands. She had the thing pointed at Tally. Mitch's heart took a tumble. She looked so frightened, her entire body shaking so much, she could barely hold the heavy gun, let alone keep it aimed. *And what the devil was wrong with the left side of her face?*

"Drop the gun, Jessie," Mitch said at once, wanting to run to her, to shield her, to protect her.

Her eyes darted and caught his, but only for a fleeting instant.

Mitch sucked in his breath. He saw no light there, no sparkle. Only terror. And something far worse. Distrust.

"They want to kill me," she stated. Her voice sounded dead.

"No, honey."

"I haven't done anything wrong. *Tell* them, Mitch! I don't want to hang."

"You won't, Jessie. I swear it."

She caught his eyes again. "I don't believe you—"

Blake made his move quicker than a striking cobra. Mitch cursed as Blake sprang, tackling her and knocking her roughly to the ground. The pistol went flying, smacking the boulder, discharging harmlessly.

"I got her," Blake shouted in triumph, straddling her, sinking his heavy rump into her middle. With one meaty hand he shackled her wrists, imprisoning her hands above her head. "Good work, Wyden. That honey-coated tongue of yours just got you another two hundred dollars!"

With a sinking heart, Mitch saw Jessie freeze, then quit struggling all together. Rage poured through him.

It took every ounce of restraint not to beat Blake senseless. Hauling the heavy man to his feet by the arm pits, Mitch shouted, "Get off her, Blake. You ever put your filthy hands on her again, I'll kill you."

"What are you talking about? Blake sputtered, stunned. "You crazy, Wyden? I got to put the handcuffs on her!"

"No, you don't. I said you aren't ever going to touch her again, remember?" He fingered the trigger on his rifle. "Now get away from her."

Backing down, Blake stepped away.

The moment Mitch had torn Blake off Jessie, she'd scrambled away, only to face the barrel of Ned Tally's rifle. Crouching against the boulder like a cornered animal, she curled up with her arms cradling her head, struggling for breath.

Beside himself with fury, Mitch ordered, "Lower your weapon, Tally, and let her be. Do it now, or I swear you won't live out the day."

Tally complied, but only after a moment of tense silence. Then, with Tally and a befuddled Blake looking on, Mitch crossed the short distance and dropped to his haunches beside Jessie. Peeling her arms away from her head, he said, "Jessie, honey, it's Mitch. Open your eyes."

She squeezed them shut even tighter.

"It's over, sweetheart. Easy now. Easy. Take a deep breath. That's it. Blake just knocked the wind out of you is all."

She shook as if she were cold, but perspiration soaked her blouse and dampened the tendrils of her hair. Her skin was flushed red as fire.

Gently, he smoothed the backs of his knuckles down her bruised cheek, and cupped her face. She didn't respond.

Spying the canteen, he reached for it. "Here," he coaxed. "Drink some water, Jessie. As much as you can. You'll feel better if you do."

When he put the canteen to her lips, she drank, but like a puppet with its strings cut. She had yet to look in his eyes or utter a single word.

Mitch swung his attention toward the two men. "Let's get her to the trees," he said grimly. "Blake, see to her horse."

# Chapter Sixteen

They made camp by the stream. Late in the afternoon, Baylor rode in, leading his semiconscious prisoner in tow.

Curtis's hands were cuffed behind his back, his body slumped over the tired chestnut's saddle like a sack of grain. Bloodstains from the shoulder wound covered most of the right side of his clothing, marking a trail clear down to the hem of his pant leg.

Mitch watched Jessie, hoping for any kind of reaction from her. Earlier, he'd made her comfortable under a tall pine, making sure she had a canteen of cold water nearby, and a soft place to lie down if she wanted. But so far, she hadn't moved or talked or looked at any of them. She just sat stretched out with her back against the tree, staring off into the distance, worrying him.

She didn't give the arrival of her cousin so much as a blink.

"I need a doctor," Curtis complained groggily, then screamed in pain as Baylor hauled him out of the saddle.

"Fresh out," Baylor replied. Half lifting, half dragging Curtis over to a tree some distance from Jessie, Baylor dropped him against the thick trunk and told him to shut up and stay put unless he wanted a few more bullets peppering his sorry hide.

"Let Jessie tend me," Curtis pleaded, his voice breathy and weak. "I'm telling you, my shoulder's about blown off."

"No it ain't," Baylor said, then strode to the campfire where a pot of beans simmered. Tally poured him a cup of coffee.

"How'd you catch him?" Ed Simms asked. "Did he give you much trouble?" Simms rubbed his sore, bandaged arm. "Hope that shoulder of his pains him good. Deserves it for what he done to my arm."

Sheriff Baylor didn't answer. Instead, he took a bite of beans and a swallow of coffee. Clearly, he was in no mood for small talk. Nobody bothered him for details again.

Mitch dished up a plate of beans, poured a tin of coffee, and took it over to where Jessie sat. He set the food down on the blanket beside her and touched her shoulder. "Jessie?" Her eyes remained fixed somewhere in the distance.

"I brought you something to eat. Come on, brat. You've got to eat or you won't have any strength to ride tomorrow."

He saw a flicker in her eyes, but then the spark died, so quickly he wondered if he'd seen it at all. He wanted to take her into his arms, but his instincts told him that trying to hold her right now would be the wrong thing to do.

"Come on," he coaxed again, lifting a spoonful of beans to her lips. "Take a bite."

At last she focused on his face, but pressed her lips tightly together.

"Jessie, don't do this. Please try and eat."

She looked beautiful to him, bruised face and all. Sweat-stained and dust-coated clothes and all. This was the first time he'd seen her wearing a skirt and blouse, and the vision of blatant femininity she presented went straight to his heart. The pretty white blouse, which she'd tucked into the waistband of her sky-blue muslin skirt, fit her perfectly and hinted at the soft roundness of her breasts beneath its folds. A white sash cinched her waist, finishing off the outfit. He drew in his breath, wanting to gather her up, remembering how perfect and right she felt in his arms.

He longed to ask her what had happened to her face, ask her the details of what had happened back at the cabin, but didn't dare. Now was not the right time for that. He had to get her to eat first. And then he'd get her to talk.

She ignored the bean-laden spoon. He watched her swallow, then lick her lips, clearly struggling to speak.

She reached for the canteen and took a swallow of water. It took a few moments, but then in a rusty voice she said, "I don't want anything from you, Mitch. Nothing. I'll be sick if I eat. *You* make me sick. Go count your reward money and leave me alone."

Feeling as if he'd just taken a body blow, Mitch set down the spoon and rose to his feet. The blood drained from his face as he looked down at her and said, "Is that the only reason you think I'm here? Because of the reward money?"

"I *know* it is."

Mitch bristled. "I ought to turn you over my knee for that."

Jessie looked away. "Tell me why you wanted to get me to Sweet Glenn so badly," she said, her voice low and smoky with emotion. "You were going to turn me in, weren't you?"

Mitch raised his chin, hurt that she'd accuse him like this, think the worst without hearing him out first. Well, he wouldn't lie to her. She asked, so he'd tell her the truth. "Yes," he told her plainly. "But I couldn't see any other option."

"You wanted the reward money."

He saw the tears trembling on her lashes, saw the tremendous effort it was taking for her not to let them fall.

"I had other reasons for wanting to get you there."

"I'll bet."

Her stubbornness made him quake with indignation. Didn't she realize the hell he'd been through the last few days worrying about her? He'd near killed himself trying to hurry back to her after his fall, and he'd put his life on the line by joining Baylor's posse and chasing after her trigger-happy cousin. He'd done it all for her. All because he couldn't bear to think of her alone, possibly hurt, and suffering in the hands of her cousin and his cohorts.

Also, as far as he was concerned, he was the only one keeping her safe from these over-zealous, justice-seeking lawmen. They all thought she was a criminal not worth an ounce of courtesy or respect. Didn't she realize that if it hadn't been for him standing between her and these lawmen, she'd be handcuffed and trussed up to that tree right now? Or worse?

"You calling me a liar?" he bit out.

She reared back a little, narrowing her eyes. "Oh. All right. So. Let me get this straight. You're saying you're *not* collecting any reward money?"

He clenched his jaw. "Let's get something straight right now, all right. Hear me good, Jessie. I'll collect what I rightfully have coming to me, and I'm not going to let you make me feel guilty about it. Those were my horses your bunch stole. Nearly a whole year's work down a rat hole. That money'll make up part of what I lost."

"You used me."

"No, I didn't."

She glared at him, biting her lower lip so hard he thought she might draw blood. Finally she said in a voice so bleak it made him wince, "Well, 'my bunch,' as you say, might have stolen your horses, Mitch, but you sure got even. In return you stole from me everything I had."

She gathered her legs in her arms and laid her forehead atop her knees. She thought she'd been quick enough. Thought he hadn't seen the tears falling at last. But he had seen, and it was like she'd just taken a dull, rusted knife and twisted it into his heart.

Because he knew what she'd meant. She thought he'd betrayed her. Used her. Thought he'd stolen her heart, taken her maiden's virtue, then like a Judas turned her over to these lawmen for the proverbial thirty pieces of silver.

"Just go away," she mumbled into her skirts.

Slowly, Mitch squared his shoulders. "You're gonna think what you want to think, no matter what I say, aren't you? It wasn't just what Blake said back there at the boulders. I'm thinking Curtis did a mighty fine job of poisoning your mind about me long before that, didn't he?"

She didn't reply.

"You're wrong, Jessie. Wrong about all of it."

He stared at her for a few moments longer. Somehow, before they got back to Sulfur Flats, he'd make her see reason. When she was calmer, and a little stronger, he'd explain everything. He'd make her see that she hadn't wasted her trust or her heart on him. He'd make her believe it when he told her that as long as he drew breath, he'd fight for her freedom and protect her with his life. He'd make her believe in her dreams again. Because he was positive that as soon as they walked into that courtroom together and presented the truth, the judge would be bound to recognize Jessie's innocence and set her free.

All right. For the time being, he'd leave her alone and see to his stallion instead. See how much, like Jessie, the animal had suffered under Curtis's brutal hand.

ᘛ ᘛ ᘛ

The trees broke away into a small meadow of sweet grass and wildflowers a short distance downstream. It was here that Blake and Simms had hobbled the horses where the animals could graze and drink their fill. The two lawmen were just finishing removing the saddles from the chestnut and Baylor's mount when Mitch approached.

"I'll see to the chestnut now," Mitch said, seething when he got close enough to assess the condition of his prized horse.

"Don't look too good, do he?" Simms said, stepping away from the animal. He gave his injured arm a rub. The strain of helping to remove the saddles had apparently taxed the wound. "Driscoll near ran him to death, by the looks of things."

"The girl's horse don't look much better," Blake added, nodding toward Belle.

"Can't say the same about the girl, though." Simms gave a small, unmistakably lascivious laugh. "Pretty as a prairie flower, ain't she? Even with that lopped-off hair of hers." He gave Blake a conspiratorial thump on the back. "Tell me again how good it felt when you had her pinned—"

"That's enough!" Mitch warned, furious. "Simms, you talk that way about Jessie again and that arm of yours won't be the only thing giving you pain."

Simms quit rubbing his arm and narrowed his eyes at Mitch. Boldly, he set his chin. "I'll talk about her any way I want, Wyden. She ain't nothing but some outlaw's whore. Sure as spit she ain't no lady, running with that gang of thieves like she done. Why, I bet every one of 'em took pleasure on her—"

Mitch lunged, grabbing Simms by the shirt front, taking the smaller man by surprise. In a steely voice much too close to the man's face he threatened, "If you value your life, Simms, you'll shut that filthy mouth of yours. There isn't a speck of dishonor in Jessie Driscoll and never was."

"Okay, okay, Wyden. Simmer down," Blake yelled, stepping in and yanking his friend out of harm's way. Putting his considerable bulk between the two men, he snapped, "Blast it, Simms, I swear you ain't got the manners of a hog sometimes. Or the brains, either. You forgetting Wyden here's sweet on the girl?"

Simms looked as if he were about to fling some more insults, but one look at Mitch's furious stance and balled fists seemed to change his mind.

"Come on, Simms," Blake said, ending the skirmish. "We're done here. Tally just made a fresh pot of coffee. Let's go get us a cup."

Mitch stood there, rigid with disgust, watching the two men retreat. Why had he allowed Blake to step in before he could defend Jessie's honor and pound Simms to a bloody pulp?

Deep down, he knew why, though he loathed the thought. It was because, if he were honest, he understood why Simms felt that it fell within boundaries to malign Jessie like he had. Jessie's reputation was in tatters. She'd ridden for months with a band of outlaws, had been cozying up with him, Mitch, for days, and these men knew all about it. Thinking back, at first even he had assumed she'd been the gang's shared woman. So how could he blame Simms and the others for assuming the same thing?

The chestnut snorted, butting his muzzle against Mitch's shoulder. He turned, his heart sinking at the sight of the weary droop to his horse's neck.

"Hey, boy," Mitch soothed, stroking the stallion's mane with a gentle hand. Picking up a saddle blanket, he gently rubbed down the horse's slick back and flanks, checking for injuries as he went along. He felt a little better after giving the horse a thorough inspection. Except for two crusted-over welts on the right rump, the chestnut hadn't suffered any serious injuries; the poor fella was just thoroughly worn out.

It was while he was rubbing down Jessie's horse that he came to a decision. Things weren't going to get any better for Jessie unless he did something to make them better. She wouldn't like what he was planning, given the sour way she was feeling about him at the moment, but somehow he'd get around her stubbornness and eventually make her see reason. After all, what he planned to do was for her own good.

He'd ask Sheriff Baylor to marry them. Now. This very afternoon. There was no way he was going to allow these men to continue to insult her—treat his beautiful, innocent Jessie as if she were no better than a backstreet strumpet. He had to protect her from that. And anyway, he argued reasonably, they'd have been married already if he'd have gotten her to Sweet Glenn before all the trouble started.

He stroked the mare with an infinitely gentle touch, as if Jessie's sweet self were under his hand. As his wife, she'd gain back some of her respectability. Maybe by the time they got back to Sulfur Flats, in the men's eyes, she'd have it all back.

He thought about the coming night. He'd been worrying about how he'd arrange it so he could lie beside Jessie and keep her close while she slept without the men making lewd comments. As his wife, he could sleep beside her without any trouble.

All right, then. His mind was made up. He tossed the saddle blanket aside and went to find Baylor.

ᘛ ᘛ ᘛ

"Come with me, Jessie." He reached out to help her up.

"Come where?"

"Not far. To the meadow."

"I don't want to go anywhere with you."

"Doesn't matter. You're coming anyway."

Mitch ignored the mulish set of her jaw and the way she stiffened up when he lifted her to her feet. When she wobbled a little, he put his arm around her waist to steady her, then propelled her with a hand on her bottom to get her moving. She looked pale and done in, but he stopped himself from giving in to the sudden sympathy welling up inside him. He was doing this for her own good.

"Quit giving me trouble, brat," he told her evenly.

"Let me go, Mitch!"

"No. And keep your voice down, or I'll carry you to the meadow. Over my shoulder. Like a sack of potatoes."

"You wouldn't dare!"

"You think not? I wouldn't bet on it if I were you."

He felt her stiffen, but she kept quiet after that and didn't give him any more trouble. She was much too tired to do anything but give in, he knew, but he wouldn't allow himself to feel guilty. She could put up a fuss and resist him all she wanted some other time.

Allowing himself a small smile, he looked down at the top of her head. Her hair was growing out, he noticed, a thrill of pleasure filling him. He didn't mind it short the way it was, but he also couldn't wait until it grew long enough for him to play with. He wanted to brush it for her while she sat before a roaring hearth. He wanted to rub the soft strands between his fingers and let them slip through his hands to tumble down her body in a silken cascade....

"She's willing?" Baylor stood under a tall pine, his hat in his hands, watching them approach. Tally stood close by, a closed, remote expression on his weather-beaten face. Beside him, deeper in the shadows, the other two men stood, rolling their hats in their hands. Simms had a surly, half-cocked smile on his face that left no doubt about what he was thinking.

Off to the left, the sunlit stream gurgled happily. *Just like church music*, Mitch thought. Above them the cloudless sky arced, bluer than a saint's robe.

*Perfect*.

Jessie looked up at him, a mixture of fright and rebellion clouding her dark eyes. He gave her shoulders what he hoped was a reassuring squeeze.

"She's willing," Mitch nodded.

"Willing to do what?" Jessie demanded. It was the first time he'd ever heard that whiskey-and-sawdust voice of hers squeak. He put his arm around her shoulders and held her close. Beneath his hold he could feel her tension peak. She began to fidget. He held on a little tighter.

Baylor shot Mitch a doubtful glance.

"To marry me," Mitch answered Jessie's question before Baylor could. Ignoring Jessie's gasp, he addressed the sheriff. "We're ready. Let's get this over with."

"*What*?" Jessie screeched, making everybody wince.

"I'll explain everything later," Mitch said quickly. "Easy, honey. All you've gotta do is just say 'I do' when the time comes."

Mitch thought he was going to lose her to apoplexy. Her face had turned white, and she'd furiously begun working a mouth that failed to form any words.

"She's so happy, she's speechless," he commented to Baylor and the others in a tone that dared them to contradict him. "Get on with it, Sheriff."

Sheriff Baylor looked as if he were about to rush to Jessie's aid. He extended his hand as if to slap her on the back to shake some words loose. Tally took a step out of the shadows so quickly, he accidentally tripped over a tree root. The other two simply stood close by, gawking.

"Wait a minute, Baylor. I forgot something." Mitch stooped to rip up a handful of blue, yellow, and white wildflowers growing at their feet. Brushing off most of the dirt clods dangling from their roots, he shoved the blooms into Jessie's hands. "Bride's gotta have a bouquet," he whispered, feeling the color rise in his cheeks. Dismissing the look of horror on Jessie's face, he squarely faced the group of men. "Okay, we're ready now."

Baylor tossed an uneasy glance at Tally. Tally stood stock still, as if paralyzed. Simms and Blake followed suit.

Sheriff Baylor cleared his throat. "You willing to take this woman, uh, Jessie Driscoll, to be your lawful wife?" he asked Mitch, hurrying through the words like a racehorse dashing toward the finish line.

"I am," Mitch said quickly.

Baylor turned to Jessie. The aging lawman's features softened as his gaze settled on her bloodless face. "And what about you, Miss Driscoll? Do you take Mitch Wyden here to be your lawful husband? Uh, to honor and obey him until…until death do you part? Sorry," he said to Mitch. "It's been a while since my missus and I tied the knot. And seeing as how I've been called to do this sort of thing only once before, I'm a little rusty."

At that, Jessie came to life and began spiting and sputtering like a wet cat. "You lousy, conniving, son of a barnyard cur!" she rounded on Mitch, cussing him out worse than that time she'd come at him with a tree limb after he'd criticized her grave digging abilities.

Mitch had already braced himself for battle. Knowing Jessie's penchant for not giving up without a fight, he'd certainly expected a skirmish once she found her voice. So, with determined, precise movements, he executed his battle plan: he silenced her rebellion by taking her head in his firm grip and kissing her soundly on the lips.

He expected a whoop or two from the men, but nobody moved. Except Jessie. She squirmed a while, beating his chest with her fists, tiny flower buds and globs of dirt flying everywhere. But after a few moments, when he deepened the kiss, her struggles began to weaken. Success came at last as he coaxed the response from her he wanted, knew deep down she'd be helpless not to give him. He knew his Jessie like he knew every muscle, bone and sinew of his horse. She loved him. And he loved her. That was all there was to it, all under God's heaven that mattered.

In the end, her knees went weak and she collapsed against him so that he had to tighten his arms around her, this time to hold her up. In a breathless whisper he said, his lips a mere hair's breadth away from hers, "Say 'I do,' sweetheart."

"I do," she whispered back, her dark eyes full of wonder as her bemused gaze searched his face.

"Good girl." He gave her a final light kiss on the lips.

"I now pronounce you husband and wife," Baylor injected quickly, clamping on his hat. "I'll get the papers ready for you two to sign back at the campfire. Tally? You got any paper somewhere in your gear? Come on, the rest of you. You're this happy couple's witnesses. You've got to sign, too."

ঔ ঔ ঔ

The campfire before Mitch blazed hot and comforting. The night was quiet except for the murmur of the stream and an occasional snort from the horses. Once in a while Curtis moaned in his sleep, setting Mitch's teeth on edge, but he could stand a few moans better than the constant whining from him they'd been subjected to all afternoon. Earlier, Tally had given Driscoll a hefty dose of laudanum, mainly to shut him up.

Mitch's thoughts turned to Jessie, who was lying on top of the blanket and bedroll he'd spread for her behind a stand of trees at the far edge of camp, well away from the men. It had taken some doing, but he'd finally convinced Baylor to trust them, to give them the privacy they needed, that they and their horses were too done in to run even if Mitch had a mind to. Which he didn't.

Jessie wasn't speaking to him, but he could tolerate that, confident she'd snap out of her sulks sooner or later. Though exhausted, he figured she probably hadn't fallen asleep yet, given her immense anger toward him—and no doubt disappointment. Imagining her lying there alone in the darkness made him ache inside. Blood surged to his temples, and the tempo of his heartbeat quickened. He forced himself to tamp down the fierce desire to go to her, make love to her.

It was early, even by cowboy standards, but the others had settled inside their bedrolls already, taking advantage of the long hours of sleep Baylor had finally allowed them. It had been an exhausting day. A hard, exhausting last few days, truth be told.

It hadn't been too difficult to convince Baylor to marry them, Mitch reflected, nudging a glowing ember with a fat stick. Once he'd explained what had gone on with Simms and Blake down by the horses, the sheriff had eventually come to agree that

Mitch's marrying "the Driscoll woman" would remedy the issue of her questionable respectability.

He'd hoped that the sheriff's convictions about Jessie might have softened after meeting her, but if Mitch were honest, he knew that the sheriff hadn't changed his opinion of her much. Which meant Baylor harbored a more practical reason for presiding over their wedding vows. By marrying them, he could avoid a good two weeks of trouble among his men during the trip back to Sulfur Flats. As Mitch's wife, Jessie would be off limits and, therefore, cease to be a constant temptation in their midst. Or, at least a temptation they could do nothing about without suffering stiff penalty.

Mitch took a deep drag on the cheroot he held between his fingers, filling his lungs with calming smoke. Shifting his legs and stretching a bit, he attempted to ease his aching muscles.

Once again, his thoughts wandered to Jessie. His Jessie. How he wanted her! Wanted her so badly he felt dizzy with such fierce desire he could barely contain it. And why shouldn't he have her? She was his wife now. Not that she hadn't belonged to him long before they'd spoken any wedding vows. He'd settled that long ago.

Just then, Mitch looked up to see a shooting star streak across the sky. *See that? Even the stars agree with you, Wyden*, he thought. Tossing the half-finished cheroot into the fire, he threw down the stick and stood.

He approached her quietly through the shield of trees and bushes, with care. As he eased down beside her, her breathing stilled, then evened out. He'd been right, then. She wanted him to think she was asleep, but he knew better. Settling another blanket over them, he unbuttoned his jeans, then pulled her tense body into his arms, hushing her little cry of protest with a gentle palm to her lips, mindful that she might still be feeling pain in her cheek.

He began kissing her, wanting her with a fierceness that staggered him. At last, Jessie was safe in his arms again. Back where she belonged, where he could hold her and protect her and feel her heartbeat beneath his hands. He could have lost her out there today. Anything at all could have happened to tear her away from him forever. The thought frightened him so much, he tightened his hold even more, crushing her to his chest as if his arms could keep her by his side for all eternity.

"Let me love you, Jessie. Please," he whispered against her hair. "I know you're mad at me, and I probably have no right to ask it of you now when things have been so rough on you the last few days. If you say no, I swear I'll accept it. You ought to know by now that I'd never force myself on you. *Never*. But be honest, Jessie. The last few days have been hell on both of us. Now we're together again, and we're husband and wife. I want you, Jessie. And I can feel it by the way you melted against me just now that somewhere down deep you want me, too."

As if she sensed his desperation, she expelled a long breath and said, a little desperately herself, "What do you do to me, Mitch? You're darned right I'm mad at you. Furious, even. But when you hold me like this, I'm lost. It's like my brain sprouts wings and flies away."

He chuckled. "Let it fly, sweetheart. You're my wife now, and I'm here, and we're together again. That's all that matters."

Burying her head in the crook of his neck, she said, "But the men. They'll hear us."

"The men are all asleep on the other side of the trees, clear at the other end of camp. They won't hear a thing."

"But Sheriff Baylor. He hears—"

"It's all right, Jessie. Trust me."

It took some gentle coaxing, but in time, Jessie forgot both her anger and her apprehensions. She began to respond, kissing him back, loving him back in all the little, precious Jessie ways he remembered. They took their time removing each other's clothes, with no one but the stars and moon keeping watch over them.

The power of his need rocked him, rocked her. And it was like the heartbeat of God pounding inside his body, consuming him, overflowing into Jessie, enveloping them, fusing their bodies into one holy being. He kissed her deeply, pouring his heart, the very essence himself, into the staggering mystery of her unimaginable sweetness.

*My wife,* he declared silently, gathering her close, rocking her to the ancient rhythm that echoed and swelled until their primal pulse-beats filled the universe. Deep within the center of his being, he declared again and again, *Jessie, precious Jessie, my heart, my wife.*

# Chapter Seventeen

Breathing heavily, Mitch withdrew from her and rolled to his back, dragging her atop his chest where he held her close against his heart. Too spent to protest even if she'd wanted to, Jessie lay in his arms like a rag-stuffed doll, listening while his racing heart slowed to normal.

The masculine scent of his heated skin filled her. The taste of him lingered like sweet morning dew on her lips and tongue. Heaven help her, she loved this man beyond all reason.

But she had a huge problem. Today, Mitch Wyden had broken off yet another fragile piece of her heart.

All her life she'd dreamed about her wedding day. Of how, months before the nuptials, her beloved would ask her on bended knee to marry her. And once she'd given her assent, as a token of his love, he would present her with a betrothal ring—perhaps a small emerald surrounded by tiny seed pearls—to seal their promise. She would be deliriously happy as she and Aunt Cora planned the wedding. Pastor Stiller would marry them in the small chapel in town where she would drift like a princess down the aisle with at least five bridesmaids preceding her. She would wear a beautiful long-sleeved gown made from yards and yards of teal blue silk and lace, teal being one of her best colors. And her veil, made of old Mrs. McKenna's exquisite, handmade Irish lace, would fall from the crown of her head down the length of the gown, nearly brushing the floor as she made her way down the aisle in her whisper-soft silk slippers.

There would be scores of guests at the nuptial celebration. The parlor and front yard would overflow with tables laden with succulent hams, turkeys, and beef roasts. Platters of vegetables and condiments would round off the sumptuous supper.

And her wedding cake. Only the most decadent would do: a rich, vanilla, feather-light confection decorated with mounds of fluffy frosting adorned with delicate pink rose blossoms.

She and her handsome new husband would dance and dance to the dreamy music of the orchestra. Then, when they were both euphoric from the heady effect of champagne and activities, he would bend to tenderly claim her lips and swear that he would love her all the days of their lives, that he would never, ever leave her.

Of course, the wedding celebration part was only a fanciful dream. Uncle Thaddeus and Aunt Cora had never deemed her worthy of a new pair of shoes, much less a fancy wedding ceremony, feast, and cake like those she'd fantasized about. Still, it was lovely to dream of such things.

Jessie pressed her lips together and inhaled deeply. Mercy. Even if she'd tried her hardest, spent days dreaming up some horrific nightmare ceremony, she never could have imagined anything as awful as the "wedding" Mitch had put her through that afternoon.

Anger at herself burned within her. Because when it came right down to it, she knew beyond a doubt that she hadn't been forced into marrying Mitch at all. The truth was, she'd said "I do" because she loved him, and she'd lost her head when he'd started kissing her. Her traitor body had gone all soft and liquid the moment his lips touched hers, melting completely at the moment he'd deepened the kiss.

It had been that way from the very beginning, she admitted honestly. All Mitch Wyden had to do was touch her and she went soft as mush inside. Worse, not a week ago, she herself had handed him the most powerful weapon of all to use against her. She'd told him from her heart that she loved him.

What a fool she must have looked like to the sheriff and his men as they'd stood by watching Mitch sway her. How they must be laughing at her, and congratulating Mitch for pulling it all off so easily. She knew he didn't love her in return. He'd never once told her he loved her. So, so.... Why? Why had he done it?

All right. "Let me love you," he'd said. But unlike her, for Mitch, what she felt for him and what they had done together were two separate things. She couldn't separate the two, but apparently men could, and they did it easily, without conscience. Mitch had just proved it.

"What's wrong, Jessie?" Mitch whispered.

Mitch had his fingers buried in her hair, gently massaging her scalp. His other arm lay heavy on her back, pressing her close. "Jessie, talk to me." His hand stilled in her hair. "What is it? Did I hurt you?" His chest expanded, and beneath her ear she could hear the quickening of his heartbeat.

*Yes, Mitch. More than I can ever say. If only you loved me, I could freely accept the events of the day, take joy in them, but....* She gave him a nearly imperceptible shrug of her shoulders.

"If I did, I'm sorry. You should have said something—"

"Don't talk, Mitch. Not even in a whisper. The men might hear us."

She felt his lips move against her hair, and she could imagine his face crumpling into a frown, his lips creasing into a hard line.

"Nobody's listening. I told you, even if they tried, they're too far off."

"If you say so."

"Jessie, stop it. I'm trying to set things straight here."

Even if they weren't listening, she could picture their thoughts, their "wedding night" imaginings. How could she ever face them again?

"I want to go to sleep now, Mitch. I'm very tired."

His fingers moved in her hair, and she could feel the tension in his hand. "I know the way I did things today aren't setting well with you, but you've got to understand, I couldn't see doing it any other way."

With all her remaining strength, she said, "Please, Mitch. Just don't."

Somewhere far away in the darkness a coyote howled.

Mitch's breath seemed to be trapped in his throat when he shifted to cup her face. As he turned her chin up he said, "I did it for you, Jessie. I did it for us. Everything's going to be all right. You've got to believe that."

But she was certain that nothing would ever be all right again. Utterly spent, with Herculean effort she once again managed to answer in a barely audible whisper, "If you say so."

☙ ☙ ☙

Mitch awoke just before dawn. Jessie lay curled at his side, her slight body warm and soft as summer rain against his skin. One weightless arm lay across his chest, and one leg lay bent so that her knee rested pleasantly against his lap. Her head lay buried in the crook between his neck and shoulder.

To spare Jessie any morning embarrassment, sometime during the night he'd helped her put her clothes back on, then dressed himself. Now, he could feel her feathery breath against the exposed skin of his throat just above the top button of his shirt.

He couldn't see her face in the darkness, yet he imagined it, his heart twisting as he pictured her kiss-swollen lips, her dark, tousled curls framing the lost expression he knew must be there. When he gently fingered a curl, her breath caught. The rhythm of her breathing broke as if on a sob. Was she crying in her sleep?

A slight breeze blew across their bodies, ruffling the blanket he held in place over her shoulders. She shifted, and with the movement he felt a chill touch the dampness of his shirt.

Well, what did he expect? They hadn't had time for a proper talk. All right, he hadn't wanted to explain anything to her before the wedding because he'd been so afraid she wouldn't listen to reason. Afraid that because she believed the worst of him, he'd never be able to convince her to marry him, no matter how noble and right his reasons were.

She shifted her knee. The movement sent pure pleasure like a bolt of electricity through his body, nearly making his toes curl. He kissed the furrows between her eyebrows, and as he did, she snuggled against him, as if seeking his warmth, moving her knee once more.

He stifled a groan, aching to make love to her again. But he wouldn't, in consideration of her feelings, the feelings he'd all but ignored yesterday and last night. It would be torture, but he somehow had to stifle his longings. For Jessie's sake. Jessie, his wife.

*Wife.* Once years ago, he'd heard his sister Laurie talking with one of her childhood friends outside the mercantile. The two girls, maybe twelve at the time and he about nine, were discussing their future weddings: their dresses, the ceremony, their respective lovesick grooms. They giggled and laughed and carried on like two twittering birds until he came out from his hiding place behind a boardwalk post and started teasing them. His mortified sister had given him the silent treatment for days afterwards.

He pressed a protective arm tighter around Jessie's shoulders. Unlike men, women cherished their wedding plans. Laurie had told him once that a girl dreams of her wedding day like a man dreams about the wedding night.

He sighed. And what had he given Jessie? A mockery of a ceremony and not quite, but a near public consummation. Yep. He'd thoroughly shattered her dreams, all right. But he'd married her for her own good. She belonged to him, and deep down he was certain that's the way Providence meant things to be. So, no matter how it had been done, he'd be hogtied and branded before he'd feel guilty about making her his wife. Or making love to her last night.

Unable to tolerate his dark thoughts any longer, Mitch carefully extracted Jessie from his arms and eased to his feet.

He looked down at her, just barely able to see her silhouette in the faint light of daybreak. Gently, he bent and tucked the blanket more securely around her shoulders and kissed her hair. She didn't move, didn't awaken.

He thought he'd been quiet enough, but one of the men stirred. Baylor, probably. Inside his camp, the canny lawman would keep one eye cracked open, on the alert for any eventuality. Nothing much got past the man.

Careful to move like a ghost, Mitch snatched up his boots and rifle and headed toward the meadow for a cold douse in the stream.

He was toweling off with his shirt when Baylor stepped from the shadows, noisily, Mitch assumed, so as not to get himself shot. *Smart man.*

While Mitch tugged on his pants, the sheriff sat down on a nearby rock, pulling up a knee and clasping it with his hands. "We need to talk," he said.

Mitch shrugged into his shirt and looked over toward camp. He'd picked a spot to wash up far enough away for semi-privacy, but close enough to where he could still keep an eye on Jessie. "Depends on what you want to talk about, Sheriff. If it's about what's personal between a man and his wife, then you can keep your talk to yourself."

The sheriff shifted. Mitch noticed the man's lips thin a little below his drooping mustache. He let go of his knee and his booted foot made a loud thump in the dirt. "As head of this outfit I've got the authority to have my say whenever I see fit."

"That so?"

"That's so. Look, Wyden, I'm only gonna say this once. I ought to be saying it strictly for the girl's sake, but the truth of it is, how you treat your wife is none of my business."

Mitch shot him a heated glare, but before he could blast a retort, Baylor warned, "My deputies *are* my business, though, so you're just gonna have to grit your teeth and hear me out."

Mitch moved to grab his rifle.

"Now, now, just simmer down. Before you end up pointing that rifle my way, try to look at things from my perspective. Jessie Driscoll is the only female for miles around, and these men haven't seen their wives and sweethearts in weeks."

Baylor didn't say more, just met Mitch's glare with one of his own.

Mitch got the picture quick enough. The others already thought of Jessie as a woman of loose morals. He highly doubted the men either saw or heard anything from him or Jessie last night, but just the thought of the two of them together must have caused the others all kinds of torment. Worse, Mitch knew that after last night, Jessie would become the sole object of all their lustful musings. His muscles tensed.

"It's Jessie *Wyden*" he corrected. "And I'll kill anyone that so much as—"

"I said simmer down. You let me handle my men, hear? Nobody's gonna lay a finger on her."

"You got that right. And another thing. I won't have her sniggered at, either."

Baylor shifted on his perch. His gaze darted to the camp, then to the barrier of trees where Jessie lay, then back at Mitch. Mitch set his rifle aside and finished pulling on his boots. A small, tense silence fell between them.

"That's not all I have to talk about. There's another matter," the sheriff said.

"Oh? And what would that be?"

"There's a possibility Curtis Driscoll's not gonna make it back to Sulfur Flats. The gunshot wound's worse than I thought." The statement fell between the two of them like the thud of a heavy stone.

Mitch stilled, considering. Would Jessie care if her cousin died? Would she be upset about Curtis's death, or relieved? Frankly, Curtis could die right now and Mitch wouldn't feel even a speck of remorse.

"Dead or alive is what the poster says, isn't that so, Baylor? What do you care if he cashes it?"

Baylor shook his head and swore. "I never figured you for a fool."

Mitch stiffened. "What's that supposed mean? Curtis Driscoll's a lowdown, sorry excuse for a human being. The world'll be better off without him."

"Maybe so, but Jessie wouldn't."

"What do you mean?"

"He's her only defense. Think about it, Wyden. You say Jessie had no idea about the crimes the Driscoll gang committed. That she was coerced into going along for the ride, was forced to participate. Right now, Curtis Driscoll is the only one you've got to confirm that."

It was Mitch's turn to swear. "And if he dies…."

"That's about the size of it. 'Course, the judge might not consider Driscoll's testimony as holding much weight anyway. With Curtis being a blood cousin to Jessie and all, the judge might figure they'd lie for each other to their mutual benefit."

"That's nonsense," Mitch protested.

"Then, too, there's the fact that Jessie resisted arrest. If she's so blamed innocent, why'd she turn her gun on my men?"

"You know why, Sheriff! Your men cornered her with their guns drawn. She thought they were going to kill her—or worse. What would you have done in her boots, Baylor? She was merely defending herself."

The sheriff eyed Mitch speculatively, then ran two fingers down his mustache. "Well, that may be. But if you ask me, right now I suggest you pray that that 'lowdown, sorry excuse for a human being' doesn't die."

Mitch hung there, speechless for a moment. It wasn't that he hadn't thought about the possibility the authorities wouldn't believe Jessie's story. It was just that he hadn't allowed himself to dwell on such calamitous prospects.

Baylor was right. Curtis's testimony could be a help to Jessie. Or maybe not. Still, if Curtis died, Jessie would lose a chance in her favor, if a slim one.

"What about Walt Conner?" Mitch said, suddenly remembering the fifth outlaw. "As far as we know, he's still alive out there somewhere. If we could bring him in, he'd be able to confirm Jessie's innocence, too, wouldn't he?"

"Maybe." The sheriff nodded. "But we don't even know where to start looking."

"I'll bet my saddle Curtis knows where he was headed when they split up."

"Maybe so, but right now Driscoll isn't in much of a talking mood."

Mitch shot a glare toward the camp. "Give me two minutes, he'll be in the mood."

"Wyden, wait!" Baylor stood, grasping Mitch's arm before he could stalk off. "Let me handle it. Since everybody's so tuckered out, I'm gonna give the men and the horses another twenty-four hours to rest up. Maybe Driscoll's condition will improve by the time we break camp tomorrow. We'll talk to him then."

"And if his condition worsens?"

Baylor thought a moment, studying the toes of his boots. Two fingers worked his mustache. "Then it worsens. Not much we can do about it."

"No," Mitch argued. "That's not the way it's gonna go. If Driscoll worsens, you and Tally and I take a sworn statement from him before he slips too far. The final testimony of a dying man ought to hold some sway with the judge."

Mitch studied Baylor's dubious expression, the lawman's obvious skepticism. "Well, you're the lawman, Baylor," Mitch exclaimed. "You ought to know that sworn, witnessed testimonies from the absent party usually hold up in court, just as if the person himself were there. Isn't that right?"

He was thinking of an innocent army friend who'd gotten into a tight situation once. Mitch, the man's only alibi, had been out on patrol at the time of the hearing and had had to send a written statement back to the fort by courier.

"That's true in most cases," Baylor agreed. "But in this one, the sworn testimony in question is coming from an alleged bank robber and possible murderer. Worse, the Driscolls are related."

Stuffing down the sick dread building in his guts, determined not to give in to nagging uncertainty, Mitch said, "At the time we get Driscoll's statement, we'll get him to tell us where Conner was headed."

"Won't hurt to try, I suppose." The sheriff sounded neither convinced nor hopeful.

Mitch wanted to punch him in the teeth for his skepticism. "Jessie's innocent," he reiterated doggedly, his tone low and desperate.

"So you keep insisting, but that's for the judge to decide," Baylor answered with maddening indifference. A long pause followed where it seemed as if the sheriff was sizing up Mitch's character all over again. The way he'd done just before he'd deputized him. "Your wife should be waking up soon," he commented finally. He clapped his hat on his head, jutting his chin toward camp. "You best go tend to her." His step as he walked away seemed heavy and slower than his usual confident gate.

"Baylor?" Mitch called after him. The sheriff turned, his eyebrows raised. "Just to be clear. Be warned that I won't tolerate anybody embarrassing Mrs. Wyden. If I hear any sniggering about last night, the guilty ones'll pay dearly for it."

Baylor gave him a curt nod. "Fair enough. But you be warned, too, Wyden. I strongly suggest that from now on you make sure you don't give them any good reasons to snigger."

# Chapter Eighteen

"Let's go," Mitch said, reaching down to give Jessie a hand up. He had her saddlebags slung over his shoulder and a small cake of soap in the other hand. "Go where?" She couldn't have kept the mistrust from her tone even if she'd tried. She saw his shoulders slump a fraction, but the hard, determined expression on his face didn't budge.

"Down to the stream. To wash and change your clothes. And take care of any...personal needs you might want to attend to."

Heat rushed to her cheeks. She did have to use the bushes. Badly. His grip as he helped her to her feet was implacable. Just like the man himself, she sighed.

Physically, she felt much better today. Not so utterly spent like she had been after surviving that hellish ordeal yesterday. Several uninterrupted hours of sleep had also helped to strengthen her resolve and waning spirit.

The flush of humiliation still burned her cheeks, however. She could feel her color rising every time she replayed the events of yesterday and last night in her mind.

Mitch led her into the meadow, downstream and far out of sight of the others. In spite of the anger she harbored toward him, she was grateful for this brief escape. She still didn't know how she was ever going to face those men, how she was going to be able to live through their humiliating whispered off-color remarks, which she knew would be forthcoming in spades sooner or later. She hadn't ridden with Curtis's men for months without learning about some of their baser amusements.

"Why so quiet?" Mitch asked, breaking into her thoughts.

She didn't answer. She wasn't going to speak to him. Ever again. Sensing his eyes on her, she didn't dare look up for fear she'd see that unsettling hunger in his eyes. A heavy arm circled her shoulders. When she tried to shrug it off, he just held her tighter.

"Jessie, don't be mad at me anymore. Let me at least try to explain."

She pressed her lips together, holding in a heated retort.

"I didn't think things through very well last night," he offered, sounding contrite. "I should have considered your feelings better, but I was just so glad to have you back safe and sound I couldn't think of anything but—"

In a burst of ire she couldn't suppress, she said, "Don't, Mitch. I know what you wanted of me last night. You don't have to spell it out as if I were a simpleton."

So much for her resolve never to speak to him again.

Mitch halted, turning her toward him. His blue eyes smoldered as he glared down at her, his hands gripping her upper arms. "Don't play the virgin martyr, Jessie. You said yes. You wanted me, too, and eventually you got lost in our lovemaking just as hopelessly as I did. And you'd be a liar if you dared to tell me otherwise."

She turned her face away, frustrated. He was right, of course. She'd wanted him, all right. Desperately. And the moment she'd felt his lips on hers, the moment he touched her, she'd sizzled and melted like butter in a skillet.

Oh how she ached to wail out her anguish over the whole sorry situation. Instead, she lifted her chin defiantly, refusing to answer him.

Just as abruptly as he'd halted, he spun her toward the stream, propelling her forward. "Come on," he grumbled impatiently. "We don't have much time. If we're gone too long, Baylor'll think we tried to escape."

"That *we* tried to escape?" she scoffed. "Don't you want me to sing a few verses of 'Aura Lee' while I bathe?" She saw his jaw tighten.

They passed the spot near the trees where their sham of a marriage had taken place. Jessie kept her chin up, though seeing it sent a stab of pain through her heart. She stumbled, and Mitch caught her, looking grim, as if he were reading her thoughts.

"I promise to give you a proper wedding, one we can *both* be proud of, when all this trouble is over, Jessie."

She gave him a sidelong glance, not believing him an inch. How could he be so cruel? He was playing with her emotions again, making promises he never intended to keep, just to keep her biddable. He didn't care one whit about her feelings and never had.

When the invisible fist squeezing her heart eased up a bit, she answered in a sharp, defensive tone, "Don't bother making any plans. I wouldn't marry you, Mitch. Not even if you were the only man alive for ten thousand miles around. Yesterday I was delirious with fear and exhaustion, which is the only reason you got away with all your hateful shenanigans. And last night…. Well, mark my words, Mr. Smart Man Mitch Wyden. I won't be duped a second time."

He tightened his jaw again, the only perceptible indication that her taunts were getting to him. Bolstered, she continued:

"What I can't figure out is why you put on that mockery of a wedding in the first place. You didn't have to marry me. You already had me, and oh yes, the reward money, neatly wrapped up. Your ridiculous actions don't make a lick of sense."

Mitch looked as if she'd kicked him. He remained quiet, but his pace quickened so that she practically had to trot to keep up. She could see they were heading for the bend in the stream where a couple of cottonwoods grew close to the bank. Their lush, silvery-green-laden branches dipped into the water, creating a sort of privacy screen.

With his face set like marble, he said, "So, we're back to the reward money again, are we? Well, you can spit and claw at me all you want, but while you're at it think about this: If I hadn't married you yesterday you'd have been fair game for the men last night. You couldn't have been so worn out you didn't notice them watching your every twitch and wiggle with lust in their eyes."

"I don't twitch! And I certainly don't wiggle—"

"And contempt, Jessie. To them you're a criminal. Worse, they've assumed you were the Driscoll gang's whore."

Jessie gasped, her head reeling. She staggered, the brutal force of his words hitting her hard.

"So the way I see it, I'm the hero here. I saved that stubborn, self-righteous hide of yours, Mrs. Wyden. And got you some previously non-existent respect in the process."

She'd stopped dead in her tracks, her face draining of color. She'd never thought...never dreamed.... These were *lawmen* for heaven's sake. Even Curtis's wily bunch, without exception, had treated her with respect.

He must have seen the severity of her distress because he wasn't forcing her forward any longer. He said in a low growl, taking the part of her chin that wasn't bruised in his fingers and making her look squarely at him, "Think about this, too, while you're at it. We've probably made a baby together by now. You ought to be thanking your lucky stars you've got a husband who'll provide for it and give it a name."

She was too distraught to say anything. To move. To breathe. He gave her a moment, but soon he was nudging her forward again toward the wading cottonwoods. She sensed the anger radiating from him, felt it, all the way to her toes. His tight, stony expression sent small ripples of fear down her spine.

He'd rendered her speechless. But he clearly didn't want to hear anything more she might have to say anyway. As they approached the river, he said, "You can take all your clothes off and enjoy a full bath, or you can spot wash. Suit yourself." He set his rifle down against a nearby boulder and handed her the soap and her saddlebags. "Just remember, it'll be two weeks or more before we reach Sulfur Flats. There might not be an opportunity to bathe again for a while."

Jessie surveyed her surroundings, glancing over her shoulder toward camp. Did he honestly expect her to undress completely with the others so near?

"Don't give it another thought, Jessie. I catch anybody peeking, they get their head blown off."

And then he did something so totally unexpected, Jessie nearly dropped the soap and her saddlebags. He jerked her into his arms, took her head in his big hands and kissed her. She tried to clamp her lips shut, but the moment he slid his tongue along the crease of her frown and gently sucked free her lower lip, she opened like a sunflower at midday.

When at last he raised his head, he warned in a voice low and fierce, "Don't ever say things you don't mean, Jessie. Like you wouldn't marry me even if I were the last man alive for ten thousand miles around. You love me. You told me so yourself, remember? So you'll never convince me otherwise, no matter how hard you try." He tugged at her lips again, teasing them, sending shivers along her spine. "The point is moot anyway, because you're already mine. Until death do us part. For better or worse, and all that. You're stuck with me for the rest of your life, brat. Get used to it."

He tasted of tobacco and coffee, smelled of soap and man. Unlike last night, his cheeks and jaw rubbing against her skin felt smooth. She realized he must have shaved this morning.

Jessie sighed bitterly. When he folded her up inside his powerful strength, she wanted so badly to give in to the urge to lean on him. To feel safe and secure again like she had back at the cabin where the dangerous outside world didn't exist and there was just the two of them. She wanted to believe in him. Trust him. Believe that he could somehow make everything right, make this terrifying nightmare go away. But she couldn't. Because clearly, the motives that propelled his actions had little to do with assuring her well-being. He wanted retribution in the form of reward money—

She broke away with a small cry, pushing hard against his chest with the flats of her hands. The saddlebags and soap spilled to the ground.

"Jessie! Stop it. I'm trying to help you, can't you see that? Why won't you listen to reason? Why do you insist on making me the bad guy here, when everything I've done, I've done for you, for *us*?"

She felt like screaming. Like putting her hands over her ears and doubling over to block out his lies.

*I will not be bullied and used!* she cried to herself. Trembling, she swiped up the soap and saddlebags, then tromped toward the bushes, leaving his words hanging in the air.

She took her time in the privacy of the bushes, gathering her thoughts, pulling the ragged edges of her sanity together. Mitch's words played over and over in her mind as she undressed. Could she believe him? Had he truly saved her from the others last night like he'd said? They were lawmen, after all, supposedly honest, upstanding officers, sworn by solemn oath to uphold justice and order. Still, she grimaced ruefully, she wouldn't trust that awful man, Simms, for anything.

She shook her head. This was nonsense. She hadn't been in any real danger at all last night. Mitch would never have allowed any of them to lay a finger on her. He'd just been making up lies to excuse his shameful deeds.

She touched her pale abdomen, considering Mitch's second declaration. Could she possibly be carrying his child? The thought both thrilled and horrified her. To be carrying Mitch's child, to know that soon she would have her very own sweet baby to love and cosset would be the next best thing to heaven, but—

For one, brief, awful moment, she pictured herself giving birth alone behind bars on a cold, dirty prison floor. The thought so terrified her, she quickly pushed it from her mind.

Instead, she concentrated on getting clean.

It felt wonderful to strip off her dusty, perspiration-stained clothes and lather her body with Mitch's herbal soap. The icy cold water numbed her skin, but she ignored the biting sting. Getting clean again was worth any discomfort. Mica flecks peppered the sandy stream bottom, reflecting the morning sun, making her feel as if she were bathing in tub of glittering gold.

Mitch sat brooding on a tall, flat boulder beside the trees with his rifle cradled in his arms, where he could survey the surrounding area and keep a watchful eye on her at the same time.

And watch her he did. But strangely she didn't mind. He'd seen her unclothed plenty of times. It was Mitch who'd taught her to be comfortable with her body, who'd told her every inch of her was perfect and beautiful. The hungry appreciation she saw in his eyes each time he looked at her touched her heart in ways he could never understand.

Heaven help her, in spite of everything, those compliments thrilled her, meant more to her than she could ever say. Her whole life Curtis had taunted her with ugly names like "scrawny" or "skinny" or "beanpole." Uncle Thaddeus and Aunt Cora hadn't treated her much better.

She closed her eyes, wishing things were back the way they used to be at the cabin before Curtis had returned. But wishes were a fool's folly. Things could never be the way they were again. She finished her bath with a cold ache clutching her heart.

"You smell good," Mitch said as she stood before him dressed in a clean change of clothes, ready to head back to camp. She heard the husky edge to his voice, sensed the enormous tension tightening his big body as his gaze traveled the length and breadth of her, finally coming to rest on her parted lips.

"It's the soap," she mumbled awkwardly.

He looked away. "Go rinse out your soiled things," he said brusquely.

"But there's no time. Aren't we breaking camp soon? My clothes won't have time to dry."

"We won't be heading out until tomorrow morning."

"Oh."

"The horses need the rest," he said, answering her unspoken question.

Grateful for the opportunity to do some laundry, and elated she wouldn't be spending the day in the saddle, Jessie headed back toward the stream. This time Mitch followed her.

A long silence fell between them while Jessie washed out her clothes. Just as she was finishing up, Mitch told her in a voice tight with tension, "I've got to tell you something before we head back. Curtis is pretty bad off, Jessie. He might not make it."

Jessie started, losing her hold on the camisole she'd been rinsing. Mitch quickly bent and snatched it before the current carried it away.

"His wounds need tending," he said gently, watching her. "Tally did what he could, but I think maybe you ought to take a look."

She felt his eyes on her but she didn't dare look up because she didn't want him to see how hard his words had struck her. Slowly, he handed her the dripping camisole. Just as slowly she took it, keeping her eyes steady on the flimsy garment, trying hard to breathe normally.

She didn't know what to say. Both anger and self-pity pierced her. Anger because Curtis had chosen a criminal's life and had forced her to go along for the ride, making chaos of her life in the process. Now he lay beneath a yonder tree, handcuffed and half dead, an utter disgrace in the sight of both God and man. She'd never felt love for her aunt and uncle, but she could honestly say she was glad they'd died before having to bear the dreadful shame their only son had brought to the Driscoll name.

Self-pity gripped her, partly for those reasons, but also because Curtis was the only family she had. If she lost him, she'd be truly alone in the world.

Yet, she asked herself sensibly, wasn't she alone already? What difference would it make if Curtis died? Ignoring a sudden wash of guilt for allowing herself to ask such an uncharitable question, she admitted in the deepest part of her that she'd most likely be better off without him. In all honesty she wouldn't miss him much. After all, he'd been mean-spirited and brutal to her all her life.

"Jessie, listen to me," Mitch insisted. This time a touch of exasperation colored his voice. He'd obviously mistaken her long silence as a refusal to help her cousin. "You've got to get Curtis to tell you where Conner was heading when they split up."

Slowly, his words penetrated, and comprehension dawned. She shook her head as if to clear it, then twisted around, squeezing the camisole in her fists, wishing it were his neck she had clenched in her hands. Stark fury flushed her cheeks as she struggled to expel the acid retort burning in her throat.

Mitch towered over her, studying her hard. Before she could choke out a reply, he snarled, "There's that self-righteous look again. Right away you've come to the conclusion it's the reward money I want, haven't you? Well, that tears it, Jessie. I'll admit I've made plenty of mistakes with you, brat, but the way I see it, I've done nothing so detestable that I should have earned this kind of scorn and hostility. At the risk of sounding like an echo, I'm going to say it one more time. *I'm trying to help you.* Why won't you believe me?"

He stood there, his rifle clutched in his hands so tight she thought he might bend the barrel. Taking in several deep breaths as if to calm himself, he continued in a more controlled tone. "I'm not going to stand here arguing with you. I've already wasted enough breath trying to explain my actions, trying to make you see reason. But you won't listen. And that's your loss, Jessie, because your stubbornness is keeping us separated, giving you an excuse to think you're all alone in this sorry mess."

He squatted down on his haunches so that he was at eye level with her and set the rifle aside. "Don't turn your head away, Jessie," he warned, taking her shoulders in his hands. "Nurse your distrust of me all you want, but if you have any sense at all, you'll find out from Curtis where Conner went. Curtis trusts you. You're the only one he'll tell. If you value your freedom, you'll set aside your low opinion of me and do as I say."

# Chapter Nineteen

In the end, she didn't have to drag any information out of Curtis. A quiet mention of Conner's name in her delirious cousin's ear had been all it took. She'd just finished cleaning his wounds when, in the throes of pain and fever, her cousin had blurted out Conner's destination without any coaxing. Mitch and Baylor were standing not a foot away when he'd done it.

"Sacramento," Baylor repeated, tipping back his hat with his thumb, then fingering his graying mustache thoughtfully.

"Conner's probably sticking to the original plan," Mitch exclaimed, grinning. "My bet is he's on his way to San Francisco."

"Sounds that way," Baylor agreed.

"Unless...do you think Curtis is just spouting nonsense?"

"Naw," Baylor replied. "Sounds to me like Driscoll's mulling over an argument the two of them had before he and Conner parted ways."

Jessie heard the excitement in Mitch's voice and winced. She looked up at him just as he turned his attention to her.

"Here. Let me help you with that bandage," he said, squatting down beside her. He held Curtis up so that she could wind a clean swath of her sacrificed petticoat around the damaged shoulder and torso. Since Curtis presented no threat in his present weakened condition, they'd removed the wrist irons to make things easier for her.

Despite the anger she harbored for her cousin, unbidden pity rose up inside her, too. Curtis had a high fever and was in a great deal of pain. He'd also lost far too much blood. She bit her lip, concentrating on covering up the ugly gunshot wound as quickly as possible. She needed to get away. Needed time by herself to gather strength, to keep from getting sick.

"It'll be all right, Jessie," Mitch told her quietly. He seemed genuinely concerned about how she was taking all this, but he didn't fool her an inch. She studied the curve of his small, satisfied smile and knew he was only thinking of the reward money he'd be claiming once he brought Conner in.

"Will it?" she asked, nearly strangling on the tight knot lodged in her throat.

She could tell by the way his breath caught and his hand jerked away that her sharp, accusing reply wasn't what he'd hoped to hear.

☙ ☙ ☙

The next morning while the men busied themselves breaking camp, Mitch had a talk with Sheriff Baylor.

"I'll get him," Mitch affirmed. "You and your men don't want Walt Conner half as much as I do."

"Maybe," Baylor said.

Mitch followed the sheriff's gaze as it swept the camp and landed on Jessie. She was sitting on a tree stump near the doused campfire, quietly brushing her hair.

"I wish she wouldn't do things like that," the sheriff grumbled, expressing Mitch's thoughts exactly. The other three men were slanting interested glances her way, too, Mitch noticed with irritation.

"You've got to watch over her for me while I'm gone," Mitch said. "Keep the men away from her. Especially Simms. I'll speak to Simms myself before I leave, but I'll rest better if you give me your word you won't let anything happen to her."

"I know how to control my deputies," Baylor retorted, clearly peeved. "I give you my word that your little gal's gonna reach Sulfur Flats none the worse for wear. Believe it."

Mitch tossed the remnants of his cold coffee into the carpet of pine needles at his feet. "Thanks," he said, forcing the word past his teeth. He hated being beholden to anyone, especially someone he wasn't certain he could trust.

Baylor said, "Blake'll give you his badge before you ride out. You may need it later on. You sure you don't want Tally or one of the others to ride to Sacramento with you?"

"No. I'll make better time by myself. Sacramento is maybe three, four days' ride from here, and nobody's got a horse with stamina enough to match my stallion. As it is, I'm gonna have to take things slow the next day or so until he regains his full strength."

Baylor nodded. "Suits me. The men are anxious to get home. They've been tracking the Driscoll gang a long time."

Mitch stifled the urge to tell the sheriff yet again that Jessie wasn't part of the Driscoll gang. Instead he said, "I'll do some investigating along the way, pass around Conner's description wherever I can. When I get to Sacramento, I'll notify the authorities that Conner might be in town, or headed in or out."

"You do that," Baylor said. "You know, that reward on Conner's head makes him mighty attractive to bounty hunters. Maybe you'll get lucky and find him already rotting in a jail cell. Wish we were closer to a town. We could wire out a few inquiries."

"I'll find him one way or the other."

Baylor nodded, then turned away to gather his gear.

"One more thing, Sheriff," Mitch called after him. "Try hard to get that statement from Driscoll. If he shows any signs he's getting his wits back, push a pencil and paper in front of him."

The sheriff turned. "Quit telling me how to do my job, Wyden. It's getting mighty irritating."

Frustrated, Mitch let the sheriff go. He was torn between wanting to go after Conner, and worried sick that when he did, he'd be leaving Jessie vulnerable, defenseless, and alone with these men.

But, he reasoned, hardening his resolve, if Curtis died, Conner's testimony might be Jessie's only hope for acquittal. Which left him no real choice. He had to go after Conner, find him and bring him back. Quickly. He didn't have all that much time before the authorities put Jessie on trial.

*What if he failed?* The thought made him queasy. Well, he wouldn't fail, and that was all there was to it. He *couldn't* fail, so no sense torturing himself by thinking otherwise.

He badly wanted to talk to Jessie before he left, but he didn't know what he'd say to her. She'd only figure he was going after Conner for the reward money, and he didn't want to face the accusations she'd sling at him, or worse, those silent, haunted looks of distrust.

He wanted to hold and kiss her and assure her that he'd come back as soon as he could. That he'd be right by her side in Sulfur Flats when she made her appearance before the judge. But even if he went to her now, she wouldn't believe anything he had to say. Not after the way he'd mucked things up between them lately.

Yeah, he'd mucked things up, all right. Badly. The brat actually tried to bolt when he'd crawled in beside her under the blankets last night, which didn't sit well with him at all. He had to put an end to her fussing with a hand over her mouth. When she finally got it through her head that all he wanted from her was sleep and peace, she finally settled down and fell asleep in his arms.

He'd kissed her awake this morning, only to find that her mood hadn't improved any. So, for now, he figured it would be best to leave her alone and let her think whatever she wanted to think. When all this was over, he'd have time enough to convince her of the truth.

He'd talk to Simms before he left and threaten him with his life if he so much as looked at Jessie cross-eyed while he was gone. It gave him only a little comfort to know that Jessie already knew to be wary of the men, to stay out of their way as much as possible. He had to trust that his wife would follow her common sense and innate, canny female intuition, especially with Simms.

One last time, his eyes lingered on the touching picture she made, sitting there with the sunlight dappling her hair and body. She was just putting the brush back in her saddlebags. A wistful expression graced her face as she tucked the silver brush away. The look of vulnerability about her nearly broke his heart.

But then she straightened, jammed her Stetson on her head, and began to buckle her saddlebags with firm, resolute motions. The vulnerability he'd seen the moment before vanished as if it had never been.

Jessie Driscoll Wyden was stronger than she looked. He bolstered his flagging spirits with that reassuring thought.

She'd be all right. She *had* to be all right.

"I'll get Conner for you, Jessie," he vowed fiercely. The whispered promise hung in the air like a thunder cloud as he turned purposefully toward the meadow and the chestnut.

# Chapter Twenty

It had been two days since Mitch had deserted her to go after Conner. Jessie sat atop Belle, her absent gaze fixed on Deputy Tally's broad back as the group pushed through the wilderness toward Sulfur Flats. Sheriff Baylor led the way, behind him came Simms, then Tally, Jessie, and finally, bringing up the rear, Blake and the barely conscious Curtis.

Her bones and muscles ached. Though, nothing hurt as bad as her aching, empty heart. The July heat became nearly unbearable as they rode toward the noon hour through open, sparse terrain where stunted, spindly pinons provided little shade. Each time she took a breath, the stench of horse and man-sweat filled her nostrils, making her stomach queasy.

Mitch had left her for the reward money. That cursed reward money was apparently more important than the safety and well-being of his wife.

For the thousandth time, hot tears threatened to spill and, doggedly, she refused to let them. She wished she could blink away as easily the terrible pain lodged in her heart. Her chest ached with heaviness. How could Mitch have left her with these four men of doubtful character who took delight in leading her into hell? Did she, and everything they had shared together, mean so little to him, then?

"You okay, Miz Wyden?" Tally swiveled in the saddle, darting her a look of concern. It took a moment before Jessie realized he was addressing her.

She looked past him to the white-hot granite walls jutting toward the empty bowl of sky in the distance. Sweat trickled between her shoulder blades. She shivered, wiping moisture off her forehead with the back of her hand.

No. She wasn't okay. Her heart was a desert, her body an empty shell. She would never be okay again.

"We'll be stopping in an hour or two for grub and to rest the horses. You'll feel better once we get to some shade."

Tally was trying to ease both her discomfort and her mind, she knew, but his kind concern only kindled the anger smoldering inside her. To shut him out, she ungraciously tipped the brim of her hat low over her eyes and dropped her head. She heard him sigh as he twisted forward again.

These men were leading her to her doom. Did Deputy Tally honestly think he, in any way, could make this trip easier for her?

Her thoughts shifted. She was all alone now. Curtis was as good as dead, and Mitch had left her. Unless she did something daring on her own, she figured she might as well be as good as dead, too.

Jessie concentrated. *What would Nora do?* Well, it was certain that her dime-novel heroine wouldn't stand for being led like a lamb to the slaughter without putting up a fight. Jessie sifted through all of Nora's many perilous situations, trying to formulate an escape plan. She remembered the time outlaws had held Nora hostage and she'd managed to slip baneberries into their food. The evil men had gotten so sick, Nora made her escape without a speck of trouble.

But sadly, there wasn't a baneberry in sight. Jessie had no mild poison in her gear, either, and no way of slipping it to the men even if she did. Blake and Tally took turns doing the cooking every night, while Sheriff Baylor made sure Jessie spread her bedroll well away from the others, bringing her meals himself. He'd made it clear that she was a Prisoner with a capital

P. Which meant, according to Sheriff Baylor, that she was not allowed to be anything *but* a Prisoner.

She wiped another trickle of moisture off her brow. Belle snorted in reply to Tally's mount's whinny. Maybe she could get her hands on some of that laudanum Tally kept dosing Curtis with....

The decision came like a sudden thunder clap.

She would wait and watch. The next time the sheriff asked her to tend Curtis, she'd get Deputy Tally to let her dose her cousin. Tonight, or maybe tomorrow night, she'd find a way to taint the men's food with laudanum. Then, while they slept a deep, drug-induced sleep, she would sneak away.

Wryly she smiled, remembering her own experience with laudanum. Just a swallow had knocked her out for hours. If she kept her courage and prayed for luck, she would be free of these mountains within days. Within a few weeks, she would be dipping her toes in the mighty Pacific, or blessedly lost in the teeming, exciting Barbary Coast streets of San Francisco.

☙ ☙ ☙

Her opportunity didn't come until two nights later. It had been a particularly difficult day. Simms and Blake had been bickering like guttersnipes since sunup, and a coughing, sniffling Sheriff Baylor complained of early ague symptoms. The stifling summer heat only magnified the sheriff's discomfort. They'd also covered a long, treacherous stretch of ground, making poor time, which had put everybody in a bad temper.

Jessie stared blankly into the night. To her despair, she'd found no opportunity to steal any laudanum, which meant that any of the men could awaken at any time to thwart her plans.

She'd sweetly asked, but Deputy Tally wouldn't let the little brown bottle out of his hand, let alone out of his sight. With Jessie looking on, he'd pointedly dosed Curtis himself. Tally watched her every move each time she'd tended her cousin, hovering over her with the pretense of sticking close in case she needed assistance.

But Jessie knew better. Tally was neither careless nor gullible. He remained, not so much suspicious as cautious of Jessie, making sure she finished her ministrations quickly. The moment she'd wound the fresh bandage in place, he personally escorted her back to her blanket where she was not allowed to stray an inch.

Jessie sighed silently. She figured the time to be an hour or more past midnight. She had no way of telling for sure because thick clouds crowded the sky, shrouding the moon and stars, snuffing out their usefulness. Clutching the blanket tightly to her breast, she listened. And waited.

Earlier, being as cautious and sly as a thief, she'd slipped her saddlebags and boots beneath her blankets. In a series of feigned stretches and wakeful shifting, she'd managed to pull her boots on and gather the saddlebags close.

Someone, she thought it was Blake, snored lightly. An ember fell inside the waning campfire, a fleeting hiss of sound. Curtis groaned softly, thrashing briefly in fitful sleep.

Fear threatened her resolve, but she firmly pushed it aside. Another fifteen minutes passed. All became quiet, except for Blake's steady snoring. *Now*, her mind screamed. *Now!*

Without making a sound, Jessie eased to her knees, gathering the saddlebags and blanket in one fluid motion. Careful to keep the blanket from rustling, she inched to her feet, thigh and calf muscles tense and straining, her breathing halted all together.

Darkness pressed in on her. She couldn't see much as she forced herself to take that first cautious step. Praying a twig wouldn't snap beneath her boots and that the thick carpet of pine needles would silence her footfalls, she slowly crept away in the direction of the hobbled horses.

Once, about half way there, she cocked her head, ears straining. Had someone moved in the camp? Silence. *Don't lose your nerve, Jess. Just a little farther.*

Desperately, she prayed that the horses would remain calm and quiet at her approach. She kept her steps light and unhurried, though the urge to run plagued her.

Squinting through the darkness, her muscles tense and straining, Jessie at last saw the horses' bulky silhouettes. She could breathe freely now that she was far enough away from camp, though she continued to place her footfalls carefully as she neared the milling animals.

A snort. A stomping hoof. Jessie froze.

Minutes passed. The night quieted except for the eerie hoot of an owl somewhere in the distant darkness.

The saddles lay in a row beneath a tall cedar. For a moment Jessie was torn with uncertainty. Should she risk the extra time it would take to snatch a saddle, or should she settle for riding Belle bareback? Chiding herself for that latter ridiculous notion, she carefully made her way toward the saddles. She'd never make it all the way to San Francisco bareback.

As quickly as efforts to be silent would allow, she threw the tack and saddle over Belle's back. She untied the hobbles and quietly led her horse into the trees, heading directly opposite the camp. Her aim was to put miles and miles between herself and the lawmen before dawn. The moment it was safe, she'd saddle Belle properly and ride, but for now, a quiet, brisk walk was all she felt she could safely manage.

From time to time she glanced over her shoulder, imagining she'd heard a twig or branch snap in the shadows. Darkness surrounded her, allowing her little sight beyond a few feet. Heart racing, she pushed on, trusting Belle's keen night vision to keep her from stumbling.

When no brawny, predatory lawmen had burst from the shadows twenty, then thirty minutes later, Jessie's heart began to beat with excitement. She'd done it. She'd escaped! She wanted to shout her triumph. Instead, she hugged Belle's neck and softly wept.

Soon she began to shiver, more from reaction than from the cool night breeze tugging her clothes and hat brim. She needed to be in the saddle, making better time. Sniffing quietly, she dabbed her nose and cheeks with the back of her wrist, and began cinching the saddle.

She had one foot in the stirrup when she heard the noise. The sharp intake of breath, the slippery whisper of sound whizzing toward her startled her, freezing her mid-mount. And then the rope enveloped her chest, pinning her arms to her sides. A hard jerk, and she tumbled backward. Her backside hit the ground with such force the breath whooshed from her lungs.

"Nice try, Mrs. Wyden," came the wheezing, raspy voice behind her. "You've got gumption, I'll give you that."

*Sheriff Baylor!*

Jessie struggled to fill her lungs with breath. All hope vanished as the sheriff leisurely walked toward her, coiling rope as he came.

He gave a series of small coughs behind his gloved hand before squatting down beside her. Quietly he said, "Did you honestly think I'd let you get away?"

Jessie sat there, frozen, her entire being cold and numb. For one, horrifying moment, she thought she was going to faint. Swallowing hard a few times, she waited for her stomach to settle and the dizziness to pass.

"Please," she managed at last. "Let me go." The desperation, the anguish in her voice echoed through the darkness like a mourner's wail.

Baylor tugged the rope a little tighter and Jessie felt the band tighten around her chest. "I can't do that," he said softly, almost like an apology.

"But I haven't done anything!"

"That's what you keep saying."

"Please," she cried again. "Let me go. You're condemning an innocent woman. Why won't you listen to me? I haven't done anything to deserve this!"

The sheriff scooped her up by the armpits and set her on her feet, holding her steady until she righted herself.

"Come on," he said loosening the rope, freeing her at last. But her relief was short-lived.

"What are you doing?" she cried as he pulled her arms, none too gently, behind her back.

"I hate to do this, but you've left me no choice." The cold bite of the wrist irons circling her thin bones made her flinch. Another wash of dizziness nearly buckled her knees.

"I wish you hadn't run," he said, rasping the words. He coughed a couple of times then finished his thought. "You might have had a chance before, but now.... You've gone and killed your odds. That's a pity."

*This couldn't be happening.* "You almost sound as if you give a care about what happens to me, Sheriff. But that isn't true, is it? You—all of you—are getting some kind of perverse pleasure out of escorting me, an innocent woman, to her doom, aren't you?"

"No."

Jessie stomped her foot in frustration. "Then why the cat-and-mouse game? Why let me think I'd gotten away before you pounced on me like a...like a lowdown, sneaking ratter?"

The sheriff gave his head a small shake. "Because I kept hoping you'd eventually reason things out. See the folly of your ways and head back to camp. If you had, I'd have let you crawl back into your bedroll thinking you'd gotten clean away with taking a chance, nobody the wiser. You honestly don't know what your running means, do you?" he asked gravely.

Jessie held her breath, too shaken to reply.

"That's probably just as well, I guess."

Jessie stumbled when the sheriff nudged her forward. The wrist irons rattled when she moved, the terrible sound ringing in her ears, filling her with sick dread.

"Let's go," the sheriff ordered, sweeping up Belle's reins.

"Are the handcuffs really necessary?" Jessie asked, choking out the words.

The sheriff looked her straight in the eyes, his expression hard, his tone gruff. "From now on you'll be treated like the prisoner you are. No more privileges. You'll be tied to your horse during the day and staked to the ground at night."

Heartsick, Jessie begged, "Don't do this to me, Sheriff Baylor. Please."

"You brought all this on yourself, girl," he shot back. "I can't trust you anymore. Now get moving. It's a long way back to camp."

# Chapter Twenty One

The loud voices outside the dank, cramped jail house that had been her home for the last six weeks startled Jessie. She swiftly sat up on the narrow cot, then swung her legs to the floor, wincing when she banged her knee on the edge of the cot's wooden frame. Lydia Baylor's husky voice seeped through the cold masonry stones and the crack beneath the heavy oak door.

"I said, let me in there, Deputy Tally. I don't care what my husband's orders were. You unlock this door and let me in to see that girl."

"Ma'am, I sure wish I could do that, but my orders—"

"I just told you I don't care about orders."

Jessie heard a loud thump and a yelp, then some scuffling.

"Ow! Take it easy, Mrs. Baylor."

"Now, are you gonna let me in there, or do you want another clout with my parasol?"

Next came mumbling, the jangling of keys, and finally the creek of the heavy door swinging inward.

"All right, all right," Tally said. "Just make it quick. And don't say a word about this to anybody, especially the sheriff. Deal?"

"Deal," Lydia Baylor agreed, sweeping into the dim interior of Jessie's cell, her skirts swishing along the packed-dirt floor. "Thank you, Deputy Tally."

"Lydia!"

The heavy door thudded shut, taking the brief flood of comforting sunlight with it.

"Yes, it's me," Lydia affirmed. "How are you holding up, dear?"

Jessie pressed her forehead against the cold iron bars of the inner cell, her hands gripping the two rods near her ears. "Not so good."

"Well, that's understandable. After that circus of a trial today, I'm not surprised." Lydia's face looked pinched, and for the first time in the six weeks Jessie had known Sheriff Baylor's intrepid wife, the woman seemed uncertain, off balance.

Jessie gripped the bars harder, until her fingers ached. "Lydia, what am I going to do? Judge Dougherty didn't believe me. Or Curtis. *None* of those men in the courtroom did. Oh mercy, Lydia. Judge Dougherty sentenced me to prison for twenty years!"

Lydia moved quickly to the bars that separated them, dropped her parasol, and covered Jessie's frozen hands with her own. "Now, now, dear. Try not to worry. There isn't a woman in this town who hasn't taken up your cause. We're all outraged by your conviction and sentence. Why, even Coreen Dougherty, the judge's wife, isn't speaking to that miserable codpate husband of hers. The idea that that man could convict you and sentence you to twenty years when it's so obvious that you're innocent astounds us all."

Jessie slumped against the bars. "Oh, Lydia. Why didn't Judge Dougherty listen to me when I tried to tell him I didn't know what Curtis was up to when he and his men were robbing the bank? Curtis tricked me. He made me stay by the horses while they—"

"I know, I know, dear. I believe your story. You don't have to revisit the whole incident again. We've been over it a hundred times." Lydia squeezed Jessie's hands, then commented quietly, "If only you hadn't tried to run away. And if only you hadn't held that gun on the deputies when they moved in to arrest you."

"I had to do those things," Jessie replied dully. "I had no choice."

"I know you were desperate, dear. Desperate because those men were taking you in for something you didn't do. No need to explain it all again to me. I'm on your side, remember?"

That much was true. The first day Jessie had been shut up in this dark, dingy, airless cell, Lydia Baylor had come, scowling like a bulldog, with a meager plate of food for the lady prisoner. Convinced of Jessie's guilt, she hadn't hesitated to let Jessie know that there wouldn't be an ounce of kindness coming her way, no matter how long it took the circuit judge to arrive in Sulfur Flats.

But over the course of the six weeks it had taken for Judge Charles Dougherty to arrive, the two women had gotten to know each other, and Lydia Baylor's antagonism toward Jessie had begun to wane. Of all things, because of a compliment Jessie had given the older woman over a finely embroidered napkin she'd wrapped some slices of bread in. In the weeks that followed, the curious sheriff's wife had encouraged Jessie to spill her story. Lydia Baylor had listened with her heart, pushing aside her indignation toward Jessie and redirecting it where it belonged: to the group of men who'd forced Jessie to do their dirty work against her will.

Lydia sniffed, squeezed Jessie's hands, then stepped away. "I've been thinking this through some, Jessie. It isn't right what's happened. There's got to be a way to turn the judge's decision around. There's *got* to be."

With glazed eyes, Jessie looked past Lydia into the gloom. "No, Lydia. The sentence has been handed down. I doubt even God Himself could reverse the decision, could change the mind of that cold-hearted, self-aggrandizing judge. I heard somebody say he's running for governor, that the decision to convict me, a woman, will make sensational headlines in every newspaper in the state of Nevada. His name will be a household word by tomorrow morning. All that's just what he needs to boost his popularity at the polls."

"The miserable goat," Lydia grumbled angrily. Slowly, she bent to pick up her parasol. She hesitated. When she straightened, Jessie saw a smile curving her lips instead of the frown that had been there just moments before.

"How can you smile?" Jessie blurted, hurt that the woman could be so insensitive.

"Because, dear. I've just thought of a way to help you."

"What? You have?"

She slapped the parasol into her palm, then outright laughed.

"*What*?" Jessie cried again. "How?"

"I'm going to pay a visit to that young new reporter, Myrna Griffin over at the *Gazette*. You leave things to me, dear. Meanwhile, muster up some more of that courage of yours and try not to worry."

But Jessie felt like swooning. She'd used up all her courage the night Sheriff Baylor had caught her trying to escape. And now her nightmares were coming true yet again, and she couldn't bear it this time. Not alone.

Mitch's image flooded her mind suddenly, sending a shaft of pain deep into her heart. Where was he? He'd sworn so many times that everything would turn out all right. Sworn that everything he'd done, he'd done to help her. That he'd be by her side when it came time to face the law. And fool that she was, oh, how she'd wanted to believe him. How her heart had held on when her mind reasoned otherwise. But again, he'd abandoned her. He wasn't at the trial to testify on her behalf, and he wasn't here now.

And yet…in spite of everything, loving him as she did, she ached with the need to have him near. Every time she lay alone on her cot, frightened nearly out of her mind from uncertainty, she longed for his touch, yearned for the comfort of his unshakable strength. The strength he infused in her whenever he folded her up in his arms and whispered soft words of encouragement and hope against her skin.

"Oh, my dear. Please try not to feel so low. I'll get Ned Tally to bring you some of the nice hot stew and muffins I brought over for my mister and the boys at the sheriff's office."

"I...I couldn't eat," Jessie said, nearly gagging at the thought of food.

"Nonsense. You've got to keep up your strength. Mind, you're eating for two now."

Lydia smiled kindly. A motherly smile that almost warmed Jessie's cold, numb heart. Almost. Stricken, Jessie stepped away from the iron bars, nearly stumbling when the backs of her knees bumped the cot behind her again. "How…how did you know?"

"Honey, I've had five babies of my own. Believe me, I'm familiar with the signs."

Jessie sagged onto the cot and covered her face with her hands. Terror gripped her, because before now she hadn't allowed herself to believe the truth: that Mitch's seed had taken root and that at this very moment their tiny babe was growing inside her. This was a disaster. How could she be having a child? In a week's time she was to be escorted to Yuma Prison, where she would begin serving her sentence.

Lydia, sounding distraught, said quickly, "I told you not to worry, Jessie. All hope is not lost. You just leave things to me."

Lydia gave Jessie a final reassuring smile, then marched to the thick oak door and rapped on it several times with the tip of her parasol. "Deputy Tally? Let me out of this dreadful hole this instant!"

In moments the heavy door swung open and Lydia Baylor swept into the sunlight. Jessie heard Tally's curt, "Yes ma'am," just before the door slammed shut once again.

Jessie looked up at the lone, barred window above the door, the only source of scant light and fresh air, and wished with her whole heart God had made her a bird instead of a woman.

☙ ☙ ☙

Four days later, two weary riders entered the town, heading straight for the sheriff's office.

"Dismount," Mitch ordered.

The battered and bruised Walter Conner slid off his horse, a difficult feat since his hands were bound behind his back. The outlaw staggered when he hit the ground, but Mitch was right beside him, an iron hand clamped to the outlaw's biceps.

"Inside," Mitch growled, giving Conner a shove.

"Wyden," Sheriff Baylor exclaimed as the two men pushed through the door. Quickly setting aside a sheaf of papers, the sheriff scraped his chair back and stood. "You made it back."

"This is Walt Conner, Sheriff," Mitch said, nudging Conner forward with the butt of his rifle.

Mitch studied the sheriff, noticing the lawman had suddenly gone a little pale.

There was a long silence. Long enough to make Mitch uncomfortable. Then: "You're too late," Baylor said, giving Mitch a pained look of regret. "The trial was held four days ago. Your wife was found guilty and has been sentenced to twenty years."

"No!" Mitch nearly dropped his rifle, his own face draining of color. Too late? He'd labored and pushed like a man possessed to get here on time, but it hadn't been enough.

"I'm sorry, Wyden. The evidence was just too convincing. The prosecution called an eye witness who identified Jessie. Jessie didn't help her case any, either. Unfortunately, she made things hard on herself during the ride back to Sulfur Flats."

"Where is she?" Mitch demanded woodenly.

"The jail house out back."

"And Curtis? Did he make it?"

"Locked up in Horace Winslow's smokehouse, awaiting trial. We thought it best to keep the two cousins separated." Baylor ran two fingers down his mustache. "That boy's meaner'n snake venom or he'd never have made it through."

Walt Conner spoke for the first time. Looking first at Mitch, then at the sheriff, he said through a stiff jaw, "Jessie Driscoll is the sweetest girl God ever put on this earth, Sheriff. She didn't do anything to deserve a sentence like that. Driscoll and I are the criminals. We deserve what we got coming, but Jessie? All she did was take orders. Driscoll forced her to obey whatever he dished out, whether she liked it or not."

"You admitting to your crimes?" the sheriff asked, clearly taken aback by the outlaw's candor.

"If it means helping Jess, well, then, I suppose I am. I got nothing to lose now." Conner looked down at his boots, then met the sheriff's eyes. "You could say Wyden here convinced me a while back that my running days are over."

The sheriff looked at Mitch. In an apologetic tone he said, "What's done is done, Wyden. I'm sorry things worked out the way they did. Truly sorry."

"Yeah, well, I'm sure you are," Mitch spat. "Where's the circuit judge? He still in town?"

"At the livery barn where he's been holding court."

"Come on then. Let's get going."

In front of Landry's Livery they found quite a commotion taking place. Men and women had formed a crowd outside the squat barn, bickering and snarling among themselves like a tangle of dogs and cats. Mitch glanced at the sheriff to find that he was just as taken aback by the considerable number of people gathered there as Mitch was.

"I say Judge Dougherty ought to reverse the decision," a plump woman dressed in dotted, yellow calico shouted above the din. "What he done to that girl is the only crime committed here!" At least twenty women cheered in agreement.

"The sentence has been handed down," a balding man with mutton-chop sideburns protested hotly. "Ain't nothing to do about it now. Why can't you women see reason? The judge made his decision, and it's final."

Another hostile uproar from the women reverberated through the crowd. One angry female voice rose above the rest. "Reason? Reason? Oh, we seen reason, all right, Mr. Chester Know-It-All Crandall. I say it's up to you men to go on in there and make that unfit, mean-spirited Judge Dougherty see reason. Because if you don't, all you men know what it's gonna be like around here for rest of your sorry days. You'll be getting more of the same as what you've been getting the last four days. Right ladies?"

Again, a mighty cheer went up, and the red-faced Chester Crandall retreated back into the crowd.

Mitch, clutching Conner, elbowed his way through the throng, Sheriff Baylor following close behind. A hush had come over the men suddenly, Mitch noticed. Then, the murmurs of "We gotta do something, Chester," and "I'll be hanged afore I'll stand for how my woman's been acting lately," filled the air. The majority of men must have agreed with the spokesperson, because before Mitch could push the livery door open all the way, the men of Sulfur Flats began pouring into the barn, stumbling over each other in their haste to get to the judge.

The rapid pounding of the gavel soon brought the crowd to a standstill. "What the devil is going on here?" the judge roared, outraged by this sudden intrusion. "Order in this courtroom!"

"It's about that Driscoll woman," Chester spoke up. During the hush that ensued, Chester politely removed his bowler hat and smoothed his oiled, neatly parted hair. "We come to ask you to reconsider your decision, Judge. About the Driscoll woman."

"What?" the judge snapped. "That's ridiculous. How dare you come barging in here, disrupting this trial in progress. Sheriff Baylor, disperse these people before I lose my temper and start handing out fines."

Chester Crandall stepped forward a couple of paces, the grim set of his features speaking volumes about his determination. Clearly, he was not going to be dismissed so easily. "We got a right to have our say, Judge. This here's our town, and we men aim to take it back from our womenfolk."

The gavel banged loudly several times to stifle the shouts and cheers of the men. "What do you mean, take it back from your womenfolk?" The judge sat back in his chair, holding up a staying hand to his bailiff, who had started toward Chester. A witness in the jury box, whose testimony had been rudely interrupted, cleared his throat, then ran a finger around the tight collar of his shirt. Another man, obviously a lawyer, took a seat behind the defendant's table, making himself comfortable, it seemed, for the duration.

"Explain!" the judge exploded, narrowing his straight, black eyebrows and training his glare on Chester.

"Well," Chester began, coloring now that he realized all eyes were upon him. He cleared his throat. "Our women ain't been...uh, ain't been wives to us since you sentenced Jessie Driscoll to twenty years in prison. They've been, uh, less than cooperative in every such way after sundown, if you get my meaning, Judge."

"That's right!" a female voice piped up in the back of the barn. "And it ain't gonna get any better if you men don't do right by the Driscoll girl!"

Again the gavel slammed down in rapid succession as high-pitched female cheers went up. During Chester's explanation, the judge looked as if he'd gone a little pale.

A small, diminutive blonde woman with a pencil and pad in her hand pushed through the crowd to stand off to the side of the judge's makeshift bench. She began scribbling on the pad, pausing only when the conversation paused.

"Who the devil are you?" the judge bellowed, slamming down the gavel for emphasis.

The woman looked up, but didn't flinch. "Myrna Griffin, Your Honor. Reporter for the Sulfur Flats *Gazette*."

The judge sobered immediately, Mitch observed. Judge Dougherty's mouth worked a few times, but it was as if he suddenly thought the better of what he was about to say. In the next instant his lips clamped shut and he turned his attention once again toward Chester Crandall.

Chester spoke up before the judge could find his voice. "We been talking among ourselves, Judge." He slanted a glance toward Myrna. "Do you know that the news of Jessie Driscoll's sentence has hit newspapers in every city in this state, and as far away east and west as Denver and Sacramento? People for miles is talking about how one Judge Charles Dougherty, candidate for governor of this here beautiful state of Nevada, went and sentenced an innocent girl to twenty years. It's my guess you ain't too popular in the polls about now, Judge. Seems to me you'd benefit some if you'd go and reverse that decision of yours."

Judge Dougherty scowled, but held his tongue while Chester continued. "Not only that, but they're crazy laughing at us menfolk here in Sulfur Flats, saying we're a bunch of frustrated roosters barred from the hen coop. They're laughing at us right good and proper, I tell you. Well, it's humiliating, is what it is. And I say it's all your fault." Another cheer went up, this time from the whole crowd.

The judge glared at Myrna. Through a sweet smile she said softly, "Telegraph, Your Honor. A downright miracle of these modern times, wouldn't you agree?"

Mitch held himself perfectly still, holding his breath. He hadn't figured on getting help for Jessie from anybody in what he'd supposed would be a hostile, prejudiced town. Yet, miraculously, it seemed as if the entire population of Sulfur Flats was on his side. The revelation staggered him.

Off to the side, Myrna Griffin continued scribbling furiously on her notepad.

Judge Dougherty took a brief moment to eye the crowd. Clearing his throat, he said, "The evidence against Miss Driscoll was irrefutable, ladies and gentlemen. Not that I must justify my decision, but there was absolutely no evidence in Miss Driscoll's favor to acquit her. No character witnesses, except for her dubious cousin, and no hard evidence, only hearsay that she had nothing to do with the robbery.

"The prosecution, on the other hand, had a solid eye witness who testified he'd seen Miss Driscoll at the scene of the crime. Further, the woman resisted arrest, and later on attempted to escape authorities. Under those circumstances, the decision to convict was appropriate."

Mitch sucked in a breath and glanced at Baylor. *Jessie had tried to escape?*

A flurry of skirts and murmurs wafted through the crowd as a buxom woman in a blue cotton day dress made her way to the front. "Excuse me, Your Honor," the woman called, stopping just short of the judge's bench. "I think you ought to know one more thing. Well, possibly two."

Baylor shot forward like a bullet, dragging Conner with him. "Lydia, what in blazes are you doing, woman?"

"I'm gonna try and talk some sense into His Honor here," she said, undaunted, turning her back on her husband. Boldly, she took another step forward and faced the judge, who eyed her with obvious distaste.

"First off," Lydia said, "You keep calling Jessie, Jessie Driscoll. You *are* aware that the girl's a married woman, aren't you Judge?"

Judge Dougherty coughed into his hand. "Seems as though I heard that once, but the woman wasn't wearing a wedding ring, and since there wasn't a man around claiming to be her husband, I didn't see any reason to—"

"I'm her husband," Mitch interrupted, quickly stepping forward.

"Well now, who in blazes are you?" the judge barked.

"I just told you, Your Honor. I'm Jessie Wyden's husband. Mitchell Wyden."

Lydia Baylor gave Mitch a thorough onceover, sizing him up and making no bones about it. Mitch flushed a little at the woman's bold scrutiny.

"See there, Judge?" Lydia said. "Jessie has a husband. I'm certain my own husband will confirm their married state, as he was the official who performed the ceremony. Won't you, Frank?" Lydia prompted sweetly, directing the question at her husband.

Bemused, Sheriff Baylor bobbed his head, his mouth agape.

"There now. So now that we've established that Jessie Driscoll is legally Mrs. Jessie Wyden, let me tell you one more thing about her. She's in the family way, Judge Dougherty."

A low roar rose from the crowd, but Lydia rushed on before the swelling voices had the chance to get rolling. "You've sentenced an innocent young mother and her child to twenty years in prison, sir. And I say innocent, because even if she did know that her cousin was about to rob the bank, which she didn't, there wouldn't have been anything at all she could have done about it, because to refuse to tend those horses would have meant a severe beating for her troubles.

"As it was, afterward Curtis Driscoll ordered his men to hold Jessie down while he viciously cut off all her hair. All along, against her will, that dear girl's been threatened, maneuvered, and coerced into doing her cousin's evil bidding. And four days ago, the one man who had the power to free her from her misery—*you*—added to it by condemning her and her unborn child to twenty years in some filthy prison. Now I wonder, Judge Dougherty, how's *that* going to read in the newspapers?" Lydia pointedly turned toward Myrna Griffin. "You getting all this, Myrna?"

"Yes, ma'am. I sure am!"

Mitch nearly fell over. *Jessie pregnant?* When he'd offered to Jessie the suggestion that she might be carrying his child all those weeks ago, he'd only said it to justify his marrying her. He'd never actually given much weight to the notion. And now....

Judge Dougherty drummed the bench with nervous fingers, his gaze sweeping the room. As if deep in thought, his pale gray eyes glazed over for a few moments. A hush fell over the livery barn, as if the crowd were collectively holding its breath.

The judge's stare came to rest on Mitch. "Well, that does change things a bit, I suppose," he said after clearing his throat. "Step forward if you please, Mr. Wyden."

Mitch glared back at the judge, his whole body tense. He had to get to Jessie. His wife was pregnant. He needed to hold her and be with her, give her his strength. With all his being he wanted to quit this place and run to her. Instead, as bidden, he stepped forward.

"I'm a reasonable and fair man," the judge began. "However, since there are no other character witnesses—"

"But there is," Mitch interrupted quickly. "I wasn't at the trial because I was busy apprehending Walter Conner, another Driscoll gang member. He'd be happy to testify on Jessie's behalf."

"Is this true, Baylor?" the judge asked the sheriff. In response, Baylor pushed Conner forward.

"It is, Judge. Conner already confirmed Jessie's story. He swears she had nothing to do with the robbery."

"That true, Conner?" the judge asked.

"Hand me that Bible, sir. I'll swear on it if you want. Jess never done anything but follow her cousin's orders. He made her do what she done. Shoot, every time we broke the law, she never even knew what we was about. I swear it, sir."

A long silence ensued while the judge did some pondering. Mitch studied the judge, sending up another rare silent prayer.

Conner had just given Judge Dougherty a face-saving way out of his own predicament. Now, if only Dougherty would take it.

"Mr. Wyden," the judge cleared his throat again. "Will you swear to keep your wife out of trouble if I reverse my sentence and set her free into your custody?" Judge Dougherty cast a quick look toward Myrna Griffin. She'd momentarily stopped scribbling.

Mitch felt woozy all of a sudden. The blood rushed like a tide through his veins then dropped to his feet. "Yes, Your Honor," he managed through a suddenly dry throat. "I swear."

The judge raised his gavel. "Write every syllable of my decision and Mr. Wyden's response down, Miss Griffin, won't you? And make sure you spell my name correctly. That's D-O-U-G-H-E-R-T-Y. I overturn my previous decision. Jessie Driscoll Wyden, from this moment on, is hereby acquitted." The gavel banged once. "Sheriff Baylor, see to Mrs. Wyden's immediate release."

Another cheer went up from the crowd. Mitch grabbed Baylor, who had a firm grip on Conner. "Come on, Sheriff!" he shouted above the commotion. "You heard the judge. I want Jessie out of that jail cell. Now!"

# Chapter Twenty Two

Another disturbance outside the jail house shot Jessie straight off the cot. Had she just heard Mitch's voice? Mercy, she must be dreaming again.

"Hurry it up, Tally. Put that blasted key in the lock!"

The solid oak door opened, and four men poured through the portal. Jessie stepped away from the bars, holding her breath. Dear heaven, were they coming for her so soon? It wasn't time yet. She had three more days.

And then, as if from a deep well, she heard Mitch's voice again.

"Jessie!"

Mitch was here, pushing the others aside, locking his fingers over the bars as if to bend them apart.

He looked angry. Angrier than she had ever seen him, turning on Baylor like a fiery-eyed wolf cornering a rabbit.

"Good God, man, what have you done to her, Baylor?"

And then he turned his anger on her.

At once the elation of seeing him faded, and apprehension shook her. Icy drops of fear trickled down her spine. Why had Mitch come? Was he here to help escort her to Yuma Prison? Oh now wouldn't that be a jolly ending to her nightmares! She took a defensive step backwards, even though her rational mind told her the move was futile.

As he watched her, Mitch's face turned to stone, his grip strangling the bars. His voice was a low growl when he said, "Unlock the cell door, Tally. Now."

What had she done to earn such raw contempt? Why was he so angry with her, looking at her as if she'd done something unforgivable? If anyone had a right to be angry, it was her!

Frantically, she looked toward Sheriff Baylor, her eyes pleading, her cold hands clenching into fists. In a far corner of her mind she recognized Walt Conner, but she had no time to form a clear image, what with her mind spinning with dread and confusion as it was.

She clung to the fact that Mitch had never physically hurt her—well, only once, but that was when he'd thought she was a boy—but that notion was small comfort. A greater fear haunted her now. "I don't understand, Sheriff. You told me I wouldn't be leaving for Yuma until Saturday. Have...have I somehow miscounted the days?"

The cell door sprang open, and Mitch roughly shouldered past Tally. "No," Mitch ground out, stopping just short of her. "You didn't miscount the days."

Jessie looked up, a vise crushing her heart as Mitch raised a hand toward her. She flinched, bracing herself against the grip that was surely going to drag her from the cell into the final nightmare.

Immediately, Mitch dropped his hand, bafflement replacing the granite creases of anger around his eyes and mouth. He shook his head as if to clear it, a curse exploding under his breath.

In a blink his features softened, and in a voice much as an experienced wrangler might use on a skittish filly, he said, "Jessie, why are you looking at me like that? I've come to take you out of here. You're free, sweetheart." Strong hands circled her shoulders, forcing her look at him, refusing to let her squirm. "Free."

Jessie swayed, the force of his words hitting her like a blow. This, this was the cruelest thing Mitch had ever done to her. Did he honestly think he could trick her into believing such a fairy tale? Did he hope that if he could get her to believe she'd been set free, she would meekly follow them to Yuma Prison, lulled into submission by false hope?

Her knees buckled.

"Jessie!"

Mitch swept her into his arms so fast she had no time to fall. She struggled against his solid chest only a moment before her strength failed her. And then she was out in the bright, warm sunlight, breathing cool, fresh air, feeling the delicious kiss of a summer breeze against her cheek, ruffling her hair.

He was holding her firmly, but with infinite gentleness, as if any moment she might break if he made the wrong move. "Breathe, honey," he whispered against her temple. "Breathe deep."

She became aware that he was climbing aboard the chestnut, taking her with him. He settled her in front of him in the saddle, his muscled arms circling her, holding her close and secure.

It was hard to remember anything much after that. Time passed in a blur. She'd closed her eyes and let her mind drift for only a moment, and then she became vaguely aware of voices and a flutter of activity. The next thing she knew, she was lying in a bed, in a small, sparsely furnished room.

She struggled to sit up. "Where am I?"

"Easy, Jessie." Mitch appeared out of nowhere and sat on the bed beside her. Carefully, he smoothed a tendril of hair behind her ear. "How do you feel?"

"I don't understand," she said desperately. "Where am I? Why am I ?"

"You're in a hotel room. Take it easy now. You've had a shock and need a little time to adjust." His cocky grin confused her. He touched her cheek, then cupped it in his palm. "How does it feel to be a free woman, brat?"

"Free woman?" She wilted back onto the bed. "Oh, don't, Mitch. Not again. I can't take any more of your lies."

She suffered a long silence where Mitch simply sat and stared at her, a muscle ticking beneath his iron-set jaw. "Don't what?" he asked at last through thinned lips. The grin had disappeared. "I haven't told you any lies." He shifted, resting his weight on one hand, leaning into her. "Somehow, I get the feeling there are things running through your mind I wouldn't like much if you told me about them. What is it? Why aren't you giggling like an idiot, or for that matter jumping up and down with the sheer joy of knowing all this sorry mess is over with? You're *free* Jessie. No more jails. No prison term. The judge reversed his decision less than an hour ago. Jessie?"

Tears came to her eyes, and this time she let them spill.

"Oh no, no, sweetheart. Don't cry. You're supposed to be laughing right now, remember?"

"But that's impossible," she replied, scrambling to her knees, swiping away the dampness on her cheeks. "Nobody believed my story. Not even when Curtis confirmed it. The judge said—"

"I know what the judge said, but I just told you that he changed his mind. Listen to me. You're free. Free as the wind."

"But how?"

Mitch told her. How the women, under Lydia Baylor's determined campaign, had schemed against their men for Jessie's freedom. How he'd brought Walt Conner to the courtroom to testify, giving Judge Dougherty substantial reason to acquit her, and in the process, polish up his tarnished name and reputation.

Yet, despite her initial elation, Jessie remained silent, her mind in turmoil. Finally, she said, "Then the judge didn't acquit me because he was convinced of my innocence, but because Lydia pointed out to him that he, a man running for governor, wouldn't fare very well in the newspapers if he stuck with his decision. Have I got that right?"

She rubbed her eyes tiredly.

"What difference does it make how it all came about, Jessie? The end result is that you've been acquitted."

In barely a whisper she said, "You just don't understand, do you Mitch? Can't you see it makes all the difference in the world?"

Mitch eyed her narrowly, then gave her an indulgent half-smile. "You're all in. So worn out, you're not thinking straight. Come on. Lie back and close your eyes. Rest. A boy will be up in a moment with a tub and hot water. Once you've bathed the stink of that stale jail cell off you and changed out of those sour clothes you'll feel more like yourself."

☙ ☙ ☙

He'd finally gotten her to lie back and rest. Reluctantly, she'd quieted and closed her eyes. Mitch covered her lightly with the thin coverlet folded at the foot of the bed and stood, looking down at her, his heart wrung dry.

*After all he'd done for her*, he thought grimly, *clear as day, she still didn't trust him.* Bringing Conner in like he had had ultimately gotten her the acquittal, but had she thanked him for it? Not a chance. Instead, she'd accused him of lying to her about her freedom and then acted disappointed because the acquittal hadn't come about the way she thought it should have.

He thought back on another one of her featherbrained notions. What the devil had she been thinking when she'd first seen him at the jail house? That he'd only come as one of the guards to escort her to prison? Most likely. Blast her beautiful hide, she was the most stubborn, exasperating woman he'd ever known.

A light rap at the door wrenched him from his musings. Turning, he opened the door with a finger across his lips. "My wife is asleep," he whispered to the young man carrying two buckets of steaming water. A second boy of about twelve or thirteen stood behind him with the tin tub and another bucket of water, along with a small package and several linen towels tucked under each arm.

The boys entered the room and hastily prepared the bath, glancing Jessie's way and whispering when they thought Mitch wasn't watching. Mitch let it go, though their fascination for the notorious Jessie Driscoll raised his hackles.

When they finished, the second boy turned to Mitch. "I went to Greer's Apothecary like you asked, sir," he whispered. "Here are the items you told me to get."

Mitch took the package, then fished in his pocket for coins, pulling up a quarter apiece. "You did just fine," he told both boys. "Come back at four o'clock this afternoon with a fresh tub and water. You can clear all this other away then. In the meantime, my wife and I don't want to be disturbed."

Dismissing the boys, Mitch eased down beside Jessie, reluctant to awaken her. Lightly touching her shoulder, he whispered, "Jessie, honey, your bath is ready."

She woke with a start, her body alert, her eyes ablaze and seeking—like she'd been used to sleeping lightly and waking up to trouble. Mitch's heart twisted in his chest. There was so much he wanted to ask her. So much he needed to know about the time they'd spent apart.

"Easy, Jessie. It's only me. Your bath's ready," he said again.

"A bath?" She rubbed her eyes and sat up.

"Come on," he said, "I'll help you undress."

She pulled away from him, taut as the bark on a tree. "I can undress myself. Go away."

"Not a chance. I'm not going anywhere. You're so weak with exhaustion you'd never make it to the tub and back."

She gave him a stubborn look, and a flash of irritation shot through him. "I'm your husband, Jessie. I'm going to help you bathe whether you like it or not. Come here."

He could see she wanted to resist him, give him plenty of trouble, but she was simply too tuckered out to make the effort. Gently, he reached for her, and with hands that had suddenly become unsteady, began unbuttoning the front of her blouse. By the looks of her, baths had been nonexistent at the jail house.

It was hard, the most difficult thing he'd ever done, but he managed to keep his touch impersonal as he peeled off her filthy clothes, layer by grimy layer. Studying the rank condition of her garments, just thinking about what she'd suffered the last six weeks, he decided he had plenty to settle with Baylor.

Groaning softly as he removed the soiled camisole, with tremendous effort he managed to restrain himself from giving in to desire, telling himself there would be plenty of time for that later.

When he'd tossed her dirty clothes into a heap in the corner of the room, he carefully lifted her into his arms and eased her into the steamy tub.

As her body sank into the warm, soothing water, she moaned with pleasure, giving him a sweet jolt of satisfaction. *Sometimes a man* had *to be high-handed with his woman*, he thought. A smile curled his lips as he took up a cloth and a cake of soap.

She reached out and started to speak, most likely to protest again, to tell him she could wash herself, but Mitch cut her off with a razor-sharp look. "You say one more word, and I won't be responsible for what happens next. Now lie back and relax."

She locked eyes with him, but only for a brief moment. "All right," she sighed, "but only because it feels so wonderful. Mercy sakes alive, Mitch, it's been so long...."

Letting out a long breath, she sank back into the water and rested her head on the tub's rim.

"Good girl."

He soaped her thoroughly, enjoying the feel of the slippery cloth sliding over the delicate dips and planes of her body. He would have lingered, ached to linger, but Jessie was already slipping back into sleep.

Quickly, ignoring her soft moan, he sat her up and washed her hair, twice, noting how much the thick, nut-brown curls had grown. The strands hung past her ears now, nearly reaching the delicate angle of her jaw. He could only imagine the glory it would be when it tumbled like a dark, reckless waterfall to the small of her trim back.

Using a bucket of warm clear water, he stood her up and rinsed her.

"Okay, out you come. That's it, honey. Let me dry you off."

The voluminous swath of linen engulfed her. Not for the first time did he realize she'd lost weight, more weight than she could afford to lose. She felt smaller and more fragile than ever beneath his hands as he patted the cloth over her frail form. Lifting her, he carried her to the bed, pulled back the covers, and laid her down on the cool, fresh sheets.

"Feels so good," she murmured quietly as her head sank into the soft pillow.

"I know, Jess. It's been a long time since you've had the luxury of sleeping in a soft bed."

He wanted to kiss her then, wanted to take her and crush her to him and never let go. But he sensed an uneasiness in her, a reluctance toward him that had him worried. She meant more to him than money, horses, the ranch in Crystal Springs, or anything else in the world. Yet somehow she still didn't understand that, wouldn't believe that he'd do anything in his power to make her happy.

The truth was, he reminded himself again, she didn't trust him. Putting himself in Jessie's shoes, he supposed she thought she had good reasons for that, but because he knew the truth, her distrust annoyed him. She'd gotten it into that stubborn brain of hers that he'd betrayed her for the reward money and had abandoned her when she'd needed him most. He also sensed that she thought he'd deliberately waited until after the trial to show up with Walt Conner.

The darkness he'd seen in her eyes when he'd first come to fetch her at the jail house had rocked him, too—until he finally figured things out. Jessie believed that he'd double crossed her. Worse, she'd assumed he'd placed himself as one of the escort guards assigned to transport her to Yuma Prison.

And that hurt.

Well, now nothing stood in his way to keep from setting things straight with her. If it took him days, months even, he'd work to gain her trust, work to make her see how wrong she'd been.

He crossed to the wash stand by the window and poured a glass of water from the porcelain pitcher. Unwrapping the small package the boy had brought from Greer's Apothecary, he uncorked the fat brown bottle of laudanum and shook several drops into the glass. He wanted her to sleep long and hard. No nightmares of hangmen and prisons. No haunting dreams of betrayal or reward money. Everything he was about to do from here on out, he would do strictly for the happiness of his woman, his heart.

He lifted her shoulders and made her sip. "That's it, Jessie. Drink it down. Are you thirsty?"

She nodded. "I guess I was," she said after draining the glass. Satisfied, Mitch rose, set the glass back down on the washstand, picked up a glass jar, and returned to the bed.

"Mitch?" Through half-closed lids, she asked, her voice husky and mellow as fine, aged whiskey, "What's that?"

"A pot of magic," he said, grinning slightly, opening the lid on the blue vial he held in his hands.

"Magic?"

"Come on, let's get you turned over."

Alarm entered her eyes, verging, he saw, on the raw edge of panic as he knelt on the mattress beside her.

"Mitch, no."

His heartbeat quickened. She'd fought him the last time he'd crawled into her bedroll and tried to lay beside her, out there in the wilderness, even though he'd only wanted to sleep. "I won't," he said, in what he hoped was a calm, reassuring tone. "I don't have anything of the sort in mind right now. I swear, Jessie. All I want to do is help you get to sleep." He gestured with the jar. "With this."

"What are you going to do?"

"I told you. I'm going to help you get to sleep. That's all. Nothing else, I promise."

A little of the wariness left her eyes. "You promise?"

The depth of her mistrust bothered him more than he could say. "I just did. Now quit fretting. Any time you want me to stop, you just say the word and I will."

When he'd helped her to roll comfortably onto her stomach, he dipped his fingers into the fragrant oil inside the jar. Smoothing his oiled hands over the taut muscles of her back and shoulders, for the first time in his life he cursed the near bone-deep calluses on his hands.

"Oh my, that smells nice. Like roses," she sighed.

Moving his fingers along the length of the tight little knobs of her spine, then spreading his palms outward across her back, he asked, "Are you feeling any better now, sweetheart?"

"Mmm. Much."

The sound of her breathing, the whisper of her husky voice, the rose-petal scent of the oil, the feel of her warm flesh beneath his palms—all of it gave him pleasure that took his breath away. Tenderness toward her welled up inside him as her body went limp and he heard her soft sigh.

He wanted her, and the overwhelming need to possess her was so strong he began to doubt he could keep his promise. To distract himself, he dipped his fingers into the pot of oil a second time.

"Feels like heaven," she said as he pressed the heels of his hands into her taut muscles, working, pressing, kneading the tension out. Carefully, but firmly, he worked his way down her back, her slim backside, down her long, willowy flanks. Not able to resist, he kissed the backs of her knees, and then moved on to the tender soles of her dainty feet. His lips lingered on the jagged scar on the ball of her left foot.

When he began to kiss her toes, one by one, Jessie's whole body stiffened, which, he sighed heavily, was defeating his purpose. He forced himself to lift his head.

"Relax," he coaxed in as soothing a voice as he could muster. *Still holding back on me, are you, brat?*

But soon she was drifting off to sleep on him. He suppressed a smile. He'd forgotten how powerfully laudanum affected her.

The scent of the slippery oil, the feel of her incredibly soft curves beneath his strong fingers, moved him beyond words. He wanted her so much he hurt. *Soon*, he promised himself. When she trusted him again, understood his reasons for leaving her, for keeping the reward money. *Soon*, he vowed more firmly. The moment she once again confessed that she loved him, then he would make love to her, fill her, make her his all over again in the most tender, sweetest ways he knew how.

And then he had another pleasant thought. Their child rested inside the cradle of her womb, he marveled, unable to quite believe the miracle. "Beautiful Jessie," he groaned.

The massage, and no doubt the laudanum, had melted her bones, had relaxed her into a deep sleep. Briefly he worried. Maybe it had been a mistake to give her the laudanum. But he shook those thoughts away. What was done was done, and he couldn't undo it. Nor did he want to. Because she slept now, safe under his watch again with all her hurts and worries buried in the land of pleasant dreams. That's all that mattered to him now.

"That's it, sweetheart, sleep," he said, easing off the bed and blotting his hands with a towel. As he tucked the sheets around her shoulders, she turned onto her side and curled up like a kitten. Lightly, he fingered her hair aside and stroked her creamy cheek, lingering in the sweet, shadowed hollow at the nape of her neck.

The sound of her quiet, even breathing eased him.

Roses. It felt as if he were drowning in them. The fresh, clean scent of roses would remind him of Jessie all the rest of his days.

# Chapter Twenty Three

He hated to leave her, but he had things to do. Important things. Jessie would sleep like a pearl nestled in an oyster shell for the next few hours. Which gave him plenty of time to do what he had to do and return before she woke up.

After scrubbing his hands to remove the rose fragrance clinging to his skin, he gave Jessie one last glance, took up his rifle, and left, locking the door behind him.

"I want my money, Baylor," he said to the startled sheriff ten minutes later, foregoing pleasantries and cutting to the quick. "Then we're gonna have a long talk, and after that I want to see Driscoll."

An hour after an illuminating talk with Baylor that left the man sorry he'd ever heard the name Jessie Wyden, followed by a highly satisfying, slightly violent session with Jessie's cousin, Mitch flexed his bruised knuckles, made sure the chestnut was safe in capable hands at Landry's Livery, then headed for the mercantile. By three forty-five he was back in the hotel room, studying the pleasant form of his sleeping wife, who hadn't moved a hair's breadth in all the time he'd been gone.

Mitch set down his rifle, tossed Jessie's saddlebags and several weighty parcels into a chair, and stretched. Exhausted, he yawned, anticipating his own hot bath.

As ordered, at precisely four o'clock, the two boys appeared at the door, carrying a tub, towels, and steaming buckets. They moved into the room quietly, keeping their voices at a whisper. Just as the boys were about to leave again, burdened with Jessie's tub and soiled linens, Mitch gathered up her filthy clothing. "Take these out back and burn them," he ordered brusquely.

The older boy, obviously the leader, cast him a look. His wide-eyed gaze slid to the bed, then quickly cut back to Mitch. "You want 'em burned, sir?"

"Right away won't be soon enough. Here," Mitch said, tossing a silver dollar into one of the empty buckets dangling from a skinny arm. "Can you handle it?"

"You got it, mister." The kid whooped in a stage whisper, grinning as if he'd just won the lottery.

After locking the door behind them, Mitch stripped, then eased into the tub. He could almost hear his tired muscles sigh as the heat of the water penetrated and soothed his tension away. He smiled, glancing over at Jessie. The only thing that would make things better right now, he mused, was if he could stretch out full length in this too-short, too narrow-tub with Jessie beside him soothing his aches away.

He lit a cheroot and allowed himself a half hour of pure luxury before he took up the cloth and soap. When he'd washed every stain of trail grime and sweat from his body, he reluctantly stood, rinsed, and toweled off. Then he shaved.

At the edge of the bed, naked, he hesitated. Then he shrugged. It was anybody's guess what Jessie's mood would be like when she woke up anyway. Might as well be in for the double eagle as in for a penny. He slipped under the sheets and gathered her close. Pressing his nose into her hair and breathing deeply, he tucked her silky head under his chin and wrapped his arms tightly around her shoulders.

She made a long, low sound in her throat, not unlike a purr. Mitch smiled, tenderly kissed the top of her head, and promptly fell asleep.

☙ ☙ ☙

Consciousness came slowly. For the first time in weeks Jessie hadn't had the nightmares...and she felt warm. Blissfully warm.

A feather tickled her nose. Brushing the offended skin with her finger, she twitched and nearly sneezed. Then she froze. Fully awake now, she realized she was lying naked on top of Mitch, who was also naked, and the feather she felt tickling her nose was not a feather at all, but Mitch's abundant chest hair.

"Easy, sweetheart," he drawled, keeping her locked in his arms. He pressed her head back down and stroked her hair. "You're in a hotel room, remember? With your husband." He seemed to add that last bit with relish. "How do you feel?"

"Let me up," Jessie said, struggling to rise.

"After you tell me how you're feeling."

"Just dandy," she snapped. He surprised her by releasing his hold and allowing her to sit up. "Whoa," she said, reeling, pressing her fingers to her temples. "I guess I did that a little too fast."

She made a move to leave the bed, but he snagged her wrist. "Don't get up yet. It's barely sunup. Stay here in my arms where it's warm."

He wanted her. She could see the familiar glow in his eyes, hear desire in his voice. Unbidden, her own body stirred, but she firmly tamped the fires as the sequence of yesterday's events came rushing back. *Not again,* she vowed. Why did she always fall so effortlessly under his spell?

"Come on, brat," Mitch coaxed through a grin. He squeezed her wrist tighter and tugged, tipping her off balance.

At once a wave of nausea gripped her. Groaning, she fell like a sack of stones against his solid chest. "Don't move," she pleaded. "If you have an ounce of kindness in you, Mitch, *don't move*."

Alarmed, Mitch sat up, taking her with him, ignoring her warning. "Jessie, what is it? What's wrong?"

Fighting to ward off the heaves, she kept the punch to his ribs she longed to give him to herself. "It's the baby. She doesn't like me much. She hates me, in fact. This is her way of telling me so." Her stomach jolted, but since there was nothing in it, nothing came up. "Oh mercy."

"What can I do?" He sounded desperate, at a total loss, his fingers gently rubbing the nape of her neck.

"Don't move."

This time he did as she asked. When her stomach settled somewhat, she took several deep, calming breaths, thankful the worst seemed to be over. "Okay, you can move now. Let me go."

He drew her against him instead. "Do you get like this often?" She heard a dusky desperation in his voice she'd never heard before, as if he were having trouble forming his words. She sensed his fear for her and didn't want to be moved by it. Refused to be moved by it.

"It's none of your concern."

"None of my.... Blast it, Jessie, what kind of hare-brained remark is that? Of course it's my concern. Are you forgetting it's my child you're carrying?"

"You don't seem an inch surprised, Mitch. How long have you known?" He went still, but answered quickly enough, "The whole town knows. I heard when they heard. Lydia Baylor broadcast the news in the courtroom yesterday, one of the more effective bits of information that eventually persuaded the judge to reverse his decision."

Her tongue felt thick. "I see."

"You still upset about the way your acquittal came about?" She heard the irritation in his voice and didn't much care for it.

She stayed quiet a long time. His hand was back in her hair, his fingers absently combing the strands. Aware of the tension there, she stayed put, though what she really wanted to do was pry one of the bedposts loose and clobber him.

"Jessie, talk to me. It's time we pull everything out of the sack and lay it on the table. What's eating at you so bad? It's clear you've still got it in that muddled brain of yours that I'm the enemy."

That was the last straw. Catapulting out of his arms before he could stop her, she scrambled to her knees and practically screeched, "Muddled? *Muddled?* You're the dimwitted dolt."

The sheets fell from her torso, baring her heaving breasts, but she was too infuriated to care. Clenching two wads of sheet in her fists, wishing she were strangling him instead, she let him have it with all she was worth. "You want everything out on the table?"

"Jessie, you're getting upset. That can't be good for the—"

"Well, all right then. You've got it, Mitch. First of all, that stupid, pompous, self-righteous judge acquitted me for all the wrong reasons. Not because he was convinced I was innocent, but because my acquittal would save his sorry backside at the polls."

"I don't see why—"

"Shut up. Don't you dare say another word until I'm finished. I'm going to have my say, Mitch.

"Lydia Baylor and I have done a lot of talking the last few weeks. Do you know that last year a woman of good standing, right here in this town, shot and crippled her best friend's husband while he was in a rage and beating his wife to death? Do you know what that brave, dear, courageous woman got for her troubles? Life in prison. Do you know what that lowdown, drunken wife beater got? He got sympathy, and the judge let him go scot-free. Is that justice? *Is it?*

"Lydia says that if an accused woman appears to be emotionless in court, she's considered cold and indifferent, hard-hearted and guilty for certain. If she shows too much emotion, she's labeled unstable and flighty, not quite right in her mind. The judge and jury—all men, mind you—then condemn her to the gallows or to prison for life, and off she goes with not another thought tossed her way. Oh, don't you see? I never had a chance. And to be freed for the sake of Judge Dougherty's bid for the governorship...well, you'd better believe I'm beyond furious about it."

"Just you wait a minute, brat" Mitch exploded. "I traveled almost all the way to Sacramento, found Conner, and hauled him all the way back here to testify for you. When it came right down to it, his testimony on your behalf is what finally swayed the judge. That's right, Jessie. I raced toward Sacramento, nearly killing myself and the chestnut to find Conner in time, and you act like that doesn't count for anything."

"Speaking of Conner, where *did* you find him, anyway?"

"Well, thank you Jessie. Nice to know you're finally interested. In Reno. In a saloon not fifty miles from where I left you, a bartender tipped me off that a man fitting Conner's description told him he was headed for Reno. To make a long story short, Conner planned to catch a train ride to San Francisco on the Central Pacific. Of course, when I found him he denied his identity, but after the brawl, which I won, I found a lock of brown hair on him tied with a bit of yellow ribbon. I had no doubts after that."

Jessie mulled over the entire account. What stuck in her mind most, though, was that Mitch had ridden all the way to Reno. No wonder he'd been gone so long.

Fiercely holding onto her anger, she argued defensively, "You left me, no, you *abandoned* me without saying so much as one word of farewell, though why I should be so surprised you'd turn out to be any different from all the other men I've ever known is beyond me. Mercy, Mitch, you abandoned me to those...those horrible, randy, ruthless *lawmen*."

Morning light streamed through the room's one window now, illuminating his suddenly bloodless face. "Did Simms try anything after I left?"

"Of course he did, you idiot. After I attempted an escape, Baylor staked me to the ground like a mongrel dog every night." She shuddered, remembering her terror, her helplessness, each time Sheriff Baylor drove the stake into the ground and fastened the wrist irons to it. "Did you think a lowdown, slimy snake like Simms wouldn't hesitate to take advantage of the situation?"

"I'll kill him," Mitch growled, flipping aside the bedclothes, the fires of hell flaming in his eyes.

"Oh, it's a fine thing to be so concerned about it now. You should have known before you deserted me like a rabbit to the wolves that Simms would try something as soon as you weren't around." She sighed deeply, wearily. "You're too late anyway. Simms didn't get very far before Sheriff Baylor nearly beat him senseless for pawing me. Simms wasn't much good for anything after that."

Mitch collapsed against the pillows. "I still owe him," he grumbled. "Plenty. Jessie, listen to me. You weren't in the mood to believe a single thing I had to say to you that morning I left. Remember? You thought I was going after Conner strictly for the reward money. Didn't you give even a moment's thought to the fact that we needed him to testify on your behalf at the trial? That that's why I was so anxious to find him?"

"Oh, yes, the reward money," Jessie spat, strangling the sheets, seeing red. "I would guess you ought to have redeemed every penny of your losses by now. Am I right?"

Angrily, Mitch sat up, hauled in a long breath, then blew it out like a locomotive letting off steam. "And then some, if you must know. Besides the bounty, Baylor turned over the five hundred Driscoll and Conner got when they sold eight of the fifteen mustangs to some rancher. And don't start flaying me with those killing looks again. I have every right to keep that cash."

She let out a sharp, anguished cry.

"Jessie, when are you going to understand that everything I did, I did for you? For us? Keeping that money means I can finally buy us the ranch in Crystal Springs. I'll even have enough cash left over to buy a small herd of breeding stock to get us started. Honey, listen. You and I have a baby coming. That money is what's going to buy us and our new family a fine future."

Jessie sat back on her heels, beyond frustrated by Mitch's lack of insight toward her feelings. The muscles in her arms began to throb, she still gripped the sheets so tightly.

"Those are your dreams," she said quietly. "And what about my dreams, Mitch?"

"What's that supposed to mean?"

"Did it ever enter your head, when you gave me no choice but to marry you that day, or when you were filling me with your—your *issue* that night, that I might have a few dreams of my own?"

He looked baffled, like a man gut-punched who hadn't seen it coming. "Such as? I told you the reasons I had Baylor marry us. It was for your own good. You said yourself you loved me, so what the devil is the problem? It was the only thing I could think of to do at the time to keep you out of trouble. Or, wait a minute. Is it the ceremony that's still got you so riled? I told you I'd give you a second wedding. One you can plan for any way you want. Did you forget about that?"

She ignored those last remarks. "Such as," she drew out through gritted teeth, "I've always dreamed of going to San Francisco. You knew that. I want to wade in the cold Pacific, hear the ocean roar, feel the damp fog on my cheeks, explore the streets of an exciting big city. I—"

"All right. I can understand that. Someday I'll take you there. Though Frisco's a rough town, Jessie. I doubt you'll believe me, but even if you never got there, you wouldn't be missing all that much."

"Someday," she repeated the word slowly, a sadness bordering on despair gripping her. That's what Uncle Thaddeus always said whenever Jesse asked for something really important and he wanted to put her off. Someday. An empty promise. Mitch may as well have said never.

She looked straight at him, wanting to hurt him, cut him in two for being so full of himself. For attempting to trample her dreams and ruin her future. Just because they weren't *his* fantasies, *his* longings, he apparently didn't think them worth any more than a pile of kindling sticks.

She shook her head. "Mitch, you just don't understand."

"Well, it sure isn't because I'm not trying."

"All right, then I'll try and explain things a little more plainly. Because of your high-handed ways, I'm now a married woman, to a man who's never once told me he loved me. And infinitely worse, this man who doesn't love me—you—has made me pregnant. So now that I've been thrown into a life I didn't choose, I have nothing left to hope for. Poof. There went Jessie Driscoll's dreams, just like that. You've dashed them all. Aren't you proud of your manly self?"

Mitch looked as if he were going to explode. Before he could make a move or say a word to interrupt her, she hurried on, refusing to let him intimidate her.

"When I left Missouri, I dreamed of somehow breaking away from Curtis and his iron-fisted ways. I dared to dream about one day truly finding happiness. In San Francisco. I dreamed of finding a good, kind, gentle man to love there. Somebody who'd vow to love and cherish me beyond his own life. A man who would love me for my thoughts as well as for my abilities, who'd never laugh at my dreams or think them foolish. Somebody who would swear to never abandon me, who—"

"Jessie stop it. Just stop!" This time Mitch did vault off the bed, in one, sure, fluid bound. He stalked to a pile of clothes on the floor, fingered through the pockets of his buckskin vest and pulled out a cheroot. When he got it lit, he blew out two long streams of gray smoke through his nose. Chest heaving, he stared at her, his gaze cold and forbidding.

*Mercy, but he was a dangerous looking man*, Jessie thought as she gathered the sheets and finally, nervously, covered her breasts. A magnificent, perfectly formed man. Oddly, though, she wasn't frightened...just rattled in a thrilling sort of way.

He stood there like some dark beast, blowing twin billows of smoke through his nostrils. Like the fire-breathing dragon ready to devour a little girl she'd once read about in a children's story. She could only hold her breath and boldly meet his smoldering stare.

His thick upper arm muscles bunched solidly, seeming to double in size with the almost electric tension she sensed running through them. The span of his broad, hairy chest, heaving with suppressed fury, drew her fascinated gaze and sent a delicious shiver down her spine.

Her breath hitched as her gaze traveled the magnificent length and breadth of him, marveling for the millionth time at how perfectly made he was. She quickly looked away, before her mounting desire could rule her foolish head.

She coughed behind her hand. "Could...could you please not smoke? The smell makes me queasy."

Mitch raised the glowing tip in front of his eyes and stared at it a long time. Then, with one vicious toss, he arched the burning cheroot into a brass spittoon in the corner, hitting it dead center. Snatching up one of the brown parcels on the chair, he ripped it open, shook out the new clothes and began to dress.

Jessie watched him silently, the first ripples of apprehension coursing through her. When he was tugging on his boots, she gathered enough gumption to ask, "Are...are you going somewhere?"

Fully dressed now in a pair of Levi jeans and a fresh, light-blue cotton shirt, he stood. "Count on it." Gathering up the remaining parcels, he dumped them on the bed in front of her. "Here. While you were sleeping yesterday I bought you a few things."

Jessie searched the room for her own clothes. The ones she'd shed before taking a bath. Mitch laughed, a bitter, and humorless effort. "You won't find them. I had them burned. Everything but the Stetson. I know how partial you are to it."

She sucked in her breath.

"Yeah, brat. Another one of my high-handed tricks. I see now I should have asked your permission first, even if those rags you were dressed in were frayed to near tatters and smelled like a drainage ditch. My apologies." He tugged on his hat, snatched up his rifle, and stalked to the door.

"When will you be back?" she asked quickly as he threw the latch and twisted the knob. He turned to face her, his jaw firmly set.

"Get dressed and go downstairs. There's a restaurant here in the hotel. Get something to eat. I don't want my son undernourished."

"Mitch?" Thrown off balance, she bit her lip and stared at the bedclothes. "Um, that would be fine and dandy, but I...I don't have any money. I won't be able to pay for the meal."

He reached into his pocket, pulled up two silver dollars and tossed them at her. They plopped near her knees on the sheets before he said, "Reward money does have its uses, doesn't it, Jessie? Oh, but if you have any qualms about spending those, just tell whoever's in charge to put your breakfast on my bill."

She wanted to throw them back at him. She really did, but she was starving all of a sudden. It seemed like ages since she'd last eaten. The nausea she'd felt earlier had disappeared. Unconsciously moving her hand over her tummy, she decided to swallow her pride. Just this once. Mitch was right, their baby needed nourishment.

"I'm going to have a girl, you know." She picked up the two silver dollars and clasped them in her palm. "I'm only taking these for her."

"Her?" Mitch scoffed.

"That's right. Her."

"Well, time will tell, won't it?"

The moment the door slammed shut, Jessie scrambled from the bed. Those packages were calling to her like candy to a child. With eager fingers, she tore into the first parcel, then stood back and nearly cried. Inside she found a lovely day dress of teal blue with a high, ruffled lace collar dyed to match. The sleeves were puffed on top, then tapered to the wrists, edged at the cuffs with matching lace trim. She fairly shook with excitement. Teal. Her very favorite color. How had Mitch known?

In the next package she found three sets of drawers, the frilly, expensive kind she'd always dreamed of owning, trimmed with white lace and tiny yellow satin bows. Three matching camisoles, two chemises, two petticoats, and several pairs of stockings accompanied the drawers.

Another package contained a yellow muslin dress with a full, flowing skirt, nipped tightly at the waist and trimmed around the shoulder seams and heart-shaped bodice with grass-green velvet piping. Also included in this package was a reticule and a pair of smart, black leather boots, accompanied by a sturdy button hook.

Racing to the small swivel mirror atop the wash stand, she held the dresses up, one after the other, straining to get a full view of both, but the mirror was too small. Frustrated, she hurried back to the bed.

Quaking with excitement, she opened the fourth and final package. Smaller than the rest, she couldn't help but wonder whatever could be inside. And then she did cry.

Two exquisite hair combs, shaped like sea shells tumbled into her hands. Sea shells. Just like the ones she'd dreamed about finding along a sun-drenched San Francisco beach someday. Like the ones she'd mentioned to Mitch back at the cabin when he'd described the roar of the ocean.

Both combs were small and exactly alike. Just the right size to allow her to gather her hair off her face at the temples and let the curls cascade behind her ears. The style would give the illusion of much longer tresses, and give her a far neater appearance.

Oh, bless Mitch. Bless him for thinking of her like this. Oh mercy. *Mitch.*

☙ ☙ ☙

Jessie chose the yellow muslin because the teal was simply too beautiful to wear so soon. Having never owned anything quite so lovely, she wanted to savor the heady anticipation of wearing it as long as she could. She'd washed her face and cleaned her teeth in record time. Using the silver brush, she secured her curls above her ears in the lovely combs, then quickly donned her new underthings and the yellow dress. After buttoning up her new boots, she gathered the reticule and two silver dollars, then left the room. Following her nose, she found the restaurant with no trouble at all.

"Jessie?" Her step faltered. She could have sworn she'd heard someone call her name.

"Over here, dear!"

Lydia Baylor and another woman Jessie had never seen before were seated at a table by a bright window beyond whose glass a flowerbox of red and white geraniums bloomed. Lydia rose halfway out of her seat and called again. Quickly, Jessie made her way over to the two ladies, trying hard to ignore the heads turning her way.

"Oh how nice," Lydia commented, holding out a plump hand in greeting. "Don't you look pretty, dear. Just like a spring daffodil, all fresh and shining new. Amazing what a bath and a fresh frock will do for a woman's sagging spirits, isn't it?

Coreen, this is Jessie Wyden. I simply couldn't wait for you two to meet. Jessie, this is Coreen Dougherty. Judge Dougherty's wife. Coreen was just leaving, so if you'd arrived a minute later, you'd have missed each other."

Coreen, a delicate woman dressed impeccably in a multi-colored, striped satin dress and a pert matching hat whose wispy veil slanted across her dark brow, extended a dainty hand. "It's a pleasure, Mrs. Wyden." The woman's grip was sure, friendly, accepting.

Jessie calculated the pretty Coreen Dougherty to be at least ten, if not fifteen years younger than her husband. "Ma'am," Jessie replied, somewhat abashed.

"Come. Sit," Lydia prompted.

Coreen lifted a timepiece suspended by a gold chain around her neck. "Oh dear, look at the time. I hate to be rude, but I really must be going. The judge has a full schedule today." She slanted an uneasy glance at Jessie. Dropping the watch, she turned to Lydia. "I'd love to stay and chat, but I really mustn't keep Charles waiting. He needs me to run an errand for him before the first session this morning." Her amber gaze slid to Jessie again, this time her expression clear and bright. "I'm thrilled things worked out so well for you, Mrs. Wyden. I surely am. We ladies made a fine statement, didn't we? Maybe someday we can band together nationwide and force the men to give us the vote."

Coreen's silvery little laugh reminded Jessie of cheery sleigh bells. The woman didn't seem to think her statement had been preposterous in the least.

Jessie nodded. "Maybe," she replied through a smile. She discovered she admired Coreen Dougherty's spunk very much.

"Perhaps we can all meet tomorrow for luncheon," Coreen said.

"I'm free tomorrow," Lydia replied. "Here, around noon?"

"Perfect. Will you be up to it, Mrs. Wyden?"

"It's Jessie, please. And that sounds very nice, though I'm not sure what my plans are yet for tomorrow." An image of an angry Mitch slamming the hotel room door flashed through her mind. Who but God knew what tomorrow would hold?

"Well, think about it anyway," Coreen urged.

"I'll do that," she promised.

A boy came to take Jessie's order, and Coreen Dougherty took her leave.

"She came along with the judge this trip," Lydia commented, taking a short sip of coffee. "She doesn't often do that. I like to think it was Providence that she did, my dear."

"What do you mean?"

"It was Coreen who most influenced the judge to bend to your favor. She joined our little cause right away. Made His Honor's life outside the courtroom simply miserable. Until he came to his senses and reversed his decision, that is." Lydia smiled, wide enough to reveal a missing upper molar.

Jessie returned the smile, but remained quiet, wishing she had a glass of water or a cup of tea to sip. Soon the smile faded as despair settled over her.

"Why my dear," Lydia said, with sudden concern, reaching to clasp her hand. "What is it? You look as grim as an undertaker all of a sudden."

"The judge is going to try my cousin today, isn't he? I saw it in Mrs. Dougherty's eyes."

Lydia's direct answer might have rattled Jessie had she not learned long ago that Lydia Baylor wasn't a woman to mince words. "Yes, dear, he is. And I don't think there's any doubt about the outcome. The men from Murryville arrived this morning with the news that the man Curtis allegedly shot died several days ago. They brought along a witness to testify at the trial. If all goes according to plan, Walt Conner will be tried this afternoon, too."

"I see."

"Did you want to...will you be at your cousin's trial? I'm not sure a woman in your condition should subject herself to such stress, but, I'd certainly understand if you wanted to attend."

"No," she said, her reply solid. Whatever loyalty she'd felt toward Curtis had died at Mitch's cabin when he'd abducted her. That had been the final straw. She owed him nothing. *Nothing.*

"Well, as far as I'm concerned, you've made a wise decision. But if you change your mind, I'm sure that handsome husband of yours would escort you. He'd look after you every moment of the trial."

Jessie looked up, startled. "Mitch?"

"Why, who else, dear? My Frank told me all about how much Mr. Wyden loves you, Jessie. Frank said that from the moment your husband joined the posse, he acted like a madman seeing to your protection. Made himself a downright nuisance over it, Frank said. And then I heard the poor, frantic man near got himself killed going after that devil, Walt Conner. All for you. Let me tell you, dear, a good, caring man like that, one who is that devoted to his wife, comes along only rarely. Why, most women live an entire lifetime never knowing what it's like to be loved that much."

A crushing sadness settled over Jessie as the boy who'd taken her order set a plate of scrambled eggs and toast in front of her. Idly, she picked up her fork and began to push a bit of egg around on her plate.

"Oh, Lydia, how I wish your words were true," she said softly, almost to herself.

"Whatever do you mean? Did I say something amiss, dear?"

Jessie looked away, not wanting Lydia to guess the depth of her misery. "You're mistaken, Lydia. Mitch doesn't love me. He doesn't care for me in the least."

To Jessie's surprise, Lydia laughed. "Doesn't love you? Oh, my dear, from what Frank says, that husband of yours is so crazy in love with you, the man's downright sappy about it. What in the world would make you think otherwise?"

Jessie chewed a bit of egg, her throat tightening up. She swallowed, nearly choking, then took a sip of water the boy had brought with her meal. "He's never once told me," she admitted quietly. "Not once has he ever told me he loves me."

Lydia laughed again, showing the black space where one of her molars used to hang. This time, the woman's laughter sparked Jessie's anger.

"You just don't know the truth, Lydia! Mitch helped me for his own selfish reasons, not because of any great love for me."

"Oh hogwash. Land sakes, girl. Don't you know how hard it is for most men to say those three magic words to a woman? I swear it has something to do with a flaw in their brains. Mark my words, they're born with some sort of deficiency, more's the pity. Why, I can count on one hand the times Frank has said to me, "I love you, Lydia." Yet no man has ever loved a woman more than my Frank loves me. And he loves the children we've made together," she added, glancing at Jessie's middle.

"Listen to some wisdom from a woman far older than yourself. Men seem to think that showing a woman he loves her is the same as saying the words. I'm telling you, it's a brain flaw. And I repeat again, they're all born with it."

Jessie sniffed, taking another bite of egg. For the first time, hope bloomed in her heart, but she dared not let the blossom mature. If she did, she'd just get herself hurt and disappointed all over again. "You don't know Mitch, Lydia. That reward money meant more to him than anything else."

"Why, if you want proof of his love, all you have to do is think back about all the brave things your man has done for you these last months. How he took care of you and kept you safe. That's right, go ahead and think about them, Jessie. I'm telling you, dear, that husband of yours is good and truly smitten."

"But—"

"No buts. Would I lie to you? Oh Jessie, you have a good man there. And together you've got a little one on the way. Don't destroy your future happiness just because the man happens to have a little brain flaw."

Jessie couldn't help it. The corners of her mouth began to twitch.

"That's a dear girl. Now, I want you to finish up every speck of that breakfast. You're eating for two now, mind."

# Chapter Twenty Four

The Quarter Moon Saloon wasn't much to look at on the outside, but once Mitch stepped through the batwings, the cool interior drew him like a parched man to a wellspring. It had been a while since his shadow last fell on sawdust, and even longer since he'd sunk into the doldrums low enough to want to drown his sorrows.

"Give me a bottle," he said to the beefy, droopy-eyed bartender. "Make it the best you got."

The aproned barkeep smacked the bottle and a glass down on the bar in front of Mitch. "That'll be two dollars," he said in a slippery drawl.

Mitch paid for the bottle, bit off the cork, and poured. He drained the glass in one swallow, then poured another. It wasn't fine Kentucky bourbon, but it would do the job.

A poker game was going on behind him. He could see things clearly in the mirror behind the bar. Four grim-faced saddle tramps stared at their cards, a pot the size of Texas spread out in the center of the table. Normally he wouldn't have been interested, but the size of the pot and the tense expressions on the faces of the players piqued his curiosity.

Feathers caught his eye. Long, bobbing blue ones, stuck like fancy skewers in a honey-blonde pile of hair. She fixed her sights on him in the mirror, but before he could rebuff the look, the lilac water-doused saloon girl had sidled up to him.

"They've been at it a while now," she said, leaning across the bar on her forearms so that the mirror reflected to best advantage the near fatal spill of her large breasts above the tight lace bodice of her dress. "High stakes. You want in on the game, mister?"

"No."

Her crimson lips parted and curved slightly, but Mitch couldn't have called it a smile. It was more like a lazy, knowing smirk. "Well then, you must want to follow me upstairs. You got a look about you says you're sorely in need of what I got. Name's Rosie. I'll do you fine, mister. Real fine."

"Sorry, honey. Not today."

He'd turned her down flat, not even tempted. The girl was young, pretty, and clean enough, and he was suffering like a frustrated bull in rut from his last unfulfilled session with Jessie. Yet, for all that, he knew bone deep that his cat-housing days were over. Like death to an era. Nobody but his wife could ever satisfy him again.

Rosie pouted prettily. "Won't cost you much. A dollar for fifteen minutes. Unless you want something fancy. Then I'm willing to negotiate."

"I'm married," Mitch said flatly. He tensed, knowing the reaction he'd get from her with that one. There was a time not long ago when he would have scoffed at that rejoinder, too, but not anymore.

Sure enough, the girl gave a short giggle and shook her head so that the blue feathers drowsed like shooflies. Her long, pink-tipped fingers reached out to stroke his arm. "Mister, half the men I pleasure are married. Don't make no difference to me."

He casually shook his arm free, then took a long pull on the whiskey. Not in the mood for polite, he fixed her with a glare. "It makes a difference to me."

The girl blinked at the rebuff, clearly stung, but soon rallied smoothly enough. "Well, if that don't beat all. A true and faithful man," she said. "Don't see many of your kind, that's for sure. Not in this town, anyways. Why, even Preacher Emmerson sometimes...well, never mind. I ain't supposed to divulge such things as that."

Rosie's tired eyes darted down the length of the bar, but the big barkeep was busy wiping glasses and hadn't heard her blunder. "Well, anyways, your wife sure is a right fortunate woman to have caught herself a handsome, true-hearted man like you."

Irritated, Mitch slammed another belt of whiskey back, reveling in the slow, lazy burn curling in his stomach. He could feel his muscles soak up the liquor, feel his bones limbering up with each satisfying swallow. *Yeah*, he thought. *Jessie sure thinks she's fortunate, all right.*

"Honey, find yourself another mark," he advised. "I told you, I'm not interested. Not today, not ever. All I want right now is a little solitude."

Rosie straightened up, her red mouth drooping like a melting gumdrop. "Well," she pouted, "you can't blame a girl for trying. I knew right off you was a horse of a different color, but I took a gamble anyways, okay?" She gave a long, forlorn sigh. "It's just a downright pity the gamble didn't pay off."

Rosie sauntered off, and Mitch's attention again fell on the card players. From the sound of things, the last round of cards had been dealt, and it was time to make the final bets. Call or fold. Winner take all.

Mitch's head started to spin. He looked down. Jessie's face floated in the whiskey glass. *Gamble. Gamble.* The word stuck in his brain like a bur. All of life was a gamble, wasn't it? A worn-out sentiment, but a true one nonetheless.

He *knew* Jessie loved him. He could see it, feel it, every time he held her close. Every time he kissed her. Every time she kissed him back and melted in his arms. Jessie made love to him with her soul. Gave him everything in her woman's heart she had to give and then some. His wife had more passion in her than a month of springtimes...and...she'd told him, *told him* she loved him.

She'd said, "I love you, Mitch," the morning after they'd made love for the first time. And before that, she'd told him she trusted him.

He'd never heard words so wonderful or so terrifying in all his life. He'd not only had her love, but at the time, before Curtis showed up again, he'd had her trust, too. Something, heaven knew, Jessie didn't give easily. Feeling overwhelmed with the enormity of the emotions running through him, at that moment he'd remained quiet, at a total loss as how to respond.

Grimly, he castigated himself, remembering. He knew she'd longed to hear him declare that he loved her too, but at the time, he honestly hadn't recognized his feelings toward her for what they were.

Well, he knew now. After all he'd done for her, after all they'd been through together, how could she think for one minute that all he wanted was to use her as a means to recoup his losses, and worse, to merely satisfy his baser needs?

He was certain of one thing only: that despite all of Jessie's ranting and raving about how he'd dashed her dreams, how he'd forced her to marry and conceive a child against her wishes, how he'd used her and like a Judas turned her over to the law, Jessie loved him.

Shouts went up from the gamblers, astonished gasps by bystanders. A trail-worn, long-haired cowpoke abruptly stood to his feet, then viciously threw his cards on the table. "You were bluffing!" he roared at a grinning young cowboy sitting across from him. "Curse you, Goddard, I folded on three deuces. Show me your hand!"

"Nope." Goddard stretched to draw in his winnings. Before the losers could catch a glimpse, he buried his cards in the heap of discards. "That's the game of poker, Montrose," he exclaimed loftily to the loser. "Glory be to heaven and back, if I don't love this game!"

Rosie streaked up to Goddard faster than a shooting star. She draped her skinny arms about his neck and pressed her abundant assets close. "And I sure do love a winner," she drawled, then squealed like a piglet when the cowboy kissed her hard and gave her a bawdy tweak on the rear.

Montrose crammed on his hat and quit the table, mumbling curses. "Man was bluffing," he repeated all the way out to the street.

Mitch carefully set his glass down on the scarred bar, his thoughts whirling. *Gamble. Bluff. Winner takes all.* Bit by tumbling bit, the pieces of a plan came together, taking shape like a detailed military operation.

He straightened up, instantly sobering. He might lose everything in the next couple of hours, but Jessie was about to learn that Mitchell Colton Wyden was not a man to trifle with. She wanted her freedom, did she? All right. He'd call her bluff.

And in the meantime he'd pray like crazy Jessie wouldn't call his.

☙ ☙ ☙

Hours ago, Jessie had dragged the room's single chair over to the window so she could sit and watch the world go by along Main Street. It was nearly three in the afternoon, and Mitch hadn't returned yet, his extended absence causing her not a little anxiety.

Having nothing else to do after breakfasting with Lydia, Jessie had climbed the stairs to the room. Someone, she'd noticed with relief, had been in to remove the bath and straighten the bed. Feeling drowsy, as seemed to be the way of things these last few weeks, she'd reclined on the bed, carefully composed her skirts to avoid wrinkles, and took a short nap.

When Mitch still hadn't returned by noon, Jessie pulled *Nora and the Outlaws* from her saddlebags, propped a pillow, and began to read. But for the first time, the story failed to hold her interest. *Where was Mitch?*

In the back of her mind she worried that she may have pushed him too far this time. That maybe, in anger, he'd taken off without saying goodbye again.

Slapping the book closed, she tossed it aside, sprang up, and began to pace. Agitated as she was, she barely noticed the sound of her full skirts rustling like the whisper of a spring breeze. At any other time the sound would have given her great pleasure. After another half hour, she took her seat by the window, her troubled thoughts her only company.

Sulfur Flats wasn't by any means a huge metropolis like St. Louis or Denver, yet surveying the bleached rooftops tinted orange now in the afternoon sun, she supposed as small towns went, it had its charm. It boasted a hotel, a bank, several saloons, and a variety of storefronts snuggled together along the boardwalk. Most all of the shop owners had placed pots of colorful flowers outside their doors, an irresistible draw to potential customers.

Jessie remembered labeling the town "sleepy" when she'd first seen it that fateful day so long ago. Her opinion hadn't changed. People moved at a slow pace here—what she imagined was a kind of peaceful, walk-in-the-garden amble through life. No wonder the bank robbery had caused such a stir among the citizens.

She watched a buckboard loaded with lumber snake its way through brief knots of pedestrians crossing the street. A little girl dressed in pink and clinging to her mother's skirts, lifted a tiny hand and waved to the buckboard driver. He whistled loudly and raised a jolly hand back. The woman laughed, sweeping her daughter out of harm's way.

Jessie's thoughts turned to her mother then. She dwelled on all the what-might-have-beens for a long time.

A key turned in the lock. Jessie sprang from the chair, her stomach doing a somersault.

"Mitch?"

"Who else?" he said, striding into the room like a king entering the royal bedchamber. Jessie would have been relieved to see him, glad even, if it weren't for the menacing scowl on his face.

He stopped short, his gaze traveling the length of her and back again. His breath had clearly caught in his lungs. Just for the briefest moment, his features softened and his eyes glowed with a gentle light. But then the light vanished and his jaw hardened again, making Jessie wonder if the sight of her in her new yellow dress had affected him at all.

During Mitch's absence, she'd done a lot of thinking. Lydia's wisdom and advice had given her a whole banquet of food for thought. Maybe Mitch truly did have a brain flaw, like Lydia said, and therefore found it difficult to express aloud his tender-most feelings. She supposed she could allow him such a lapse. Especially if, like Lydia insisted, most men suffered the same impairment.

And when she'd analyzed Mitch's actions, spread them out and looked at them closely, she could see where a man of Mitch's strong character and military inclinations would automatically take charge of things, leaving no room for contradiction or insubordination.

"Take a seat, Jessie. We have to talk."

Jessie started, sharpening her focus. So much for making allowances. Mercy, but the man could be overbearing at times. With hackles good and truly risen, she said, "I'll stand, thank you. I don't want to sit. I've been sitting waiting for you all afternoon."

Inwardly she sighed. Could she help it if contradiction and insubordination were part of her nature? All her life she'd had to tamp down her innermost feelings, suppress the rebellion or suffer punishment for her troubles. Well, no more. She was tired of bullies telling her what to do and when to do it without her having any say-so. Mitch included.

"Suit yourself." He drew near and handed her a brown envelope.

The scent of whiskey, tobacco and, good heavens, lilac water filled her senses. Had Mitch been drinking? Had he spent the greater part of the day at a saloon? With some fancy bawdyhouse woman?

"Open it," he commanded stiffly.

Such heaviness settled over her, she struggled to reach for the envelope, her arm leaden. When she'd finally grasped it, her fingers remained still on the stiff paper.

Mitch gave her a strange look, then dropped his gaze. That look puzzled her. It was as if he were trying hard to hide the fact that whatever she did next was extremely important to him.

"No," she said. "I have a feeling I'm not going to like what's inside." She stared at the envelope. "What is this?"

Mitch blew out a breath. "A stage ticket to Reno." There wasn't an ounce of emotion in his voice. His tone sounded flat, final. "The stage leaves tomorrow morning at seven."

"You're going to Reno?" Jessie said, her throat suddenly dry.

"No. You are. And from there you'll be catching the train to San Francisco. I'll be heading the opposite way, toward Crystal Springs."

"What?"

"You heard me right." He went to the window, pushed aside the lace curtain, and studied the street. At length, he turned to face her. "I've done some considerable thinking since our little spat this morning. And I've come to the conclusion that even though I've tried my hardest to win your affections, I've failed."

"Mitch—"

"Don't interrupt. So it simmers down to this: I won't be saddled with a wife who can't believe in her man. Who thinks he's nothing but a selfish, dream-crushing bully."

Jessie's head spun. What was happening here? Going to San Francisco was what she'd always wanted, but not like this.

He pulled another envelope out of his vest pocket. The paper was white this time, but considerably wrinkled and stained, much like an old, discarded glove. "Here. I got this from Baylor. It's our marriage papers."

She refused to take the second envelope so he tossed it on the bed. Stunned, Jessie watched with glazed eyes as the parchment fluttered like a felled dove to land upside down on the sheets.

"If I were you I wouldn't destroy them until after the child is born, though."

Jessie blinked. "Destroy them? Mitch, what are you saying?"

"Isn't it obvious? I'm giving you your freedom, Jessie."

"My freedom?"

"With conditions attached."

"Conditions." Mercy, she sounded like a trained parrot. Her head was spinning and her heart was pounding so hard she could hear it booming in her ears.

"Yeah, conditions. This is how it's gonna go: There's a nice, middle-aged gentlewoman named Virginia Reeves whom I met at the stage station an hour ago. She was buying tickets to Reno for herself and her two nieces. We talked. In the end she said she'd be happy to watch over you until you caught the Central Pacific in Reno, headed for San Francisco.

"Once in San Francisco, I've arranged for old friends of mine, Hank Kendall and his wife Julia, to take you in until the baby's born. I'll be sending you a monthly stipend to keep you comfortable, enough to more than cover living expenses and doctor visits, plus I'll be sending compensation to the Kendalls for their kindness."

"Mitch, stop! What is all this? I could never impose upon strangers—"

"Hank and Julia aren't strangers. Not to me. I've wired them already and told them you're coming. You'll stay with them, Jessie, because I refuse to worry every minute about the safety of my unborn child for the next seven months. Subject closed."

A long silence fell between them. *What about my safety?* Jessie screamed silently. Clearly, Mitch was putting her under the Kendalls' care for the child's sake only. It was true, then, what she'd sensed all along. He cared nothing about her welfare at all.

Jessie was afraid to speak, afraid to move, sensing an even more terrible hurt to come. She didn't have to wait long.

Mitch gathered himself to his full height, the set of his jaw intimidating, the look in his eyes cold and foreboding. "As soon as my son is weaned, I'll send for him. He'll live with me on the ranch in Crystal Springs. Once he's safely in my care, you can tear up or burn those marriage papers. Once they're destroyed, you can begin using your maiden name again, and start living the carefree life you've always wanted. The ceremony was a sham anyway, right, Jessie?

"You'll be happy to know I got those papers from Baylor before he had a chance to register them at the county seat."

Jessie thought about that. If she destroyed the papers, there would be no record that the ceremony had ever taken place.

"Just think, Jessie. You'll be free to find that man of your dreams you've pined for all your life. The man whom you've made perfectly clear, isn't me."

Jessie had gone still, one hand clenched at her breast, the other unconsciously splayed across her abdomen. Above everything Mitch had just dropped in her lap, one thing stood starkly out above the others. Give up her child? She could never do that. Not ever.

In a shaking voice she said, "How could you think I would ever give up my daughter? You can't have her, Mitch." She sounded distraught, near frantic with distress, but a force beyond her control goaded her to come to her unborn child's defense. "I'll never give her up. Never!"

He actually grinned at that. An unpleasant grin. "Oh, stop it, Jessie. That's what you want, remember? Complete freedom, to do as you please, with nobody—man or child—holding you back, telling you what to do, keeping you from fulfilling your dreams? I'm making it possible for you to have everything you've ever wanted."

"But a baby needs its mother. Nobody knows that better than I do."

Furious, Mitch rounded on her. "I won't give up my son, Jessie. I'm willing to allow you think what you will about me. I'm even willing to set you free from your marriage vows. But allowing my son to grow up with a mother who never wanted him in the first place—who believes the absolute worst of his father—" He clenched his jaw and balled his fists. "I'll never allow my flesh and blood to suffer a lonely, loveless childhood and a lifetime of shame under that kind of stigma."

"Oh, Mitch. How could you? How could you think that I would be so cruel as to cause my own little girl such anguish? I want her so much! She'll be my own little bundle to love and cherish all the days of my life."

"Little boy," Mitch corrected coldly. "How could I think such a thing? Because of your own words, Jessie. You've been telling me over and over again how much you resent our wedding vows and that our baby—the baby you and I made *together*—is nothing but a burden keeping you from fulfilling your dreams. Well, believe whatever you want. But know this: you aren't going to pass on those beliefs to my son. I won't have him growing up with a mother who wishes he was never conceived. You can fight me all you want, but I warn you, you'll lose. I won't give him up, Jessie. You aren't going to raise him, and that's final."

"But...you can't mean that, Mitch."

"Can't I? I mean every word. Now, about our marriage. Or, wait a minute. How did you put it the morning after when I took you to bathe down by the river? Oh, yeah, you told me the ceremony was just another one of my hateful shenanigans. Well, think what you like about that, too, but if I were you, I wouldn't tear up those papers just yet. They're all you've got to prove you're not an unwed, pregnant, fallen woman. They're all you've got to keep your reputation spotless and the question of my son's legitimacy beyond doubt.

"Which reminds me, I almost forgot. Here." He reached into his pocket. "Hold out your left hand."

When she didn't move, didn't even blink because all of a sudden her limbs locked up and the blood, she was sure, ceased to flow in her veins, he expelled a short, exasperated breath and grabbed her left wrist. She tried to pull away, but he wouldn't allow it. "Hold still!"

The gold band was warm from lying snug against his body. He slipped the ring, shining and heavy on her finger, the weight of it settling like a ton of sorrows squarely on her heart.

Nonplussed, Jessie stared at the ring, words failing her. She could have sworn Mitch hesitated, his fingers lingering on her wrist and palm for the briefest of moments, as if he couldn't bear to let her hand go. But then he did let go. He dropped it as if it were a live ember searing his fingers.

Bemused, she fisted her left hand, her heart breaking. He was letting her go. He really was. He was giving her everything she'd said she always wanted. Her freedom, San Francisco, a chance to look for a good, fine man to marry and make her happy. Then why did she suddenly feel as if her whole world had just fallen apart?

"What's the matter, brat? Why aren't you giggling and jumping for joy? Total freedom and San Francisco are within your grasp. Thanks to me, you're gonna live happily ever after. You ought to be kissing my boots."

Her legs were going to buckle any moment now. She was sure of it. To be safe, she backed up toward the bed, and the moment the backs of her knees hit the mattress, she dropped like a stone. Lifting a shaking hand to her suddenly throbbing temple, she closed her eyes. The room spun.

This was it. This was her Waterloo. Except that Emperor Bonaparte couldn't have felt half as defeated as Jessie did at this moment. How could she live in a world without Mitch? Oh, mercy, she loved him so much it hurt. All afternoon she'd mulled over Lydia's words, thought about the complexity that was Mitch, his bluster, his tenderness, his endearing high-handed ways.

Whoa. *Endearing* high-handed ways? She must be losing her mind to admit such a thing. But then, Mitch's ways *were* endearing. Never once after he'd found out she was a woman had he used his strength to physically hurt her. Never once had he lied to her, even though she'd suspected he had, even though the truth had sometimes hurt her terribly.

Whenever he took her in his arms she felt as if nothing harmful could ever touch her. And when he made love to her—oh how her body leaped toward his gentle ministrations, ached for his thrilling kisses, his tender endearments as he brought her to the very heights of heaven itself.

It hit her like a thunder clap. There wasn't another man in all the world whom she could love like she loved Mitch. If she searched San Francisco from top to bottom, found a million Prince Charmings wandering those teeming streets, none would ever compare to the amazing, wonderful prince glowering down at her right at this moment.

She covered her eyes, feeling like a fool. Feeling sick. If only he wanted her again. Life on a ranch, owning their own piece of land, their own spread, raising their children together, well, that would be all the happiness she'd ever need. Oh, if only she hadn't driven such a wedge between them!

"You okay, Jessie?" Mitch had dropped down on his haunches in front of her. He peeled her hands away from her face. When Jessie opened her eyes, she saw that his expression had changed. He didn't look quite so frightening now.

"No. I'm not."

"Is it the baby?"

"No."

"What is it then? Aren't you excited? San Francisco is only a stage and train ride away."

"Oh stop. Please stop. I can't bear anymore."

"Jessie, what's the matter with you? I thought you'd be happy about all this. I swear, you're the most confusing, confounding woman I've ever known. Heaven knows I'd do anything in my power to see to your happiness. All I'd thought about for weeks was how I was going to get you acquitted, how afterward we'd start a family, how we'd build a life on the ranch together. How I'd be the proudest, happiest man alive with a woman like you by my side. But you've scorned every single thing I've done. So now that I've made it possible for you to follow your heart, have your own way, you're upset about that, too?"

Jessie took a deep breath, Mitch's words going straight to her broken heart. "Just leave me be, Mitch. Please."

"Jessie, look at me. If making you happy means that I have to let you go, then I will. I never once laughed at your dreams, did I? Answer me, honey. Did I?"

"No."

"And I'm not laughing at them now. I know how much independence means to you, now that all the trouble with the law is over and happiness is within your reach. What kind of a monster would I be if I tried to take all that away from you? Against your will?"

Jessie sagged, her whole body rubbery, as if she'd been stuffed head first through a knot hole. Mitch had gone so still, she wondered if he'd quit breathing again.

A vision of San Francisco flashed through her mind. And then she saw herself clinging to her daughter, bleakly going through the motions of life, unhappy, merely coping. Without Mitch. She would never give up her child, would fight to the death for her, but having her daughter grow up fatherless just as she had was out of the question.

"I don't want to go," Jessie blurted through a watery knot lodged in her throat.

Mitch dropped his head and shook it, his far-too-long hair brushing his shirt collar and shadowed cheeks. "I don't believe I heard that," he said. "Say it again."

"I don't want to go," Jessie repeated, too distraught to reveal any more of her heart.

Mitch eased to his feet, pulled her up and crushed her against his chest, his strong arms circling her back, supporting her. The burning kiss he gave her was long, deep and slow. "Ah, Jessie, Jessie. You had me scared near to death."

Jessie clung to him, afraid to let him go, afraid that if she did she'd never again feel the comforting warmth of his embrace. "I love you so much, Mitch," she whispered against his shirt.

Mitch put her away from him a little. "You sure?" he asked, the corners of his mouth curling upward. She saw concern mixed with triumph in his eyes, and when she saw it, she clung to him even harder.

She nodded, rubbing her cheek against his shirt. "I'm sure." But she couldn't smile back. Not when such a vital piece of the picture was missing.

"Then what's the matter, brat? Tell me."

"I need...."

"What?"

"I want you to say it back, Mitch. I want you to tell me you love me. Just once. And if you really mean it, I'll never ask you to say it again. Only once is all I ask."

Mitch smoothed a wayward lock of hair off her brow, then tipped her chin up with his fingertips. He looked at her hard. "I like your hair the way you've got it fixed. It looks just as pretty as I imagined it would when I saw those combs at the mercantile. And you look good enough to eat in that new dress."

She nervously patted her hair. "The shell combs are lovely. Thank you for all the...gifts. Everything you bought for me is...is beautiful beyond words."

"You're beautiful beyond words. Do you know that?"

Jessie shook her head in denial, hurt racking her. He still hadn't said the magic phrase.

"Well, you are. The most beautiful woman God ever made. And you're stubborn and infuriating at times, and it pains me to think that I may never have your complete trust. But considering how you were raised, I can understand that and I'll live with it for a while. But be warned. Your trust is something I plan to earn back."

"You don't love me, though. If you did, you'd say it."

He gave an exasperated sigh. "Don't love you? Jessie, how can you doubt it? I admit that in the beginning I didn't recognize what I felt for you was love because I'd never cared for any other woman before like I cared for you. But, for heaven's sake, brat, just because I never said the words, didn't you realize how deep my feelings ran for you? I know I showed you every way I knew how.

"Ah, Jessie, I love you. *I love you.* And I'll tell you a million times a day if that's what's going to keep you happy. Never doubt it. Never for a moment."

Tears came to Jessie's eyes as a flood of warmth began to thaw her cold limbs.

"Here," Mitch said, scooping the brown envelope up off the floor. "Look inside this."

"I know what's inside. A ticket to Reno."

"No. Come on, take it."

She stepped away, studied the envelope for a moment, then lifted the flap. Hesitantly, she peered inside. "There's nothing in here," she said, astonished.

"That's right. Nothing. Come on, Jessie. Do you honestly think I would allow my pregnant wife to travel all the way to San Francisco without me there to protect her and keep her safe? Don't you know me better than that by now? Don't you know that there would be no purpose to my life without you in it? I would never have let you go."

"You wouldn't have tried to take my daughter away from me?"

"Your son. And no, I wouldn't have."

"Oh, Mitch. But you said—"

"I said I love you, Jessie. This whole scene was a bluff. All of it. One big, all-or-nothing gamble."

"What!"

"Don't be mad, Jess. Throw away your anger and just try and understand that, like everything else I've done since the day you rode into my life, I did this for you. For us. I had to come up with a way to force you to finally face your true feelings for me and realize once and for all that we belong together. This was it."

"Wonderful," she said, not sure whether to laugh or cry, or better yet, find something to cudgel him into pulp with. "You did it again, didn't you? Tricked me, played me for a fool."

"No, Jessie. No." He hesitated. "Well, all right. I admit that my tactics were a little extreme, but they worked, didn't they? Didn't the end justify the means?"

"I'm not sure," Jessie said sadly. "Mitch, I won't live with a man who can't respect the fact that I have intelligence and feelings. A man who doesn't think my opinions count."

"I do understand all those things about you, Jessie. Look. I was raised to believe that a man takes care of his woman. In all things. From the moment I discovered your true identity back at the cabin, I've been taking care of you the best way I know how. Maybe I went a little too far at times, but I swear, everything I did, I did because you mean more to me than my own life."

Jessie pondered that and could come up with only one solution to her dilemma. "We have to settle something right now. I'll learn to accept you just the way you are, but you'll have to do the same with me. That means you're going to have to put up with my tongue from time to time, because I'm warning you, Mitch, I'm going to tell you about it every time I sense you're up to one of your high-handed tricks again."

Mitch gave a short laugh, but answered in all seriousness. "Agreed. Say whatever you want to me, whenever you want to say it. How else am I going to know what you're feeling? We'll talk and share our feelings and work everything out, Jessie. Together. I swear it."

Jessie's eyes glowed as she took him at his word. After a short pause, though, she brought up one more thing that needed settling. She sniffed and said, "Have you been drinking, Mitch? Don't answer. I know you have. And there's a faint smell of lilac water about you, too." She looked away as her smile drooped a little. "I've grown accustomed to your smoking too much, Mitch, but I'll not tolerate drunkenness in my house, nor will I tolerate a husband who cheats on his wife. I...I couldn't bear that."

Mitch looked at her hard, then as if settling the matter, he said, "I'm not going to even qualify that with an answer, Jessie. Listen good and know this: if it takes me the rest of my life, I'm going to earn your trust. Count on it.

"And another thing," he added, his voice softening. "I meant what I said about taking you to San Francisco. I never lied about that. It's just going to take a while to get there, is all." He reached for her and took her in his arms again. Gently, he gripped her nape and tilted her head up. "Jessie, look at me. Square in the eyes, brat. The moment the ranch begins to hold its own, we'll go. From now on we'll dream about the trip together. We'll make it our belated wedding trip."

"Together," she repeated in a delicious daze. Then she lost her voice all together when he crushed her close and kissed every doubt she'd ever had into oblivion.

# Epilogue

"Mitch! Watch Robbie. He's getting too close to the surf!"

"I've got him," Mitch called, sweeping his giggling three-year-old son onto his shoulders.

Jessie cuddled their second son, James, close to her breast, feeling young and carefree as a schoolgirl. Playfully, she kicked an arc of water and sea foam, delighting in the lovely way the droplets caught the light and pelted the receding wave like a shower of sunbeams.

She was here. Finally here, wading, bare-toed in the mighty Pacific. *With her family.* Sometimes she had to pinch herself to believe it all wasn't just the dream she'd held in her heart for so very long.

Mitch caught up with her, still carrying the squealing Robbie.

"Down, Pa," Robbie insisted, bouncing his little rump against Mitch's shoulders.

"Down you go, then," Mitch said, but warned as he swung his son to the sand, "Stay close, Rob. Mama worries when you get too close to the water."

As soon as he righted his balance, Robbie squatted down to examine a shell lying in the glistening sand. "'Kay," he answered his father obediently.

The day was warm, bright, and perfect. Jessie tilted her head up as several white seagulls circled the blue sky above where she stood, then winged away out to sea. "Thank you," she said to

Mitch as he fell into a lazy pace beside her. "This is everything I've ever hoped for, more than I've ever dreamed it would be."

"That's what I want to hear," Mitch said. "But you've got a faraway look in your eyes. Is something wrong?"

"No. It's just that being here made me think of Curtis, is all. He could have had this instead of a life in prison. That's sad, isn't it?"

"I guess. But he could just as well have hung for his crimes. At least he's still alive. And he's got Walt Conner for company, remember."

"I suppose." Jessie pressed her bare foot into the wet sand and watched, fascinated, as a brilliant halo circled her toes.

"Curtis had a choice, Jessie. It isn't anyone's fault but his own that he ended up at Yuma. Come on. Don't think about it anymore. Don't spoil the day."

"I've been thinking about other things, too," Jessie said. "About your parents. You know, we really need to plan another trip, Mitch. To Denver. It isn't right that your mother and father haven't seen their grandsons yet. Besides, Robbie and James need to know their family, too. They have aunts and uncles and cousins. I want them to know every last one of them. I want them to have everything I never had."

It had taken time, but she'd finally convinced Mitch that he needed to reconcile with his family. Life was too short to bear grudges. Family was important.

Mitch remained quiet. After a moment he bent to pluck up a sand dollar before a sneaky wave could sweep it away. The shell was as big as his fist and perfectly formed.

"Oh!" Jessie cried. "Robbie, come see what your pa has found."

Robbie toddled up to his parents and peered into his father's large palm. "Flower," he said, remarking on the petal design imprinted in the center of the shell.

"That's right, flower," Mitch agreed, handing the shell to Jessie. "Pretty as your mama," he said, then reached down to take Robbie's sandy little hand.

Jessie blushed as she adjusted the baby and put the delicate shell into her skirt pocket to keep company with all their other sea treasures. When she looked up at Mitch again, the breeze caught her hair and it billowed in thick streamers behind her, catching the light. Mitch put his free hand to it, then let the strands drift like sand through his fingers.

"I suppose we could arrange a trip to Denver," he allowed. "But not until well after our daughter is born."

Jessie grinned. She was pregnant again. And here little James was only six months old. Mercy, she'd barely had time to catch her breath and bang, they had another little Wyden on the way.

"Daughter?" she challenged, furrowing her brows.

"Yeah, daughter. You've always wanted a girl. So I gave you a girl this time. We'll call her Claire."

Vaguely irritated, but more amused, Jessie chuckled softly. "Claire, is it? You've decided? Which means you're certain, then, it's a girl this time?"

"I'm sure."

She shot him a look.

He chuckled back. "Well, when's the last time I was wrong about the gender of our kids, Mrs. Wyden?"

She had to admit, he did have a point. Obviously, he hadn't once been wrong, blast him. Still, she needed to make her own wishes clear.

Jessie looked out toward the horizon. The wind had picked up, and far out to sea she could see a white bank of fog closing in. She took a deep breath of misty, salty air and said, "I'll be happy to bear your daughter, Mitch, but we most certainly won't be naming her Claire."

Mitch hesitated. "Why not? Claire is a perfect name."

"Because we're going to name her Lucinda. After my mother."

She flashed him a radiant smile, knowing there wouldn't be a whole lot he could object to about that.

Over time, they'd learned to talk out their differences. And whenever they disagreed, they'd learned to respect each other's views, to lovingly accept each other's personalities and quirks instead of trying to change them. Marriage had taught them, especially Jessie, plenty about the meaning of trust, selfless love, mercy, and giving. Jessie had no doubt that they would find a way to work out the matter of their daughter's name in a way that would satisfy them both.

"After your mother?"

"If she were here she would be over the moon about it."

A soft light shone in his blue eyes as he kissed her lips, then smoothed a thick strand of wayward hair from her cheek. His fingers finally came to rest on the top of James's downy head.

"Lucinda Claire it is, then," Mitch said.

*Paula L. Silici grew up in San Francisco where romantic tales of the Old West, the 1849 Gold Rush, and Western Expansion never failed to set her imagination on fire. She began writing her own tales in grade school and never stopped. Paula's award-winning fiction, nonfiction, and poetry have appeared in both national and regional publications, including Award Winning Tales, numerous editions of Chicken Soup for the Soul, Ideal/Guideposts, and others. Her first published novel, A Way in the Wilderness, was a Colorado Authors League Book-length Genre Fiction finalist. She lives with her husband near Denver, Colorado.*

Made in the USA
Coppell, TX
05 July 2021